Praise for
BRAIN STORM

"Ambitious...*Brain Storm* contains one outrageously brilliant character: a lunatic judge named Stang....His withering tirades against the absurdities of the legal system alone make the book worth reading."
—Steve Szilagyi, *The Cleveland Plain Dealer*

"Wildly, laugh-out-loud, wake-up-your-spouse-to-read-passages-aloud funny."
—Joann C. Gutin, *San Jose Mercury News*

"Finds a place both in the beach bag and on the shelf as part of one's permanent collection...That *Brain Storm* often makes for riotous reading because of Dooling's wit and general sense of humor alone should commend it, but there is much more to it."
—William Domanarski, *San Diego Commerce*

"Dooling has such a gorgeously rampaging take on brain chemistry, hate-crime law, and the grounds for contempt of court that you may find yourself, like Joe Watson, losing sight of the brilliantly overinflated conflict at the heart of this postmodern fable."
—*Kirkus Reviews*

"*Brain Storm* is simply brilliant—hilarious, thought-provoking, and masterfully crafted. The characters are fantastic and irresistible but completely believable, and their banter is so witty and natural that a reader can forget they are debating ideas at the cutting edge of brain science and philosophy. *Brain Storm* is also suspenseful, entertaining, and completely satisfying."
—Steven Pinker, author of *How the Mind Works*

"If there is any justice in the world of letters, *Brain Storm*...will establish its author as the foremost legal novelist in America today....*Brain Storm* is packed with episodes of inspired lunacy, but beneath the laughter it provokes, it's a slyly serious book."
—Joel Chineson, *American Lawyer*

"With his mad new novel, *Brain Storm*, Richard Dooling has joined the ranks of the real satirists....Dooling has mastered the vocabularies of law, computers, and neuroscience, and his performance reaches beyond parody into the realm of art."
—John Wilson, *The Weekly Standard*

ALSO BY RICHARD DOOLING

Critical Care

White Man's Grave

*Blue Streak: Swearing, Free Speech, and
Sexual Harassment*

Brain Storm

BRAIN STORM

RICHARD DOOLING

Picador USA
New York

Picador® is a U.S. registered trademark and is used by St. Martin's Press under license from Pan Books Limited.

For information on Picador USA Reading Group Guides, as well as ordering, please contact the Trade Marketing department at St. Martin's Press.
Phone: 1-800-221-7945 extension 763
Fax: 212-677-7456
E-mail: trademarketing@stmartins.com

Library of Congress Cataloging-in-Publication Data

Dooling, Richard.
  Brain Storm / Richard Dooling.
    p.   cm.
  ISBN 0-312-20399-3
    1. Trials (Hate crimes)—Missouri—Saint Louis—Fiction._
  2. Lawyers—Missouri—Saint Louis—Fiction.   3. Saint Louis (Mo.)—
  Fiction.   4. Legal stories. gsfad   I. Title.
  [PS3554.O583B72]
  813'.54—dc21
                                                          99-22390
                                                              CIP

First published in the United States by Random House, Inc.

First Picador USA Paperback Edition: May 1999

10 9 8 7 6 5 4 3 2 1

A.M.D.G.

FOR CARLO AND MOQUAH

BRAIN STORM

CHAPTER 1

"The beheadings are almost identical," said Joe Watson, placing his memo on the walnut expanse of Arthur Mahoney's worktable. Watson resisted the impulse to retrieve the memo on beheadings from the senior partner's elbow and check it again for typos. Arthur Mahoney—silver-haired mentor and the partner in charge of young Watson's career at Stern, Pale & Covin—had been less than enthusiastic about the last two memos Watson had done for him, and Watson feared that another unsatisfying piece of work might jeopardize the comfortable, protected niche he'd made for himself as research and writing factotum to the head of the litigation department.

"Almost identical?" asked Arthur. He set aside the stack of correspondence and enclosures he had been reviewing, swiveled in his recliner, and attended to his young associate and the press of the business at hand: decapitations.

"Yes," said Watson, panicking as he suddenly realized he had forgotten to use the spell checker himself (instead of just having his secretary do it), so he could activate the homophone feature of the firm's word processing software and double-check for words that were spelled correctly but were misused, like *discrete* instead of *discreet*, or *principle* instead of *principal*. He'd used *stationery* instead of *stationary* in the last memo, and Arthur had filled the margins with a handwritten screed on the importance of precision.

"Is this something more than look and feel?" asked Arthur. "We've seen so many of these damn beheadings. And you associates tend to make wild, very serious, highly theoretical allegations without thinking about the weeks of courtroom labor you'll need to prove them. How do you distinguish one beheading from another? I'll have to rely on young people to teach me about decapitations. We didn't have such grisly spectacles in my day."

"Both heads are severed at the third cervical vertebra—right here," said Watson, running a finger across the back of his own neck by way of illustration.

"So?" said Arthur. "Seems a likely enough site."

"Similar-sounding crunches occur when the blades strike the vertebra. The arteries and veins sprout like seaweed and spurt blood everywhere. I'm having the splatter patterns analyzed to be sure, but the splotches look identical. The heads topple forward and then roll down stairs—three stairs, to be exact, with three kerplunks. The animated victims turn their headless stumps toward the gamer and squirt blood through the windpipes onto the screen. The heads themselves are mounted on pikes, and in both cases the heads say, 'Ouch, that smarts!' in a kind of cartoon voice, at the instant of impalement."

Arthur made a small steeple of his index fingers and tapped it against his pursed lips. "Joseph," he said with a benevolent smile, "I can imagine myself arguing to a federal district judge that one beheading is identical to another. I can imagine myself arguing that one beheading is wholly distinguishable from some other beheading which has been served up by way of comparison, but I'm straining somewhat to imagine myself arguing that two beheadings are *almost* identical. Instead of issuing general proclamations of their near identity, perhaps your analysis could commence with a succinct delineation of the difference or differences, however slight, between the two beheadings. I'll speak plainly: What is keeping our almost identical beheadings from becoming completely identical beheadings?"

"A halberd and a scimitar, sir," said Watson.

"A halberd," said Arthur.

"It's kind of a combination poleax and pike mounted on a six-foot handle," Watson explained. "You've probably seen knights and beefeaters and whatnot holding them. Or maybe if you've been to a museum you've seen them leaning against suits of armor. The Met in New York has quite a collection."

"I know what a halberd is," said Arthur.

"I knew you would," said Watson, deciding not to mention that he had exhaustively researched the subject of halberds to the tune of six or seven billable hours, had viewed the Met's collection of halberds on-line at http://www.nycmet.com/medieval/halberds, and had submitted his time under the heading "Research Look-and-Feel Issues Involving Ancillary Armaments, 6.75 Hours."

"In CarnageMaster, the Crusader's head is cut off by a Maltese knight with a halberd, but in Greek SlaughterHouse, Medusa is beheaded by Perseus, who uses a blazing scimitar."

"And a polished shield for a mirror?" Arthur asked eagerly.

"No," said Watson, "I don't think our clients are up on their Greek mythology. Perseus just kind of looks right at Medusa and whops off her head with a scimitar he must have stolen from a vanquished Turk after doing a little time traveling. Now, you're probably thinking, That's different—Perseus and his scimitar are different from a Maltese knight with a halberd. But when the weapons are displayed later, the blood drips in precisely the same patterns from the blades to the same reticulated stone floor of an identical castle—the Castle of Skulls—which was designed by our client's multimedia programmers."

"Sounds like more than a coincidence," said Arthur, "but is this copyright infringement? Something more than look and feel? Has CarnageMaster stolen the story of Greek SlaughterHouse? The characters?"

"CarnageMaster has stolen the *soul* of Greek SlaughterHouse," Watson said.

"Hmmm," said Arthur. "So we have these 'almost identical' beheadings, and we have the 'very similar' dungeon torture sessions, followed by the 'almost identical' disembowelments."

"That's right," said Watson. "Don't forget the nearly identical large-breasted blondes wearing see-through chain mail shackled to ringbolts and stones inside pink, secret chambers. In both games, male assailants brandish flesh-colored broadswords at them."

"We need more," said Arthur. "Subliminal Solutions and the SlaughterHouse team want to be absolutely certain of their position before amending their complaint and adding a request for punitive damages.

We need to be sure this is all—what are the magic words?—'well grounded in fact and warranted by existing law,' or we risk Rule Eleven sanctions. More research is indicated."

"Yes, sir," said Watson.

Arthur took a call. Watson gathered his papers and headed out, back to his office, a windowless cubicle one fourth the size of Arthur's spread. Arthur had the big office, the ancient measure of partner power, but he didn't have a 600 megahertz Pentium VI 3-D system with a sub-woofer and a twenty-eight-inch flat-panel display, which the firm had installed in Watson's office to assist him in analyzing copyright litigation claims for the firm's software clientele. Arthur didn't "do" computers, had no use for them. He was an example of that dying breed of lawyer who still pined for the days when former fraternity brothers and family friends paid dearly for sage advice and legal guidance. The old guy had barely an inkling that modern corporate clients were no longer interested in sage advice (they could get that from the in-house lawyers they had on staff). They had all the family friends and wise men they needed; they came to Stern, Pale looking for armies of ruthless litigators and information dominance, so they could massacre their opponents in court.

In the twilight of his august career, Arthur was still dispensing advice and memos to clients, but these days those memos and that advice consisted of information that had been winnowed, gathered, and compressed by associates using powerful computers and search technologies. For young lawyers, like Joe, legal prowess increasingly depended on computer expertise, which meant that one had to curry favor and cultivate relationships not only with senior partners, who played real golf, but also with the management information systems (MIS) people, who played 3-D Microsoft Golf and who controlled access to the machines and the software a young associate needed for optimum research capabilities.

For instance, Arthur barely knew the head of MIS—a shapeless, rumpled dweeb, affectionately known as Inspector Digit—who was Watson's buddy and primarily responsible for getting Watson into his high-end equipment. Digit was, in the language of the trade, a guy with lots of MIPS but no I/O. Plenty of brainpower, but subject to trap errors, freeze-ups, and system hangs when it came to interacting with humans. When Digit opened his mouth, argot and acronyms, techno-linguistics and programming instruction sets came out. Most lawyers said only

"Uh-huh" and "Fix it" to Digit, which was why Digit valued Watson's friendship. Watson, in turn, looked to Digit for the very latest in beta browsers and processing power.

Officially, the lawyers were allowed to use only firm-issued desktop PCs (referred to by the information elite as "beige toasters") that were hooked to the network and ran five-year-old firm-approved software (hopelessly dated stuff, referred to as "stone knives and bearskins"); third-party programs of any kind were strictly forbidden, for obvious security reasons. But unofficially, Inspector Digit and the MIS people gave Watson and a few other silicon turbonerds high-end machines and let them deploy and test the latest Web browsers, agents, robots, and legal systems software. It was the best way to test the stuff before implementing it throughout the network. Watson and the other tech-headed lawyers were always clustergeeking around the new machines, running beta software, crashing supposedly crashproof software, or cycle crunching the networks on purpose, so that the MIS people would order them stand-alone workstations. Also known as propeller heads, spods, and terminal junkies, these associates knew the antiviral and security drills, so there was no point in limiting their use of third-party programs. Besides, restricting the serious user's choice of software is the equivalent of thought control.

Let Arthur have a big office, thought Watson—I'll take the workstation with two gigabytes of RAM and the beta software.

His screen came back to life when he moved the trackball, and Watson returned to the Castle of Skulls, ready for another thirty or forty billable hours of dismembering 3-D medieval warlords.

A blinking light on his Personal Information Manager (PIM) indicated that he had external voice mail waiting. He pressed the button. "This is Judge Stang's clerk, Federal District Court, Eastern District of Missouri, calling Joseph T. Watson, attorney number 76892. Pursuant to the court's local rules, Judge Stang has appointed you to represent an indigent defendant in Case Number 2002-CR-30084-WJS. For more information about the case and for a copy of the information and the bill of particulars, please call the court at . . ."

His appointed case! In the Eastern District of Missouri (St. Louis) and in many other federal districts, the district courts have a long-standing tradition of assigning every new lawyer admitted to practice in the district a pro bono case, usually an indigent criminal or civil rights plaintiff who, for whatever reason, cannot be represented by the federal public defender. It's a rite of passage for new lawyers who don't know which end is up in a drug conspiracy trial, and it's the bane of big law firms, whose partners lose hundreds of billable hours' worth of new associate time to the defense of guilty criminals or the filing of often frivolous prisoners'-rights or discrimination suits.

Watson knew he was due for his appointed case, because three of his classmates who were sworn in with him had already received theirs. He'd had secret hopes for a criminal case, because back in law school— before becoming husband to his wife, Sandra, and father and provider for their children, Sheila and Benjy—he had aspired to being William Kunstler, Gerry Spence, or Clarence Darrow. A legal warrior and protector of downtrodden outcasts. Instead, he became an overpaid silk-stockinged Westlaw geek for the partners of Stern, Pale. A criminal case might satisfy some of his former cravings for glory. But big criminal cases usually went to the federal public defender. Besides, a federal criminal appointment would tear some ragged, deep valleys in Watson's 180-day moving average of fifty billable hours a week, because all of the appointed work would be nonbillable. In his day, Clarence Darrow probably didn't turn in time sheets to the management committee, or answer to the wife and kids when he passed on the family vacation and took a case for no pay. Or if Clarence answered to a wife, she probably didn't have Sandra's withering contempt for professional frolics and detours—like defending guilty criminals—that would do nothing to advance the welfare of their traditional family.

He called Judge Stang's clerk and exchanged pleasantries with a pleasant young woman. He patiently waited for her to tell him he had been assigned a nice Title VII employment discrimination case, an inmate wanting his sentence corrected from 580 years to probation, or a Social Security matter—maybe helping a destitute widow make a claim for benefits.

"It's a murder case," the woman said pleasantly.

"Murder?" Watson choked. It was criminal, all right—beyond his wildest dreams, verging on his wildest nightmares. "Since when do they have murder trials in federal court?"

"Let's see here," she said. "Looks like the murder occurred on an army base, in the on-base housing where the defendant was staying with his wife, who is in the reserves. That's military reservation, meaning it's federal jurisdiction, which puts it in U.S. district court. And the U.S. attorney is seeking the death penalty under the Hate Crime

Motivation or Vulnerable Victim provisions of the new federal sentencing guidelines. It's the federal version of all those state penalty-enhancement statutes."

"It's a hate crime?" asked Watson.

"Why don't you read the Complaint and Affidavit? It probably came through on your fax machine a few minutes ago. It's murder, and the government is saying"—Watson heard pages riffling—"here we are, paragraph seven: 'The defendant intentionally selected his victim as the object of the offense because of the actual or perceived disability of the victim—deafness.' "

"Deafness? And they're saying what?" Watson asked, amazed that there was such a law and doubly amazed that prosecutors actually used it. "You mean they're saying he shot a deaf guy because he hates deaf people?"

"I guess so," said the clerk. "Hold it. It also says"—more riffling—"paragraph eight: 'The defendant intentionally selected his victim as the object of the offense because of the actual or perceived race of the victim—African-American.' The victim must have been a deaf black guy."

Murder! Joseph T. Watson, Esq., recent graduate of Ignatius University Law School and winner of the Computerized Legal Research & Writing Award, was the attorney of record for a hate criminal accused of murder! He panicked and did the noble thing, which was to argue his own incompetence, taking the defensible position that he was not a real lawyer.

"This must be a mistake," he said. "I'm not a real lawyer. I do computerized legal research. I'm a Webhead and Westlaw expert. I'm not an officer of the court. I've never even been to court, except to get sworn in. I spend roughly eleven hours a day foraging in computerized legal databases retrieving precedent—cases that support the legal theories of senior partners who pay me handsomely for my skills."

Even as he was attempting to beg off out of fear, he was tempted—exhilarated even—by the prospect of doing something—anything—besides fifty hours of legal research per week, every week. All he had had to say was "Yes, ma'am," and he could play at being a real lawyer, a trial lawyer, a criminal defense lawyer. But a first-year associate taking on a murder case for the sake of trial experience was like a med student dabbling in a little brain surgery.

"It says here you do discrimination work, Title VII cases, and so on," said the clerk.

"Employment discrimination," said Watson. "I've done computerized legal research and written legal memoranda for partners who defend large employers who have been unjustly sued by disgruntled employees, but—"

"Judge Stang said these bias crimes are a lot like discrimination cases," said the clerk. "Think about it. Killing somebody is the ultimate form of discrimination. You shouldn't have any trouble."

"But I've never uttered word one in a courtroom!"

"Which puts you in the same boat with all the other young lawyers who get appointed every day," said the clerk. "Besides, you work at Stern, Pale. It's the best firm in town. I'm sure you'll do a better job than most of the appointed lawyers we see down here."

Again, the prospect of a real case—his very own case!—beckoned, but he also vividly imagined his normal workload, his billable hours, and his performance profile all ravaged by a murder trial in which he would be representing a nonpaying client. What would Clarence Darrow do? Selflessly think about the poor client, probably.

"I am not a trial lawyer," he continued, wondering how much trouble he could cause the government by filing a dozen vigorous, well-aimed pretrial motions. "Stern, Pale hired me because I have a certain facility for answering essay questions on law school exams."

"I'm looking at the judge's notes," said the clerk. "He says you wrote a law review article called 'Are Hate Crimes Thought Crimes?' in the Ignatius University law journal."

Watson was flattered that Judge Stang had noticed his student comment but alarmed that anyone would think it qualified him to handle a murder case.

"That's me," he said. "But that's just footnotes, research, and so on. That's not murder!"

The clerk sighed. "The case has been assigned to you. I don't know if there's such a thing as a Rule Forty-nine Motion to Withdraw Because of Your Own Incompetence, and I don't think your client can claim ineffective assistance of counsel until you lose the case, but if you want to file something, see Judge Stang at informal matters after the arraignment. I'd wear a helmet if I were you."

The clerk added that Watson could watch *Channel 5 Live* at ten if he wanted to know more about the case, that newspaper people were calling, that Lawyers for Deaf Americans, lawyers for the National Organization for Women, NAACP lawyers, civil rights attorneys, and hate crime experts were all calling for information about the case, so maybe he would be able to fob it off on an attorney for a special interest group or on some other eager young defense lawyer willing to work for nothing while building his or her reputation.

"This is an academic discussion, however," said the clerk. "You've been appointed. I can't unappoint you. Only the judge can do that. Do you know Judge Stang?"

Legends and war stories came immediately to Watson's mind. The time Judge Stang—a cantankerous graduate of the Roy Bean school of jurisprudence—ordered an attorney to put a bag over his client's head, because the judge was sick of the man's supercilious grin. The time he ordered a federal marshal to handcuff two squabbling attorneys together and lock them in a holding cell. The time he flew into a blind rage (later diagnosed as *furor juridicus,* a species of judicial seizure activity) and attacked thirty lawyers with the courtroom's iron flagpole because they were unable to settle EPA Superfund litigation after three years of discovery. He had more nicknames than any other judge. Some called him Ivan the Terrible, others, Blackjack Stang; still others referred to him as the Grand Inquisitor, Darth Vader, Beelzebub, the Gowned Avenger, or the Prince of Darkness.

"I'll tell you this," she said, "if you try to withdraw from an appointed case, and your only excuse is that you lack trial experience, Judge Stang will fine you for contempt, and then he'll cut your ears off with a butter knife."

CHAPTER 2

Stern, Pale policy and procedures required a conflicts memo to be sent via E-mail notifying the firm and its 572 lawyers in offices all over the world of any prospective new clients. The clerk's fax was long on charges and short on facts. *"James F. Whitlow,"* Watson typed in the new-client box—the first time he'd made such an entry. *"United States v. Whitlow,"* he typed in the new-matter box. He sent the conflicts memo and then selected the West CD-ROM version of Title XVIII of the United States Penal Code—the title that dealt with criminal offenses— took the disk home, and looked up all of the crimes charged in the complaint.

The next morning's *Post-Dispatch* was more helpful than the conclusory legalisms set forth in the clerk's fax. SUSPECT'S SLURS PROMPT HATE CRIME INVESTIGATION. Watson read it in his office while waiting to see Arthur, who had left an early-morning voice mail after reading the conflicts memo. He had asked Watson to see him about "taking steps to be certain his new criminal appointment would not interfere with his responsibilities to the firm's clients."

According to the *Post-Dispatch*, the murder had occurred in the defendant's bedroom. The defendant's wife, serving in the army reserves, was the only witness. No mention of what the wife, the victim, and the defendant were doing at the time, who got there first, or last. The story had the heady breathlessness of breaking news, garnished with the usual journalistic sociology: a warning of a local and national epidemic of hate crimes. Throughout the 1990s, the FBI had collected statistics on hate crimes, pursuant to the Federal Hate Crimes Statistics Act. Then, in 1999, new categories were added to the statute providing enhanced penalties for attacks motivated by pro-choice or antiabortion sentiments. Now, all fifty states and the federal government had laws against hate crimes, and those laws had in turn spawned task forces—hate crime investigation units staffed with hate psychologists and forensic psychiatrists—and more laws designed to prosecute hate criminals for a growing variety of prohibited hatreds.

According to the article, the victim, Elvin Brawley, was a locally prominent artist, an engraver, a craftsman—"a black William Blake," in the words of one African-American professor at the local community college. "Elvin Brawley designed and printed his own poetry books, worked at a local computer-graphics boutique, and still found time to be active in both the deaf community and the black community," said the professor. Others praised Elvin's knowledge of computer science and how he had tirelessly worked to develop and implement computer technologies, especially for the underprivileged and those with special needs. A local civil rights leader proclaimed that Elvin Brawley's death was "an outrage and a waste of the human spirit, a tragic loss to the black community and the deaf community, who now console one another in sorrow and grief and cry out for justice."

The accused, James F. Whitlow, was a native South St. Louisian—a working-class Catholic boy who had been a year behind Watson at Ignatius High, though Watson hadn't known him and now, seven years later, had only the vaguest memory of Whitlow's name and none of his face. But Watson vividly recalled Whitlow's reputation as a hothead, including one specific episode he'd heard recounted a dozen times in high school, told and retold by various witnesses who seemed at once intrigued and sickened by the incident.

Whitlow had gotten into an argument with another kid, a two-hundred-pound right tackle—Terril Williams, a black potential All-American—at a south-side White Castle hamburger joint. The manager had told them to take it outside, and Whitlow, holding up his hands in apparent capitulation, had said, "We are on our way outside right now. Aren't we?" His adversary nodded in response and prepared to leave.

Whitlow reportedly had put both of his hands on the metal chair he'd been sitting in, as if to push it in, and then had swung it aloft in a split second and brought it down on Williams's head. Williams had sat out the rest of the football season with a fractured skull.

Charges were dropped because of Williams's own record of criminal assault and the traces of PCP and amphetamines that had shown up in his blood at the hospital. Whitlow—who had magically gotten away with nearly mortal violence—acquired the school-yard reputation of an Al Capone, cunning and ruthless. He wasn't very big, but he had one formidable weapon—his proven willingness to damage seriously and permanently anybody who crossed him.

By the time Watson met with Arthur, his boss—a former prosecutor—had already called around for the inside dope on the case.

"This is bad," said Arthur, pacing behind his tribunal-size desk, while Watson cowered in a hard-back chair in front of him. "High profile *and* bad. We're talking about weeks of preparation, research, pretrial motions, followed by a murder trial, appeals. This could go on for months. Years. We need a way out of this one.

"You need to file a motion to withdraw," Arthur insisted, glancing at his desktop, where James Whitlow's mug stared back at him from the front page of the *Post-Dispatch*. "Failing that, the best you can do for the unfortunate fellow is plead him out on a lesser included charge—manslaughter, or something."

"Lesser included charge?" said Watson. "In this case the lesser included charge is first-degree murder. The U.S. Attorney is trying out the new federal sentencing guidelines for hate crimes."

"What's the old psycho thinking?" Arthur muttered—an apparent reference to Judge Stang. "There must be a conflict in the federal public defender's office. And you came up on the wheel. You don't have an iota of trial experience. You need to withdraw."

"On what grounds?" asked Watson. "When was the last time Judge Stang let anyone out of an appointed case because of a lack of trial experience?"

"I thought you said this fellow went to Ignatius High?" Arthur said. "He was in your class, wasn't he? It's a potential conflict, at least. I think we owe it to Judge Stang to bring your relationship with this fellow to the court's attention. At the very least, I would call it the appearance of impropriety."

"What relationship?" argued Watson, his misgivings about trying the case and his concerns about the effect it would have on his firm performance profile momentarily supplanted by his resentment at being ordered to get rid of it. "He wasn't in my class. I barely remember the guy's name. I wouldn't know him if he spit in my face. What are the legal grounds for withdrawing? I need search terms to feed into the computer."

"Computers are no good in gray areas," said Arthur, "but of course you young associates don't know that yet. The accused was almost a classmate, and as such he qualifies as a former acquaintance. Take a stab at a memorandum in support of a motion to withdraw, call it the appearance of impropriety, mention your complete lack of trial experience, indicate your dearth of expertise in criminal law. Let me worry about what to do if he denies the motion. File it on Monday at informal matters before Judge Stang. I'll call and try to soften the ancient bully with some kind words. He and I were fellow travelers many years ago in the U.S. Attorney's office. It may be a simple mistake, in which case we want to provide all the excuses he'll need to assign it to another lawyer."

"And if he doesn't let me out?" said Watson. "I can't plead a guy out on a murder charge. It sounds like plain-vanilla voluntary manslaughter. A classic case of provocation. You can't plead a guy to life, or death, for that. He found his wife in bed with another man."

"And murdered him," said Arthur. "Not just murder. The hate business is very problematic. What was it he said? Before he shot the poor man?"

Watson ground his teeth and tasted acid. Arthur seemed to revel in the lurid details of this case while tirelessly working to dispose of it. This was the second time during their meeting that Arthur had asked him to repeat his client's alleged statement upon finding his wife in bed with another man.

"Didn't he say, 'Looks like I'm gonna kill me a deaf nigger'?" said Arthur, with a look of happy revulsion on his face.

"That's the wife's version of the story," said Watson.

"And she says that your esteemed client burst in on her and her sign language teacher, brandished a nine-millimeter semiautomatic, and threatened to kill both of them."

Watson was on the verge of rebuttal on behalf of his brand-new client—Arthur seemed to be reliving his past as a prosecutor while enforcing his present as a partner concerned about the bottom line—but the contemplation of a future without Stern, Pale & Covin paychecks and benefits gave him pause. Arthur pressed on, savoring the unsavory: "According to the wife, your new client pointed the gun at the man's head and threatened him. And she screamed, 'He's deaf, he doesn't know what you're saying!' Then the gun was pointed at her, wasn't it? And your man said something to her about sign language, didn't he?"

"The defendant hasn't told us what happened yet," said Watson. "You're convicting him on the basis of some reporter's reading of the police report."

"It gets worse, doesn't it?" said Arthur. "Because the defendant's seven-year-old son is deaf. And after he killed the poor man, he forced his wife at gunpoint to call military security and report an attempted rape. He didn't want her taking sign language lessons. He kept insisting the boy could lip-read and learn to talk. Cruelty itself against the specialness of the child, which builds into the federal bias-crime charges. This fellow has a malignant, displaced hatred of some kind, a short step from hating deafness to hating the deaf. And the poor wife, not knowing where to turn in her desperate attempts to learn the language of the deaf, falls in love with a deaf man who gets killed for his trouble."

"Are you the prosecutor?" Watson exclaimed, stopping just shy of a shout and tempering what could have been an outburst with an ironic smile.

"Just getting the bad facts out where we can deal with them," said Arthur.

"What about the good facts?" asked Watson. "Let's say he's a faithful husband with a seven-year-old son. He comes home from work in the middle of the day and finds his wife holding on to the headboard with another man on top of her. And the government comes along and says his motive was deafness or race?"

"The circumstances go to the murder charge," said Arthur. "The remarks put him under the hate crime enhancements. Didn't he say, 'You want me to learn sign language? Teach me some sign language. I need to know three signs—dead, deaf, and nigger'?"

"I haven't asked him what he said yet," Watson replied. "I haven't met him yet. So far, she has the luxury of doing all the talking, because she's not in jail."

"We'll know more when we get the reports from the army's Criminal Investigation Division," said Arthur. "Because the defendant is a civilian, the FBI will come in, too, under the Posse Comitatus Act. All we know now is that this case is trouble. And the client is a bad client."

"How do we know that?" Watson asked, deciding at the last second not to suppress an argumentative tone.

Arthur sighed and assumed the demeanor of Fermat teaching the multiplication tables to an eight-year-old. "Good clients are friends of yours seeking assistance in conducting their affairs and businesses. You give good advice to good clients; it saves them money and trouble, and they gladly pay you."

Arthur stabbed his desk with a forefinger, clearly ticked that Watson would even consider a trial instead of a suitable plea. "Bad clients are also seeking assistance. But when you give good advice to bad clients, they don't pay you, and after you represent them for little or no fee, they sue you for your trouble. This fellow is a bad client. I know. I used to put his kind in jail."

"The government doesn't just want to put him in jail, they want to execute him. And you don't stop being a good lawyer just because you're stuck with a bad client, do you?"

"Of course not," said Arthur. "But we—this firm—and you, in the interest of our professional integrity—and, yes, in the interest of our financial well-being—we do our best to avoid bad clients and cultivate good ones. You should be investing your time establishing relationships with our good clients. An appointed case is a nuisance to be summarily disposed of in the most expeditious fashion. If you have a different idea, then . . ."

The unthinkable met the unutterable. Stern, Pale was the best firm in town. Many lawyers and most corporate counsel knew that; the only question for corporate clients was whether they could afford the best. And the only question for Watson was whether he wanted to work at the best firm in town or at another, one that was not the best. Worse, how about going to a firm that was not the best, having left the best firm two weeks before semiannual bonuses were due?

He broke into a sweat just imagining the explanation: *Sandra, remember that job I had at Stern, Pale? The one I got because you put me through the last two years of law school, so I could study real hard and graduate in the top ten percent of my class? Well, San, guess what happened?*

The look on Arthur's face convinced him this scenario was possible if Watson chose, now or later, to put any real work into defending his hate criminal.

"You may have noticed that our firm doesn't do criminal law," said Arthur.

That wasn't quite true. The firm represented white-collar criminals with money. Drug dealers, murderers, and rapists had to go elsewhere, whether they had money or not. Drug dealers, murderers, and rapists who happened to also be immediate family members of huge clients also went elsewhere, but their cases were quietly supervised by Stern, Pale lawyers whose names appeared nowhere on the pleadings.

"I know people in the U.S. Attorney's office," Arthur said. "I'm going to tell you this once: I want to know the instant anyone contacts you with an offer. Hear me? This case will not go to trial."

"Wouldn't the trial experience be good for me?" Watson implored, again not quite sure he wanted a murder trial but resenting Arthur's interference in his appointed case.

"Withdraw," Arthur commanded. "Failing that, plead him out."

CHAPTER 3

"You don't know what to do?" asked Sandra through the door of the powder room, where she was getting ready for bed. "Arthur told you what to do. Get out of the case if you can. If you can't get out of it, then get rid of it."

Watson was propped against the headboard in his underwear, his state-of-the-art subnotebook computer supported by a pillow in his lap. He was scrolling through the memorandum in support of his motion to withdraw from the Whitlow case, which he was scheduled to present to Ivan the Terrible at informal matters in federal district court, 10:00 A.M. tomorrow. Like most associates, he often worked at home, but not even he worked in bed . . . except in emergencies, which happened only once a week or so. Even then, he didn't ordinarily bring files or his computer to bed—he simply thought very deeply about the matter at hand and made a billing entry the next morning to account for the time.

Watson had written a succinct, compelling memo about how an inexperienced first-year associate could easily *lose* a death-penalty case, creating crabbed constitutional bugbears, not to mention loss of life, which could, in turn, engender ten years of postconviction litigation on the issue of ineffective assistance of counsel. The memo appealed directly to Judge Stang's renowned hatred for being reversed on appeal and getting the case sent back to his crowded docket.

Arthur had reviewed the memo, crossed out half of Watson's carefully crafted sentences, and stuffed the paragraphs with rambling, deniable assertions about how the defendant was Watson's "acquaintance" at Ignatius High and how the appointment would create at the very least "the appearance of impropriety." The old meddler had also added three pages of grandiloquence belaboring the obvious, namely, that the district court (Judge Stang) had near absolute authority to exercise its sound discretion in interpreting its own local rules, and had finished with a barely disguised insinuation that a talented young associate of Watson's caliber, working in a firm of Stern, Pale & Covin's stature, should not be ordered to sully his reputation and the firm's good name by defending common felons.

"You have no decision to make," said Sandra brightly, opening the door. "Just do what Arthur told you to do."

She came into the bedroom, still steamy from her shower and looking distinctly unmomlike, a shimmery, green-apple teddy clinging to curves that were still brave, free, and in high relief despite two pregnancies. Kids? In bed asleep. She slithered her way across the sheets and cuddled up next to him and the computer, her bowed head nuzzling him somewhere between his chest and his waist, spreading frothy, wet black curls across his torso and the keyboard. The scent of conditioner wafted aloft and further distracted him.

Her warm, damp hand prowled under the sheets and settled on his thigh. He watched the cursor arrow skid around the screen as he fingered the sponge-tipped TrackPoint III device embedded in the keyboard, right about where his navel would be but for the subnotebook. She kissed one of his ribs, then moved down a rib or two, where he could feel her breathing against his skin.

"I mean, you can't expect them to pay you a six-figure starting salary," she murmured into a roll of his baby fat, "so you can turn around and squander three months defending some racist murderer for no pay."

He pushed the nib of the TrackPoint again, and one of those forbidden thoughts blossomed on the screen of his imagination, as he realized that if Sandra went any lower, into even more erogenous sectors, he could—if he were vile, lewd, carnal—call up that multimedia clip he'd downloaded from the Sultan's Seraglio of Sin Web site—the MMX video of Tanya going down on Sophia in high res, 3-D, 65,000 colors (it was work-related, honest!)—and he could mute the audio and watch it, while Sandra . . . Vile. Lewd. Carnal.

Or he could argue with her. His first duty was to his client, not to his employer; and a federal district court judge had ordered him to defend a human being accused of a capital crime. Arthur was free to give him advice, but it was Watson's case and Watson's client. How would it look if Judge Stang denied his motion to withdraw, and then a week later an ignoble Watson was back in court with a client he had talked into taking a shitty government deal?

Her lotiony hand moved slightly higher on his thigh, her head moved imperceptibly lower. He activated the laptop's pause/resume feature.

"Obey King Arthur," she said. "We have two small children. Do we need to worry about losing your paychecks? Or, I could go back to the accounting firm, I guess."

Shorthand. She was dangling a carrot and waving a big stick. If he agreed to take Arthur's advice and put aside this whimsy about jumping off partnership track and grandstanding in some murder case, she would be happy and affectionate. Otherwise, she would make more noises about going back to work, and they would have an argument about how they had agreed to keep the children out of day care by having one full-time parent stay home. Either way, he wouldn't be playing with what she called his "second penis" (the subnotebook), and if they argued, she wouldn't be playing with the first one.

"I'll probably end up taking Arthur's advice," he said, sliding his fingers around a plump, well-formed, satin-covered breast, suddenly willing to say or do just about anything to keep her hand and head in convergence.

"Good," she said.

Happy and affectionate she was, and so was he. After his blood cooled and his head cleared, he thought about reopening the conversation on the strength of his *probably*, as in: I'll *probably* take Arthur's advice. And could an argument be made that taking Arthur's advice meant *listening* to Arthur's advice, and was that semantically different than *following* Arthur's advice? Instead, he watched her roll onto her back and drift off, while he retrieved his subnotebook and tried to salvage his memo from his boss's depredations. In a spasm of defiance, he renamed the memo ARTHUR.BAK, split the screen, and retrieved his own version, then spliced in just enough Arthurisms to protect himself in case anybody ever reviewed the file.

She was onto something, calling his laptop a second penis. Like cars, computers were perfect vehicles for displaced male sexual impulses. But her phallic imagery was all wrong. Computers are women, not penises. Total infatuation with the love-object, fetishistic behaviors, how-to manuals. Love, followed by the labor and headache of system maintenance: configuring drivers, updating software, applying corrective service diskettes and fixpacks. He diddled the nib of the little cherry-colored TrackPoint device embedded in the middle of the tactile keys. Just the right size and shape . . . Vile, lewd, carnal.

She moaned softly from somewhere far away in the land of nod. He switched off the notebook and studied her sheet-draped swells and curves. When she breathed, her chest bloomed under the silk teddy, and he vividly recalled just why he had given up his dream of being a criminal lawyer and civil rights warrior. Blame it on her breasts. Here he was lounging next to a beautiful woman in a nice house in Ladue, Missouri. He could trot downstairs and fetch another cold beer from the refrigerator, or watch a sporting event on a big-screen TV. He had two cars in the garage and a nice high-end subnotebook. And where was James F. Whitlow sleeping tonight? Less than ten years ago, they had attended the same high school, read the same books, had the same Latin teacher. Now Whitlow was sleeping in a cage of concrete and steel. No possessions, except maybe a toothbrush and a prison-issue Bible. No women. No children. Only criminals and stone-hearted guards.

Like many lawyers, Watson originally went to law school because he had been unsettled by the prospect of graduation from college. If, as Clausewitz observed, war is a continuation of politics by other means, then perhaps, for young Watson, law school was a continuation of college by other means. Good Catholics have vocations, not jobs. Teachers, parents, priests, nuns—they all had solemnly admonished Watson and his brothers and sisters to listen in their heart of hearts for a tiny whispering voice, which would summon them to their calling in life, the way he supposed his father had been called to serve others as a psychologist, helping people solve their problems and tame their demons. But Watson had realized, as he stood on the steps of Ignatius University with his undergraduate diploma in his hand, the tassel depending from his square cap and swinging in the periphery, that he had no calling. He had just completed eight years of quality education administered by Jesuits and was still picking up nothing in the way of a voice summoning him anywhere but to Ladies Night at the nearest Happy Hour.

As for career interests, the only proclivity he'd noticed in his undergraduate studies was a pronounced fascination with evil characters, usually encountered in the pages of literature. Thus his major: World Lit. It probably started back in grade school with the story of Satan's fall. As the nuns told the tale, Lucifer had been at the head of the elite class of archangels. But then the star pupil, the brightest light among the cherubim and seraphim, had turned on his Maker. Rebelled, bit the hand that had made him, fell from grace, and chose to live in darkness and damnation rather than heel and serve at the foot of his master. "Better to reign in Hell than serve in Heaven."

Even as a little boy, Watson wanted to know more. Not about God, who seemed monolithic and as unapproachable as a beam of eternal light, but about this headstrong fallen rebel angel who had willfully condemned himself to the darkness visible. By the time he found the story again in Milton's *Paradise Lost*, Watson had seen the same theme tricked out in hundreds of variations and derivations. If literature is an exercise in empathy, Watson had so far affiliated himself with the unsavory scions of Satan who inhabited the fringes of human endeavor in the novels he had read. It's possible to develop a certain affection for the romantic strains of criminal psyches when one encounters them primarily in print. Raskolnikov from *Crime and Punishment*, Julien Sorel from *The Red and the Black*, Anna Karenina, Macbeth, Richard III—fascinating rogues, one and all. What's it like to be a ruthless criminal? Somebody once asked Albert Einstein what it was like to be a genius, and he said, "What does a fish know about the water in which it swims every day?" Literature offered an easy fix for Watson's curiosity about sin and sinners, with none of the risks involved in actually committing crimes or consorting with criminals.

How noble, if he could say that a love of imaginary criminals had prompted him to attend law school. Instead, having caved in to the fear of beginning adult life without a vocation, he consoled himself with the notion that if law was to be his rather haphazard, default destiny, then he would not become just another nameless, greedy, suburb-living, big-firm lawyer. He would be Clarence Darrow, lawyer for rebels and criminals. He would be a courtroom hero with a gifted, extreme sensibility, driven by ideals instead of by cash, placing himself and his literary sensibility in the service of defending monsters from the society that had created them. In his legal memos and oral arguments, he would quote Terence, the Roman slave and self-made man of letters, *"Homo sum; humani nil a me alienum puto"*—"I am a man; nothing human is alien to me." He would be the kind of advocate who could wind up a passionate closing argument by leaning on the bar of the jury box and delivering a tender rendition of Portia's speech to Shylock from *The Merchant of Venice.* "The quality of mercy is not strain'd, It droppeth as the gentle rain from heaven . . ."

He imagined the jury reaching for their hankies by the time he closed.

Instead of following in old Clarence's footsteps, Watson met Sandra. He fell in love with her first, even before he had taken off her clothes, but when he undid the three clasps over her backbone for the first time, then lifted the lacy cups and planted his head between them, her breasts had inspired the biological equivalent of a religious experience. There was no stopping him, or her. They went at each other every which way, every day, morning, night, lunchtime, under the table on the kitchen floor, in the parking garage on the hood of her car, on the stone benches in Forest Park.

Sandra's breasts were perfectly formed, like the breasts adorning the statues of Greek goddesses: *Nike,* from the balustrade of the Temple of Athena; the *Dying Niobid;* or Praxiteles' *Aphrodite of Cnidus.* Sandra's breasts, worthy of serving for all eternity as archetypes, made him believe in the concept of Plato's Forms.

Once he had met her, law school, which had never been a passion, was minimized, idling like a desktop utility in the background under other, more important programs. *Now this,* he could recall thinking at the time, *must be what life is all about.*

Contrary to the way they behaved, time did not stand still. And barring some violent dislocation of the natural order, a law student will become a lawyer, as surely as a fetus left unmolested usually becomes a human being. The imagery might seem extreme, except that he and Sandra had some misgivings about the more reliable methods of birth control. The misgivings they should have had about premarital sex seemed unimportant, because they assumed—knew!—they would marry. Sooner than they had planned, as it had turned out, when a certain reproductive miscalculation produced what Catholics refer to as a person.

The proper procedure was to say nothing about the new cellular person, get married immediately, and pretend that little Sheila, who appeared seven and a half months later, during his third year of law school, was born premature, even though she weighed ten pounds.

And, later on in law school, after clerking between first and second year with Myrna Schweich, a very good solo practitioner specializing in criminal law, he'd had to decide where to work between second and third year, the year most law students intern for the job they expect to have upon graduation. He had had offers to choose from, most of which were from large firms for good money. Or, as he had explained to Sandra, who was big with Sheila at the time, he could go work with Myrna for about half the money but get almost immediate trial experience and hands-on criminal lawyering, with an eye toward someday going into practice for himself.

Sandra had some stark alternatives for him. She came from a family where the men—heirs and shareholders of the closely held R. J. Connally & Sons Technology Investment Group—made lots of money, while the women ran the households and reared the children. But this was the beginning of the twenty-first century. She was willing to be flexible. With a kid on the way, it seemed to her they had two options. "Either I stay home," she had said, "with the baby, while you go out and make a lot of money. Or you can stay home, and I'll go out and make a lot of money. Either way, strangers will not be raising our children." The plural was a given. Having a family with one kid would be like having a rosary with one bead, or a place setting with only a salad fork. Not done among Catholics, unless God so willed it. Sandra had two brothers and two sisters; Watson had two brothers and three sisters.

Sandra's father, the head of R. J. Connally & Sons, put it a different way. Watson asked R.J. for his daughter's hand in a cigar-and-brandy ceremony that could have happened three hundred years earlier. Cigars had come back in fashion and so had brandy—they were missing only the English drawing room. Instead, R.J., a trim but balding fifty-two-year-old ski-hound who did everything in moderation (except make money and ski), was showing off his big-screen, high-definition, flat-panel plasma monitor and its remote-control pointing device. He had a football game going in a square at lower right, the Tokyo bond markets running in real time at lower left, the Silicon Investor Web site, www.briefing.com, and *The Wall Street Journal* Interactive all running somewhere in the middle in cascading tiles, Microsoft NBC news coming in at upper right, and what he called his "personal small-cap tech portfolio" at upper left, featuring a highlighted bottom line of, ahem, $810,000.

Watson tried and failed to work up the nerve to pop the big question, namely: "What's the personal *large*-cap tech portfolio look like?" So, instead, he tried working up the nerve to ask for Sandra's hand. R.J. clicked and dragged frames around the four-foot-square plasma screen, bragging about how he'd bought two thousand shares of Cisco Systems before anybody else ever heard of it, nervously filling every space of silence with more tech talk. He seemed to sense what Watson was getting ready to ask him, or maybe the women in the family had already let slip why Joe and Sandra were in such a rush to get married. Eventually, Watson asked him. And R.J. put on a solemn look and gazed into the middle distance, as if peering into his daughter's future; then he delivered the first rendition of a speech Watson would hear many times: "The Working Fool and Real Money" speech.

In the Connally household, this speech inspired the same reverence and gravitas that the entire nation had probably felt for William Jennings Bryan's "Cross of Gold" speech or FDR's "Nothing to Fear but Fear Itself" speech. As R.J. saw the world, a young man had to go out and make his first half million in seed money on his own by being a working fool, doing something arduous and not very lucrative: law, accounting, medicine, banking, a profession, or a small business. But only working fools labored in these professions for life. Nothing wrong with being a working fool (he was always careful to point this out, especially when the room was full of them); it could even be a compliment, as when he would remark that someone was a "working fool of a surgeon" or a "working fool of a lawyer." This meant that the person excelled at their profession and indeed had even accumulated skills that could be very usefully hired on occasion. But it went without saying that these people suffered from a congenital lack of market savvy and investment wisdom, because they never took their seed money and aggressively invested it to make what R.J. called Real Money.

A guy with any brains ultimately couldn't help seeing that the Real Money was in the stock market. And that's where you put your seed money—the money you had earned the hard way in your raw youth as a working fool. Only then was it possible to log on before going on vacation, pull up your personal small-cap tech portfolio, and check it at, let's say, $750,000. OK, then you go on vacation for two weeks to one of those time-share condos down in the Gulf Shores (write it off, because you are exploring other time-sharing investment opportunities down there). You come back home, pull up your small-cap tech portfolio, and see that it is now at $810,000, for a net of $60,000 earned while on vacation.

That was Real Money and the market at work. And Watson (so far utterly seedless) could see that he would be in for some serious flacking around the Sunday-evening dinner table out at the Connally's in Ladue if he didn't make big seed money and apprehend the wisdom of the stock market before age forty. Before his second year of law school was over, he had sworn allegiance to his future wife. He put in for the internship at Stern, Pale & Covin, so they could buy a nice house, settle down, and raise more little interlopers, who competed with Watson for access to Sandra's breasts. And soon, Clarence Darrow had become an all-purpose, computerized, legal-research working fool on a big-firm salary. It wasn't altruistic or socially redeeming labor, it wasn't satisfying or particularly difficult, but it paid well and was therefore presumptively respectable. And if he and Sandra ever stopped spending, why maybe seed money would appear.

And what sort of career had Whitlow chosen? he wondered, just before slumber took hold of him.

He drifted off into a dreamscape populated by phantoms born of his apprehensions about what would happen at informal matters before Judge Stang. The only historical detail about Ivan the Terrible he could recall from his undergraduate studies suddenly played itself out in the nether courtrooms of his nightmares. Ivan the Terrible, robed in black after the fashion of Judge Stang, had just seen St. Basil's Cathedral in Moscow—that Disney-looking conglomeration of multicolored turrets and onion domes always prominently featured in news photos of the Moscow skyline. The story goes that Ivan had commissioned the best architect in town to build it for him. And when it was done, and Ivan saw how beautiful it was, he promptly feared that the architect would go on to build an even more beautiful building for someone else. So he had ordered the poor man's eyes to be put out.

Watson, prostrate on the cold flagstones of some multimedia castle of nightmares, unable to breathe, covered his eyes and screamed in anguish, while Judge Ivan Stang pronounced judgment from above.

Arthur stood in the galley, solemnly shaking his head in disapproval.

And Sandra leaned out of the jury box and said, "I warned you, didn't I?"

CHAPTER 4

The court reporter slipped into her booth, switched on her computer, and began clattering on her keyboard. The courtroom deputy tapped the microphone and announced: "Informal Matters, Courtroom Twenty-seven, Federal District Court, Eastern District of Missouri, St. Louis. Twenty-four June 2002. Time and date stamp entered."

The court deputy clicked the gavel icon on his computer screen and a computer-generated sound clip of a gavel banging issued from the courtroom's sound system. "All rise!" he cried.

Young Joseph Watson, Esq., and twenty or thirty other lawyers of all ages, sexes, races, ethnicities, sexual orientations, and legal persuasions abruptly ceased their subdued wrangling, broke up earnest conferences with opposing counsel, stood up from cushioned benches, and faced front.

Watson had been in the old federal courthouse once before, when he was sworn in during a dimly remembered ceremony—at the time he had just finished back-to-back all-nighters doing document productions in two different securities fraud cases and was barely able to find the courtroom. (He went first to the St. Louis city court by mistake.) His next contact with the federal court had been the clerk's phone call announcing his appointed case.

He had no trouble finding the new courthouse: It was the third-tallest building in town. The Thomas F. Eagleton United States Federal Courthouse. Thirty floors, over a million square feet, the largest courthouse in the country, a hub of federal justice for seven states. At a cost of almost $200 million, it was a monument to the explosion of federal laws and federal rights. Twenty-nine courtrooms were arranged in four towers around elevators, lobbies, holding cells, and offices filled with lawyers, litigants, judges, clerks, deputies, court reporters, jurors, prisoners, federal marshals, and expert witnesses—all participants in the booming twenty-first-century industry called litigation.

Watson carried a folder with his motion to withdraw, memorandum in support, and proposed order neatly printed on 100 percent bond, proofread, spell-checked, and signed with his Mont Blanc fountain pen, a graduation gift. According to Arthur, Judge Stang was an old colleague who might read between the lines of the memorandum in support and maybe make an exception to the rule that nobody was allowed to withdraw from an appointed case.

A twenty-foot ceiling vault soared overhead and echoed with the sounds of clearing throats and soft coughing. The benches, the dais, the witness stand and jury box, were all paneled in cherry wood and capped with slabs of marble. Computer monitors were mounted around the jury box, on all four counsel tables, on the dais, in the court reporter's booth. Running transcripts of all proceedings scrolled by on the screens, which could also be used to display everything from police reports and deposition transcripts to MRI films.

Federal District Judge Whittaker J. Stang walked in from his chambers and gasped with exertion (he was an Eisenhower appointee and a heavy cigar smoker) or despair (he nourished a notorious hatred for the legal profession) as he climbed two steps, turned left at the entrance to the witness box, and took two more steps up behind the bench, where he enjoyed the highest vantage point and suffered the eye of every lawyer in the courtroom.

He tugged at the collar of his pleated black robe, muttering under his breath and over his shoulder at his clerks—two petite recent law school graduates, a blonde and a brunette—who tiptoed in behind him and took seats in the empty, sweeping curve of the jury box. Along with the usual battered leather portfolio, Judge Stang carried something pale and rectangular, which looked like a long white book until he brandished it. It was a length of two-by-four about a foot long—a piece of lumber. He set it on end and drew everyone's attention to it by carefully adjusting it so that the breadth of it faced out. Watson assumed it was an exhibit or a piece of evidence—a bone of contention in a motion to be argued later on.

Judge Stang groaned as he pushed aside two three-foot stacks of bound pleadings and pretrial papers.

"It's Monday," he announced, looking up suddenly. "And despite the fond hopes of some of you, I am not dead."

He produced a white handkerchief from a slit in his robe and blew his nose, as one furious eye peered over his hand and probed the congregation.

"I thought I hated Mondays," he said, deftly returning the handkerchief to its place under the robe. He stopped and looked down again. "Look at them out there!" he cried, pointing at the lawyers while addressing his clerks, both of whom smiled and obediently looked out over the heads of the lawyers. "It's not Mondays. It's the goddamn lawyers who show up on Monday mornings seeking continuances for the trial dates I set for them four years ago! That's what I hate!"

About half the audience stopped breathing.

"Is this informal matters?" he hollered, glancing at his clerks. The heads of the two young women nodded in unison.

"I like my clerks smart, young, and pretty," he said to the lawyers. "And if anybody doesn't like it, they can sue me for sexual harassment, age discrimination, and—I don't know—*brains* discrimination, how's that? Can they sue me for intelligence discrimination yet? Never mind. I'll send the government lawyers over to explain a little concept called absolute judicial immunity to them. Take note! I've hired black ones five or ten times at least. They were also smart, young, and pretty."

He paused. "Is this informal matters?" he hollered, glancing again at his clerks. The heads of the two young women nodded in unison again. "See? Attentive, responsive, and they're both great writers who've decided for some reason to defile themselves by placing the English language in the service of a lower human urge called litigation.

"Well, if it's informal matters, let's be informal, shall we? Informal it shall be then." He looked down onto the lawyers thronged before him. "Look at my face!" he shouted, placing a rigid index finger just under his chin. "See what it's done to me? Sitting here watching you mounte-banks and carnival barkers wag your forked tongues at me for forty years? Forty years of mummery and flimflam, travesty and sham!"

Several lawyers coughed, a few others politely covered their mouths and quietly cleared their throats again. Watson wondered if he could get away with leaving. Not a single eye strayed from Judge Stang's face.

"I detest lawyers," hissed the judge. His arm shot out in the palm-out gesture he used to stop his court reporter. Her fingers instantly rose from the keys, and the transcript of the proceedings froze on the com-puter monitors. "And I am a goddamn lawyer," he said, his false teeth clacking. "A federal judgeship doesn't change that. Nothing changes that, once the brain has been reformatted by the case study method, but I hear they are having some success using frontal lobectomies in lawyer retraining programs out on the West Coast."

Twenty or thirty lawyers shifted their collective weight from one leg to the other and looked askance at one another, thinking that this was going on just a tad longer than usual. They sighed and carefully kept their impatience invisible. They were plaintiffs' lawyers, corporate lawyers, U.S. Attorneys, federal public defenders, members of the crim-inal defense bar, big-firm lawyers, solo practitioners, feminist lawyers, AARP lawyers, NAACP lawyers, ADA lawyers, LAMBDA lawyers, NRA lawyers, Lawyers for the Homeless, Lawyers Owned by Large Corporations, Lawyers 4 Christ, Lawyers for the AIDS Coalition, Lawyers Protecting the Rights of Fatal Viruses, Greenpeace Lawyers Against the Dioxin Incinerator at Times Beach, Lawyers for Drunk Drivers, Lawyers for Mothers Against Drunk Drivers, Lawyers for Specially-Abled Children Abused by White Male Republicans, Lawyers for Battered Male Spouses, Lawyers for Affirmative Action, Lawyers for Negative Action and Reverse Discrimination, Lawyers of Color, Lawyers for Promise Keepers, Lawyers Against the Stigmatization of Deadbeat Dads Who Can't Help It, Right-to-Life Lawyers, Abortion Lawyers, Lawyers for a Bar That Looks Like America, Lawyers for an America That Looks Like a Bar, Lawyers for the Beautification of St. Louis, Lawyers Against Lawyers, Lawyers Against Judges—all of whom found a way to keep silent and respectfully listen to an outraged old man pour bilious lava on their heads. It was informal matters, held on Mondays, Wednesdays, and Fridays at 10:00 A.M.—excluding federal holidays—but Watson had been told to call ahead, because sometimes Judge Stang was constitutionally unable to bear the sound of a lawyer's voice, and on other occasions he was under strict medical orders from his cardiologist not to expose the cochlear nerves of his inner ear to sound waves from the vibrations of an attorney's vocal cords.

He bowed, then looked up suddenly.

"As you know, I cannot be fired. I am an Article III federal district court judge. President Eisenhower appointed me for life. And unless I commit a felony, or a high crime or misdemeanor, nobody can touch my paychecks. They can discipline me. They can reverse me on appeal, they can whine about me in the newspapers. If they get two thirds of the U.S. Congress to go along with them, they can impeach me. They can complain to the bar committees and the rules committees. But the practical truth of the matter is I can't be fired unless I commit a felony, and guess what? Over the last forty years, I've become intimately acquainted with exactly what constitutes a felony, and I am not going to commit one. You're all stuck until somebody sends me a mail bomb.

"As you also know, I'm somewhat reticent when it comes to expressing my feelings."

The courtroom erupted in nervous laughter.

"Hah! Hah! Hah!" he shouted, anfractuous veins flickering and standing out in blue relief between his skin and his skull. "Stop laughing," commanded the judge. "I'll be on my deathbed soon. My whole life will be flashing before my eyes, and I don't want to see myself giving the likes of you any pleasure.

"See this?" he shouted and pointed again at the stacks of bound pleadings from dozens of different cases. "Papers filed by all of you. Do you want me to read them? I'm calling every one of your clients so I can personally tell them how much it costs them per word for these learned treatises which I do not read. I cannot read them. I cannot begin to wade through the high tides of bilge that flood this place every day. Do you think I need another fifteen-page regurgitation of the Eighth Circuit's current standard for reviewing an order granting a motion for summary judgment? I can admit to you and to your clients that I do not read any of these papers. Do you know why I can admit it? Not reading them is not a felony. Admitting that I do not read them is not a high crime or misdemeanor.

"There you are. And here I am.

"Don't misunderstand, I'm an avid reader, that's why I can't bear this tripe. Lavater said, 'God protects those He loves from worthless reading'—a sentiment that has me very worried about meeting my Maker."

The lawyers inhaled, prepared polite laughs, then recalled that Judge Stang had ordered them not to laugh.

"Maybe some of you are familiar with a very famous lawyer turned author. He wrote one of these blockbuster legal thrillers. Probably the first blockbuster legal thriller. It's called *The Trial*. It even sounds like a blockbuster legal thriller. That's right, *The Trial*, by old Franz Kafka. A real finger-burning page-turner. Can't put it down! Hold on to your ottomans! Clear out the weekend, unplug the phone. I'm sure you've all heard of old Franz, his novels have been published in five hundred and seventy-two different languages, and if he was still alive he'd be getting advances of several thousand dollars at least. Anyway, he was a lawyer, too. I'm told he never practiced, couldn't quite go that low, but he went to law school and passed the bar. And he had the perfect description of what it's like to read this stuff.

"Old Franz said that reading legal briefs was like being 'intellectually fed on sawdust which had already been chewed by thousands of other mouths.' I don't think he could bring himself to contemplate what it would be like to *write* the stuff, but you all know, don't you? You know what it's like to sit there with your Dictaphone on, droning forth polysyllabic Latin derivatives carefully arranged in the passive voice, with nine dependent clauses and a few semicolonic afterthoughts tacked on for good measure. Every once in a while you get up and go into the john and retch a few times, and then you come back and settle in for some more yammering. Your secretaries put it in their computers, push a button on the printer, and then you send it over here.

"Well, I've been reading that stuff for decades. And guess what? It's all the same! Over and over again! It's eternal damnation! You've all heard about the Eternal Recurrence of the Same? How about the eternal recurrence of the same IRS regulations, of EEOC regulations, of OSHA advisories, and EPA wetlands restrictions, and of lawyers by the dozen explaining them over and over in prose that's even more obtuse than the statutory language. I remember when the Tax Code was twenty-five pages long! Now it's housed next door in several rooms. Nobody's read the whole thing. It takes too many lifetimes! But a tax case would be stimulating compared to the reams of papers I receive about drugs, guns, and civil rights! The Republicans keep passing laws telling me to put everybody who smokes pot in jail. Guess what? Everybody the marshals drag in here smokes pot, and probably half the marshals do too! But that's not enough. Vote the Republicans out, and here come the

Democrats passing laws telling me I have to hold a three-week jury trial every time a woman, a black person, a Jewish person, an old person, or a crippled person gets harassed in the workplace. Guess what? Ninety percent of the population is old, female, Jewish, or black, and one hundred percent of the workforce is harassed every day, which means nine out of ten employees are entitled to three-week federal jury trials. And you want to know why we are backlogged for five years in civil cases!

"Open the floodgates! We need more justice. Look! Here comes Pugnacious Plaintiff and Demonic Defendant—why, I've never heard from them before. Is it justice, peace on earth, equal rights, and goodwill toward men they want, or are they looking for money damages? Punch versus Judy for assault and battery! Romeo et al. versus Juliet d/b/a Capulet Consulting for detrimental reliance and promissory estoppel, Bert versus Ernie for homosexual palimony, Tristan versus Iseult for loss of consortium, Hamlet versus Claudius et al. for negligent infliction of emotional distress.

"This Kafka fellow also said, 'Sometimes I think I understand the Fall of Man better than anyone.' Hah! What does he know about the Fall of Man? He wasn't even a judge! How can he know the first thing about fallen human nature until he's sat through one of these drug conspiracy trials—or how about a sexual harassment case? Let's go ahead and set one of those four hundred and ninety-two sexual harassment cases we have waiting on the docket for trial. I can't wait to listen to another two weeks of testimony about who told what dirty jokes in the workplace."

The clerks bowed their heads and whispered. Some of the attorneys did the same. The brunette rose and tiptoed behind the judge and out of the courtroom.

"I can tell you where she's going," he said. "She's worried about me. She thinks my heart medication is causing some psychological side effects. She's calling my doctors. But before they get here, let's grab the bull by the pizzle and get this over with.

"How many of you are here seeking continuances for trials?" he asked.

About half the crowd looked down at their hands and shuffled their feet. Several attorneys closest to the door took a step or two back and looked for an opportunity to bolt.

"How many?" Judge Stang yelled. "I want everybody who is seeking continuance of a trial date for any reason, including, but not limited to, deaths, vacations, missing witnesses, missing lawyers, drunk lawyers, the press of other business, a conflict in another court—any reason. I want all the lawyers seeking continuances to step over to my right."

A cluster of six or seven lawyers drifted over. Another cluster of seven or eight conferred in low whispers and then followed. Another ten or twelve lawyers looked down at the motions for continuance of trial setting they had drafted up in their offices and desperately tried to think of something else they could make a motion for on short notice.

"Now!" he hollered at this last group. "Over there!"

They hung their heads and shuffled over to join the others.

"Is that it?" he asked, eyeballing the other half of the lawyers. Two more lawyers skittered under his gaze and joined the others.

"OK," he said. "Now I want everybody who is seeking leave for additional time to file any motion or memoranda whatsoever to also move to my right and join the learned counsel who are seeking continuances of their trial settings."

Ten or twelve lawyers walked to the right and joined the others.

"This will include but not be limited to motions for leave to file anything out of time, late responses to motions and memoranda, late answers, late responses to discovery . . ."

Attorneys moved in clusters of three and four to the right as the judge uttered each new category of requests for additional time or for leave to file something out of time.

"Is that it?" the judge asked Watson and the one other attorney left standing next to him, a stout man in a yellow tie and a gray suit.

"Judge Stang," the lawyer said, taking one step toward the bench.

"Did I ask you to approach the bench?" Judge Stang demanded.

"Sorry, Judge," the lawyer took a large step backward. "Judge, I represent the Klaxon Corporation, and we've had a default judgment taken against us because—"

"Because you missed a filing deadline," hissed the judge, his face swelling and purpling with rage, "and now you're seeking leave to file a late answer. Over there!" he bellowed with the authority of Minos sending a damned soul down to the lowest rung of Hell.

Joseph T. Watson tucked the folder containing his motion to withdraw under his arm and tried to meet the apocalyptic stare of Judge Whittaker J. Stang. Watson's throat locked up, his palms were slick against the folder, his heart fluttered like a bird with a broken wing.

"What are you here for, Counselor?" asked the judge.

"I've . . . I've been appointed by the court in the case of U.S. versus Whitlow," said Watson.

"U.S. versus whom?" asked the judge.

"U.S. versus Whitlow," said Watson. "The defendant's name is Whitlow. James Whitlow, he . . . or, I mean, the government is saying he committed murder."

"And you're seeking leave to withdraw from the case," said the judge.

"Well, yes, actually, I am," said Watson. "I don't know if perhaps Mr. Mahoney phoned ahead from Stern, Pale?" asked Watson. "Never mind. The partners of my firm have decided that I am not going to be doing trial work. Uh, I've never been to court. This is my first time. I do computer research mainly. In addition, it seems the defendant, or the alleged defendant, I mean the alleged suspect, the accused was . . . We went to the same high school. He was a year behind me at my high school, and so he was an acquaintance of mine, which my partners feel creates at least the appearance of impropriety."

"Approach," said Judge Stang, with a single flap of his hand.

Watson kept his knees from buckling and approached the bench of the most senior federal judge in the Eastern District of Missouri.

"I have one question I want to ask you in your capacity as an officer of this court," said the judge. "Was this man a friend of yours?"

Judge Stang stared down with a face beyond human. It belonged to the Overman, an oracle, a force of nature, an ancient Greek god who had heard all the lies of everyone who had ever lived, including lies formulated by the best, most highly compensated liars in the history of Western Civilization.

"Technically," said Watson, "no, Judge. He was not a friend, per se. But he was my high school classmate, in the sense that we went to the same high school, and therefore I believe use of the term *acquaintance* is warranted in the papers I have to file in this court. I believe my firm is concerned about the appearance of impropriety."

"The appearance of impropriety?" asked Judge Stang, recoiling slightly, as if he had already eaten one dish of his least favorite vegetable for dessert and was being served another. "Mr. Watson, at my age everything has the appearance of impropriety. I am only surprised when those appearances are deceiving, which happens infrequently these days."

Judge Stang grabbed the two-by-four from its place on the bench and handed it to Watson.

"Your motion has the appearance of impropriety, as well as the odor of impropriety, about it. I want you to take this piece of lumber back to your office and chew it into sawdust. Very fine sawdust. I don't want to find any chunks in there when you're done. And I'm going to weigh the whole mess when you bring it back to me in a few weeks with all of the pretrial materials you'll be filing in your murder case. Do a good job now, because next week some other lucky lawyer is going to be coming along behind you and rechewing your sawdust, understand?"

The judge faced the mass of lawyers on his right and spread his arms like Charlton Heston doing Moses.

"All the requests for continuances, all the requests for additional time and for leave to file out of time, are hereby denied.

"Lord," he cried, looking up into the sunlit vault overhead, "send my white head down to the netherworld with grief!"

Then he looked down again at the lawyers.

"If you want a written order," he said with a grisly smile, "see the docket clerk!"

CHAPTER 5

On the sidewalk in front of the courthouse, Watson held another *Post-Dispatch* in his trembling hands. A typical American adolescence spent imagining fame had done nothing to prepare him for the shock of seeing headlines for the first time from the inside out. It did not say, FAITHFUL HUSBAND KILLS WIFE'S LOVER. It said, HATE CRIME CHARGED IN SLAYING OF DEAF MINORITY.

The sensation of being a *person's* lawyer was also new. Judge Stang had spoken, and Watson had a client. Instead of doing legal research and writing for Arthur Mahoney, instead of summarizing deposition transcripts for PizzaFax, managing documents for ChipsMacro, or playing Greek SlaughterHouse for Subliminal Solutions, Inc., he would be defending a human being in mortal peril. The *Post-Dispatch* and most of St. Louis had already tried, convicted, and sentenced his client. And the prosecutors wanted the penalties doubled or tripled under statutes that punished not only the loathsome crimes, but also the alleged bad attitude with which they were committed. Now, this forlorn citizen's only hope was Joseph T. Watson, Esq.

Photos of the victim, Elvin Brawley, showed him performing his poetry in American Sign Language on a stage for deaf children at a Festival of Language on the Hands. A sidebar featured examples of his computer-generated artworks. In another frame, captioned "A Tireless Advocate of Using Technology to Overcome Disabilities," Elvin Brawley held up a pocket-size VTD—Voice Transcription Device—for the hearing-impaired—a handheld computer capable of displaying spoken words on a liquid crystal screen. He was eulogized as a deaf poet, an "enabler and proponent of empowerment . . . a leader capable of transcending race and disability."

Next to the deaf poet, the photo of James Whitlow captured the requisite spitefulness of the accused—his eyes glowering in the slits of a major frown. ("I'll make you a deal," Watson imagined the photojournalist saying to the officer escorting the defendant. "You tell him to fuck himself and keep the baby, and I'll take the picture, OK?") Whitlow looked mean and scrawny, as if instead of working out he burned fat with a daily regimen of energetic hatred.

Great, thought Watson—*the victim was St. Francis, and my client looks like John Dillinger.*

Over a million people would see this despised felon's photo. In the safety of their kitchens and offices, they would sample another lurid newsprint episode of human depravity, savor the usual blend of horror and intrigue with sips of morning coffee. If Watson hadn't been holed up in the firm conspiring with Arthur to find a way out of the case, he probably could have appeared in the photo with his client, over the caption "The accused, James Whitlow (left), with his lawyer, Joseph Watson." His daydream vanished at the thought of Arthur opening the front page to find a photograph of his associate in the same frame with an accused murderer. As it was he had to make do with a glancing reference in the last sentence of the second-to-last paragraph: "District Judge Whittaker Stang has appointed Joseph Watson to represent defendant James Whitlow, who is indigent." The publicity would be a big hit with the firm's partners. And what about Sandra? The kids? "Sandra," people would say, "why is Joe defending that hate killer?"

He read his own name again and realized that while everyone else would be reading about gore and musing over photos of the alleged murderer, Watson would be interviewing his client and meeting the creature himself—in the catbird seat, the public would think, able to find out what they really wanted to know:

1. What went through your mind when you aimed your gun at the victim's chest and pulled the trigger?

2. Have you spoken to your wife since the night of the murder?

3. What does it feel like, knowing you're going to watch a needle poke a hole in your vein and fill you full of death?

Once in his Honda, Watson grabbed his firm-issued communicator—a combination handheld computer, fax/modem, PIM, and cellular phone—known among the associates as "the tether." It allowed any lawyer in the firm to contact any other lawyer in any of the firm's twenty-five offices all over the world just by entering their initials, or a three-digit ID. He rarely got to play with the communicator out in the field, because he was usually logged on to Westlaw doing computerized legal research at his desk. He was spending so much time on the computer that when he found himself behind the wheel of a car, his first instinct was to look for the keyboard and the pointing device. *"How much memory we got in this thing? Where's the operating system?"*

"Arthur?" he said, after being shuttled from voice mail over to the operator, up to Arthur's secretary, and in through the back door on line three. "I guess you didn't get ahold of Judge Stang."

"Tried to, Joe," said Arthur, "but his clerk said he was on the verge of anaphylactic shock triggered by an allergic reaction to lawyers. After that, one of my old law school classmates who represents the Klaxon Corporation called to tell me you're becoming a lumberjack." He chuckled.

"Paul Bunyan, Esquire," said Watson. "I'm taking a two-by-four to lunch, and then I'm going to the Des Peres County Correctional Center where they're housing my client."

"You'll need to get some kind of story from him before too long," agreed Arthur, "but I want you back here first. I have an expert witness on her way down who might be able to help us."

"What kind of an expert?" asked Watson. Perhaps he should risk insolence and just tell Arthur: *"I'll get my own expert if I need one. Thank you."*

"Have you thought about a medical angle?" Arthur asked. "I mean, what if there's some mental incapacity? A mental disease or defect? That might give you some leverage in bargaining a plea with the government."

"I—" began Watson.

"She's from an old St. Louis family," continued Arthur. "The firm's done their trust and estate work for decades. She went to Harvard. She may be able to help you with the new behavioral testing and some of these scanning technologies. She's a forensic neuropsychologist, a neurologist. It's easier to say what she's not," he said, "but I'll let her do that. Stop by when you get back."

"I was headed over to see my prisoner," Watson said.

"Well, don't," said Arthur. "Come back here first."

Watson punched the phone's END button and felt the despair of indentured servitude mollified by the thrill of being a real, road-warrior lawyer. Pretty soon, he'd be getting twenty or thirty calls a day on his car phone from people willing to pay his hourly fee plus the tab for both ends of a cellular call, just to talk to him sooner rather than later. He had half a mind to pull over and celebrate his first day as a real lawyer by plugging his laptop into his cellular phone and sending an important legal memo back to his own desktop PC at the office via time-sensitive E-mail. To: Joseph T. Watson, Esq. From: Joseph T. Watson, Esq. Re: Important Legal Matters.

He pulled into an ATM for some cash, wincing when he read the balance, $2,489.26. Just enough to cover the automatic withdrawal for the mortgage payment, not counting any checks Sandra had written in the interim, with ten days to go until the next paycheck and two weeks to the semiannual bonus. Instead of staying in the rented two-family in South St. Louis, Sandra had insisted on overbuying in Ladue, where the schools were better and the houses bigger. Money. If he didn't make more of it quick, she would start threatening to go back to the accounting firm. Her newest project was getting the gravel driveway paved, not in asphalt but in concrete, like the rest of the upscale neighborhood. And if she went back to work? No mother at home for the children. No wife at home for the lawyer.

Instead of hastening to his needy client's side, Watson obeyed Arthur and the note-holder on his mortgage, and returned to the firm's parking garage.

He snagged the latest batch of Arthur's memos from his in-box. As usual, Arthur's explicit verbal instructions looked slightly different when confirmed by way of his ubiquitous memos, which quaintly still arrived typed on paper, transcribed by his secretary from Dictaphone tapes.

TO: JTWatson
FROM: AFMahoney
RE: US v. Whitlow

As per our discussion Friday morning, you are to provide this
client with the best possible service and representation. Acquit
yourself and our firm to the best of your abilities pursuant to the
district court's orders. Please explore settlement while keeping a
vigilant eye on the interests of your client.

AFM

To the uninitiated, the discrepancy might seem duplicitous. The difference between "Plead him out" and "provide the best possible service
and representation" was more than mere semantics. But Watson barely
noticed. Arthur's memos were simply good lawyering, five-hundred-
dollar-an-hour ass-covering. Remarks, verbal instructions, comments,
oral promises, spoken threats, questionable suggestions—like pressuring an associate to plead an appointed client to murder one—vanish as
soon as they leave a person's mouth. They are as insubstantial as
wishes, dreams, and Freudian slips. Memories fade, people remember
incorrectly. Years later, if accusations surface, or if blame needs to be ap-
portioned in a particular matter, the first thing lawyers do is retrieve the
files from storage. The files contain tangible evidence—like Arthur's
memo showing he specifically instructed his associate to vigorously
represent James Whitlow, never mind his privately expressed wishes.

The last in-box memo had a yellow sticky attached that said: "See me.
AFM."

His boss seemed incongruously cheerful.

"I sent your memo on decapitations to Ben Verruca, the in-house
counsel at Subliminal Solutions," said Arthur. "He loved it. He thought
your analysis of the scorekeeping similarities was right on the money."

"Virtually the same in both games," said Watson. "I'm glad he liked
it."

Arthur smiled. "You told me about the scorekeeping, but I'm not remembering," he said, with a wave at the stacks of documents and correspondence on his desk.

"Of course," said Watson. "In Greek SlaughterHouse, there's a puck-
ish, Till Eulenspiegel–ish prankster who follows the game protagonist
from room to room in the Castle of Skulls, keeping score by stabbing

freshly decapitated heads with a pikestaff and depositing them in a seabag slung over his shoulder. After each new head is collected, the prankster turns, winks at the gamer, and paints a red hash mark on the screen with a bloody finger. It's virtually the same in CarnageMaster, except the head collector is a satyr or faun type, with goatish horns and bedraggled hindquarters, who turns, winks at the gamer, and paints hash marks with a bloody, caprine hoof. Same pikestaff. Same seabag. Blatant rip-offs."

"I remember now," said Arthur. "Fine work."

Whew. One more crisis averted in the daily triage of career-threatening disasters that erupt in the life of the lowly associate. Subliminal Solutions was a huge client, and Ben Verruca was one of Arthur's old law school pals. For years, SS was just another also-ran in the multimedia gaming industry, with a couple hundred-thousand sellers called Tower of Torture and Anthrax Avenger. Then one Sunday in Lent, 1998, gamers all over New Mexico and Arizona witnessed what one of them decided was the Blessed Virgin Mary appear midway through Tower of Torture, version 3.11.

The site of the appearance was Hans the Headsman's turret in the Tower of Torture, where Hans did his bloody executioner's work, decked out in spiked and ringbolted black leather armlets, a ventilated cast-iron jockstrap with worms poking their heads through the mesh holes, and jackboots covered with scorpions and roaches. The graphics work on Hans's upper body had won the gaming industry's coveted Styx Award because it was so anatomically precise that, with a video driver capable of delivering 65,000 colors at a screen resolution of 1024 by 768, gamers could actually pick out the origin and insertion of every one of Hans's bulging muscles. Phat graphics. Anyway, beginning at 12:01 A.M., Mountain Time, on that fateful third Sunday of Lent, gamers also claimed to see the face of the Blessed Virgin Mary in the polished reflection of Hans's dripping, bloody broadax.

The scene featured Hans, known to gamers for years, as a Headsman who approached his work so zealously he usually peeled skin off of his victims or jammed his thumbs into their eye sockets before beheading them. But in version 3.11, Hans's workday included the task of decapitating the ravishing, nubile, buxom Princess Althea—condemned to die, alone in the tower, under Hans's ax. When Althea bent her gorgeous head of marcelled blond locks over Hans's chopping block, her breasts (billowing and heaving with sobs) spilled forth from the neckline of her sackcloth garment. At this point in the program, according to the user-market surveys and the real-time, live-site studies, 37 percent of male gamers between the ages of eighteen and twenty-nine clicked on the pause button and studied Althea's lissome frame all bent over the chopping block. Survey results indicated that most of the pause-mode gamers lingered to consider whether—with Althea all bent over and due to be executed forthwith—wasn't there a way to find a silver lining in this dark cloud of death? At screen right, a pixel's toss from Althea's breasts, an ad-box applet for Zap high-capacity storage drives had a click-through rate of 14 percent, yielding some 178,000 visitors to the Zap Web site from its connection with the Hans/Althea Tower of Torture scene.

It was a hot site even before the Virgin Mary sighting. Once that happened, *Cyber Hour* did a special. Then *Night On-Line*. Live footage showed what devout gamers claimed was an image of the Blessed Virgin Mary appearing in the blade of Hans's broadax, as well as supposedly actual teardrops beading up on their computer monitors, blood oozing from the seams of their joysticks, and the soothing voice of what gamers were now calling Our Lady of Multimedia, audible even though their sound systems were turned off! When the computer code was disassembled and debugged, an instruction set showed a subroutine calling the image of a feminine face, but the Subliminal Solutions programmers had remarked-out the code so that it was nonfunctional. The designers claimed they had originally planned to have the estranged head of Althea reflected in Hans's broadax, but now the line of code was plainly inoperative.

Tower of Torture sales took off, then the mania spread to Anthrax Avenger, and later to Greek SlaughterHouse, because gamers nationwide were inspecting the blades of all the weapons for hints of other avatars and incarnations. Subliminal Solutions's stock doubled, split three for one, then doubled again, despite a price/earnings ratio of 127 to 1. SS was now one of the hottest companies in the burgeoning multimedia gaming industry, and Arthur was perpetually anxious about losing the account because of his own dearth of technical computer expertise. Enter new law grad Watson, who was comfortable talking pixel density, dot pitch, MPEG, MMX, Ultra QuickTime for Windows, VRAM, and video drivers.

Keeping Subliminal Solutions happy was important, because keeping Arthur happy was important. In a huge outfit like Stern, Pale—one of the biggest law firms in the country—associates like Joseph T. Watson are fair game, hirelings, who can be summoned to work for any partner, anytime, doing the most tedious research known to the profession—unless they are protected. Watson achieved protected status by working primarily for Arthur Mahoney and by doing such a good job that Arthur in turn made sure his associate's time was not squandered doing document productions or flying to Newark to do some due diligence on a struggling fertilizer concern. Intrafirm patronage. Not that the work he did for Arthur was any more meaningful or fulfilling than flying to Newark, but it was predictable and manageable, kept him at home with his family, and involved dealing primarily with machines instead of obnoxious lawyers and demanding clients.

Arthur's intercom beeped; he motioned for Watson to stay put.

"Yes, yes. We're just wrapping things up. Have one of the receptionists show Dr. Palmquist back here."

"Your appointed case," said Mahoney, switching off his intercom as his eyebrows converged in a frown. "The Business Committee met this morning. They're concerned about the amount of time these appointed cases are consuming. Yours came up by way of example."

"I don't have much choice about it now," Watson said. "Do I?"

"Well, as I mentioned, I've been busy with contingency plans."

Watson tried to think of a polite, respectful way to tell Arthur that he would prefer handling his own appointed case. And the district court's local rules were on his side—appointments are made to individual lawyers, not firms.

Arthur smiled again. And Watson smiled back, until he realized Arthur was smiling right past him at someone standing in the doorway behind Watson's head.

"Come in, Dr. Palmquist," Arthur said, rising from behind his oversize desk and opening his arms.

Watson stood up and jumped in his clothes at the sight of a woman who looked as if she'd been assembled in the lobby by a team of health and beauty experts. A wife, two kids, a Catholic's fear of adultery, and an early apprenticeship in sexual harassment litigation had endowed him with a reflexive aversion to attractive women, especially in the workplace. Back in his single days, he would have tagged this one with a field-programmable microchip tracking device, so he could chase her down and explain his uncontrollable impulse to be with her, to know her. But those days were long gone, and those drives subordinated to hearth, home, family, spouse, God.

When he helped himself to another view during Arthur's introduction, he was alarmed to discover that she looked even better up close. Black tresses raked around to one side and swept up in a French twist. Steel rims, sheer coral lipstick, same color on the nails. The hint of darkness under her eyes suggested sleeplessness and made him want to solve the mystery of what was keeping her up at night.

When she and Arthur pecked cheeks and talked of family friends, Watson studiously suppressed the gawking reflex and busied himself with the books and papers that had been in his lap when he stood to meet her. Then he looked past his reading materials to suede pumps, nylons somewhere between pearl and nude, hem a notch below provocative, and up, his eyes ascending the shapely lineaments of Dr. Palmquist—"Rachel," to Arthur.

Not normally one to notice clothes, Watson kept noticing hers: The nylons, which indeed turned to nude when she moved them; a lustery blouse that heaved with competitive archetypes in full bloom. A thin, rainbow-colored mist of refracted light clung about the nylons and the sheeny blouse. He trained a gimlet eye between the lapels of a royal blue double-breasted silk suit, where the blouse was just sheer enough for him to make out the ghost of a floral motif on whatever she was wearing underneath.

Married, he thought. *Gotta be.*

"I still see Jim," said Arthur.

"I don't," she said, with a shrug.

"Good," said Arthur, taking her hand up in both of his. "It's for the best. And things have ended as we thought they might. Remember—we predicted this?"

Watson felt a pang at all the physical contact Arthur was getting out of the deal. He was reminded of another path not taken in his undergraduate studies. He spent a semester or two absorbed in anthropology, primatology, evolutionary psychology—any epistemology that studied protohuman behavior, humans illuminated by way of monkeys, apes, lawyers, and so-called "primitive" peoples, primal motives played out on a parallel stage. He recalled a passage about male vervet monkeys he had read in a book—*How Monkeys See the World*—assigned to him by his Evolutionary Psychology and Primate Science professor, a man who had been his idol and mentor for all of three months, until Watson found out what associate professors make a year: "Once he has entered a new group, a male interacts with other males primarily in the context of competition for access to sexually receptive females." For young human males, Watson had concluded, the observation could be altered to advantage by changing "primarily" to "exclusively."

He might need to see her again. She was some kind of expert in a field he might need to know a lot about. And it was fun watching Arthur—a heavy hitter who bowed to no one—fawning at the altar of physical beauty.

"We were discussing weighty legal matters relative to the subject of beheadings," said Arthur with a half laugh, motioning her into a chair and summoning Watson to join them.

"Frequently a symbol for castration, according to Freud," she said, wrinkling an eyebrow and mocking her own erudition with a lilting chuckle. "The eyes stand in for the testicles, or so the psychoanalysts say. I once wrote a paper on it. I think you should hire me as an expert on beheadings. I'm quite knowledgeable on the subject."

"You don't say," said Arthur, retreating to the safety of his desk and lining up a few pencils that were already lined up. "How about that, Joe?" Arthur joshed. "An expert on beheadings and castration."

"Very Oedipal," said Rachel. "Freud gets into it with the usual Greek myths. Oedipus rips out his eyes instead of castrating himself, because he has seen the forbidden sight of his mother's genitals, Medusa's head—that which no man may look upon and live."

Watson held in a smirk and watched Arthur become nonplussed at the discussion of maternal genitals. She had a dreamy, vacant look about her, until she opened her mouth and made like Dr. Knowledge. And her limbs seemed to be loose in overlubricated sockets, off on their own, until she needed them. Head? Eyes? Watson had heard them called everything from Big Sam and the Twins to the Devil banging two bowling balls on the gates of Hell, but this cephalopeniform, oculotesticular eyewash was a new one on him. She was having the old guy on, and Arthur didn't even know it.

Another gander at the nylons made Watson a little goosey and short of breath. Under orders to kick in his own doors and arrest himself for discrimination of any kind, he knew he would never inventory the wardrobe of any male professional he met in the course of a day's business, which meant—what?

"Astonishing," Arthur said. "We were just discussing Medusa's beheading the other day. But in the context of these blasted computer games."

"Greek SlaughterHouse?" said Rachel. "Are you guys into Greek SlaughterHouse? My nieces and nephews love it."

Arthur looked from Rachel to Watson and back again. "You see what an old man misses when he won't sit down in front of a computer."

Watson mentally ticked off the forbidden categories to which she did not belong: she was not a secretary, not a client, not a Stern, Pale & Covin associate. He was the one mired in forbidden categories: marriage, commitment, wife, son, daughter; at least this was happening in Arthur's office, so he wouldn't have to show her a photo of the wife and kids.

He knew his boss and the firm well enough to know that Arthur would immediately segue out of the discussion of Greek Slaughter-House, even though the chance of a breach of client confidentiality was minuscule. It was part of the Stern, Pale code. ("You get paid well for your legal skills," Arthur had once advised him. "You get paid very well for keeping your mouth shut.")

"Enough about games," said Arthur. "Just now our problem is defending a young man whose own head sits somewhat ticklishly on his shoulders because the federal government, speaking figuratively, wants to cut it off."

"I've read the papers," said Palmquist. "And the materials you sent me."

"What materials?" Watson asked. It was his case! What was Arthur doing sending his client's shit to people without asking him first?

"The police reports came in," said Arthur, without looking away from Dr. Palmquist. "I faxed them to her," he said, with a single glance at Watson.

"I'm sorry," Watson said, "I must have been distracted by the précis on castration. What is it you're an expert in?"

"I'm a neuroscientist," said Dr. Palmquist.

"She's a brain scientist," said Arthur.

"Oh," said Watson, wondering how she went about studying brains.

"I'm especially interested in forensic neuropsychology. In criminal cases we are sometimes called to testify at sentencing hearings as mitigation specialists, or sometimes at trial we are expert witnesses on the subject of the behavioral implications of neurological disorders. I'm part of a team. Have you heard of the Gage Institute? Ignatius University Medical Center Campus? We study the neurophysiology of violent criminal behavior. We are trying to find out if there are anatomical, neurochemical, metabolic, magnetic, or electrical differences between the brains of violent criminals and normal brains."

"She called me," inserted Arthur.

"I did," she said. "A so-called hate crime presents certain issues of motive and intent, or what you lawyers call mens rea, the mental state necessary to find a person guilty of committing a crime, issues that are of particular interest to neuroscience. I can send you abstracts from some of the studies we're doing on automaticity, neuropathologies, violence, and neural networks."

"Suppose your boy has a mental defect of some kind," urged Arthur. "Seizures, schizophrenia, psychosis, or some other organic malfunction. Suppose Rachel could find something like that for you. Wouldn't that operate in his defense?"

"The defendant has a history of impulsive behavior, if you believe the newspapers," she said with a smile. "We don't know if there's a history of drug or alcohol abuse. If we're lucky there's a history of epilepsy or seizure activity—which sometimes manifests itself in impulsive or violent behavior. There's a report that he's had at least one episode of antisocial behavior in the past, for which he received psychiatric counseling."

"What report?" blurted Watson.

"But it's the hate business that's earning him a death sentence," interrupted Arthur.

"We don't know if we have deliberation or premeditation," said Rachel. "And then there's the question of the hate motivation." She nodded at Arthur. "The government seems to be trying out a mixed-motive argument. They want to enhance the penalties here because the defendant was motivated in whole or in part by ill will, hatred, or bias because of the race or disability of the victim. So proving the defendant was enraged by sexual jealousy doesn't help us. Under the law, they have the burden of proof, but in fact we do. We're forced to prove a negative. That he was not also motivated by bias, despite his remarks. If he is a bigot, we have to prove that he was not motivated in whole or in part by bigotry in committing the crime."

Watson hadn't been a lawyer for very long, but he had deposed enough doctors to recognize Palmquist's syndrome: She was a doctor whose favorite hobby was being a lawyer.

"Isn't a question like that beyond the realm of medical science?" asked Watson. "I mean, are you suggesting you can test the guy and tell us whether he's a bigot?" He laughed.

"No," she said, without smiling. "But I wouldn't be a bit surprised if the prosecution tried just that. They have a brand-new Bias Crimes Unit set up over there—investigators, hate psychologists, prosecutors, expert witnesses—just waiting for cases. The new testing techniques combine standard behavioral testing for automaticity and unconscious bias with functional neurological scans to produce a personality and neurofunctional profile of the defendant. Then you combine the profile results with all the other evidence of bias—comments at the scene, membership in hate organizations, earlier threats against protected minority groups—and you make a case that the crime was bias-motivated.

"It used to be that these neurological workups were used mainly in the sentencing phase. Lately, both sides have been trying to sneak them in at trial, either to prove a mental defect, or to suggest to the jury that the defendant is a remorseless bigot and an incorrigible criminal. In this case, the charge has more to do with the U.S. Attorney's mental state than your client's. Black votes for next year's Senate elections. African-Americans are sick and tired of seeing these bias-crime statutes used on people of color who intentionally pick white victims. Remember the U.S. Supreme Court case of Wisconsin versus Mitchell?" she asked.

Arthur stared blankly.

"I wrote an article about that case," said Watson. "Wisconsin doubled the sentence of a black kid because he intentionally picked a white victim and assaulted him."

She nodded. "And here's a chance to get a white guy for using the n-word during a violent crime."

Her neurolegalistic bafflegab was impressive, but he remained skeptical; he took notes and tried to get enough of it down, so he could look it up in the privacy of the library or find a relevant Web site. He wrote "Wisconsin v. Mitchell" "automaticity," and "neurofunctional profile" on his notepad.

"You get a full, free medical workup on your man," said Arthur. "The newest and best scans. Have you seen the pictures they're taking of the brain? Why, you can almost reach out and touch it. Rachel tells me these devices are so sensitive and sophisticated—it's to the point where she can scan you and see if you're full of hate or sexual deviance."

"Arthur," she said with a laugh.

"I'm not saying your man is full of those," he continued. "What if he's schizophrenic? Suppose he has some kind of malignant, hate-bias, anti-social deviation syndrome?"

"Suppose he has," Watson said, perhaps a bit too curtly. He wasn't sure he could stomach another enthusiastic denunciation of his client from Arthur. He wanted to suggest that he meet with Dr. Palmquist somewhere outside of the firm and away from Arthur, where he could maybe learn a little bit more about sexual deviance.

"Try this," she interjected. "You stop by the lab next week, and I'll show you what we do, and the potential relevance of a workup for your client's defense. If you don't like the looks of it, or if he doesn't want to try us, then forget we ever met."

Not likely, he thought. "I'll stop by," he said.

"Excellent," said Arthur.

"I know you gentlemen are busy with decapitations," she said playfully, "and I've got to get back to the lab and study some heads which are still attached to bodies."

Arthur reached for another pencil. Watson took another eyeful and wondered how she got interested in brains, and if heads are penises and eyes are testicles, then brains are—what?

Serried, leather-bound spines loomed behind her. Her chest expanded and shimmered with another laugh. Against the backdrop of inert volumes filled with symbols, the flesh of her face and hands seemed at once transcendent and delightfully corporeal.

Arthur came out from behind his desk—a little boy seeking more affection, a look of sad longing at the last glimpse of her leaving. His phone trilled.

"Uh, Doctor," said Watson, deciding to make a move while Arthur was admiring her exit and feeling for his phone.

She turned on a heel and smiled.

"This report you mentioned," he said, continuing to move past her and leading her out of Arthur's office. "And the history of impulsive behavior. Is that from a medical report? What kind of impulsive or antisocial behavior are we talking about?"

She laughed as they moved down the hallway. "You've been reading the *Post-Dispatch*," she said. "If you want unreliable dirt in St. Louis, you need to read the *River City News*. They claim that your client had a few run-ins with the law and was tossed out of college five years ago after he painted a swastika on a water tower in southern Missouri. Sounds like a fraternity prank, but unfortunately it also fits right into his hate crime résumé."

They stopped outside Watson's office, where she noticed the name plaque. "Your place?"

"My place."

"Could we?" she said with one glance at her watch and another one into his office.

"Sure," he said.

Once inside, she closed the door. The place felt like a closet after Arthur's corner-office real estate.

"Shall we sit?" she suggested, showing him one of two hard-back chairs in front of his desk.

Watson pointedly did not look at her legs when she crossed them.

"I've been an expert witness often enough to know how these appointed cases work," she said. "Your job is to look the case over and then plea-bargain. Maybe the government would agree to drop the hate crime charge, if you'll agree to murder one. But natural life without parole for plain old manslaughter?"

"Sounds like he needs a good criminal lawyer," said Watson. "Maybe you and I could hold a bake sale and raise enough for a retainer fee."

"I'll be straight with you," she said. "I want your client. I want to scan him. I want to map his neural networks. Some of the other people I work with want to administer certain neuropsychiatric batteries. It's research."

"And if we plead him out," said Watson, "you won't get to do that?" He was relieved to discover a self-interested motive—it made her more trustworthy.

"I've done a decade of research on violent criminals," she explained, "but so far it's been mostly postconviction—sentencing and mitigation reports. The neurosciences are finding their way into the courtroom. But nobody wants to invest time and money in a neuropsychological defense until it impacts on a few high-profile verdicts. How long has DNA been admissible evidence in criminal trials?"

"I don't know," he said.

"Less than twenty years," she said. "And it came in the first time only because a lawyer got together with a scientist and tried it. Do you follow me? I study criminal brains, including what motivates criminals, and in this case motive is an essential element. Modern crimes, especially these new hate crimes, require proof of the defendant's mental state—mens rea, motive, whatever you want to call it. Was there deliberation? Intent? Was there hatred against a protected group? Just plain hatred? How about hatred against an unprotected group—ugly people or fat people, stupid people or lawyers? Is there a mental disease or defect? Modern neuroscience is increasingly able to provide objective data about mental states, and the law is increasingly interested in that data. At some point, the two fields will intersect." She smiled, as if she would be proud to be directing the traffic at such an intersection.

"What do you need me for?" he asked.

"I need a lawyer willing to try something new in defending a high-profile case," she said. "I think the science is there, and it can be used to convict, acquit, or mitigate sentencing. I need a lawyer to get the client's consent and file the necessary motions. If we find anything, I need to be called as a witness."

She leaned closer to him. "Ever wonder where that 'I' you take for granted inside of you comes from?" she asked, pointing just behind the intense green of her eyes in their dusky hollows.

"Yeah," he said, "sort of," even though, at the moment, he was more interested in sending the 'I' inside of him off somewhere, so the other parts of him could lose control of themselves and go thither in response to her come-hithering. Was she wearing tinted contact lenses, or were her eyes really that green?

"I'll show you what I do for a living," she said. "And I'll show you what I can do for your client. And you'll get a free glimpse of the future of neurotechnology."

Their wordless stare lasted too long without being the least bit uncomfortable.

"When are you going to see him?" she asked.

"After lunch," said Watson, "I think, unless Arthur—"

"You're probably a very good lawyer," she said, mocking him with an overdone bat of her eyelashes, "but would I be out of line if I came right out and said you don't know shit about criminal law?"

"I know *shit* about criminal law," said Watson, "which means, as you said, I don't know shit."

"Good," she said. "No ego problems. Let me tell you what I think. Arthur is going to let you blunder up this case quick. Because the sooner you bonehead your way into the boneyard, the faster you'll plead the guy and forget about it. But we don't want that, do we?" She wagged a finger at him, a finger he suddenly wanted to touch, maybe even taste. "So, what you need to remember this afternoon is: Don't let your client tell you what happened, yet."

"Why?" asked Watson, puzzling over this apparent discrepancy between the criminal law and his witness interviews in civil cases, where he was always trying to dig up facts.

"Nothing gums up a criminal case worse than bad facts. In the meantime," she said, opening her folio and handing him a typed form, "we need any and all medical records. Get his signature on here and tell him that if the government wants to ask him about ultimate issues he should tell them to call you."

"Right," said Watson, taking the form.

"The time sequences are especially important," she added. "We don't want him having any time at all, understand? Because if he has time, it may mean he either deliberates, or he stops and thinks about how much he hates deaf black people, follow me?"

"I think so," said Watson, suddenly relieved at finding an ally who seemed to know something about defending the client instead of just getting rid of him. More important, he understood the part about not wanting too much time for deliberation. He wanted to go somewhere with her, before he had time to think about the consequences.

"You're smiling, Mr. Watson," she said. "If I had injected water tagged with a radioisotope like oxygen-15 into your antecubital vein and had you under my PET scanner, I could tell whether you are smiling because you are happy, or smiling because you are voluntarily moving your facial muscles."

"Go on—really?" he asked.

"Ever wonder why photographers tell you to say 'cheese'? When you execute a voluntary, unemotional smile, you are using portions of your motor cortex to get the job done. When the same facial muscles exhibit the so-called 'true' smile of an emotional situation, they are being controlled by a different part of your brain. According to electrophysiological recordings, pretend smiles generate different brain-wave patterns from real ones. The true smile is controlled by our limbic cortices," she went on, uncrossing her pearl-nyloned legs, "sometimes called the 'older' or 'lower' parts of our brain."

Watson felt a tingle in the older, lower parts of his brain.

"The same parts of your brain are responsible for the four F's of neurobiology: feeding, fighting, fleeing, and . . . family matters."

Another comfortable look.

"Is that a true smile you have going there, Mr. Watson?"

She pulled a card out of her pocket and added a home phone number with a pen from his desk. "Call me and tell me what happens."

CHAPTER 6

Accustomed to the efficiencies of computerized legal research, and unaccustomed to midday traffic patterns on one-way streets, Watson took a wrong turn in his Honda and noted again how much of lawyering outside the office seemed to consist of roaming around in search of the right building to appear in and then finding a place to park. He drove past what looked like a courthouse twice before he realized it was the Des Peres County jail. The concertina of razor wire around the top story should have tipped him off. Maybe all of his online legal know-how had been acquired at the expense of a corresponding measure of practical knowledge, like knowing the location of the courthouse, or thinking *jail* when he saw barbed wire around the top of a building. In the future, with the aid of two-way videoconferencing and a loaded multimedia PC, he would be able to appear at informal matters, file documents in court, and interview his clients without leaving the office, and this annoying waste of time spent grooming, buttoning cotton shirts, knotting silk ties, and transporting well-dressed flesh in real time through meat space could be avoided.

A U-turn landed him in traffic three blocks deep. He was delighted when his car phone rang, but Arthur's voice quickly dispelled the road-warrior glow.

"Remember what I told you about good and bad clients," he said. "And before you go in there, think about this jailbird recounting every word you say in open court three years from now when he sues you and us for malpractice and ineffective assistance of counsel. The attorney-client privilege protects him, not you. Hear me? The less you say, the better."

"I hear you, Arthur," said Watson. "The less I say the better," he added, knowing his sarcasm would be buried in cellular static.

"And start softening him up for a plea to life, because that's what he'll get, unless you go to trial, in which case he'll get the death penalty."

"I'll see what kind of shape he's in first, Arthur."

"Don't bother," said Arthur. "I used to do this for a living. A whiff of the death penalty turns them into trapped animals. All they want is a claw hold, a crack of daylight, a glimmer of fond hope on the long walk to the chamber. Scare him. Tell him to count himself lucky if they'll let him plead to life."

Watson hung up and imagined his client sitting alone in a cell, a desperate human being, a victim of twisted fate and uncontrollable circumstances, not a friend in the world . . . except his court-appointed lawyer. Arthur had a point. But a federal district judge had issued a superseding order, calling Watson to a higher and lower duty. According to Arthur, Watson was romanticizing his client, hearing the siren song of the civil plaintiff and the criminal defendant—the downtrodden and dispossessed, desperately needing representation, lacking the means to pay for it. Maybe he'd seen one too many major motion pictures about Clarence Darrow and Gerry Spence. For some reason, in Hollywood's estimation, a lawyer representing the venal interests of individuals was less despicable than another lawyer representing the venal interests of corporations or governments. Perhaps it was a question of magnitude—it was nobler to represent the lesser and feebler of two evils. A curious distinction. If, as a lawyer, you can see your way to represent venality and evil, wouldn't it make sense to represent the *greater*, moneyed, and more powerful evil—and increase one's chances for a success at trial?

He entered the prison with a burst of enthusiasm, as if he meant to announce to the prison officials and employees that it was his first day on the job as a criminal lawyer, and that he wanted to be the best criminal lawyer he could be in the shortest possible time. Joe Watson, movie lawyer, to the rescue. Then it occurred to him that they might not sympathize with his aspirations.

A rotund black woman in a uniform and a spectacular headdress of cornrows sat inside an octagon of painted steel screens. She stared intently into a screen where she was absorbed in a government-subsidized game of Microsoft Hearts, expertly shuffling and clicking her way to victory over her three software opponents, Anna, Lynda, and Terri—the virtual banes of employers nationwide, and another example of the profound impact of computer software on our nation's productivity.

A guard lounged in a booth and buzzed people in and out, a green bulb flashed over a metal detector and an X-ray machine.

"Name?" asked the woman, her eyes tagging him once from a government-issued mask of bureaucratic insolence.

"Joseph Watson," he said.

"Prisoner?" She tapped an antique keyboard through a filthy plastic spill-guard, not bothering to conceal her intense irritation at being forced to abort her attempt to shoot the moon.

A red bulb flashed somewhere behind the Plexiglas, and a loud buzz made him jump. An automatic door opened, and a uniformed man pushed a gurney bearing a sheet-draped human silhouette. A body? Joe smelled a waft of disinfectants, followed by the stench of urine.

"Prisoner?" she repeated.

"Whitlow," he said. "James Whitlow. I'm his lawyer," he added significantly, but it did nothing to dispel the woman's conspicuous opinion that he was completely insignificant.

Watson signed a ledger and selected the cleanest of a half dozen vinyl chairs. He tried to brush it off, only to discover that the filth had long ago become part of the chair. No one asked him for ID or checked his name against any list to find out if he was indeed a lawyer.

Ten minutes later, a guard brought James Whitlow through a steel door into a conference room windowed in painted steel and chicken-wired Plexiglas. The defendant's stature fell something short of his crimes—well under six feet, with the same physique Watson recalled him having in high school, the sort of frame young bucks achieve with a fat-free diet of caffeine, nicotine, and hard liquor. His pasty skin appeared to be shrink-wrapped around muscles and tendons, which looked pegged and drawn taut at the joints. His granny glasses were clean, his mustache brushy but neatly trimmed. In his orange jumpsuit, he had the look of a sanitation worker or an auto mechanic ready to put in a day's work, if somebody would only get the cuffs off of his hands and feet.

Watson sat across from his client at a scarred table with an ashtray and a buttonless, dial-less phone between them.

The guard gave Whitlow two cigarettes and handed Watson a small box with two matches in it.

"Pick up the phone when you're done," he said, and turned to leave.

"What if I got to piss?" Whitlow asked suddenly, stopping him at the door.

"I just took you to piss," said the guard. "You wanna piss again?"

"Not now," said Whitlow, "but before we get done here, I might have to." He squirmed and tugged at himself under the table. "I told you it's an infection. They took me down to Sick Call and now they want to make me wait until the test comes back before they give me back my medicine."

The guard stared through the Plexiglas, waiting for Whitlow to quit talking, then he looked back at him and said, "If you need to piss, pick up the phone," then left.

"Joe Watson," said Watson, putting his right hand out over the table. Whitlow extended his manacled wrists, and Watson said, "Oh."

They managed a shake in spite of the hardware, Watson's tender keyboard pinkies snagging on the prisoner's scaly calluses. The cracks and creases of his skin were paint-speckled and patinated with chalk or white dust, prompting Watson to recall reading that he had worked for a painting and drywall outfit, because he had been laid off at the packinghouse, after he was fired from a night job as a computer technician, after he was thrown out of Southwest Community Technical College when he was a freshman for having painted the swastika. His client was a manual laborer who had fallen off a carousel of part-time jobs into prison. Maybe going to law school hadn't been such a bad idea after all.

Watson pulled his firm-issued computer out of his briefcase, set it on the table between them, booted up, and opened a new file.

"That government lawyer kept asking did I have money to hire me a lawyer," said Whitlow abruptly, talking fast and coughing to camouflage the quavers in his voice. "I told him I got no money. So he says I got to take my chances with an appointed lawyer. Then he came back next day and said I was lucky because I got appointed a lawyer at the biggest firm in town. Said you wrote an article about this hate bullshit."

"The judge appointed me to be your lawyer," said Watson, "but—"

"And I got lucky," Whitlow interrupted, "because I got one from the best firm in town, is what they told me."

Watson suddenly realized that his client was almost motionlessly hyperventilating; only the rapid constrictions of the rib cage and the faint rushes of air hunger gave him away. The knuckles of his cuffed, clenched fists seemed ready to burst through the skin. Watson missed being able to read the lettering of a purple tattoo on the left forearm, which blurred and flashed out of sight when Whitlow took his elbows off the table. He smelled urine again and wondered if it had soaked into the stones of the place, or if his client had—

He stifled a swell of pity—a sentiment he'd never experienced in civil litigation, where money was the most valuable thing at stake and the misfortunes were usually corporate ones. Arthur's instructions were to give the client the facts—namely, that Watson had never handled a criminal case before, that he had never even watched a jury trial, that he had been appointed by the court to handle a murder case in which the government was seeking the death penalty under the new federal sentencing guidelines for hate crimes. He was to use all of his persuasive powers to present the facts, which would lead even the most obtuse defendant to conclude that pitting a bright, young legal researcher like Watson against a seasoned federal prosecutor in a murder trial was like putting Microsoft's Bill Gates in the ring with Iron Mike Tyson. Once the defendant was suitably terrified, he would make some phone calls and muster up money from family and friends and hire a criminal lawyer.

"You're a good lawyer, aren't ya?"

"I'm a good lawyer," said Watson. "But I've never done criminal law. I've never been to trial. My firm doesn't do criminal law. We do business law, mostly for big corporations."

"So I ain't lucky enough to get a criminal lawyer," he said bravely. "But leastwise I got a good one." He searched Watson's face for confirmation. Then he made claws of his shackled hands and raked his goatee. The skin of his face and arms was paler than the whites of his eyeballs. "That delousing shit they sprinkled on me itches worse than the crabs," he said, gouging his chin again and grimacing around a set of gray teeth. He tried a tough guy's laugh and didn't make it.

Watson sustained a blast of rancid breath and stared at the gray teeth. Antibiotics, he realized. One of his first assignments as a new lawyer was to go to a building with a team of six other Stern, Pale associates and sift through boxes of documents produced by the plaintiffs in a massive class action suit brought against PharmChem, Inc., one of the firm's biggest clients. The plaintiffs had taken tetracycline as children and gotten stained teeth because of it. The stained teeth in turn caused intense emotional distress, loss of income, suicidal depression, astronomical medical and dental bills, failure to thrive, loss of self-esteem, and posttraumatic stress disorder. But above all, for much of his first six months as a lawyer, the stained teeth provided Watson with roughly sixty billable hours a week, which in turn put him three fourths of the way to bonus-track billables in half a year's time. Then the case had settled, and all that was left of it was Watson's fat performance profile and his profound, intimate, well-financed knowledge of exactly how and why antibiotics stain teeth, the frequency of discernible stains in random demographic samples, the two thousand or so depositions of emotionally disturbed adolescents whose mental afflictions were caused by stained teeth. Murders; suicides; spontaneous, idiopathic hebephrenias; gout attacks; pancreatic malignancies; and failed marriages—all brought on not by the antibiotics but the resultant stains, which in turn caused such plagues of catastrophes they would have persuaded Pharaoh to let Moses and the Twelve Tribes leave Egypt.

It was all he could do to keep from asking, "Your teeth—tetracycline, right?" But he was fighting a new war now. A murder case, where instead of being a biomedical lottery ticket, stained teeth would be just another flaw in an unlikable defendant, which would make it easier for a jury of sturdy, death-penalty-minded citizens to do their duty.

Perhaps Watson could achieve justice with a blended martini of civil and criminal litigation by having one of his law school buddies sue PharmChem on behalf of Whitlow, thus obtaining an expedited settlement and enough money to hire a criminal defense lawyer?

The prisoner lifted his arms and stuck an unlit cigarette in his lips. Watson was so distracted by the litigable gray teeth that he missed the tattoo again, except for the word JESUS in purple ink and . . . snakes? They both looked at the matchbox.

"So you got to represent me, even though I can't pay, is that it?" asked Whitlow.

Watson noticed one huge vein, bulging like a seam in his client's left bicep, blue as a bruise under the smudged white skin. Does shooting drugs make your veins bigger or smaller? Smaller, he thought—had to be, because in movies and novels they are always looking for veins. Right? It seemed improbable that an Ignatius High grad would be mainlining, but, then, it seemed just as improbable that one would land in prison. Maybe Whitlow had surrendered to the authorities because he knew what the Jesuits would do to him if they got hold of him first.

"The judge appointed me to be your lawyer," said Watson, "but you may want to think about whether there is any way you can get yourself a criminal lawyer, a specialist."

"How do I get me a criminal lawyer?"

"Those you hire," Watson said, trying to think of a way to convey the looming peril of having a first-year associate and Westlaw geek for a trial lawyer. "You'd need money for that. A retainer of some kind, as I understand it."

Watson didn't know the first thing about signing up a client, because he'd never done it before. He worked for WorldAgri and BioKinetix; a retainer was something you put in your kid's mouth.

"I got no money," said Whitlow. "What if I ask the judge to appoint me a criminal lawyer?"

"You may ask the court to appoint you a different lawyer," explained Watson. "But you don't get to pick your specialty. If the request is granted, you'll probably get another new lawyer with no trial experience. That's how it works in this district."

And, he thought, *you'll probably get one that graduated in the bottom tenth of his class, instead of the top tenth, one that works at the worst firm in town, instead of the best, and you will have pissed off Ivan the Terrible, the meanest judge in the Eastern District.*

"Is there anybody you could borrow money from? Any relatives who might lend you a retainer fee?"

"There's money on my wife's side," he said.

"Yeah," said Watson, "well—"

"Maybe some . . . other people might help," said Whitlow guardedly.

"Other people?" asked Watson.

"Friends," said Whitlow. "I have some friends who might do it. But they wouldn't want anyone to know they were doing it. And I wouldn't want anyone to know either. It wouldn't be good for me if people knew I got money from them."

"Really?" asked Watson.

"It's like a club. We all promised each other a long time ago that if anything happened to one of us, the others would . . . help him out."

"I see," said Watson. "Well, if you can get the money from your friends at the club, I would hire a real criminal lawyer."

"Well," said Whitlow, "one of my friends in particular—his name is Buck—and Buck could maybe get me lots of money, except I got a problem with my car."

"It has a lien on it?" asked Watson, groaning inside, wondering how to politely tell his client that borrowing against some decomposing Ford Escort with cloth seats and gunny sacks for floor mats would roust up about a tenth of a criminal lawyer's retainer. Whitlow had what Sandra's dad would call a Real Money problem requiring a working fool of a criminal lawyer.

"Yeah," said Whitlow averting his eyes, "sort of like that. It got towed the same day of the . . . killing. And so Buck can't get to it. It's got a Hide-A-Key under the back bumper. But he don't wanna go out to the impound lot till he knows why the cops or the MPs towed it. What if they towed it because they was thinking it had something to do with the killing?" Whitlow fixed him with a single, cautious glance. "This shit is all privileged, lawyer talk, ain't it? Right? I know that. But still, Buck wouldn't like it if I told you he was gonna try to get at my car."

Watson couldn't tell if Whitlow was rambling and confused, or just desperate for any chance to get a real lawyer. "Who's Buck again?"

"Just a friend," said Whitlow quickly. "But if he could just get to my car, he could maybe get me money. See, last year my old car got towed from the same spot, because of Lucy Martinez, who don't like people parking in her spot. And maybe she called it into base security again, just coincident, and that's why they towed it. But Buck is worried because it got towed the same day the nigger got shot, and he's afraid if he goes after the car—" Whitlow swallowed and looked away again "—then the cops might start asking him about the nigger getting shot. And Buck don't want that. Shit, I don't either. Buck is a buddy, and he don't like cops any more than I do."

Whitlow needed another stern lecture on the relationship between the n-word and the death penalty, but if the car somehow led to money, Watson could leave that chore for a lawyer who would be paid by the hour.

"Either way, the cops will know it was your car, right?" asked Watson. "Never mind why it was towed."

"Well," Whitlow said, "not really, because it don't have plates at the moment. I bought it off a guy a few months back, but it still ain't registered. Like I said, this happened to me once before with a different car. They ain't gonna let nobody have that car unless they show up with a title and a photo ID. And if she finds the title, they gonna make her register it and buy plates before they gonna let her take it."

"Her?"

"My wife," said Whitlow.

Watson kept waiting for a point to be made and, while waiting, worried about his client's coherence, his ability to testify on his own behalf in the unlikely event he ever took the stand.

"So, anyway, long story short. Buck could ask Lucy his own self if she called and got the car towed, but Lucy don't talk to him because she's afraid of him, and she wouldn't fess up to it anyway. So, we sorta need somebody else to find out if it is OK for Buck to go and see can he get at the car, or will he get arrested if he goes after it?"

Watson had shifted his attention to the notebook computer, which was making more sense than his client. He barely realized what was being asked of him. "Me?"

"Well," said Whitlow, holding his cuffed hands out, "you could call the tow lot maybe and pretend you are the owner. Or maybe you could go see Lucy Martinez and maybe say you are a lawyer and ask about the day of the killing and all. Then maybe slip in and ask like no big if she seen my car get towed, or better still was she the one who called it in and got it towed."

Watson looked askance at his new client.

"I can see you ain't never had your car towed," Whitlow said angrily. "If they think the car had something to do with the killing, it is going to be locked up tighter than a fourteen-year-old virgin, and if anybody tries to get at it, they will get arrested. But if it's just a dead car towaway, it's gonna be out in the general impound lot, which is a ten-acre spread with nothing but chain-link around it, which means Buck could get at it, if he had to. Does that make sense?"

Watson wanted to say no, but his client's agitation was mounting. "I'll see what I can do," said Watson.

"Hell," Whitlow urged, "you probably gotta talk to Lucy anyways, right? What if she has evidence about the day of the murder? Maybe she seen something, right? She's only two units down. She maybe heard the nigger going after Mary? Or maybe she heard Mary yell, 'Help, James! The nigger is comin' after me!' If there's a God He heard her say it, too. But mainly, I can guarantee you that if it's just a dead tow, Buck could maybe get me some money. Enough to maybe get me a real criminal lawyer, and you wouldn't have to do all this appointed lawyer work. Maybe we could even get some money for you. Who pays you?"

"No one," said Watson. "Appointed lawyers don't get paid. I have to do it because I'm a new lawyer. I'm supposed to be willing to devote my time to helping people who can't afford lawyers."

"But you ain't willing, right? You don't want to do it? Or maybe you would do it, but only if you was getting paid?"

"I didn't say that," said Watson quickly. "A federal district judge has ordered me to be willing. But a judge can't order me to be able." Played back in the courtroom of his imagination, as per Arthur's instructions, this seemed a little too stark.

"I'm not saying I'm not able," added Watson unconvincingly. "A judge has concluded I am able and ordered me to be willing. I'm just advising you of my qualifications."

Whitlow shuddered and scanned the activity on the other side of the Plexiglas, as if he expected personnel in the next room to let loose a few man-size rats, turn the conference room into a big shock cage, and get on with some behavior modification. "I need a fucking lawyer, man," he said in an angry rush. A single tear beaded at the rim of one eye and quirked its way down his cheek. He sucked in a few more breaths. Scared past shitless, he was on his way to respiratory arrest. "The government lawyer said you filed some bullshit telling the judge you can't be my lawyer because we were buddies in high school. What is that? I don't know you from shit, motherfucker."

Watson felt sweat burning in his pores—the clammy liar odor wafting off of him. The Apaches were right, you don't need a polygraph to detect skin galvanic response, just line up the suspects and smell them.

"Your name was so familiar to me," said Watson, desperately prevaricating while he tried to think of a few lines that would stand up in court three years from now, when another lawyer would transform this wretched, all-but-sentenced criminal into a civil rights and legal malpractice plaintiff, suing Watson for attempted client desertion.

A lawyer owes the client the duty of zealous representation, or however it goes in the Model Code of Professional Responsibility, another doomed attempt to codify morality with conditional precepts.

"I'm your lawyer," said Watson, peering into Whitlow's jumpy eyes. "If you scrape enough money together, I will help you get a criminal lawyer. If you can't get money, I will do my very best to defend you. I promise. If I don't know the law, I will learn it. But I can't learn trial experience in three weeks."

Whitlow took fast, shallow breaths, opened his manacled hands, flexed his fingers, and made white-knuckled fists again. "They want me dead," he said, holding a deep breath. "I need a real lawyer."

Watson resisted the impulse to console the poor guy with his qualifications. Things could be worse. Although he was a new lawyer, he had graduated ninth in his class, won the Computerized Legal Research & Writing Award, been on the law journal, and now worked at the best firm in town. Stern, Pale didn't hire just any old law grad. He was capable of researching any area of the law better than most of the other lawyers he knew, and so would at least be able to write a bang-up brief appealing the disaster that would surely occur at trial. He'd hold off talking about the odds of reversals in criminal appeals until his client could stomach fat chances and percentages in the lower single digits.

Watson fingered the little TrackPoint device of his computer and noted how quickly he was able to scroll through the outline of his witness interview. He inwardly congratulated himself on ordering the extra 256 megabytes of RAM and the tertiary cache.

The two men stared at each other across the scarred table.

"You understand the charges the government is bringing against you?"

"Sure," said Whitlow. "Government bullshit. Murder ain't enough. It's murder and what? Discrimination, I guess? I shoulda waited till my wife was being raped by a white guy."

"This is a federal crime. Federal prosecutors who work for the U.S. Attorney's office are going to be trying to convince a jury that you should get the death penalty."

"Shit," said Whitlow, swatting away another tear.

"If the jury decides you killed this man in the heat of the moment, because he was . . . let's say, sleeping with your wife," said Watson, "that's voluntary manslaughter. That's anywhere up to ten years in prison. If they find that you planned it, or that you stopped first and had time to think about it, and then deliberately, or willfully, or maliciously killed him anyway, that's first-degree murder, thirty to fifty years."

Whitlow shook his head bitterly and looked at his manacled hands, splaying white fingers on the black tabletop.

"This bullshit was not supposed to happen," said Whitlow.

"If the jury finds that part of the reason you killed him was because he was black or deaf . . . that's a hate crime."

"DEAF?" shouted Whitlow. "What's *deaf* got to do with it?"

"The statute . . ." began Watson.

"What statute?" said Whitlow, "the same that says you get extra for killing niggers?"

The n-word temporarily locked up Watson's central processing units and triggered a series of automatic professional behaviors. He reached into his briefcase and extracted a photocopy of the relevant federal statute.

"It's a sentencing guideline," explained Watson. "So it assumes that the jury has found the perpetrator guilty or he has pleaded guilty or nolo contendere to a crime against person or property." He fished a yellow highlighter out of his suit coat and deftly marked the relevant passage as he read it aloud: " 'If the finder of fact at trial'—that's the jury— 'determines beyond a reasonable doubt that the defendant intentionally selected a victim . . . as the object of the offense because of the actual or perceived race, color, religion, national origin, ethnicity, gender, disability, sexual orientation, or viewpoint on the issue of reproductive rights of any person, increase by six levels.' "

"I never heard of nothing like that," Whitlow complained. "Where did they get that from?"

Watson took the question literally and avoided admitting that, until his appointment, he had never heard of the statute either.

"It's from the United States Code Annotated, Title Eighteen. From the looks of it, it's modeled on the California Hate Crimes Act. But all fifty states have some version of bias-crime legislation. You're being charged under the federal version. See where it says 'disability'? That's where the deafness comes in. The government is charging that you allegedly killed this man, in whole or in part, because he was black. And if that doesn't work, they'll try to prove you killed him in whole or in part because he was deaf. And if they succeed at either, or both, then the maximum penalty for, let's say, voluntary manslaughter is enhanced under the terms of the statute six levels, or even twelve levels, since the enhancements are cumulative, then the maximum penalty gets boosted up to the maximum penalty for first-degree murder, which, as you know, is death."

"Jesus Christ," said Whitlow, "musta been a nigger thunk up that law."

Rachel Palmquist's warning about how bad facts gum up the case had revived a dim memory from a law school exam in Ethics and Professional Responsibility, an alarm bell, something about not allowing the client in a criminal case to commit to a version of the facts until you decide whether you are going to call him as a witness.

"What the fuck would you do?" he asked, sudden red splotches burning in his white cheeks. "The nigger was goin' after my wife! She's screamin' for help. She said so when she called 911! I was standing there! I heard her!"

"That's what the police report says," Watson interrupted. "But then, it seems, she changed her story and said you found her—" he paused "—in your home with her sign language instructor."

Whitlow's eyes flushed red. The muscles in his neck arched under his waxy skin. "He's a fucking sign language instructor?" said Whitlow. "Then I'm Martin Luther King."

"Then who was he?"

"Never mind," said Whitlow. "You're my lawyer, right? If it ever looks to you like I'm going down for death or in for natural life, I want you to tell me, understand? Before trial, got it? Because I ain't going alone. Swear to God I'll take her with me! Understand me?"

Good forceful eye contact, Watson thought, *probably had a firm handshake as well, when uncuffed.*

Whitlow sniffled and whipped his head to one side, wiping his nose on the short sleeves of his jumpsuit. "As for deaf," he said, "are we gonna get to cross-examine her?"

"Her?" asked Watson.

"My wife," he said bitterly. "I seen in the paper where she's supposedly the queen of sign language now. Fuck me five times every Friday if that's the truth."

"It's not true?" asked Watson.

"My boy's deaf. Born that way. Couldn't hear the space shuttle if it took off in the backyard. Deaf as a box of rocks, which means he can't talk neither. So, the oral school here in town, they teach deaf kids to talk and read lips and they don't use sign on them. Now, we coulda sent him there, or we coulda sent him up to Fulton at the residential school. Let him be with his own kind and learn sign. What would you do?"

"I don't know," said Watson with a frown.

"Some doctors and teachers claim you ain't supposed to use sign language on your kid if you ever want them to learn to talk. They had a deaf girl on *60 Minutes* who learned to talk. And as soon as I seen the girl talking, that was what I wanted. So I decided to keep him away from sign and give the oral school a try."

"OK," said Watson, studying his client's twitching facial muscles and trembling hands.

"That girl on *60 Minutes* was happy," said Whitlow, "because she could lip-read and talk."

This sounded like one of those syllogisms from a formal argument. But a premise seemed to be missing, and Watson was therefore uncertain of the conclusion. Either the sudden ability to lip-read and talk had made the girl happy, or happiness was impossible for her until she could lip-read and talk. More important, for Watson, either sign language had something to do with homicide, or his client was nuts.

"I decided about the oral school and I paid for it," said Whitlow. "Mary don't care about nothing but cold beer and *Days of Our Lives*. According to her, Charlie was deaf because my uncle was deaf, so it was my problem. She didn't give two turdballs either way. Now, all of the sudden, she's Miss Sign Language with a sign language instructor? I shoulda seen it coming," he said, banging the table. "Then Charlie flunked out of the oral place. Next thing I know, all this bullshit happened."

"Because he flunked the oral school? Because of the sign language instructor?" asked Watson, trying not to sound like he needed some serious help with the story.

Whitlow sneered and nearly spit sideways. "He weren't no fuckin' sign language instructor, lawyer. I told you that."

"Well?" asked Watson. "Then who was he?"

Whitlow took a deep breath, as if about to tell him, then shook his head in disgust. "Forget it."

"Maybe you were defending yourself or your wife against an intruder in your home. You didn't sign a confession, did you? You didn't give them a statement, did you?"

Whitlow shook his head. "I ain't dumb enough to talk to the cops. Only the Queen of Sheba, Mary Whitlow, is dumb enough for that. She's trying to fuck me good and proper," he said, squaring his shoulders and hyperventilating through his nose. "She's trying to fuck us all! We'll see about that." He pointed at himself in bitter triumph. "We'll see about that."

Watson sat up and pushed the computer aside.

"At this early stage," said Watson carefully, "I don't really want to know if you did it—and if you did it, I don't want to know why you did it, yet."

"If I did it?" cried Whitlow. "What would you do?"

What would you do? There it was for the third time. The cardinal inquiry of the nonprofessional. Clients and patients routinely asked this question; doctors and lawyers did not answer it. It was an oral invitation to a professional malpractice suit.

"If we decide you should take the stand in your own defense," said Watson, "the Rules of Professional Responsibility will not permit me to ... A lawyer cannot knowingly present perjured testimony to the court."

"I think I just got amnesia," said Whitlow with a sharp, scared laugh.

"That's entirely possible," said Watson brightly. "Severe psychological trauma can induce amnesia to concurrent events. Which brings me to my next proposition. There are expert witnesses, doctors or psychiatrists, who can test you for certain mitigating factors. Medical, or psychological disorders, which may have manifested themselves in uncontrollable behaviors."

"I have amnesia," said Whitlow. "And I'm nuts."

"I'll find out more about the medical or psychological defenses," said Watson, "and then I will advise you about whether the tests will help us. I'll need your medical history. Any psychiatric treatment? Are you taking any medications?"

"Dilantin," said Whitlow. "I used to have fits awhile back."

"Fits?"

"Seizures," he said. "Epilepsy, I guess, but not bad. Only twice, I guess."

Watson opened the file containing his notes from his first meeting with Dr. Palmquist. There it was: "If we're lucky there's a history of epilepsy or seizure activity."

Watson retrieved the medical release form Dr. Palmquist had given him, put a pen on it, and pushed it across the table to Whitlow.

"How often do you take Dilantin?"

"Every day," he said. "Sometimes I forget, but I generally take it. And they give it to me in here, too. I had the bottle on me when they brought me in."

"And how long have you been taking it?"

"Since my one year at the community college. My first seizure. Six, seven years."

"How about medical records of these seizures? Where can I find those?"

"Seen lotsa doctors," said Whitlow, "mostly at Doc-in-the-Boxes. Can't remember them all. I guess I went to the clinic at Southwest Tech the first time. Then . . . Hell I can't remember them all. You want me to sign this," he asked, "for the medical records?"

"Yes," said Watson. "Did you take your medicine on the day . . . of the murder?"

Whitlow looked over Watson's shoulder. "Would that be good? Or bad? Or do I have amnesia?" Watson held the paper for him, while he signed the release. "I'll try and remember whether I took my medicine. This seizure shit might be important, huh?"

"I don't know," said Watson, placing the form back into his briefcase. "Maybe. I've talked to one doctor. She seemed to think seizures might be important."

"In that case," said Whitlow, "I still have amnesia. I can't remember why I'm nuts. I don't know if I took the medicine or not, and maybe I forgot a lot of jumbo seizures."

"How about the infection you complained to the guard about?" asked Watson.

"Oh," said Whitlow, looking off the edge of the table. "That's some other medicine I'm needing. It's personal. It's got nothing to do with seizures or being crazy. It's just a piss infection. No big deal. They said I can have medicine once they get done testing my piss."

Watson typed *"urinary tract infection"* into the computer.

"So, you got *'Lucy Martinez'* written down in your computer?" asked Whitlow.

Watson nodded.

"And my car's a ninety-two Ford Taurus. Gray. No plates, like I said."

"And you need to know what?" asked Watson, typing in the information.

"Just tell them you are the owner and can you come pick it up," said Whitlow. "Fort Sheridan Base Towing and Vehicle Impound Lot, Craig, Missouri. If it's being held for evidence, they'll tell you no you can't get it. If they say bring the title in, register her, and she's yours, that means it's in the general impound lot."

Watson typed. "And this helps us do what? Get you some money?"

"Never mind money," said Whitlow. "Let's say it will help me get some evidence for my side of the story."

"Which is?"

"I thought you said you didn't want to know if I did it," complained Whitlow, "and then you said that if I done it, you don't want to know why I done it, yet?"

"Right," said Watson, chagrined. "Never mind. I'll try to find out about the car."

"That would really, really help," said Whitlow.

He squirmed again in his chair. "Fuck me," he scowled, "I gotta piss right now." He picked up the phone and tucked it between his chin and his shoulder.

"Piss," he said angrily. "I gotta piss again."

He lifted his chin, let the receiver drop back into his hands, and hung it up. Then he raised his manacled hands, put the unlit cigarette in his mouth, and steadied it.

"Are you gonna light this?" he asked.

Watson saw the tattoo on the left forearm, which was now facing out and lit by the fluorescent ceiling fixtures: a mauve heart spidered in black coronary arteries, which zigzagged around the heart and unfurled in a small bouquet of snake heads spewing forked tongues around the purple text, JESUS HATES NIGGERS.

Watson stared at the tattoo and panicked. He heard the sage and seasoned voice of Arthur Mahoney within him: *This is a bad client.*

"Match," said Whitlow. "Hello, lawyer?"

Watson, still staring at the tattoo, lit the match and held it to the end of the cigarette. Whitlow took a drag and blew out the flame with a puff of smoke and foul breath. Watson dropped it in a round steel ashtray and watched a white fume rise from the charred tip.

Why had he, a fairly bright bulb, ignored the advice of a senior partner with forty years on him? Watson wondered. The head of the litigation department at Stern, Pale & Covin, one of the best lawyers at the best law firm in St. Louis, Arthur Mahoney was right. The sun rises in the east, water flows downhill, this is a bad client.

Whitlow offered him the other cigarette.

"No thanks," Watson said with a wave.

"Go ahead," said Whitlow. "I'm a Christian."

"I noticed," said Watson.

Whitlow took a puff. Watson inspected the purple heart attack on the dirty white arm while his client exhaled blue streams of smoke.

"The tattoo," said Watson.

"Yeah," said Whitlow, glancing down and flexing muscles under the inky flesh. "Only cost me forty bucks, because the guy was a buddy."

Whitlow took another puff and turned his arm for a better view. His face suddenly went limp, and he glanced up at Watson. "Hey, this won't . . . This don't mean anything, does it? I mean . . ."

Watson took a big breath and eyed the computer's battery gauge.

"I saw it hanging on the wall of a tattoo hut where I went to get some ink done ten years ago," he stuttered, flushing in splotches and squirming in his chair. "I thought it was funny. It's a goddamn joke!"

Watson mentally slipped into law exam mode: May the government compel the display of the defendant's tattoo and enter it into evidence, or would that violate the Fifth Amendment's guarantee that no person shall be compelled in any criminal case to be a witness against himself?

"Am I fucked?" pleaded Whitlow. "I'm remembering something. I'm remembering that a girl I used to date gave me this tattoo once while I was asleep."

Watson sighed.

"Look," begged Whitlow, "it don't say 'I Hate Niggers,' does it? Read it, lawyer! It says, 'Jesus Hates Niggers.' What if it said 'Jesus Loves You'? It don't mean I love you, does it?"

CHAPTER 7

L
ess than twenty-four hours after meeting with his tattooed client,
Watson was on cellular hold, waiting for Myrna Schweich—the
only criminal lawyer he knew personally—who had taken another
call. He had the receiver of his communicator pressed to his ear, trying
to listen for her return while following Rachel Palmquist's faxed page of
directions as he hiked through the interlocking corridors and lobbies of
the Ignatius medical-industrial complex, dodging swarms of patients in
street clothes and striding lab personnel in white coats. He'd worked
for Myrna the summer between first- and second-year law school, had
done research and written an appellate brief for her—his only brush
with the criminal law—before leaving for Stern, Pale and the big bucks,
according to Sandra's wishes. But he often looked back longingly at the
path not taken. Two or three of his law school classmates had gone into
criminal law. And when he saw them at lunch, or at happy hours, or
parties, they seemed to be having all the fun—if wild stories were any
indication. Watson and the rest of the studious, law review types from
the top of the class were working at huge firms, reading ERISA regulations or summarizing the depositions of forty plaintiffs whose panic
disorders were allegedly caused by inhaling fumes from CleanWhite's

toilet bowl cleaners or from eating too much monosodium glutamate at Wu Fong's.

He had called Myrna the day before, after Judge Stang had made it clear the Whitlow case was his and Arthur had made it equally clear that he wanted the case disposed of at the first opportunity. Myrna had already heard about his appointment. She had offered to look at the complaint and affidavit and the military police reports that Joe had received from the government's lawyers, to maybe give him some pointers. He'd faxed them to her, and now he was calling for advice.

While waiting for her to come back on the line, he was reminded of her incongruous, near comic appearance—she was less than five feet tall, with orange hair, tiny freckled hands, and childlike features. She had big blue eyes that were always aimed up at him from at least a foot lower than what was usually called stature. If you didn't know her, *diminutive* came to mind—until she opened her mouth. From four-eleven land, Myrna projected an aura of absolute authority. She picked up words like clubs and used them to beat the bloody shit out of men who were twice her size. She'd been trained in the trenches at the county public defender's office for a few years and then had gone solo. Just before she'd put him on hold, he'd asked her the typical rookie criminal lawyer question: What if his client was guilty as charged?

Myrna came back on the line and resumed control where she'd left off. "It doesn't matter if he's guilty," she said. "It doesn't matter if he's a racist. Nothing matters, except making the prosecution prove every single element of their bullshit case. Your job is to make the government do its job. Because if you don't, then tomorrow we might as well move to Russia, where they can arrest anybody they want, including defense lawyers, and put them in jail."

Myrna was a real lawyer, not a glorified businessperson. He had visited her office in Clayton several times to pick up research assignments. She had a .357 magnum loaded with Rhino hollowpoints in her right-hand desk drawer and a minirefrigerator stocked with Heinekens. She left the office every day at five o'clock sharp, and went home to her two little girls, who didn't know much about what Mommy did for a living. Like almost everyone else, her husband was afraid of her. He worked nights as a cardiac pump tech out at Barnes Hospital and spent the rest of the time saying, "Yes, Myrna."

Watson had met the girls once at Myrna's office after he'd graduated.

Both were redheads, like their mom. "Are you going to be a lawyer for people with lots of problems, too?" they had asked him.

"No," he'd said, "I'm going to be a lawyer for people with lots of money."

Myrna's voice nattering in the earpiece of his communicator brought him back to the present: "You gotta make the government do its job."

"But what if they prove he's a racist," argued Watson, "and what if they prove he called the victim a, you know," he said, jerking his head around and dodging a clutch of nurses on the skywalk, "and what if they prove he killed him. Then?"

"Then geese farts," said Myrna. "If you find a guy in bed with your wife you're gonna call him a nigger, a honky, an asshole, an ugly fuck-head, a rotten douche bag, a filthy cocksucker, and anything else you can think of before you kill him. That doesn't mean you killed him *because* he's a nigger, a honky, an asshole, an ugly fuckhead, a rotten douche bag, and a filthy cocksucker—does it?"

Watson spun around again, wondering if anybody else in the swarm of medical-center pedestrian traffic could hear Myrna's legendary profanity.

"Suppose the victim sucked cocks," said Myrna. "OK? He's bisexual or homo, or whatever. He sucked cocks, and we can prove he sucked cocks. We put Joe Blow on the stand, and we ask him, 'Did the victim suck cocks?' And Joe says, 'Yes, Your Honor, in fact he sucked my cock on several occasions.' OK? Now, your guy calls the victim a cocksucker and shoots him. Does that mean he shot him *because* he's a cocksucker? Does that come under hatred because of sexual orientation, or whatever? Only if you're a prosecutor. Your guy shot the victim because the SOB was porking the old lady in the wedding bed! And if you let them tag him for anything else, you're not a lawyer, you're a dickless, glorified paralegal in silk stockings. Christ Jesus! My clients are all black, and I have to explain to a mostly white jury why they carjack decent people, shoot them, and take their money. You? You have to explain why a white guy might want to shoot a black guy who's shtuping his wife in living color. Mother of Christ!"

"OK," said Watson, gasping for breath, "never mind name-calling. What about the medical?"

"Check out the medical," Myrna said patiently. "What's to lose? But stop letting that old fart down there fuck with you. What's his name? Mahoney? Baloney? Fuck Mahoney. Must I explain?"

"OK, OK," said Watson, "What else?"

"I breezed through those field reports you faxed me in about eight minutes, before I ran out to a hearing. Coupla things, then I gotta go. If it's a rape, where's the mess? The MP reports make it sound like a Holiday Inn after the maid came. And—big question alert!—where was the gun? Did he have to go somewhere and get it? If so, is he thinking the whole time about how much he hates deaf niggers and how nothing would give him more pleasure than killing his wife's special friend? Or was it right there loaded in the nightstand? If it's an affair, why didn't Mr. Hothead Racist kill her, too? Or at least beat her up real good? Then blame everything on the nigger? ABC. That's what usually happens. You talked to this guy, didn't you? Is he real dumb?"

"I can't tell yet," said Watson. "He's either dumb, or smart enough to play dumb."

"There's a line in that second MP report," she said. "What's it say? Something about a nursery monitor? Hold it." He heard her pawing through papers on the other end of the line. "Yeah, here we go: 'Before leaving the premises with the suspect in custody, an operational nursery monitor was found in the living room of the quarters. Responding officers checked the premises for unattended children or infants. None present. Suspect states he has one seven-year-old son, who was visiting relatives.' "

Myrna coughed, then cursed her cigarette. "That sounds funny," she said. "Find out about that. What's a nursery monitor doing in a house where there's a seven-year-old deaf kid who's not home? Could be nothing. Could be something. Could be nothing more than a day care, or a white-trash intercom. But find out. Get your investigator on that and the affair. How long had she been doing the deaf black guy? Did it start before or after the sign language lessons? Did Barney Bigot know about it? If so, when? Any domestic abuse calls? Divorce actions? How much do they hate each other? Regular marital hate, or the killing kind? Et cetera."

"OK," said Watson.

"Listen, I gotta go. I gotta find a way to keep one of my clients in jail because five different gangbangers want to kill him. Call me later about the pretrial motions. You gotta find a way to keep all this 'nigger this' and 'nigger that' horseshit out of evidence. Call me. Bye."

/   /   /

Tunnels and skyways took him over, under, and across the Orthogenic Institute for Mental Dissonance, the Ignatius Home for Qualified Client Bodies, and the Outpatient Cybercash booths, until he wound up in the lobby of the building called the Gage Institute for Neurosciences. Access to the elevators was controlled by a security desk, where he gave his name to the guard. Dr. Palmquist's offices were in a secured area, where he needed a badge or an escort with a badge, so he took a seat in a stuffed vinyl chair while the guard called up.

Watson opened his briefcase and retrieved the most recent issue of the *River City News*. It had come out the same day as the first *Post-Dispatch* story, but Watson had missed seeing it, until Rachel Palmquist put him onto it. He had snagged a copy from the firm's library en route to see Whitlow. Front page again: RIGHTS GROUPS DEMAND DEATH PENALTY FOR HATE KILLING. Next to the photo of Mr. Hate, a picture of the Mrs. streaming tears. "My husband refused to accept our son's deafness. And he hated people of color. That's why he killed Elvin," said the quote next to the photo.

A spokesman from the NAACP and another from Klanwatch recited the latest statistics: upward of seven thousand hate crimes per year in the United States, 62 percent of which were directed at African-Americans.

A spokeswoman from Women Against Domestic Violence said it was another brutal expression of male sexual jealousy in the ongoing campaign to oppress and subjugate women. "Usually women are the victims of the jealous male's violence. Mary Whitlow was lucky, that's all."

Deaf activists explained how the killing was a violent example of the usual cultural chauvinism of the hearing world, which assaults deaf culture daily by abolishing deaf residential schools, promoting cochlear implants, and failing to teach deaf children American Sign Language, the true language of the American deaf. "He couldn't kill deafness in his own son," said one deaf activist by way of an interpreter, "so he killed a deaf man instead."

Two paragraphs covered the Terril Williams incident. No mention of Terril's record of criminal assault. No mention of the drugs in his system. Instead, he was described as an "All-American, African-American running back who had been savagely attacked by James Whitlow during Whitlow's junior year at Ignatius High."

According to the *News*, the swastika incident had occurred at Southwest Missouri State after a drinking binge; the defendant had bet his fraternity brothers that he could scale the water tower at midnight. A former frat brother said that the swastika had been part of the dare, intended to prove that Whitlow had actually climbed the tower. Like the *Post-Dispatch*, the *News* played up Whitlow's education at Ignatius High, a Jesuit prep school, after which he'd gone to computer technical school and then to work for a data processing company, until he was fired for computer sabotage.

Elevators opened and closed, an incessant paging system issued a stream of coded messages. He resolved to focus on Whitlow's defense and not notice Rachel Palmquist's wardrobe, her hair, her makeup. His new duty was to his client, not to his firm, not to a smart, witty, beautiful woman who was offering to teach him about criminal brains. He was here for one reason: to find out if her tests and her testimony about those tests could help him defend Mr. Jesus Hates Niggers.

She came out of an elevator at the opposite end of a lobby dwarfed by soaring white arches and sun-filled clerestories. All this true smiling would eventually lead to trouble, he thought, as they smiled at each other through the crowd and held the smile during her long walk across the lobby.

"Welcome to the Gage Institute for Neurosciences, Mr. Watson," she said with her usual lilt of self-mockery.

"Nice place," he said, rising from his vinyl chair and shaking her hand. "And look," he said, showing her the headline, "I'm now a *River City News* reader."

Maybe the new science of evolutionary psychology or some biology of beauty theory could explain just why he ignored his own resolution and studied her running shoes, her faded denims, a long white lab coat over a tight, black Lycra shirt, the shallow arc of pearls at the neck. Maybe it was all caused by pheromones, plumage, some as-yet-unidentified psychomagnetic brain wave of hers he was tuned into. RADIATION SCIENCES was stitched in red on the lab coat, just above the swell of the left breast—nice! "Swell," as Wally Cleaver would say, even sweller than Watson remembered—and an ID badge with R. PALMQUIST, and below that LEVEL 5 CLEARANCE, PSYCHON PROJECT in bold black on an orange stripe. The makeup gone and no harm done; her hair indifferently bound, with stray wisps wreathing her smile. A pen stuck out of the tresses above her right ear. Her lips . . . had nothing to do with why he was here. "Big place!" he added, following her easy, loose-limbed lope to the mirrored elevator banks, extending his neck slightly and homing in on a faint whiff of perfume.

Five or six other white lab coats followed them into the elevator. She stood in front of the control panel and spoke in a conversational tone, as if they were alone. "I live on Five. That's Neuroimaging. If we have time, I'll take you down to Neuropsych on the third floor."

"This whole building—it's all brain science?" he said, as they stepped off on Five into a vestibule with a huge, square metal door.

She unclipped her ID badge and plugged it into a slot in the door.

"Neuropharmacology, neuropsychology, neurophysiology, neurobiology, neuroimaging, neuromagnetism. We just had the Decade of the Brain." She chuckled. "Now, my colleagues and I are neuromaniacs in a building full of big brain toys."

She led him down hallways and past signs: MAGNETIC RESONANCE PHYSICS, MAGNETIC RESONANCE SPECTROSCOPY, POSITRON EMISSION TOMOGRAPHY, FUNCTIONAL MRI, ELECTROPHYSIOLOGY, COMPUTED TOMOGRAPHY.

"And Mr. Whitlow," said Watson. "I know what you want to do, but I'm unclear about just how it helps him."

"You file a motion notifying the court and the government that at trial you intend to introduce expert testimony of the defendant's mental condition. Let them think you're going for a traditional mental defect or disease. You request that he be transferred to the Federal Medical Center in Rochester, Minnesota. It's hooked up to Mayo's. There, he is screened, scanned, and tested. We get the images and the test batteries piped back here via file transfer protocols and display them on our systems and monitors. Not only do you get free testing, you also get an extra forty-five days to accommodate the travel and the testing. After that, he comes back here for trial. They do the scans and the procedures, we interpret the results."

"What kinds of tests?"

"Day one, cerebrospinal fluid, urine, hair sample for gas chromatography and drug testing, tissue biopsies for genetic and biological markers. Day two, we do the psychological testing and profiles: Wechsler, Halstead-Reitan Neuropsychological Battery, Bias Profiles, automaticity testing. Day three, neuroimaging, CAT, MRI, fMRI, PET, MEG, ABC, DEF, GHI . . . Do you know what any of this means?"

"Not really," said Watson. "But, you're looking for what? A disorder of some kind? Insanity? Oh!" he exclaimed, his palm to his forehead, "the seizures. He's had seizures. He takes medicine. Dilantin."

"Nice," she said. "That may help. Slim chance of a lesion. We can tell Arthur that's what we're looking for, or we can tell him we're pursuing the seizure business." She turned right down another corridor. "If we are lucky enough to find an abnormality, we have half a dozen neuropsychologists who could testify about the behavioral repercussions."

"This guy is creepy," said Watson, "but pitiful, at the same time. I can't really describe— Well, he has this tattoo that says 'Jesus Hates Niggers.' "

"Mmm," she said, "possible religious delusions."

"Yeah," said Watson. "And he—"

"Quiet," she said. "You're telling me too much. I'll get my data from the scans."

They passed a vault with huge block red letters that said: CAUTION: EXTREMELY POWERFUL MAGNETIC FIELDS and a special icon resembling the radiation symbol.

"MRI," she said with a wave. "Magnetic Resonance Imaging. We call them magnets. As for insanity, that's what we call a 'soft' disorder. Most of them went out back around the era of the Twinkie defense. Remember the trial of Dan White for killing George Moscone, the mayor of San Francisco, and Harvey Milk, the city supervisor? Mr. White got three years for a double homicide, because his lawyer successfully argued that junk food had addled the defendant's brain and predisposed him to murder. Then we went through the Menendez phase, where it was abuse that created killers, not Twinkies. But even there the defense was neurological. In the first Menendez trial, they had experts comparing the violent responses of the defendants to the gill-withdrawal reflex of sea urchins. But if all else fails, we could have one of our therapists elicit some soft recovered memories of abuse."

She pointed at a vaulted door with block red letters. "Another magnet."

"Can we go in and see one?" he asked.

She stopped suddenly and looked him up and down. "Pen, watch, belt, phone. You probably have keys. We're talking about extremely powerful magnetic fields. The walls, ceilings, and floors around here are eight feet thick. If you have any metal components in a prosthesis, a pacemaker, orthopedic screws, shards of shrapnel in your eyes, those pretty much get ripped out of you. No, you can't go in."

Watson held on to the pens in his shirt pocket and walked on by.

"Then there was the Crocodile Man," she said, "another real-life case. The defendant picked up two hitchhiking teenage girls and beat them over the head with a stonemason's hammer, stopping just short of killing them. The defense called an expert witness from Harvard Medical School, who used a book called *Violence and the Brain*, written by two Harvard neurosurgeons, to argue that the defendant had an organic brain syndrome called 'episodic dyscontrol syndrome.' It was based on the old triune brain model. It doesn't matter whether you call it superego, ego, and id, or neocortex, limbics, and brain stem, the theory is that there are violent urges from our collective reptilian unconscious hiding like trolls under the bridges of our higher brain parts. And when the neurological functions responsible for holding these paleopsychic urges in check malfunction, out comes the Crocodile Man. So it's not attempted murder, it's episodic dyscontrol." She tittered. "The judge and jury's eyes glazed over, they nodded their heads, and the defendant got a suspended sentence and six years' probation for bashing in the skulls of two girls."

Watson wondered if the syndrome could manifest itself sexually, in which case he could recall a few episodes of dyscontrol back in college. He pointed at a white vault emblazoned with PET in red. "I know it's a scan of some kind," he said, "but what does P-E-T stand for?"

"Positron Emission Tomography," she said. "PET scanner. Probably one of the first scans they'll do on your client. Imagine taking a big metal donut filled with radiation detectors and putting it around his head." She made a circle around her head with her hands. "Then they inject a positron-emitting radioisotope into his veins, which allows them to take pictures of where all the blood is going in his brain and which parts are using sugar and oxygen, while he is, say, watching videotapes depicting scenes of graphic violence, scenes of children playing, scenes of couples engaged in sexual intercourse."

"PET," said Watson. "What about heavy petting—where's that done?"

"In the primate labs," she said, as if on cue, "where they keep your relatives. We have a couple of amorous baboons and a chimp named Cham, who gets it whenever he wants it by pushing a big red button with his girlfriend's picture on it. I'll take you down there, later . . . if you want."

She continued leading him down hallways and past small cubicles where intense academics were hunched over computer keyboards and hemmed in by stacks of journals and printouts.

She opened a door. "My place," she said, showing him a tower computer and two monitors on an L of worktables. Two of her four walls were crammed with books on shelves, including a fat tome entitled *The Amygdala*, which drew his attention more than the others.

"What's the amygdala?" asked Watson, mispronouncing it and bending over to read the subtitle. "It's an African antelope, right? No, wait, it's a Chevy, came out after the Impala?"

"Remember the older, lower parts of your brain I was talking about?" Rachel said, grabbing a model of a human head, finally opening the hinged plastic skull, and removing colored brain parts, showing him two grape-shaped structures at the base of the brain. "*Amygdala* is Latin for 'almond.' Along with the hippocampus and the hypothalamus, it's part of the limbic system. It's kind of a switching station for powerful emotions—rage, violence, fear. Back in the sixties, it was all the—sorry —rage to insert electrodes into the amygdalae of violent criminals and stimulate them like rats."

"And, what happened?" he asked.

"Irresistible urges for sex and violence," she said, "or a total absence of urges for sex and violence, depending upon where the electrodes hit."

"Electrodes?" he asked.

"Yup. Implanting electrodes went the way of lobotomies. Trying to stimulate something as complex as an amygdala with an electrode is a bit like trying to tweak the insides of a Pentium chip with a claw hammer."

"Oh," he said.

"Dramatic, fascinating results," she added, "but wildly unpredictable. And if you can't duplicate what you get, it ain't science."

She picked up one of her phones. "Hi, Walt. Hey, I'm bringing somebody down to see Cham."

Watson retrieved *The Amygdala* and opened it, finding a lot of eight-syllable Latin derivatives fastened together like Legos.

"No," she said, "he's not a journalist and he's not from the ethical groups. He's a lawyer on our side. Do you have an estrus female? Good. Load the environment, and we'll be down in ten or fifteen. Thanks."

Watson returned *The Amygdala* to its niche on the shelf.

She regarded him with sham suspicion. "You're not one of them whirling-dervish, bug-fucking animal-rights activists, are you?"

"I love animals," he said. "Medium rare, rolled in olive oil, cracked black pepper, and chopped garlic."

She laughed. "Leave your stuff here," she said, pointing at the table. "We'll tour."

They walked past more red-lettered vaults and office spaces.

"Do you know what a CAT scan is?"

"Yes," he said. "Of course I do. It's . . . like X rays, only better, right?"

"I thought so," she said. "The young, healthy, immortal male. Imagine I wanted to slice up your client's brain into forty-eight very thin horizontal layers and look at them to see if there are any structural abnormalities or lesions. Now, imagine you can slice it on any plane, transverse, sagittal or sideways, coronal, even diagonal if we had to. We can do that."

"Wow," said Watson.

"That's the boring part," she said with a laugh. "Because now imagine shaving his brain into even thinner slices, but instead of static structural images, you construct temporal images so you can observe function over a period of time, whether it's measured in glucose uptake, oxygen consumption, blood flow, or electrical or magnetic activity, and then make a movie of various functions occurring in all these different slices."

"Heavy wizardry," said Watson.

"That's still boring," she said. "Because now take a scan of a slice with very precise structural detail, such as MRI, which has a spatial resolution approaching one to two millimeters, and then take another scan which is sensitive to function, like PET, and superimpose the PET picture showing function in the slice on top of the picture showing the structural detail, and voilà, you have a very good idea which neuronal groups are active at any given time."

"A brain movie," said Watson.

"Now," she said, "cut to the chase. Suppose I administer some standard behavioral testing or cognitive testing, but I couple it with neuroimaging. I make a movie of the brain working while it solves problems or reacts to controlled stimuli. And from the data and the images we assemble a neurofunctional profile of your client's brain. Then a powerful computer using recurrent networks compares his profile to thousands of other brains and profiles. We record the subject's responses to, say, black faces as opposed to white ones, his capacity for empathy when confronted with images portraying human suffering, his attraction or revulsion to depictions of violence."

"*A Clockwork Orange*," said Watson.

"Better," she said. "That was behavioral modification. Imaging techniques noninvasively detect and diagnose behavior at its source, inside the human brain."

More labs, offices, testing booths. They stopped in front of an elevator bank and waited, while she paced and held her chin in her hand.

"Seizures," she mused aloud. "Very nice. Maybe we can argue he has Tourette's syndrome." She assumed a lawyerly demeanor. " 'He calls everybody a nigger, Your Honor. He can't help it.' " Her eyes opened wide. "We could put him on the stand and have him call me a nigger, you a nigger, the judge a nigger. 'What's more, Your Honor, he is afflicted with religious delusions. He thinks Jesus will save everyone except for us niggers.' Did he say how many seizures he had?"

"Sounded like not very many and they've been controlled with medication for six or seven years."

"Did he stop taking his meds?" she asked. "Did he take them the day before? The day of?"

"I asked him that," said Watson. "He, uh, doesn't remember."

"Oh, good," she said warmly. "We not only have a lawyer smart enough to ask, we have a client astute enough to not remember."

They rode the elevator to the second floor. She put her badge in another white door. This one said PRIMATE LABS, AUTHORIZED PERSONNEL ONLY.

They entered a huge, high-ceilinged room, warm and humid—unlike the air-conditioned chill in the rest of the building—and lit by blazing drumlights. He heard screeching and smelled urine before he saw the deep cages lining the walls: a sauntering baboon, a pair of orangutans grooming each other, chimpanzees hurling monkey epithets at him from perches in artificial trees. Ventilation fans hummed overhead. Four-foot-high interlocking partitions divided the cavernous room into examination areas and controlled environments.

He followed her to a large glass booth. Someone had taped a printout page on the booth's door with CHAM'S HOUSE written in black marker. Inside, he saw stacks of computer equipment, monitors on steel shelves, and the back of what looked like a barber chair with hairy limbs strapped to it.

Rachel walked around to the front of the chair and smiled at Watson as he followed her.

"Meet Cham," she said proudly.

Watson was unprepared for the sight—the merciless drumlights made the monkey strapped in the chair glow in vibrant, unnatural colors: purple skin, mother-of-pearl teeth, a textured, vermilion tongue. Eight Velcro cuff restraints, one for the upper and lower parts of each limb, and a thick Velcro belt restrained a male chimpanzee bolt upright in the straight-backed chair. The legs were spread, the arms strapped to retractable slats. A steel crown vice had immobilized the cranium with four bolts screwed into the chimp's shaved head. Absolutely painless, Dr. Palmquist insisted. The bare skull was studded with hundreds of dental-cemented electrodes sprouting color-coded wires, which rose up like a surreal fright wig of rubber hair in neon hues and then spun up into an armature overhead.

The chimp laughed at Watson, an expression of emotion that seemed oddly contrived, because only the mouth and eyes moved; the rest of him was motionless. With all the wires, electrodes, leads, sensors, cuffs, and tubes coming out of him, Cham looked like the mutant offspring of a mother chimp who'd done it with a Cray supercomputer, a hideous crossbreed from a modern bestiary, a high-tech hippogriff or a silicon centaur, half computer chips and wires, half organic flesh.

Watson felt his gorge rise, tugging his lunch up behind it.

Cham's right hand rested on a small console of big buttons. A few feet in front of them was a sheet metal partition with closed chutes and what appeared to be a door for a four-foot dwarf.

Rachel picked up a phone. "Walt?" she said, looking at the sheet metal wall. "You got everything loaded on the other side? . . . Elsa will be fine. . . . Great. We'll start."

Rachel stepped up behind a small, elevated worktable that looked down on Cham. She flicked a switch, and the console under Cham's right hand lit up. Each of the big buttons or keys had a colorful backlit graphic: a banana, a toy, a chimpanzee's face, a glass of water, a smiley face.

"What are the buttons for?" asked Watson.

"I'll show you," she said, swiveling on a lab stool and bringing a bank of big color monitors to life with a touch of a pointing device. Her fingers clattered expertly on the keyboard.

Watson stepped up next to her, tuned in to her perfume again, and settled in for a view that included the dark plumage of her hair and her smooth, capable hands.

"What would you like Cham to be?" she asked.

"Be?" asked Watson. "You mean, like, would I like him to be a marriage counselor or a tax lawyer?"

"No," she said. "Do you want him to be horny? Hungry? Happy? Thirsty? Violent?"

"Hungry," said Watson, trying to be delicate, even though "horny" sounded more interesting.

She selected a sliding gauge on the computer screen with her mouse pointer and elevated it by clicking and dragging.

"Let's make Cham hungry," she said, as if she could make him anything she wanted.

She brought up a red three-dimensional grid in the shape of a brain and rotated it on the screen using her mouse. "We use computer algorithms to warp the data from Cham's brain and fit it into a standardized model of a chimp brain space. Then we select coordinates for areas of stimulation, creating electrical impulses in the neural bundles of the brain, very similar to the impulses generated by the brain itself."

She clicked on a small cube in the lower half of the grid, and it lit up.

"That's the hypothalamus, which contains neural networks intimately associated with hunger, among many other things."

Cham hooted and shrieked, again without moving, though his lips parted, showing a row of teeth the size of Chiclets. Then his index finger extended and pressed the banana button. One of the sheet metal chutes opened, and a large fake banana attached to a telescoping armature extended itself and stopped directly in front of his mouth.

"It's hollow plastic," she said, "filled with banana mash."

Cham wrapped his lips around the nozzle and snarfed banana mash with gusto. When he sucked and got nothing, he screamed at the plastic banana and sucked again. The armature retracted, the chute closed.

"Wow," said Watson.

"Now what?" she asked. "As if I don't know." She clicked open a few menus and dialogue boxes on her screen.

"Pay attention," she said. "Learn something about sex and the brain."

She flicked a switch, and the four-foot door in the sheet metal wall slid open, exposing another chimp, a female, without scalp electrodes, but similarly restrained in an identical chair, genitals swollen and exposed.

"Hi, Elsa," said Rachel. "Are we feeling romantic?"

Watson noticed for the first time a steel track embedded in the floor and running between the two chairs.

"Cham gets it fairly regular," she said, "so the sight and smell of an estrus female is mildly arousing, but, as you can see, he does not press the button with his girlfriend's picture on it. And we pick up impulses just slightly above baseline in the medial preoptic area of the hypothalamus."

"Medial optic what?" asked Watson.

"The medial preoptic area of the hypothalamus. Part of the limbics, which we talked about earlier. Remember the four F's?" She giggled and winked at him. "I said, pay attention. The medial preoptic area modulates male sexual behavior: mounting, pelvic thrusting. It's very sensitive to visual and olfactory stimuli. I'll show you."

She flicked the switch, and the small door slid shut, concealing Elsa again. "And we ventilate," she added, flicking another switch, which set a large exhaust fan whirring overhead, "to remove any lingering scent of estrus."

"And now," she said, moving the cursor of her tracking device to another cube on the grid, and then to a sliding bar at the periphery of the screen, "we juice him with millivoltage to the medial preoptic area. We attempt to mimic the same sort of impulses his brain would produce if he were engaging in sexual behavior."

Cham, stirring slightly under his restraints, cooed and gave a couple of hoots.

"We receive a pleasurable response. But, as you can see, he still does not push the Elsa button."

"Now," she said, opening Elsa's door with a flick of the switch. "We present estrus Elsa, and we stimulate the medial preoptic area." She clicked and dragged a sliding bar.

Cham's index finger promptly punched the red button with the chimp face on it, and Elsa's chair moved along the steel track toward Cham. Watson watched Cham's purple tool stir in the hairy undergrowth of his pelvis.

"And we begin picking up impulses of fifty or more per second from the cells we are monitoring in Cham's hypothalamus."

Watson noticed there were cutouts for the chimps' legs in both chairs, allowing the chairs to come flush together, permitting copulation in situ.

Cham tilted his pelvis and shrieked. Watson felt light-headed, as if his brain, not Cham's, were suspended in space by colored wires.

Rachel said, "I want you to appreciate the biotechnical obstacles we had to overcome to get this right. The electrodes allow us to stimulate or record. And we are one of the first labs to successfully monitor the electrical activity of individual hypothalamic neurons while the animal is engaging in sexual behavior. Energetic sexuality usually dislodges the microelectrodes from their placement coordinates. But here the cranium is immobilized, so we can get stable recordings, even during orgasm, which"—she moved her mouse and clicked—"should be happening any second now."

Watson felt sweat bleeding from his pores as he watched the immobilized chimps struggling against each other and shrieking.

"Sexual behavior is complex," she said. "Even in males," she added with a titter. "The medial preoptic area does not simply produce a motor pattern—mounting, let's say—but instead seems to generate a mind-set which is exquisitely sensitive to sexual messages from the female."

As he stood looking over her shoulder and the aromatic swath of her dark hair, she moved the tracking device, and her elbow brushed the upper part of his thigh.

"If an estrus female gives the proper cues, stimulation produces mounting and pelvic thrusting."

Watson inhaled her perfume and felt a curious mixture of nausea and arousal, as he watched the chimps bumping their restrained pelvises together.

"Simon LeVay wrote a book called *The Sexual Brain*," she said, "describing an experiment very similar to this one, first performed at Kyushu University in Japan. His conclusion: 'Love will find a way.' No slight intended to the song as sung by William Bell, Jackie DeShannon, or Amy Grant. Ah," she said, just as Cham's and Elsa's grunting achieved a crescendo. "There it is. The big O. During copulation, the neuronal discharge rate actually falls and then ceases altogether after ejaculation."

Watson did his best to lean against her arm in the confines of the booth.

"Well," she said, clicking and dragging, opening and closing boxes on her screen, "Cham and Elsa are ready for cigarettes, and we better get back upstairs to finish the tour."

Watson stepped down and looked at Cham, still panting from exertion. Elsa's door opened, and her chair went through the partition on the steel track. Cham's spent erection slowly wilted like a dying tuber.

"Thanks, Walt," called Rachel.

"No problem" came the voice of Walt through the sheet metal.

Three shrill beeps erupted from Watson's personal communicator. He retrieved it from the inside pocket of his suit, opened it, and read the message displayed in liquid crystals on a gray pop-up screen:

JTW SLO. ORG. WL4, BC A1–A4.

"Fuck," said Watson.

"We can do that," she said. "We make fuck happen all the time around here. We can put you in Cham's chair and bring Elsa back."

"Code Orange," said Watson, and then deciphered the abbreviations aloud: "Joseph T. Watson, St. Louis office, Westlaw expertise level 4, billing code first-year associate to fourth-year associate. I need to go back downtown and log on. A partner needs emergency computerized legal research."

"We're not done," she said. "The tour is incomplete. You haven't finished telling me how the interview went. Can't you call them and tell them to get somebody else?"

"Whoa," said Watson with a cautionary shake of his head. "Not done. You respond to a Code Orange first, and argue about it later. I have to go." He let her know with a doleful grimace how much he wanted to stay.

"Well," she said, "you have to come back. That's all."

"I will," said Watson, summoning his calendar onto the screen of the communicator. "When?"

"Tonight," she said, lifting one eyebrow in a parody of mischief. If he was not mistaken, she beamed one of those true smiles at him from her stool at the console.

"Tonight?" he said. "It's a Code Orange. I might be down there till midnight."

"Well, if we're going to play 'Who Works the Most?' I live here," she said happily. "So there. And you're still loafing along at the glacial pace of the civil law. Remember the speedy trial provisions from your law school courses? I've been an expert witness enough to know that civil law moves like a bus in a school zone, and now you're on the freeway of federal criminal law, with the cops after you and your client."

"Shit," said Watson.

"If you can't make it, call," she said. "But we really should . . . finish up."

"I'll call," said Watson, putting the communicator back in his pocket and looking for his folder.

"Joe," she said.

Joe? he thought. Yes, of course, Joe. It was turning into a big date. "What?" he said.

"Before I shut this down. Do you want to see what your boy looked like on the day of the murder?"

"What?" asked Watson. "You mean Whitlow?"

"Yeah," she said. "Watch Cham. I'll show you exactly what happened to your client."

Cham was still breathing deeply, murmuring contentedly, and drooling banana paste from one corner of his mouth.

Watson heard a single mouse click and watched Cham's entire body buckle violently under the restraints. His bared teeth opened in a violent, ear-piercing shriek. Arcs of contracting muscles rose from his neck and shoulders, tendons stretched under his hide like twisted ropes. The skin of his immobile, shaved scalp crawled and bunched itself in wrinkles where the bolts held his skull. Watson lost his breath and felt the visceral impact of Cham's rage, channeled into the only parts of the monkey's body that could still move freely—vocal cords and facial muscles. Another primal shriek, this one so loud he was forced to cover his ears.

"Hey," yelled Walt from the other side of the partition. "Lay off the amygdala, would ya?"

Watson panted for air and swallowed, then tore his gaze from the spectacle of Cham's shrieking, grimacing face.

"That's your man," she said grimly, the colored light from the monitors swathing her features in the chiaroscuros and morbidezzas of a painted Venus.

"You're warped!" he said. "Don't do that again!"

"Hey," she said. "You asked me about the amygdala. I showed you the amygdala."

CHAPTER 8

S EE ME. AFM.

Arthur's note was a yellow sticky stuck on another *St. Louis Post-Dispatch* article—the third one in a row!—page A4: COURT APPOINTS LAWYER TO DEFEND ACCUSED HATE CRIMINAL. The clipping teetered on the precipice of Westlaw printouts that overlooked Watson's desk and several adjacent mesas of draft motions, buttes of research summaries, cliffs of photocopied cases—all research that he had compiled during the last three days on the issue of hate crimes, penalty-enhancement statutes, and First Amendment challenges thereto.

His hands shook as he scoured the boxed twin columns of newsprint from page A4:

> Federal District Judge Whittaker Stang appointed attorney Joseph T. Watson, of the St. Louis firm of Stern, Pale & Covin, to serve as counsel for the indigent defendant, James F. Whitlow, who was taken into custody last week.

He flushed with pride at seeing his own name in print, but his cheeks burned for another reason when he read the next paragraph:

Attempts to reach Mr. Watson were answered by Arthur Mahoney, the Chairman of Stern, Pale's litigation department, who explained the district court's long tradition of appointing private attorneys to represent indigent clients.

"Neither Stern, Pale nor Mr. Watson has any expertise in this area of the criminal law, but we will strive to provide the best possible representation for this client because the court has ordered us to do so. At the same time, we will petition the court to reconsider its appointment of a first-year associate to represent an accused murderer facing the possibility of the death penalty."

Mr. Mahoney was unable to comment further on the case.

Watson set the article aside and instantly noticed that the cross-hatched heaps of hate crime cases, statutes, and law review articles he'd left scattered all over his desk had been disturbed—snooped into?—then reconfigured. By . . . ? His secretary never touched documents unless they were in the IN, OUT, or FILING baskets, which meant . . .

He'd recently completed a memo for Abulia Systems (one of Arthur's clients) on a private employer's near absolute right to search the workplace, including an employee's desk—a virtual desktop made of software or a real one made of metal and wood. Never once, during its research or composition, had Watson thought about his own files being ransacked. Intracorporate espionage is perfectly legal, he had concluded in his summary to Abulia's Human Resources Department, especially if the personnel manuals contain proper warnings, thereby removing any mistaken expectation of privacy. And only now did it occur to him that just about everybody else in Stern, Pale's litigation department had at least one locked file drawer.

Surveying his desk for a moment through Arthur's eyes, Watson saw stacks of work product bearing the client-matter name and numbers for U.S. v. Whitlow—paper evidence of excessive nonbillable hours scattered everywhere.

Line one trilled twice. Inside call.

He lifted the handset. "Joe Watson."

"Oh," said Arthur, "you *are* in. Did you see my note?"

"I was on my way over to see you," said Watson. "I was at the Gage Institute, talking to Dr. Palmquist about our prisoner. Until I got a Code Orange on my communicator."

This was Watson's way of letting King Arthur know that his trusty associate had been unable to complete his assigned mission, because some overweening junior baron had presumptuously summoned him back here to do rinky-dink Westlaw research. If bluntness had a place in the feudal hierarchy of big-firm politics (which it didn't), Watson could have said, "Boss, some foul usurper has defied you by commandeering your protégé and right-hand man."

"Sorry to bring you back," Arthur said coolly.

Watson lost a lungful. "*You* brought me back?" he asked as respectfully as possible.

"Yes," said Arthur, using the same crisp timbre, "Todd Boron has an urgent project, and I told him you had time."

Todd Boron? Watson thought. *Boron the moron?* Boron was the most junior partner he could think of, a legal robot, a paper-processing R2D2. He had made partner by billing 3,500 hours a year, every year, for nine years, which averages out to 67.3 billable hours per week, every week, which comes out to 11.2 billable hours per day—if you assume he took Sundays off for spiritual upgrades—and 9.6 billable hours per day, every day—if you assume he didn't. That's billable hours; it doesn't count nonbillable hours, for things like recruiting interviews and lunches, timekeeping, firm luncheons, meetings, repairing a hangnail, client golf outings, pro bono work, continuing legal education, bending a few paper clips, taking a call from an old girlfriend or a buddy from law school, or logging on to "Ask the Contessa" at the altsex.org Web site.

At an average Stern, Pale associate billing rate of $200 per hour, Boron's nine years of 3,500 hours amounted to over $6 million in firm revenue. He was a legendary figure capable of superhuman feats of mental drudgery, the first associate in Stern, Pale history who had made partner not by rainmaking or big verdicts, not by ingratiating himself with big clients or moving the family to open the Hong Kong office, but solely by dint of sheer Herculean labor. He had no personality, no clients of his own, no rapport with in-house counsel, no flair for firm politics, no pizzazz for wowing or lulling summer associates into the firm, nary an extralegal thought or sexual peccadillo to distract him. He was Mr. Grind, a highly compensated drudge, a dumping and transfer station for massive, menial legal projects—the kind of stultifying toil normally reserved for paralegals. But if the client was oblivious or obtuse enough, or, more likely, smug and flush enough to insist that all of their legal problems were too special or complex for lowly paralegals, then attorneys were called in to do essentially the same work at twice the rate. For these "special" clients with massive legal projects, Boron and any unprotected associate hirelings were locked up in off-site warehouses with computer terminals and boxes of documents, or sent to the library and ordered to compile summaries of the Bureau of Weights and Measures regulations for all fifty states.

Senior partners with big cases loved him, because they could take him down to the loading dock and say, "Todd, in four hours, two semi-trailer trucks are going to pull up at this dock with nine tons of documents produced in our client's litigation with Aileron Ballistics Corp. Those documents must be scanned by optical character readers, summarized, indexed, and they must be retrievable by author, recipient, witness, subject matter, and keyword before the first of the month."

Whereupon Boron would say, "The first of the month? Why, that gives us twelve—wait, thirteen days? Cakewalk with cherry pies and duck soup. Fish in a barrel of gravy." But between these performances he was shunned and pitied like an off-duty circus freak.

The quality of mercy was strained and no rain in sight for the first-year associates who were locked up in document warehouses with Boron. A diet of Mountain Dew, Jolt, No-Doze, Snickers, and espresso. Keyboard-induced carpal tunnel syndrome and radiation sickness from computer monitors. The firm provided family law services free of charge when the spouses of Boron's minions filed for divorce and custody of the children. The one suicide on Boron's watch had been covered up and blamed on "personal problems."

Why was Arthur allowing Watson to be summoned back to the office to work for the likes of Todd Boron?

"From the looks of things, you seem to have plenty of time on your hands for nonpaying clients," said Arthur, "and Todd has a Code Orange for a real client, so I told him you were available."

From the looks of things? The old ferret wasn't even going to pretend he had not been in Watson's office sifting documents.

"It's right up your alley," said Arthur. "More handicap discrimination. Pick up Nancy Slattery and meet Todd and the client up in the main conference room on twenty-four."

/   /   /

At the briefing, Boron presented the facts of the Code Orange. The client was Gateway Steel, and the plaintiff was a male steelworker named Mikey, who wore fishnet nylons, a merry widow corset, a chiffon bustier, and Magenta's wig from a *Rocky Horror* dress-up kit out to the line on a Friday morning, and was summarily terminated. Mikey promptly hired a lawyer and sued for reinstatement, back pay, and punitive damages, claiming that Gateway had fired him because he was a transvestite, a handicap allegedly protected under the terms of the Illinois Human Rights Act. The litigation department was in eleventh-hour settlement negotiations on the night before Gateway's summary judgment motion.

Seated at Todd's right hand was Spike McGinnis, the line supervisor who had done the firing, a short, stout authoritarian with a bench-presser's physique, who interpreted any attempt at resolving the dispute short of trial as a direct challenge to his authority. He needed only a bearskin admiral's hat with a white-and-amaranth cockade and a lapel to tuck his right hand under to round out his Napoleon complex.

When Boron introduced Nancy as the department's expert on state and federal handicap laws, Watson could tell that Spike felt the firm was shortchanging him by pawning a female lawyer off on him in his hour of need. His attitude was not lost on Nancy, who dealt with assholes for a living, two of whom were sitting across the table from her. She listened intently to Boron's and Spike's descriptions of Mikey's escapades, nodding and asking for additional details. What kind of hose did he have on? Was Magenta's wig artificial? When they got to the bustier and the corset and the termination, Nancy flatly declared: "That's completely inappropriate."

"You mean, it's not covered under the Illinois Human Rights Act?" asked Boron. "You mean the firing was inappropriate?"

"I didn't say that," she said. "I'm saying it's completely inappropriate to wear *both* a corset and a bustier. One or the other, fine. But both? He's not a transvestite, he's a fashion victim."

Spike took the position that if Gateway wanted to settle the case they would have hired an East St. Louis firm with offices next door to the ambulance service for eighty bucks an hour, but instead he had come to Stern, Pale and paid three times as much, which in his considered opinion entitled him to some legal authority for the proposition that he was right and Mikey was wrong. Nancy took the position that Gateway had paid its money for an accurate appraisal of Gateway's legal position, good or bad, and if Spike didn't like it . . .

Three hours later, Watson was hunched over his monitor. Outside, rush hour was beginning, and Boron's Code Orange was still in progress. *"Transvest! /s discriminat! or handicap! or disab! but not transsex!"* Watson tapped the search query at the command prompt on Westlaw, sat back, and waited for more relevant case law on the subject of transvestism as a handicap to appear in window one, the upper right-hand corner of his twenty-eight-inch monitor, which was now a patchwork of open windows and dialogue boxes, all of them relating to different client matters.

Pretty exciting stuff for a Boron assignment—and Watson counted himself lucky—but not exciting enough to keep him from reading the *Post-Dispatch* article three more times between searches. Arthur had put him to work for the likes of Boron when the case of a lifetime was unfolding on the front page of the *Post-Dispatch*. (For the first time, he dared to consider the delicious scandal, the trajectory of his career, if he actually managed a defendant's verdict. Far-fetched, yes. Possible? Of course.) Instead of researching hate crimes, calling Dr. Palmquist, getting on the Web to find out more about forensic neuroscience, he was on-line trying to find a court opinion that might suggest that transvestism is not a handicap protected under the Illinois Human Rights Act.

Unlike the federal Americans with Disabilities Act, which explicitly excluded from its coverage the more controversial mental disorders (kleptomania, pyromania) and sexual disorders (pedophilia, transvestism, transsexualism), the state handicap laws often had no such exclusions. When these popular, well-intentioned laws were passed, many of the people with conventional disabilities—blindness, deafness, paraplegia, mental retardation—were either already happily working, or they were at home avoiding any W-2 income, which might disrupt their Social Security, food stamps, Medicare, and Medicaid payments. But nothing feeds the legal imagination like new laws with undefined terms, and soon, under the expanded coverage of state and federal handicap laws, just about any "disability" was good for a lawsuit seeking "reasonable accommodation." Pandemic outbreaks of heretofore unheard-of, undiscovered, undreamed-of physical or mental impairments that "substantially limit one or more major life activities" claimed victims nationwide, and lawsuits poured in from hypochondriacs, people with bad backs, phobics, transvestites, transsexuals, junkies, alcoholics, narcoleptics, insomniacs, women who believed they had a man trapped inside of them, men who believed they had a woman trapped inside, sufferers of something called "chronic lateness syndrome," the obese, people with low or high metabolic rates, bulimics, neurasthenics laid low by the rigors of indolence, distressed citizens with irritable bowels and spastic colons. Later, no less crippling for their strangeness, came disorders such as Prominent Facial Birthmark syndrome and excused absenteeism for "experiencers" and alien abductees raped in outer space.

Watson proceeded to spend several billable hours on-line, scouring legal databases for any opinion containing *transvest* and *discrim* or *disab*—but not *transsex*—in the same sentence. He scanned case summaries on the screen and found even more of them that were not going his way. He was dreading another phone call from Boron and Spike; they were upstairs in a conference room gorging on catered food . . . waiting. He was finding administrative opinions in other jurisdictions declaring that a male transvestite's desire to wear women's clothing is a "physical or mental impairment that substantially limits one or more major life activities"—magic words, which meant that employers were obligated to reasonably accommodate the predilections of transvestites by allowing them to cross-dress in the workplace. Watson would have to tell Todd and Spike that Gateway might be better off letting Mikey return to work as Magenta because of potential liability under the Illinois Human Rights Act—sort of like telling the Ancient Order of Hibernians that an injunction had been issued giving Boy George and a shaved transsexual called the Leather Tinkerbell of Castro Street the right to march in the St. Patrick's Day Parade.

His eyes strayed from the Gateway window of his monitor over to the upper left-hand corner, window two, where a helicopter gunship equipped with air-launched Cruise missiles was poised to fire at a Level Four Minotaur on the Planet Anthrax. In the lower left-hand corner, window three, was a downloaded graphic from On-Line NetErotica called STACY.JPG, featuring a snake-hipped Stacy with implants the size of cantaloupes; she was lounging in a nest of feather boas and dreamily dandling a computer joystick with one hand, while the other was busy somewhere down at the convergence of her legs. The graphic image invited the viewer to attend at the moment just before Mother

Necessity gave birth again and Stacy invented a new application for the featured peripheral.

In the lower right-hand corner, window four, his personal information manager was open, the cursor bar highlighting the entry for Dr. Rachel Palmquist. He saw his notes, which he'd entered after his first meeting in Arthur's office: *Neuroscientist, potential expert witness, mentioned Sup. Ct. hate crime case of Wisconsin v. Mitchell, divorced, knows Arthur, major babe . . .* with the dialogue box open and the software prompt: "DIAL WORK NUMBER FOR THIS ENTRY?"

The program waited patiently for him to click YES or NO. The stark options didn't do justice to the complex moral and professional implications of calling the good doctor just because he wanted to see her, to hear her voice, to visit her for the second time in one day. He needed a PERHAPS or IT DEPENDS, or an Ethical Event Planner, which could display projected marital repercussions with a click of his pointing device.

"Are you ready to be faithful?" he recalled his father asking him, when Joe had told him he wanted to marry Sandra.

His father was probably thinking about the revolving ensemble of nubile babes Watson had been parading around since high school.

"I think so," Joe had said, vividly recalling how the question had caught him off-guard. He had assumed that fidelity would be a natural by-product of marriage, not something he had to be concerned about. But his father seemed worried about whether Watson was capable of it.

"Being faithful to your wife and your children is not optional," his father had said. "It's required. Unless you want to spend the rest of your life thinking about how you committed adultery. My advice would be to make damn sure you're ready to be faithful to her. Otherwise you'll end up divorced."

Watson recalled his father's chilly warning and recalled thinking at the time about how certain women seemed to produce gravitational fields or tractor beams, and how, once touched by their force fields, he fell into an orbit, where it was almost impossible to think about anything else. Dr. Palmquist was one of these celestial bodies—the first one he'd been alone with in a while. Probably best to stay away from her. But he couldn't, could he? What if his client needed her? What if he was already in orbit?

Palmquist's entry was linked to the Whitlow file, and a click took him to his notes from his first client interview, where the words *"Lucy Martinez"* and *"Fort Sheridan Base Towing & Vehicle Impound Lot"* scrolled by and caught his eye. *Why not?* thought Watson. And who knows? Maybe it would lead to exculpating evidence. He called information and got the number.

A woman answered: "Vehicle Impound."

"Yes," said Watson. "I'm looking for a 1992 Ford Taurus. A gray one with no plates. I'm told it was towed seven or eight days ago from base housing at Fort Sheridan."

"Hold on," she said. "It's in the system. A woman came for it yesterday afternoon."

"Oh. Right. That would be my wife. I'm out of town," Watson said, "and, um, I haven't talked to her since yesterday. But she asked me to call and find out what we needed to do to get it back. If she already got it, then never mind."

"She don't have it yet," said the woman, "it's still here. It's got no plates and an expired registration. Your wife was here saying she needed to get your briefcases out of the trunk because they had your credit cards and checkbook in them and she would need those to pay the towing charges and register the car, but she didn't have the title papers. We can't give her access to the vehicle unless she shows us title and proof of ownership. She said she was going back home to try and find them."

"Oh," said Watson. "I see. So she's coming back for the car then?"

"She needs title and a photo ID," said the woman. "Until that happens the vehicle has no owner, because it ain't registered and has no plates. When we ran the Vehicle Identification Number through the computers we got an expired registration. Either you or her needs to come in with title papers, and then you will have to register the vehicle and get new plates before you can drive it off the lot."

"I see," said Watson. "So the vehicle is in the impound lot."

"That's right, sir," said the woman.

"It's not being held for any other reason?" asked Watson.

"Title and a photo ID," said the woman, "and you will have to register it, pay any back taxes and licensing fees. Then, it's yours."

"Thank you," said Watson, typing the information in his contact database in a window at lower left.

Watson hung up and stared at the phone. *"Your wife was here saying she needed to get your briefcases out of the trunk because they had your credit cards and checkbook in them"?* No time to wonder about that one, because, back in the upper right-hand corner on Westlaw, the Code Orange was still in progress. He returned to the PIM and selected YES for a call to Dr. Palmquist, while his eyes strayed back over to window three, where Stacy was looking like Leda with a swan by the neck. The line was busy.

"Busy?" Nancy Slattery appeared at the door with a flashy striped envelope. "A courier left this at the front desk," she said, setting the priority envelope on top of the stacked, cross-hatched, sliding piles of paper covering his desk. Then she handed him a diskette. "Survey of state handicap laws and transvestism," she said. She glanced down at his monitor. "Taking a break?"

"Breaking my back with labor," said Watson. Using his trackball pointing device, he began at upper right and proceeded counterclockwise to identify the client and matter occupying each window. "One, Gateway Steel, disability laws research. Two, Subliminal Solutions, intellectual property analysis for Anthrax Avenger. Three, People Against Nudity on the Internet and Cyberporn—PANIC—a nonprofit organization filing an amicus curiae brief with an appendix of downloaded graphical samples—it's work, you see. And over here, window four, my appointed case, U.S. versus Whitlow."

"True multitasking," said Nancy.

"I have a program that keeps track of which window I'm in for how long, enabling me to accomplish continuous, interleaved billing."

"Wired, not tired," said Nancy as she moved toward the door. "I saw the *Post-Dispatch* piece," she added, sticking her head out into the hallway and looking both ways, then leaning back into his office. "Don't plead him out," she said with a comradely smile. "And, uh, let me know if Stacy has a boyfriend I can bill some time to."

Adding insult to the ignominy of working for Boron, yet another Arthur memo arrived advising Watson that the management committee had appointed Arthur as the firm's public relations officer on the Whitlow matter. All outside calls for Watson were to be routed to Arthur's administrative assistant, who was to supply the standard formulation Watson had read in the *Post-Dispatch*. If contacted by the press, Watson's instructions were to say only that he was unable to comment on the case at this time.

But that hadn't stopped the mail. The citizenry had strong feelings about lawyers, especially lawyers who could sit at the defense table with a hate killer. The mail had started trickling in the day after the newspaper ran the first story about his appointment. Some handwritten, some typed, most anonymous, even a couple of E-mails.

The first letter came in a blue envelope, typed on matching blue watermarked bond, no handwriting anywhere:

Dear Mr. Watson:

The Post-Dispatch says about you are going to be a lawyer for that white hate killer who shot Elvin Brawley. Maybe you should think how your kids would feel if an African-American called you a honkey and blew a hole in your chest? Then think how Elvin Brawley's kids feel because the man what you are defending has broken the Commandment Thou Shalt Not Kill by murdering their Dad.

For my ownself, I will wait until Judgment Day, because I want to see you stand up in front of the human race and explain yourself to your Creator.

May God damn you to Hell for all Eternity,

Concerned Citizen

The second came inside a hand-addressed envelope, but the letter had been typed on lined notebook paper.

Dear Joseph Watson:

I have no legal background, but maybe you can explain a thing to me. Why ain't Mary Whitlow on trial for adultery stead of Whitlow being on trial for shooting a colored in bed with his wife?

Is it the end of the world?

Confused in Florissant Mo.

He tried Rachel again. Busy. He reread his fan mail with a twinge of anxiety. Concerned Citizen's prose gave off the odor of a threat—oblique, to be sure, but ardent nevertheless. Was the writer suggesting that he would *show* Watson's kids how Elvin Brawley's kids felt? Perhaps help Watson shuffle off his mortal coil, so God could damn his soul to Hell for all eternity? He decided the letter was mostly cathartic anger, not a threat, which allowed him to resume thinking about Dr. Palmquist again.

If he went back to the Gage Institute he would be late getting home. Very late. Which meant he should sample storm conditions on the home front, perhaps issue a warning; then, later, decide whether to actually go to the institute. He called Sandra at home. She answered, but her voice was promptly drowned out by barking dogs and screaming children.

"Uh, San?"

"Just a minute," she hissed, "the dogs are chewing holes in the kids' new clothes."

Watson held the phone away while his wife screamed at the kids and swatted the dogs with a rolled-up newspaper. Then she screamed at the dogs and swatted the kids with a rolled-up newspaper. He could hear his son, Benjy, yelling over the racket.

She came back on the line, only to be drowned out by the dogs again.

"San, put the dogs outside," he pleaded.

"You're the one who wanted a dog," she said.

"I bought Lilith, one dog," he said. "You bought Hannibal. Not me."

"Because no one played with Lilith," she said. "Everyone just ignored her." Pause. Long enough for them both to think: *the same way everyone ignores me.* "You can't buy an animal and ignore it. Now, I feed them. I walk them. I groom them. I worm them. I get the kennel arrangements when we go to the Ozarks."

More barking and screaming.

"San, a bunch of stuff has come up."

"You mean, stuff that doesn't usually come up?" she asked.

"Yeah," he said. "I've got that appointed case now, and . . ."

"You mean, the hate killer?"

"San, he's not a hate killer. Not the way you think."

"Did he kill that deaf, black poet? The computer artist?"

Watson paused. "Probably."

"OK," she said. "He's a killer. Now, does he hate black people?"

"Uh," said Watson.

"That's what I thought," she said. "He's a hate killer. Just a minute. Lilith bit Hannibal."

He held the phone away, until he heard her voice surface again out of bedlam.

"I think I understand," she said. "You would rather stay down there late working for a hate killer for no pay instead of coming home to eat dinner with your family. Sheila's preschool teacher is concerned about her self-esteem. She asked me if the home environment included a strong father figure."

"San . . ."

"So what has come up?"

"I—I'm going to be late. That's why I called."

"Late?" she said. She dropped the phone on the countertop and screamed some more at the dogs and kids. He heard air whistle by the mouthpiece when she picked it up again. "Late? I thought you said something had come up? And by that I thought you meant something *different* had come up. Late isn't different. Late is the *same*."

"San, I . . ."

"I have to go. Your son is being attacked by your dog. Good-bye."

She hung up. His gaze fell again on STACY.JPG. Did Stacy yell at her significant other when he worked late? No, Stacy would probably be eternally grateful if he worked late trying to excel at his chosen career so he could bring home plenty of bucks for bigger implants and more interesting computer peripherals. And if things got dull, Stacy could check out the Orkin Man's computer peripherals.

All of his problems would be solved if he had more time and more money.

He tore the flap of the courier envelope. His PIM announced an external call with two short beeps and opened a window in the foreground, wiping out his view of Stacy's implants. A dialogue box followed, advising him that the caller's number did not match any entry in his contact database, so it was not Sandra calling back. He picked up the phone. The only other person he'd given the new number to was . . .

"Attorney Watson?" said the voice of James Whitlow.

Watson paused. "James?" he said uncertainly, unable to decide what to call his client on such split-second notice, knowing only that a reciprocal "Client Whitlow" would be ludicrous.

"They said you maybe was coming over again early tomorrow morning, and I was wondering about some things."

"I had planned on tomorrow morning," said Watson. "What's up?"

"Well, sir. My health is in big trouble here. I was talking to some of the other prisoners about the living conditions. Like the food, which is making us all sick. Also when it gets hot, they won't let you take off your shirt, and when it gets cold they won't give you an extra blanket. I've got criminally insane cellmates and they scream all night. Anyway, some of the other prisoners' lawyers got them special diets and extra blankets, and I was wondering if I could get me a special diet, like maybe a little meat that don't give you ptomaine and the trots. Right now I'm getting what the prisoners call fuck-you meat. You ask the help what kind of meat it is and they say, 'Fuck you.' "

"A special diet?" asked Watson, writing "special diet" on a stray legal pad.

"Yeah. That buddy of mine named Buck. Remember Buck? One of those friends of mine that I told you about. When Buck was in prison, we . . . or, I mean, he got himself a lawyer and sued the warden saying Buck had a constitutional right not to eat preservatives, because he was allergic to them, and so Buck got meat and you could see that it was chicken or beef, instead of the fuck-you, which is kind of like squares of runny yellow soybean loaf with shiny green scales on it."

"I'll have to ask someone if there is anything I can do," stammered Watson.

"You want the name of Buck's lawyer? Because Buck's lawyer got him a extra blanket and two-ply toilet paper, too. The lawyer said two-ply was part of Buck's constitutional rights. The other thing is there are a lot of Afro-Americans of color in here. I don't mean anything by that. Some of my best friends are friends of people who have talked to friends of Afro-Americans. You maybe saw on the news where a lot of men of colored end up in here because they are discriminated against or whatever. You maybe also remember that tattoo you seen on my arm, the one we was talking about? I'm getting a little, uh, worried." His voice was quavering. Watson heard him take a breath. "Concerned, I guess, that one of these men of colored might not understand about how it's just a joke. So Buck said I might have a constitutional right to get my tattoo taken off before I suffer some cruel and unusual punishment, which is against the law, according to Buck."

"I'll have to see what I can do," said Watson uncertainly. "Why don't we talk tomorrow morning."

"Yeah, OK. Like maybe I need some administrative confinement or isolation or something." His voice was shaking again. "Like soon. Or maybe they could send me off for those brain tests you was talking about and get me somewheres where there ain't so many Negro-Americans of colored in the prison system. It ain't just them—I got other problems in here too. Let's just say it ain't healthy here, and I need to get out quick. If you want the name of Buck's lawyer it's right there in the yellow pages of the phone book. Big boxed photo says to call if you get a spinal cord injury from driving while intoxicated. Buck's lawyer is famous and has got him completely off more than once besides getting him the special diet and the extra blankets."

Watson scrawled "Tattoo removal, blankets, two-ply, Minnesota, administrative confinement" on his notepad, as Whitlow kept talking.

"Buck's lawyer said you got to file—hold it a sec, I wrote it down— under Section 1983 of the civil rights laws claiming—yeah, here we go —claiming 'deliberate indifference to medical needs and extreme conditions of confinement.' "

"What medical needs?" asked Watson. "I thought you said they were getting you your seizure meds. You said that during our interview."

"I'm getting my seizure meds," said Whitlow. "And they even give me the meds for the piss infection. I guess the trots and food poisoning would be serious, indifferent medical needs which could be fixed by serving real food. And maybe getting killed by Afro-Americans of colored would be like a permanent extreme condition of confinement. I think I need a constitutional special diet and relocation." He was pleading now. "And like I said, it's either cold or hot. And the crazies in here are giving us sleeping disorders. Buck also said I should see can I get my laptop computer in here so's I can help with my own defense and do some legal research of my own."

"Laptop, cold, hot, sleeping disorders," said Watson. "I'll look into it, and we'll talk in the morning."

"Don't forget about the administrative confinement. Buck's lawyer also said . . ."

Outside call. His information manager appeared again on the screen with a double beep. His clients had the new classified number. He'd also given it to Whitlow, Sandra, and—well, Dr. Palmquist needed it, didn't she? But the information manager was again showing no match.

"I have another call," said Watson. "We'll talk about Buck's lawyer in the morning, OK? Oh, and I called the impound lot for you."

"Oh, right," said Whitlow. "Never mind about that. We took care of the impound lot. Which reminds me of the most important thing. Buck found some money. Some good money, actually. Buck's lawyer said you might need some to get a decent investigator and to pay experts and so on so . . ."

Watson froze. The other line flashed. "You're getting money? Enough to hire a criminal lawyer?" he asked.

"Why would I do that? They said stick with you, but that I should tell you they got some extra money for expenses and medical testing and stuff. They said insanity or a mental defense takes a lot of money. They said it was a rich man's defense and we couldn't win without we had enough money to do it right."

"Let me get this other call," said Watson. "I need to talk to you about this, OK? Don't hang up. If you have money, I can't . . ."

"It ain't my money," said Whitlow. "It's Buck's money. Remember?"

"Don't hang up," said Watson. "Stay there, and I'll tell you about the impound lot—"

"Fuck the impound lot," said Whitlow. "We took care of it."

"We—you took . . ." said Watson. "Stay there, I need to talk to you about the money."

He punched the other line.

"Hello?"

"Mr. Watson," said a smoker's voice. "Mike Harper, U.S. Attorney's office. I'm on the other side of you and this bigot killer Judge Stang sent you for your appointed case. How the Hell are ya?"

"Fine," said Watson, "I guess." Watson watched the other line blinking. "I'm on the other line, can I . . ." The blinking light went dead. "Shoot. Never mind." He sighed. "I guess they went away."

"Sorry," said Harper. "Hey, I don't know about you, but I prefer a working relationship when it's possible. So, I thought I'd call, and we could maybe figure out what to do with this guy."

"Release him immediately," said Watson. "Dismiss all charges and bring this gross miscarriage of justice to an end."

They laughed together, until Harper stopped abruptly in mid-guffaw and said, "Mr. Watson, I never show all my cards, but this time I have such a great hand I can't help it. Mary Whitlow is Mrs. Death Penalty. I thought the only fair thing was to give you an idea of the kind of evidence I have on the penalty enhancers. This guy is going to look like Adolf by the time we get finished with him. I sent ya a little sample by courier."

"Yeah," said Watson. "I'm opening it."

"As I was saying," Harper continued, "I'm just trying to be fair, being as how you got appointed to this back-alley abortion."

Watson skimmed some of the headings—"Excerpts from Affidavit of Witness Mary Whitlow"—and the introductory paragraphs, which essentially tracked the elements of the offense. Then his eyes landed on a section entitled "Evidence of Intentional Selection of Victim Because of Actual or Perceived Race and Disability" followed by more numbered paragraphs:

(13)   The defendant's wife, witness Mary Whitlow, will testify that when the defendant, James Whitlow, first met the victim, an African-American and a deaf American Sign Language instructor, at his South St. Louis home, the defendant declared, "Deaf is deaf, I can't do nothing about deaf. But you ain't bringing a nigger into my house."

(14)   Upon information and belief, neighbors of the defendant will testify that on recent occasions prior to the charged felony, the defendant had made public statements to the effect that he did not want any blacks in his neighborhood because it would destroy his property values. . . . When African-Americans came to the neighborhood to look at houses, the defendant displayed a Confederate flag from the balcony of his home.

(15)   Upon information and belief, educators and health care providers who cared for the defendant's hearing-impaired son will testify that the defendant expressed a violent antipathy for deaf culture, for American Sign Language, and for hearing or deaf people who communicated in his presence using American Sign Language, allegedly because the defendant did not want his son to use gestures and instead wanted him to learn to read lips and speak.

"You want to have somebody testify that he wanted his kid to learn to talk and he was worried about his property values?" asked Watson incredulously.

"I win any way I can," laughed Harper. "Evidence of motive. And maybe conspiracy. We're toying with amending to conspiracy, and that means we can put the plumber who fixed the kitchen sink on the stand if we want to. And we haven't said anything about the tattoo described in the police report. The jury will love that."

"What's the jury going to say about Mrs. Death Penalty calling military security and reporting a rape, then changing her mind once she gets to the emergency room. It wasn't a rape, it was an affair. What's her story today? It wasn't an affair, it was their first date?"

"She has one story," said Harper, "her husband pointed a gun at her head and made her tell the rape story. The jury will have no problem with that. We can prove up the affair and the sign language lessons."

"Prove them up with what?" asked Watson. "More of her testimony?"

"I'm making copies of some TDD printouts for you. Why am I telling you this?" Harper asked cheerfully. "Do you know what a TDD is, Mr. Watson? A telecommunications device for the deaf. Formerly known as a TTY, or a teletypewriter. It looks like a typewriter only you plug it into a telephone jack. It's how deaf people talk on the phone. They hook up a TDD to a normal phone line and they type back and forth to each other, or even to hearing people using Missouri Relay, which is provided by the phone company."

Watson knew what a TDD was because he'd written memos about the Americans with Disabilities Act for employers who were trying to provide reasonable accommodations for their deaf employees.

"The victim had a TDD," said Watson, thinking out loud.

"Sure," said Harper, "and Mary Whitlow had one too. So she could keep in touch with her son, who needed special schooling up at the deaf residential school in Fulton," said Harper with facetious tenderness.

"OK," said Watson. "They both had TDDs."

"And guess what? Most of these devices have little adding-machine-size printouts attached to them, in case you want to print a conversation while you're having it, or review the printout afterward to help you remember what was said. Follow me? Handier than a pocket on a shirt."

"And you have TDD printouts from the victim's machine?"

"Yup," said Harper with a chuckle. "Good ones, too. Because, every time Mary Whitlow called Elvin to arrange a sign language lesson, or just to make a little lovey-dovey, he apparently kept the printouts. You know—" Harper chortled "—the way you keep love letters when you're having an affair with somebody?"

"Are the copies in here?" asked Watson, flipping through the papers and looking in the envelope.

"Not yet," said Harper. "They're long, skinny things, and I didn't want to taint the evidence, so we brought in somebody independent to cut them up and mount them for us. You'll see them soon enough. I can read you a few to tide you over till then." Harper's voice moved into a falsetto: " 'Elvin, I am ready for lesson three in the sign language syllabus. I'll pay you for the lesson when you get here. Thanks, Mary Whitlow.' Or how about this one, 'Elvin, please come for another sign language lesson. I will have the money as usual.' And here's one when they were getting down to the end, probably one of the last things the poor guy read in his life, 'Elvin, I want another lesson. But also I just want to be with you. No one makes poetry with their hands the way you do. I just want us to be alone together. And next week, James will be gone to Nevada. I want to see you and have you touch me with your signs.' "

Watson felt his face burning. Harper wouldn't make up shit this good, which meant things looked dire for old Whitlow.

"Of course," added Harper merrily, "you can always put old James on the stand so he can give his version. I wouldn't mind cross-examining him about how much he likes the n-word. You ever heard the word *nigger* used in a federal courtroom?" Harper laughed. "I'll try to be sure we got extra marshals on hand, so they don't try to string him up right there from the chandeliers."

Watson didn't know much about criminal law, but he had done enough motions in limine—pretrial motions designed to keep evidence out of the courtroom—to know what was called for here. Lots of paper—motions and supporting memoranda—aimed at keeping bogus evidence away from the jury. If the TDD printouts were real, they would come in—but racial remarks made who knows how long before the murder? What Watson didn't know was his opponent. In another era, he would have sized up opposing counsel by the cut of his clothes, the make and model of his car, his address, his alma mater, his firm, his military service or lack thereof. Not anymore. Watson wanted to know what kind of machine Harper had, his operating system, whether he used Westlaw or Lexis, his Web browser, his Internet search engines.

"Let me look through this stuff and send you an E-mail," said Watson. "Is it a dot gov address?"

"A what?" asked Harper.

"Dot gov," said Watson. "Dot com? Your E-mail address. What is it?"

"I don't do typing, Mr. Watson," said Harper with an audible sniff. "I'm a trial lawyer. If you want me to look at something from Westlaw or the Internet or something, mail it to me, or we have a girl here in our office who gets that stuff for us. I can put you in touch with her."

Watson feared for his life in a jury trial, but in the paper wars that were sure to occur before and after, his opponent had just confessed to being technologically impaired. This realization and the ensuing rush of information dominance made him feel better.

Harper laughed good-naturedly, as if this case was going to be not only easy but fun, too. "Look, if you were one of those pit vipers from the criminal defense bar, I'd have sandbagged you until the week of trial, and then I would have mailed you this stuff two days before I blew it up on overheads and read it aloud to the jury. But I'm not like that. You were appointed to represent this hellpuke, so I thought I'd let you know early on what you're up against. Maybe if we try real hard, we can get rid of this thing."

"Get rid of it by—?" Watson asked.

"By pleading this racist hate killer to natural life," said Harper, "so he won't be hunting down any more disabled citizens of color."

"Hunting?" Watson jeered. "In his bedroom? Now he's hunting disabled people of color in his bedroom? I'll take your offer to my client, because I have to, and then I'll tell him not to take it." He instantly sensed the spirit of Arthur brooding over this conversation, but he couldn't fight his advocacy instincts.

Harper chuckled again. "I don't know what you do over there at that big, fancy law firm you work at, but I make my living in federal court talking to juries. Think about it."

"Fair enough, Mr. Harper. You talk to juries. I make my living writing appellate briefs. I make my living on Westlaw finding cases that say you can't put half of this bullshit into evidence. How about your jury verdict getting reversed on appeal? Think about it."

Watson heard clapping at the other end of the line. "Good speech, kid," said Harper, "and on short notice, too. I want to hear you give a speech like that when you've got twelve heads and twenty-four eyeballs staring you in the face. Tell your boy he can take life, or he can hold his breath for a week at trial and see if the jury wants to roll up his sleeve for the big needle."

CHAPTER 9

H e tried to call Whitlow back at Des Peres County Correctional Center but failed to rouse a human being. Then he left his transvestite research on Nancy's desk with a note—probably not proper Code Orange protocol, but he wanted to avoid another forty-five-minute conference with Boron the Moron and Spike. He snuck out down the back stairwell at 6:15 P.M.—lunch hour for Stern, Pale associates—and left.

Once in his Honda, he put Rachel Palmquist on cellular speed dial—an act the nuns would have called malice aforethought. He also needed to call Whitlow. His client was a power user when it came to gall. He seemed to think he could accept the services of an appointed lawyer and supplement them by hiring pretrial services with cash from his pals. When he made it through to the jail on the third try, he got a taped message about telephone privileges and client contact hours.

Still plenty of traffic. It was only six-thirty. He could be home by seven. Early for a change! And if the nuns were riding in the backseat, they would say, "Yes, go home!" He had plenty of socially acceptable tasks to perform. He could do something obsessive and harmless, and forget about doing something obsessive and dangerous.

He had done his duty to his client. Now all he had to do was go home.

He speed-dialed Palmquist, resolving to tell her he would not be able to make it tonight. They could finish up some other time during normal daylit business hours, instead of planning the second half of a date, meeting under cover of darkness, after flirting with each other all day. She was too much the babe. Too smart. Too funny. Too irresistible. And he was terrified of what he might find if he undid the clasps over Dr. Palmquist's backbone. Even a small chance of something happening was too great a risk. He manfully focused his thoughts on Sheila and Benjy. Think about them, he told himself, conjuring up images of their happy faces. How those faces would look if they became specular reflections of adultery and marital discord. The incoherent bitterness of abandoned innocence. Think about them.

No gas, he realized with a glance at the gauge. No money either. And the credit cards were stacked. He went back around the block to an ATM. His first transaction was a request for a balance—$42.86: the mortgage payment had been automatically withdrawn. He took out ten and hoped Sandra hadn't written any more checks. He put five in at the pump and stared at the lone five left in his billfold.

The wolf was at the door, and his name was Credit. Thank God Watson took care of the bills himself—Sandra would go cardiac if she spent a day in the credit control tower with him, rotating money among bank and credit card accounts, checks flying blind, interest rate turbulence, dizzy excess, stock accounts only points away from crashing into margin calls.

The nuns had also taught him a concept called "avoiding the near occasion of sin," which was what he needed to do right now. All he had to do was pick up the phone, push her cellular speed-dial button, and tell her that he absolutely had to go home. He picked up the phone. Pushed the cellular speed dial once again. The charmed third try found Dr. Palmquist via the institute's paging system. His lips parted. He inhaled. He spoke.

"En route," he said.

"Cham?" she said. "Is that you?"

He heard her laugh softly in his ear, and he squirmed in his car seat to accommodate the vascular events in his lap. His foot felt the floor under the gas pedal, and the Honda's pistons sang in their cylinders.

"My name," he said, soaring up the ramp onto Highway 40, "is Australopithecus Robustus. Similarly ranked males call me Rob. Females call me Mr. Robustus. Elsa, is that you?"

They traded wild, stupid laughs over the airwaves.

"I'll go down to the lobby and wait for you. Bye."

Harmless, he told himself. Just a meeting. It'll be over in an hour, and he could go home and help put the kids to bed.

The campus, the buildings, the lobby, were all easier to find the second time, and so was her increasingly familiar manner. If he was not mistaken, she'd found time to freshen her perfume.

"Another grant proposal funded," she gushed.

"Congratulations!" cheered Watson. Should he—what? Playfully cuff her on the shoulder? Shake her hand? Would a hug be overkill? "Nice work, Dr. Palmquist. What's the research on?"

"The brain chemistry of violence and aggression," she said. "In this case, we are studying genetic aberrations in the brains of aggressive mice. Male mice to be precise—did I need to add that? The defective gene makes them so violent they kill all the other rodents in the cage if you leave them together overnight."

"These are Mafia mice?" asked Watson. "Crips and Bloods mice?" He took a look around at the dim corridors and dark rooms. "Just how late do you work?"

"As late as I want," she said. "No kids. I got rid of the big kid I married. And I won't have my own kids until I get myself a wife." She slipped into an antic John Wayne brawl. "A good little cook with a strong back. One a them there househusbands, is what I want. I wanna be like you. A mother at home nurturing the children, while I go out to conquer and acquire."

They walked into an elevator and rode to her floor.

"I talked to my client, and I talked to the prosecutor, and I have concluded that my client is probably a person of hatred," Watson said.

"Not a crime as far as I know," she said. "Not a medical condition, either—yet."

"Think about it," she continued, marching along and waving her hands, her running shoes squeaking on the marble floors. "Hate could be important to the evolution of the species. What if, as some have suggested, the species evolves with optimum efficiency when there is a very exquisite balance between love and hate, good and evil, predators and victims, positive and negative emotions? What if, without hate to compete with, love gets fat, lazy, and self-interested?"

"Now wait a minute," he protested.

"Neurotechnology will soon give us the tools to make a very precise, efficient excision of the circuits in the human brain that are responsible for hatred and violence. Biomedical, pharmaceutical, radiological, microlaser surgery—pick your technology—it's going to happen. Should we do it? Should we reformat human neural networks with gamma knives? It's no longer a question of *whether* we will figure out how to erase or neutralize hatred. We will. But should we? What if the networks enabling desirable aggression and undesirable violence are the same? What if low serotonin not only provokes serial killers, but also stimulates fearless soldiers and brave cops?"

"And what sort of person would Whitlow be without his hatred?" Watson asked. He patted his folio. "I brought my notes from my interview with him."

"I don't need to know anything else about Mr. Whitlow," she said. "Not from you, anyway."

Watson was flabbergasted. "But I thought you said you wanted to hear about the interview?"

"A ploy to get you back here," she said bluntly and merrily. "When I testify about Mr. Whitlow, I'll be speaking on the basis of what I learn from his neuropsychological test batteries, his neurofunctional profiles, his personality profiles, his genetic and biological markers, his medical history, and so on. I will be testifying that I have never met Mr. Whitlow. I have not interviewed Mr. Whitlow. I have not received any extraneous information about Mr. Whitlow from anyone, except maybe the *River City News*. I will know more about Mr. Whitlow than he does, or you do, without ever meeting him." She turned right down a short hallway and opened a white door that said MAGNETOENCEPHALOGRAPHY.

"There's a fresh toy in here," she said, leading him into a room with a big, square box that looked like a bank vault with thick glass windows. There was a console against one of the windows. She turned a wheel on the door and opened it.

"Those other rooms I showed you are designed to keep powerful magnetic fields generated by the MRI devices in. This room is designed to keep magnetic fields out."

Inside, it felt like a dentist's examination room, except that the reclining patient's chair sat under what looked like the hood of a monster hair dryer that rose eight feet up in a space-age white column.

"What is it?" asked Watson, bending over and looking up into the hood and inside a helmet fitted out with an array of shiny disks.

"You are looking at a Neuromag 278-channel whole-head magnetometer. It measures magnetic fields in the human brain, the cerebral cortex mainly, but more channels allow us to see deeper. We call it the ten-million-dollar hair dryer. It picks up even very weak fields from the brain—that's why we keep all the other magnetic fields out with these walls. After analog filtering and analog-to-digital conversion, the computer makes pictures from the magnetic fields called magnetoencephalography, a direct measure of activity in different parts of the brain. It's completely noninvasive. Have a seat," she said, gesturing toward the chair.

Watson felt slightly claustrophobic. The walls seemed to absorb all sound, her words seemed to die in the air before he could hear them.

"I'll show you some pictures of your brain moving your finger."

Through a window in the wall, he could see the console flanked by a series of twenty-eight-inch monitors displaying images of transverse and sagittal sections of brains, some black-and-white, some glowing with eerie splotches of color, like fluorescent Rorschach inkblots, some showing geometric shapes, planes, vectors, and arrows, looking almost like tectonic plates on brain grids.

"First," she said, "we've got to get you away from dated, wrongheaded ideas about how the brain works. I'll start with a concept that may become a building block in our neuroscientific theory of your case. It's called the delay of conscious intention."

"Philosophy?" asked Watson.

"Neurophilosophy," she said. "Most of what we do every day is unconscious behavior, *automatic* would be a better word, and I'm not talking about sleep. Whole portions of our brains are devoted to activities we are not consciously monitoring, like absent-mindedly brushing our teeth, driving on autopilot right past the interstate exit we wanted, because we usually get off at the next one. Dialing an old phone number. Calling your wife by your secretary's name. It happens in the brain, the brain directs the body to perform the action, and the action is accomplished, all before the so-called subjective consciousness is aware of it. At such times we smack ourselves in the head and say, 'What was I thinking?' or 'Why did I do that?' "

"You mean, like why am I listening to you instead of just pleading our prisoner out?"

She picked up a twisted cable of colored wires that ended in a tangled net of electrodes. "Hold that thought," she said. "I'll come back to it later.

"How long does it take to shoot a man?" she asked.

Watson opened his mouth.

"Don't answer," she said. "First, let's shave the event into slices of neurological time. Be careful—" she giggled, wagging a finger at him "—you might hurt yourself. This is heavy-duty, state-of-the-art, cognitive neuroscience. It's not for amateurs."

"In that case," said Watson, "it's not for the jury. But go ahead."

She paced in front of him. He settled back into the device's chair, put his head under the scanner, and enjoyed the view.

"Now, as you've said, you and the other members of the jury know nothing about brain science. You are what we call 'folk psychologists.' You imagine a fictional mental construct called 'free will,' which is kind of like believing in leprechauns or UFOs to a cognitive neuroscientist. You still believe in what we call Cartesian dualism, meaning you believe there is a material world, including your material brain in that material world, but you also believe that somewhere inside that material brain is a central processing arena—call it the mind, the pineal body, the spirit or soul, the third eye, the Cartesian theater—a place where a unified consciousness reviews stimuli from the external world and then makes decisions and issues commands to your physical body, the place where you experience the sensation of 'I.' 'I want to rob a bank.' 'I want to cheat on my wife.' 'I want to be a lawyer.' "

Watson visibly flinched under the impact of proposition two. Did she wink at him?

"As a dualist," she continued, "meaning one who believes the mind and the body are two different, albeit inseparable things, you believe that shooting a man goes something like this. One, the defendant—his mind, his soul, his central processing unit, his 'I' or his pineal body, whatever—intends to kill the victim. Two, a burst of neural activity in the motor cortex of the defendant's brain initiates movement by sending a message to the trigger finger. Three, the trigger finger actually moves."

Watson mulled that one over and watched her plugging leads into the sensor net of electrodes, a kind of hair net with disks imbedded in it, with wires from each disk leading to the cable, which spooled around an armature and up into a socket in the wall.

"Sounds good," he said.

"Sounds good is right," she said. "But it has no basis in fact. It's been disproved by dozens of experiments and fifty years of neuroscience.

"If I put one electrode in your brain," she said. "Here." She reached up and touched a spot somewhere on the apex of his skull. The reclining chair of the imaging device put his head even with her chest; when she leaned over him a fold opened in the white lab coat and one of the Lycra-bound breasts nuzzled his cheek for a fraction of a second. The sudden warmth made his face flush in a backdraft of perfume. He stared at two plump, blood-warm, shapely near occasions of sin. His nightmare: contending breasts adorning a woman every bit as beautiful and interesting as his wife.

"Right here," she said, touching his scalp, "a microthin wire in your motor cortex."

She stepped back and took his right hand in her own soft, dry hands. "And another one here," she said, touching the back of his hand, below his forefinger, "where the muscle contracts and moves your index finger.

"If the wires to my recording device are the same length, I can tell you precisely, in milliseconds, how long it takes from the moment cerebral activity begins in the motor cortex to the instant the finger actually moves. It ranges from five hundred to six hundred milliseconds, over half a second."

"Where's the motor cortex?" he asked, hoping she would lean over and touch the top of his head again.

"Wrong question," she said. "The right question is: When are you subjectively aware of your brain's intention to move your finger?"

Watson made a face.

"Hold on to yourself. This won't make sense," she said. "It goes against everything you've ever learned about thought and behavior. But pay attention, because it's important, and it's hard science, not a theory. I can prove this to you. You become consciously aware of your intention to move your finger approximately three hundred milliseconds, or almost a third of a second after cerebral activity for the finger movement begins in the cortex and approximately two hundred fifty to three hundred milliseconds before your finger actually moves, assuming you choose not to interfere with the original signal."

Watson made an even uglier face, while hers took on a certain radiance as she warmed to the task of explaining how brains work.

"Uh-huh," he said with a nod.

"You just said uh-huh to a trap," she observed. "What is the *you* in assuming 'you' choose not to interfere with it?"

"Uh," said Watson.

" 'Uh' is right," she said. "If you questioned the population on the subject, you'd probably get at least half of them to reject Cartesian dualism—the spirit or ghost in control of the brain machine—but then they fall right into what we call Cartesian materialism, meaning they still want to think that some central part of the material brain is in charge of all the other parts."

"And that's not true?" he asked, almost wistfully, sensing that he was about to lose a cherished notion under the advancing army of her remorseless logic.

"We live and breathe Descartes," she said. "Even if you've never heard of the guy. Mr. Think-Therefore-I-Am. His shadow falls over all of law and medicine. Descartes claimed that he'd had a series of dreams and based his philosophy on them. Revisionist psychoanalysts have concluded that Descartes probably suffered undiagnosed epileptic fits. He created an entire philosophy to explain the terrifying chasm that epilepsy had opened between his thinking brain and his uncontrollable body—a dream solution to the problem of failed self-control. So—" she chuckled "—the classic formulation of the mind-body problem was probably inspired by brain damage. Does irony come in more delicious flavors?"

"But human consciousness?" said Watson. "You can experience it, analyze it, study its electrical activity. But you can't *explain* it. What's the word? Ineffable. That's it. It's ineffable."

"Right," she said sarcastically, "like the Hebrews couldn't say Yahweh. Because it's your faith, which is a word you use to mark off parts of nature you will not try to explain. You need to go off and join one of those neurophilosophy sects, where they sit around all day reading Thomas Nagel and asking themselves, 'What is it like to be a bat?' We are talking about one hundred billion neurons, one hundred trillion synaptic connections, with each connection capable of assuming different strengths. A combinatoric universe, but, so far, no evidence of a central processing unit. So the narrative which most accurately represents the neuroscientific sequence of shooting a man goes like this: One, a burst of neural activity in the motor cortex initiates movement by sending a message to the trigger finger. Two, after three hundred milliseconds, the defendant becomes subjectively aware that an impulse to kill has originated somewhere in his brain, and that a signal is being sent to his trigger finger. Three, during the two hundred to two hundred fifty milliseconds after awareness and before actual movement occurs, other parts of the brain decide whether to interfere with or counteract that signal, which was launched preconsciously, almost half a second before. Four, the brain either stops the action, or allows the trigger finger to actually move."

Watson squirmed in his chair. "Isn't this just a fancy elaboration of what used to be called unconscious behavior?" he asked, slightly exasperated by her millisecond hair-splitting.

"*Pre*conscious," she said. "Not unconscious. Big difference. By definition, you're unaware of unconscious thoughts. Preconscious cognition is brain activity that occurs *before* you are aware of it. The scary part is that it initiates actual movement in the physical world. Your consciousness, if you want to call it that, simply observes activity which originates somewhere else in your brain. Whether consciousness actually modulates brain activity is a question for neurophilosophers. Many doubt it.

"Think of your brain as a complex arrangement of networks and parallel processors. From time to time, some are conscious of themselves, but most aren't. Imagine a three-hundred-millisecond moral void which opens just after the brain triggers behavior and before the brain becomes consciously aware of it."

"And for Mr. Whitlow, this means what?"

"Mr. Whitlow sees his wife in bed with another man," she said, folding her arms and pacing. "He is provoked, enraged. The law describes his mental state with catchphrases: it's a crime of passion, it's voluntary manslaughter, he lost his self-control in the heat of the moment. He goes on autopilot. He points his gun and pulls the trigger.

"According to the federal government's theory, Mr. Whitlow sees his wife in bed with a deaf, black man. He is provoked, enraged by his wife's infidelity, but he does not go on autopilot. Instead he takes an additional mental step, that of being motivated, at least in part, by a hatred of deafness or blackness. He points his gun and pulls the trigger. And," she continued, putting her hands on the armrests and leaning over him, "until Mr. Whitlow tells us something different, this all happened in three hundred milliseconds. One third of a second?"

Watson's mouth fell ajar, he looked up into her face. "You should be a lawyer."

"No way," she said. "Too much work, not enough pay. And dull as dry toast." She laughed. "Unless, of course, the lawyer has the good fortune to happen his way into a criminal case with neuroscientific possibilities."

"Of course," he said.

"Now," she said, "back to Mr. Whitlow. A good brain scientist might ask about the timing, the sequence, the neural hardware required to transmit these two emotions or motives—rage and bigotry. Where do they originate in the human brain? What neural networks conduct them to the level of what the law calls 'consciousness' or 'intent'? What if rage caused by marital infidelity originates in the amygdala, and bigotry descends from the prefrontal cortex? Rage triggered by a front-row view of your spouse's infidelity is not the same thing as hate inspired by bigotry. Rage for one reason, and hate for another reason? Can the brain produce them simultaneously? Can they coexist in what you folk psychologists call subjective consciousness? Can they coexist in the subjective consciousness in the space of one third of a second? What if one, neurologically speaking, overwhelms or displaces the other?"

"You've convinced me," said Watson. "I vote for acquittal."

"Why?" she said. "You don't understand the first thing about how brains work."

"But it sounds so good," he said.

"You're nice," she crooned. "Do you want to see pictures of the nice magnetic fields a nice brain like yours gives off?"

"Why not?"

"OK," she said. "This sensor net allows me to take a simultaneous thirty-two-channel EEG. And, if you want the jumbo, bonus, extra-special value of an EKG and skin galvanic response, I need you to get the tie off, unbutton your shirt, and undo your belt buckle."

He glanced up at her.

"Don't worry," she said with a smile. "It's science. I'm a doctor. And you? You're a big blob of protoplasm. An unformatted human male from one of what I call the corrupted zones of human endeavor—the law."

He draped his tie over one of the armrests and modestly left the shirt flaps closed after unbuttoning.

She tore two foil packets open and expertly smeared clear jelly on several leads. She parted his shirt with the backs of her hands and started pasting leads on his torso. He felt goose bumps ripple across his chest like a cool breeze, then the tiny, cold shocks of jelly.

"That preconscious lag works both ways," she said. "Not just from the brain to the body, but from the body to the brain, and from the environment to the brain.

"Stimuli, sensations," she said, pasting an electrode on each shoulder. "They get processed preconsciously, important mental decisions and representations are made before the brain is self-consciously aware of them."

She gently set the clutch of wire leads in his lap.

"This is . . ." he began, then took a breath.

"Harmless," she said. "Completely harmless. A free look at the magnetic fields generated by your own brain. It's like being one of the first people to look into a microscope or a telescope."

She put on her favorite mock-professorial pose, pushing her horn-rims down her nose, tugging her chin, and peering at him.

"When Goethe's Wilhelm Meister looked into the telescope for the first time, he warned the astronomers around him that these instruments would have a morally bad effect upon men because they would see things beyond the powers of their inner faculties of discernment. The invention of the microscope prompted a similar response—terror— and it was banned. Goethe said only a superhuman culture could harmonize the inner truth of man with this inappropriate vision from without. And remember old Michelangelo had to sneak around under cover of darkness for anatomy lessons on corpses? Why? Because the Church outlawed human dissection. They didn't want to know if men dissected looked very much like their cousins, the animals. Imagine what old Goethe would have said about this gizmo? Talk about an inappropriate vision from without! And we are"—she grinned—"the superhumans?"

"I'll be watching myself think?"

"Not quite," she said, "that might put us both to sleep. But you'll be seeing visual representations of the magnetic fields generated by your brain. We put each other under the hair dryer all the time around here. But even slight movement in the torso causes artifact in the tracings, so I must restrain your arms and legs. May I?"

She showed him the Velcro flaps of the wrist restraints on the arms of the device.

"Sure," he said uncertainly. "Why not?"

The flaps were thick and strong, and she expertly bound his arms and legs. If he really wanted to, he figured he could free himself, but when he tested his hypothesis by flexing his right bicep against the Velcro, he realized he was held fast—just as she was finishing up his left leg.

"Trapped," he said, playfully struggling.

"Like Cham," she said.

She reached down and picked up the leads from his lap, plucking and sorting them like the stems of flowers, setting one tangle back in his lap. She spread the sensor net with her hands and leaned over him, brushing his cheek again with glands that had nourished the human race from day one, putting the web of electrodes over his head, and gently pushing him back under the hood of the device.

"Sometimes sensory input is processed in that preconscious lag I was telling you about," she said, still leaning over him, adjusting the leads, touching his hair, his neck, "until the mental activity acquires a certain momentum. The autonomic nervous system comes into play before the brain is self-consciously aware of the parallel processes, what is sometimes referred to as 'losing control' or 'losing your head.' "

She checked the connections on the armature overhead.

"Mr. Watson," she said, lowering her face and looking at him intently, "according to the readings I'm getting, your brain registers intense pleasure when I lean over you."

"This thing is *on*?" he gasped.

She walked to the door of the vault, turned, and smiled. "Not yet."

She slipped out and appeared on the other side of the window at the console. He heard a distant hum and watched the monitors come to life. One displayed shapes of the human head from different angles with what looked like topographic maps in different shades of pastel and citrus colors. Another monitor was full of squiggling lines. A third was blank.

She came back through the chamber door, stooped, and put her head next to his, looking out through the window with him at the monitors.

"Those colored patterns represent magnetic fields of different strengths, a direct measure of the neuronal activity in your brain. You are one of the few people on earth who've had the pleasure of witnessing images of their own neuromagnetism unfolding in real time. The squiggles on the other one are the EEG. All recorded and stored in the computer. I can print color films for you."

She came back around to the front of the chair and lifted the remaining leads out of his lap.

"I told you to undo this," she said, looping her little finger under the tongue of his belt and tugging it free. "You disobeyed. I need a lead on top of each thigh for the skin galvanic responses. Now I'm getting lubricant all over your belt."

"Hey," he said weakly, surging against the restraints.

"Relax," she said. "Don't be a stress puppy. I'm a doctor."

She dabbed jelly on the two remaining leads, brushed his pants open with the backs of her hands, and pasted the leads in place.

With her hand on his thigh, she glanced out through the window as the third monitor blinked and then displayed horizontal rows of squiggles.

"Um," said Watson. "I think . . ."

"That's it," she said, smiling at him again. "You're hooked up. A Neuromag 278-channel MEG, a simultaneous 32-channel EEG, and a 12-lead EKG, and skin conductance response all being recorded, analyzed, and stored in our computers—the first components of your neurofunctional profile. What's it feel like, watching all that magnetic and electrical activity roaring up and down your spinal column between your brain and your erection?"

Watson swallowed moisture down the wrong pipe and coughed violently. He struggled again—mentally more than physically.

"Maybe we should stop now," he said unconvincingly.

"Move a left finger," she said.

He did.

"Move a right finger," she said.

He did.

"Southpaw," she said. "Heavy Pavlovian circuits laid down in the right hemisphere. Were you a Portnoy?"

"I don't know . . ."

"Don't get mad," she said, strolling to the chair and bending over him, her eyes peering into his. "I'll do us both a favor," she offered, grabbing another jelly packet.

He tried to move, for no particular reason, and failed.

"Do you know the hoops I'd have to go through to get permission from the FDA to obtain a magnetoencephalographic record of an event like this in a human male experimental subject? Four years, at least, to get it approved. With your help, I can get it in about four minutes."

"Look," he said, protesting a little too little and late. "I don't want to do this. I'm married."

"I know," she said, squeezing clear jelly onto the fingertips of her right hand. "We can see that on the monitors. In male brains it shows up as washed-out splotches in the limbics. We lose resolution at that depth, it shows up as gray or beige, June Cleaver's meat loaf. It indicates a stimulation deficit associated with chronic monogamy, a fundamental lack of diversity in sexual partners and experiences. It's treatable."

His forearms bulged under the thick Velcro pads and straps.

"In male rats," she added brightly, "we call it the Coolidge effect. A male rat who has just ejaculated will mount a new female more speedily than he will remount the same female with whom he has just copulated. What do you think of that?"

"I need to think . . ." he said.

"Do," she said. "We're into that around here."

She touched him carefully, tenderly.

"Control lost," she observed with a friendly smile. "Your neural networks are phase-locked. Resistance is down. Rheostats open. You're servomechanical. IRQ. IRQ. IRQ. IR-ACK. We have bus connection to the joy port. I'm sampling directly across the modal-spectrum of sympathetic and parasympathetic nervous systems."

Her voice was soothing and sincere, a warm reverberation in his spine. Cool jelly. Smooth hand. "A single . . . stroke," she murmured, "and the circuits open, and they are all one-way."

He took a few deep breaths and watched the tip of her tongue move across her upper lip. She settled herself against him on the arm of the chair.

She undid whatever was holding her hair together and shook it loose.

"Breathe through your nose," she said.

She craned her neck and took a look at the monitors. "We have olfactory," she said.

"It smells good," said Watson, "but—"

"Bodies cast shadows," she said. "Brains throw off consciousness. But consciousness doesn't control your brain any more than your shadow tells your body what to do."

"Yeah," he said. "But—"

"Your vocalizations, your moral reasoning, your sham protests are all what we call epiphenomena—accessory events, secondary artifact. Your brain wants to make you feel better about something it decided to do on its own, without your permission."

She bent over him, still alongside, her hand manipulating him expertly to orgasm. He looked over her shoulder, through her dark tresses, through the booth window, and saw the colored tectonic plates of the graphic representation of his head turn red and orange.

He felt her warm chuckle in his ear. She put her head alongside his and watched the monitors.

"Generalized muscular tension, perineal contractions, involuntary pelvic thrusting with a periodicity of zero-point-eight seconds, white-hot medial preoptic." She giggled. "The lateral hypothalamus brings accessory networks into play," she whispered. "Houston, we have bursts of impulses in the hypothalamic supraoptic and paraventricular nuclei, down the axon terminals. Heart rate climbing. Skin flushed. Vasodilation. Muscle spasms. Involuntary vocalizations . . . *Aaaand* . . . Boom! Massive discharge of oxytocin from the posterior pituitary gland."

He turned his head, panted, and moaned.

"Neuroscience," she said. And kissed him.

CHAPTER 10

N ot only had he missed dinner, he had missed baths. Dinner he missed two or three times a week, but missing the kids' baths was a marital war crime. If there were Codes or National Situations at the firm, he missed baths, and paid dearly in downtime given over to fielding incessant remonstrations from the Memsahib. He heard her upstairs, already doing bedtime reading. He knew he was in for a look that was older than time, the same look that paleowife Lucy and her hunter-gatherer sisters probably gave to their protohuman husbands when the roistering cads returned late from the hunt with meager results, a look that said: *I know a few similarly ranked males who bring home twice the meat with half the effort, and then devote their leisure time to mentoring and nurturing the children.*

To make things worse, he'd been pawed at, nuzzled, and slavered on by a rival female whose scent was smeared all over him. Sandra was not the jealous type, but he'd seen some pretty ferocious displays over the reported infidelities of their married friends.

"Is that you?" she called down, her tone suggesting she'd be just as happy with a gentleman burglar or a competent baby-sitter.

"What's left of me," said Watson, seized by a sudden urge for cold beer, wondering if this desire for a depressant in beverage form had erupted somewhere in his preconscious, which was causing his hand to automatically grab the refrigerator door, open it, tear the pop-top . . . and other parts of his brain were not stopping that impulse.

"I met with those doctors who want to scan my appointed guy, then I had to go back to the office for a Code Orange in L.A.," he loudly explained, neatly omitting the return visit and the hand job he'd received from a gorgeous neuroscientist.

Danger made him trust his instincts. And his instincts told him to come up with entirely new subject matter for the Code Orange, because a description of Gateway and Mikey would come too near the topic of sexual behavior. "They wouldn't let us off-line in L.A. It was a hostile takeover, we were trolling the information services doing due diligence all night, looking for white knights, greenmail, poison pills, shark repellent."

"FEED THE DOGS," she yelled, then continued reading to the children. " ' "I know some new tricks," said the Cat in the Hat. "A lot of good tricks. I will show them to you. Your mother will not mind at all if I do." ' "

The truth was he'd blown off the Code Orange and left Nancy Slattery behind to explain the cases he'd found, while he ran off to see Dr. Palmquist. And Boron was just the sort to keep his list, check it twice, and enter *naughty* on the upcoming performance evaluation.

He grabbed the phone and called into the firm's voice mail; the synthetic operator told him he had twelve minutes of messages. He started the playback, with his finger on the SKIP button.

Arthur came on and told him to report on his meeting at the Neuroscience Center. (Maybe he'd visited the place himself and wanted to compare notes.) Then he started in again on plea bargaining. "I know people in the U.S. Attorney's office," he said. "I specifically instructed you that I wanted to know immediately if anyone called you to discuss a plea."

Watson froze. "Fuck!"

"Please!" Sandra hollered down from upstairs.

"Sorry, San," he said. He had forgotten to tell Arthur about Harper's call! Deep shit was one thing—now he was under full fathom five.

SKIP.

In-house counsel from PizzaFax, re: discovery matters. SKIP.

He heard Sandra's voice again: " 'But our fish said, "No! No! Make that cat go away! Tell that Cat in the Hat you do *not* want to play. He should not be here. He should not be about. He should not be here when your mother is out!" ' "

Boron with Spike McGinnis on speaker, going ahead with the summary judgment motion. "What about cases analyzing whether transsexuality—wait," said Boron the Moron. "Which is he, Spike?" he asked, his voice fading as he turned from the speaker. "Which one has to do with clothes?" His voice came back full: "Yeah, not the clothes one, whether the other one, transsexuality, is considered a handicap under Illinois law? Since we can't find favorable stuff on trans-, trans-, whatever. You get the idea. Would those be relevant?"

"No, ass-wipe!" said Watson. "We talked about that at the Code Orange briefing." SKIP.

"Who are you swearing at down there?" Sandra asked shrilly. "Are you on the phone again? Will you stop the language!"

"No one," he said. "No! Yes, I will stop the language." *I'll get a Glock 19 semiautomatic instead.*

"Did you feed the dogs?"

The next message began. "Attorney Watson? This is James Whitlow. They don't let me use the phone much. I got cut off from you. I did not hang up. I don't know if they tape or bug these calls, but I had another idea to tell you why I ain't guilty of discrimination. I have seen many Afro-Americans and many hearing-impaired people and have never tried to kill them, until I seen one trying to fuck my wife. Plus my own boy is hearing-impaired and I ain't tried to kill him yet. Are they saying I only try to kill people who are *both* hearing-impaired and African-American? In fact, I had seen the deaf . . . I mean, the hearing-impaired African-American several times before and had never tried to kill him, but I guess they would say it was because when I seen him it was in church.

"Anyway . . . Oh, yeah. I talked to Buck and some of my friends, and I think I told you we got some good money. Anyway, even though Buck has good money, Buck's lawyer says I might be better off with you as my lawyer, at least until we get to trial, because there are so many legal theories on this hate stuff that need sorting out and lots of research, which would be very expensive, and, what do you call them? Motions, yeah, motions. I wrote this stuff down. And, anyway, Buck's lawyer said you might be pretty good at that part of the business being as how you were on law journal and because you work at such a big firm, and you would be free, too. They said worry about trial later. Or maybe, they could get another lawyer to help you later, a good criminal lawyer. And Buck and his lawyer said to let them know if you need extra money for investigators or medical experts or whatever, or maybe even some extra money for yourself. Whatever. But of course if the government asks, we both know I ain't got no money. Right? And even if I could get some money, I might forget that because of that traumatic amnesia we was talking about. I'm running on, so, never mind, I will call tomorrow in the morning if they let me."

Watson's spider sense tingled. *"Buck's lawyer says I might be better off with you as my lawyer"?* Sap alert! Now he was being used as a patsy to do research! *"And you would be free, too"?* "Shit," he said, and promptly heard his wife's foot stomp over his head. *"Extra money? Or maybe some extra money for yourself"?*

"Oh, yeah," Whitlow's message continued, "I'm getting pills for the infection, and they are giving me the Dilantin, too. They said something about could they get the medical records from the doctor who prescribed the medicine for the infection when I was still . . . before I was in jail. I don't think they should have those because that is private shit. So can we just tell them no?

"I have thought about what you said about how you don't want to know nothing yet, but I still say, what would you do if you come home to that one day? Anyway, I will see you in the morning."

Watson pushed PAUSE, then replayed the message. The other lawyer, the extra money, the medical records. And, there it was again—Whitlow asking him, "What would you do?"

He resumed voice mail where he'd left off.

A message from Rachel Palmquist, whose voice tripped a circuit and opened his pores, so he could bathe in the sebaceous slime of the guilty. A power surge in his autonomic nervous system triggered irregular heart rhythms. Pitter-pat and butterflies for the young and single; mortal terror and angina for adulterers with children.

"I'm not chasing you," she said. "I called to tell you I got a slot for your man. I called the Psychon Project director in Minnesota. I made a place for your guy, and I'm supposed to provide any support you need for your Rule Twelve motion. As for your own criminal, neurofunctional profile, I reviewed the films of the big event right after you left. Hot pink and electric orange, high magnetic fields in the medial preoptic region of your hypothalamus, indicating extremely aggressive, male-typical sexual behavior—mounting, pelvic thrusting . . . I think you need a doctor to take a look at it for you. Permission to seek confirmation with a PET scan and functional MRI? See ya."

While his cheeks burned, he heard his wife's voice again.

" 'Then our mother came in and she said to us two, "Did you have any fun? Tell me. What did you do?" '

" 'Should we tell her about it? Now, what *should* we do? Well . . . What would you do if your mother asked *you*?' "

It was too late to go up and offer token assistance. The Battle of Putting the Kids to Bed was over; the vanquished had surrendered in tears, taken baths, brushed their teeth, relinquished toys, fallen under the spell of reading. Now Papa, a pacifist and stranger to the toils of bedtime civil war, had shown up for the spoils and the goodnight kisses, and lessons in the use of foul language. Instead, he went through the mail and discovered that some of the concerned citizens and *Post-Dispatch* readers had looked up his home address in the phone book:

Dear Attorney Watson:

I know there are a lot of fancy legal theories what you will use to try and keep James Whitlow from getting what he deserves.

Lawyers forget that true laws are simple. One of them is: HATE IS ALWAYS WRONG.

Your client don't deserve death—what he needs is SLOW DEATH, which I would watch if I could. Better, I could help with the torture aspects, because that would make me feel better.

When I get to heaven, I will look over the railing and see you and James Whitlow burning in Hell.

Remember. HATE IS WRONG. Period.

Gabriel

The next one came in an envelope on the letterhead of the American Association of Handicapped Americans, featuring a logo of Sisyphus in a loincloth pushing a rock up a hill, or maybe it was Atlas trying to climb a mountain while carrying the world on his shoulders.

Dear Mr. Watson:

I have spent twenty years of my life as an advocate for citizens
with special needs. I have seen the indomitable spirit of the disabled and I have seen the hatred and disregard of the rest of our society for those with special or different abilities. James Whitlow
hates anybody and anything different than a phenotype of a white,
low-intellect, extremist mentality, which is to say he hates everybody but himself and a few other tattooed, militia-minded thugs
who shoot pool in bars and like to beat up people with different
abilities or lifestyles.

My deaf clients consider Mr. Whitlow's intentional use of violence
against a deaf person and his public disdain for American Sign
Language to be an affront to their culture and their self-esteem, and
a threat to their very existence. This morning we will be mailing
5,000 letters to Senator Bond and Congressman Gephardt asking
them to be certain this administration and the federal prosecutors
in this case settle for nothing short of the death penalty.

Yours very truly,

> Amanda Wright
> Vice President
> American Association of
> Handicapped Americans

In the shower, he thought about Pontius Pilate and Lady Macbeth,
even though it wasn't his hands he was washing. Afterward he peed,
drank three glasses of water, scrubbed his face again, clipped his fingernails, brushed, flossed, finished brushing, swabbed cerumen out of
his ears with Q-tips, peed again, and trimmed his nasal hairs. The flurry
of purification rituals did nothing to assuage his contamination anxi-
eties. Irrational, neurotic fears to be sure. Diseases from a hand job? Yes!
What about the monkeys and rats she was always handling? He should
have stopped her and insisted on a latex glove. *"I don't want you to do
this, but if you do it, please use a latex glove."*
At bedside, he turned around three times looking for his reading
light, his glasses, his book, then got under the covers. He had a sudden
urge to retrieve his subnotebook and defrag its hard drive. Run a new
antivirus utility he'd downloaded at work. Update the video driver

with a beta version that had just come out. But he'd left his machine in the car. Nothing but trouble if he went and fetched it. She'd probably find a gun.

Instead, he stared up at the dark ceiling and tried to think of himself as a complex animal, a distant relative of Cham, an organism fitted out with a brain that was evolution's crowning glory, a biochemical marvel refined by centuries of neural Darwinism and programmed to do whatever was necessary to protect and transmit his genes into the next generation. That's it, he thought, I'm a male biological force. Females can produce, at most, one child per year; it behooves them to be highly selective when mating. But males have every evolutionary incentive to mate with the highest number of desirable females and create as many offspring as possible.

In other words, adultery made perfect sense, biologically, and he was only fulfilling his genetic destiny by chasing a beautiful brain scientist. *Honey, don't blame me! Get Darwin on the line and tear* him *a new asshole.*

But wait, he thought, calming himself. True to form, he was overreacting. A semivoluntary hand job, adultery? A *prelude* to adultery, perhaps. Certainly not sexual intercourse. Petting, the nuns would have called it. A teenage infraction, worse than staying out past curfew to be sure, but not adultery. Not a mortal sin.

His father's words rang in his ears: *"Are you ready to be faithful to one woman?"*

He recalled a vivid, recurring dream, in which he was making love to . . . well, not Sandra. An old girlfriend, a secretary, a stranger. And on waking, the dream changed into a nightmare, because for a half-minute space of time, his heart squirming in his chest, he knew and could recall being unfaithful to his wife many, many times, separate episodes, graphic details. But because he had such morbid, Catholic fears of committing adultery, he had blocked the memories of these indiscretions from his conscious mind. Only the recurring nightmares provided glimpses into his true bestial nature. In these very brief, waking moments, he saw his real self and felt . . . How did the renegade Catholic Jimmy Joyce put it? "I had sunk to the state of a beast that licks his chaps after meat." (This from a guy who thought he was throwing off mind-forged manacles?)

Formerly, Watson could always wake up from these persistent nightmares and breathe deeply of the consolations of the real world. *It was only a dream!* He was still a good and faithful husband. Could he still say that? Maybe not. Now he had to settle for some specious ratiocinations about how adultery made perfect evolutionary sense.

Next to him in their queen-size bed there would soon be another complex animal with advanced language capabilities. He jumped when she sat on the edge of the bed. She had a different satin teddy on, this one a rose-petal pink. She set the alarm on her clock radio by stabbing the button repeatedly.

"It's your turn if they wake up," she said curtly. "There's a bottle in the refrigerator. Don't forget to change him or the bed will be wet."

Still angry about him being late? But why the teddy? Not the usual cotton T-shirt? Did she just grab it? Or was she in the mood? Again? That would not be good, because what if he couldn't so soon? Or what if the turmoil of guilt jangling his nerves kept him from—? What if he said no? She would suspect something. Home very late, and then turning down sex? Her husband, Joe Watson? She wouldn't suspect, she would *know*.

"Arthur called," she said irritably, slipping under the covers. "Did I tell you that?"

"No," he said, suddenly unable to breathe. "What did he want?"

"He was looking for you," she said. "Where were you?"

"When?" asked Watson. "I was at the brain place. Then, I was back at the firm. I was probably still there; he just couldn't find me. That's happened before."

"He said you weren't there. He tried you on the communicator. And he paged you."

"Then I was at the hospital. I had to leave the communicator in the doctor's office because of radiation and magnetic fields."

She sighed long and hard.

"I'm not making dinner anymore, unless you call and tell me before four o'clock that you will be home before eight-thirty."

"Fine," he said. "Once this appointed case is over, I'll be getting home by seven every night."

She was definitely ticked and not in the mood, which made him feel better. But Arthur? Calling him at home? To bitch about not reporting Harper's call? And the teddy was still making him nervous. What if she got in the mood? He would be on the spot. Only one thing to do. Risky to be sure. Pretend he was in the mood, while she was still peeved, betting that she would rebuff him the way she usually did when she was pissed because he had come home late.

He snaked one hand out and rested it on her thigh.

"I don't feel like it," she said.

Whew.

She rolled over and stabbed buttons again on the clock radio.

"Arthur is killing me," said Watson. "It's worse than golden hand-cuffs, it's more like being bound and gagged. He's a black widow. They have liquefied my insides, they are siphoning my guts."

Another of her sighs filled the air with poison vapors. "Maybe you could pass on a few of those PizzaFax golf outings and get some work done?"

"Can't," he said bitterly. "They're required."

He suddenly felt like Raskolnikov after the ax murders. Watson had let a brain scientist convince him that the *conscience* was a vestigial, evolutionary device that had served its purpose in the village setting and was no longer useful in the modern world. As usual, Shakespeare had come true, and conscience had become an obstacle, a thing beggaring any man who keeps it. Living well meant trusting yourself and living without it.

He had invested years of daily human industry in building a family, only to merrily risk it all for an episode of *Erotic Science Quest.*

Big fun. Now what?

"So what are we doing about this appointed case?" she asked. "Are you getting rid of it?"

"Can't do that yet," he said. "The government is going for the death penalty."

"Because he's guilty, right?" she asked. "That's why they want the death penalty. It's not like he's innocent."

"He probably killed the guy, OK?" said Watson. "But I don't think he did it on purpose. I don't think it was malicious—"

She cut him off with a smirk and rolled over to face the other direction. "He called a black man a nigger and shot him in the chest, but it wasn't malicious? Is this one of those legal theories you develop after spending weeks reading cases you downloaded from the computer? I didn't work for two years at the accounting firm, putting you through law school, so you could defend a destitute racist. I think you better hurry up and do what Arthur told you to do."

"Arthur ain't his lawyer," said Watson.

"*Ain't?* So you'll be trying to get a hate killer off, I guess, is what I'm supposed to tell people."

"He ain't getting off," said Watson, thinking: *If only!* He'd be the hottest new legal talent in town if he could manage anything less than life, much less *off.*

He closed his eyes and replayed his client's phone message in his mind's ear. *"Or maybe some extra money for yourself"?* The guy had cheek a mile wide. And that question again: *"What would you do?"* One more time, and Watson promised himself he was going to answer that question. He mentally rehearsed his answer.

What would I do? I would say to myself: I am experiencing an acute, domestic relations crisis. . . . I have an almost uncontrollable impulse to kill my wife and her spare significant other, a disabled African-American. I am contemplating the ultimate breach of the laws of Church and State, the taking of human life—serious criminal conduct with profound, lifelong legal consequences. Didn't I go to Ignatius High with a fellow who's now at Stern, Pale & Covin, the best law firm in town? Sure, Joe Watson. I'll put the safety back on my weapon and give old Joe a call.

Once I reached Joe, we would have caught up on old times, and Joe would have immediately referred me to the firm's domestic relations specialist, Drath Bludsole, Esq. Drath's advice would be to rethink the murder option. Murder, he would probably explain, can be an important estate-planning device, or a tool for resolving domestic relations disputes short of trial in divorce court. However, because of certain niggling statutory and common-law prohibitions, murder almost always requires careful planning and expenses related to the hiring of third-party experts. Was this something I had thought out in advance after consulting with my attorney and deliberating with the aforesaid specialists and consultants? No? Drath's opinion would be that impetuous decisions to use murder as an alternative dispute resolution device almost always expose the client to unnecessary legal sanctions ranging from loss of a driver's license to fines or even imprisonment.

"Let's think about this," Drath would say. "What is it we're after? I don't know you all that well, but I sense at least a passing desire for revenge, which you'll savor for all of two or three minutes if you select murder as your modus operandi. And for that, you risk prison? Skip the prison sentence," Drath would have sagely advised. "Let's make them suffer horribly for years, while you and I stay completely within the letter of the law."

After he made sure the gun was put away, it would be routine. Drath would probably take another call and turn me over to the firm's family law paralegals, who would have told me in simple numbered sequences exactly what to do.

1. Do nothing to betray your knowledge of the affair.

2. Hire a private investigator with a telephoto and get some pics of her and the African-American significant other desecrating your conjugal bliss. If pics are unobtainable, hire somebody to rear-end them in front of his house and get a copy of the police report with both of their names on it.

3. After you get the pics or the police report, clean out all joint accounts and take the proceeds in cash. Cancel all joint credit card accounts and tell them to send her the bills.

4. Decide which car you want, then strip the other one of all cellular phones and valuable electronic devices. Carry anything out of the house that is portable and worth more than $500, except her jewelry and family heirlooms.

5. Take the kid and move to Texas, which has a homestead exemption and some very traditional laws about things like alimony and marital infidelity. Move the cash offshore and stir it through a few numbered accounts, put what's left in the new house, which no creditor, including your soon-to-be former wife, can touch.

6. File for divorce and sue for custody of the kid.

7. Get a court order for a medical and psychological examination of the kid. After the forensic psychologists and the recovered memory experts help the kid through posttraumatic stress disorder, he may be able to remember that the African-American once acted like he wanted to sexually abuse him, or that he may have offered drugs or said suggestive things, in sign language, I guess. Or claim the guy brainwashed the wife and kid with deaf-culture delusional systems. It's a stretch, but if it's handled properly, somebody in the district attorney's office might charge her or the African-American with child abuse.

8. Get custody of the kid.

9. Get the wife's attorney to agree to waive maintenance and alimony in favor of a huge property settlement including assets A, B, and C. If they sign onto that, file an immediate Chapter Seven bankruptcy, which discharges almost all debts, including the property settlement, but which would not discharge maintenance and child support payments, of which there are now none.

Result: Instead of employing the firm of Smith & Wesson, I would have consulted Stern, Pale & Covin. Instead of sitting in the jaws of Hell looking at life in prison or death by lethal injection like you, I'd be barbecuing in the backyard with my kid in Texas. The little deaf guy would be attending the local oral school and learning to lip-read, the African-American would be in jail awaiting trial, the wife would be destitute and in agony. All would be right with the world.

That's what I would do.

CHAPTER 11

Arthur's flame phone message of the night before left him two choices: He could go in early, grovel for forgiveness, and have his arm twisted to make Whitlow take the plea, or he could sleep an hour longer, phone in on the way to see Whitlow, and avoid a face-to-face encounter. He chose the latter. He waited in the turn lane with a crush of Ladue commuters, looking at freshly groomed occupants in nice cars on their way to the office, fairly sure that he was the only commuter whose work was taking him into a secure conference room with a murderer.

How to tell Whitlow about the sucker plea offer from Harper? Suppose he advised him not to take it and the jury came back with death? The explanation might be a little strained. "James, buddy! Never in a million years did I think they'd do that! Myrna Schweich said no way would they send a white man to the chair for shooting a black in bed with his wife."

Instead of Arthur, he got Arthur's voice mail.

"Arthur, it's Joe," he said, as Watson maneuvered the Honda onto the inner beltline. "Got your message late last night. I . . . will talk to you this morning around ten-thirty, eleven, if it's convenient, after I get back from Des Peres. As for Mr. Harper, he called me late yesterday afternoon"—*Lie, it was early or mid*—"I tried to call you, but you were . . . on the phone, I guess." *Bald mendacity!* "I'm seeing Mr. Whitlow this morning to recommend the government's offer to him." *Recommend rejection, that is, or had he misspoken?* "I will also recommend Dr. Palmquist and the neuropsychological testing, and then I will come straight to the office. I'll keep the phone and the communicator with me, of course," *even if I happen to let the batteries die.*

Maybe he had simply made a mistake, Watson thought, the kind normal people are allowed to make, because they are not being paid an entry-level salary of a hundred grand a year to not make mistakes. So far, these lapses seemed to happen only when he was working for Arthur, perhaps because he was unconsciously rebelling. *"I know people in the U.S. Attorney's office."* The timbre of Arthur's recollected voice tingled in the roots of his hair. *"I'm going to tell you this once. I want to know the instant anyone contacts you with an offer. Hear me?"*

At the Des Peres County Correctional Center, the same overweight black woman sat at her computer inside the octagonal kiosk of steel screens; she had another sumptuous arrangement of cornrows beaded in new colors—burnt sienna, fuchsia, indigo, madras, and mauve—and a new game of Microsoft Hearts on the screen. New wallpaper on the screen of her virtual desktop, too—a Kente cloth background pattern with Africa outlined in the video-graphic equivalent of a watermark. She had an impeccable sense of design and color, which might explain her lack of feeling for a job that trapped her in such drab surroundings.

This time, she didn't bother to look up. She played the last three hearts in her screen hand, and said, "Shit," when software opponent Terri took the last heart trick with a nine over her seven. "Your mama makes housecalls with a mattress," she muttered to the monitor.

Watson cleared his throat in an attempt to call attention to himself. She clicked out to the desktop and into her database.

"Name?" she said.

"Joseph Watson," he said.

"Prisoner?" She tapped at the keyboard, leaned over, and puckered up to a straw smudged with lipstick and stuck into a can of Coke.

"James Whitlow."

A burst of typing, then she stared blankly into her screen and rolled a wad of purple gum between her tongue and her gold-filled incisors.

"Ain't here," she said, retracting the gum and snapping it with her molars.

"Beg pardon?" said Watson. "James Whitlow. I sat in that room with him the day before yesterday. The prisoner's name is James Whitlow. W-H-I-T-L-O-W."

The gum reappeared, formed into a purple bladder by her tongue. He watched it slowly inflate—its surface speckled here and there with streaks and flakes of crumbling rose-colored lipstick—until it burst in a muffled explosion. Her mouth opened and, as she typed the name again on the keyboard, a muscular tongue emerged and rounded up the shreds of detonated gum from around her lips.

"W-H-I-T-L-O-W," she said—in a special tone of voice meant just for him. Then she stared into the screen. "Ain't here," she said again, glancing up once with a look that gave him to understand that she had no intention of doing any more typing for him.

"My prisoner is not here," said Watson. "OK, I guess that means he's been, what? Transferred? Executed?"

The woman barely frowned and put on another look, this one letting him know that providing therapy for his mental illnesses was not part of her job description. She shifted her comfortable, government-fed girth in her chair and stared at him, patiently waiting for him to shut up and go away.

"I am the attorney representing Mr. James Whitlow, who is being held here on a murder charge. If my client is not here, I would like to know where he is, and then I would like to speak with him as soon as possible."

The woman slowly shook her head and stared at him through the wire mesh, her eyes as placid as a grazing cow's. Closer scrutiny revealed that she did appear to notice him, maybe even observe him with passing interest, as if his ability to get worked up over something like a prisoner's whereabouts were a rare and fascinating personality disorder—nothing she intended to do anything about but an interesting quirk in the otherwise tedious spectacle of daily human depravity.

Watson had an almost irresistible urge to open her personality's config.sys file, REM-out the line that was causing her intense indifference, and reboot her. But they were addressing each other across the insecure, organic network known as regular human interaction, so he did not have access to her system files. If only.

"My client, please," he said, cycling into busy-wait mode, watching another purple bubble explode onto her lips.

She dandled the gum between her tongue and teeth a few more times and regarded him with a look of vague mistrust. The purple wad took another trip or two around the inside of her mouth, whereupon she concluded that the recent turn of events might call for a syllable or two. She took a big breath and shifted her weight again, then said, "Reggie."

On the other side of the wired Plexiglas barrier, a large, thick-necked man in a uniform lifted his pumpkin-size head out of a file cabinet and sauntered out into the octagonal cage.

"It's a lawyer," she said, eyeballing Watson, the manageable nuisance on the other side of the screen from her, "askin' 'bout a prisoner who has been turned to the Marshals Service."

"Can't do that, sir," the man said cheerfully. "Once they go to the U.S. Marshals Service, ain't nobody can ask about them for twenty-four hours. That's the rules. Call the Marshals Service if you want, but they'll tell you the same thing."

"Call the . . . Marshals Service," Watson repeated vacantly. "You mean they took him somewhere?"

The woman hissed under her breath, then stuck out a tongue sheathed in purple and began inflating another bubble.

"OK," said Watson looking helplessly from her to the smiling man in the uniform. "James Whitlow is not here, and the Marshals Service has taken him somewhere else?"

The woman shook her head in disbelief and returned to her screen, pointing and clicking to somewhere as far away as possible from Watson.

"That ain't necessarily so," said the man. "You see, he's been turned over to the Marshals Service. Once that happens we don't know nothing about him. He could be here with the marshals, he could be in California with the marshals, he could be in court with the marshals, or he could be on the moon with the marshals. Not to mention the marshals could have taken him somewhere and turned him over to someone else. What we're saying is we can't supply any information about him for twenty-four hours once he has been turned to the Marshals Service. That's a rule."

Watson looked from Ms. Microsoft Hearts to Reggie, who was still smiling sincerely, with a look that said, "Ain't this a bullshit world we live in? But we all got rules to go by."

Watson's brain had been trained to attack bullshit rules, but first he needed to know the bullshit source and authority for the bullshit rule. Was this a prison bureau rule? A municipal ordinance? An administrative guideline, a state statute, a federal regulation? Was this something that had been read into the U.S. Constitution by the Supreme Court? Probably a product of the doctrine of original intention. Clear as a glass nose on a plain face. The Founding Fathers didn't want anyone asking about prisoners who had been turned to the Marshals Service.

If, as Myrna Schweich had opined, he needed to make the government do its job, he was so far failing miserably. He stared into the cage, then beyond the wired Plexiglas, into the bowels of the prison itself, and realized that criminal law should be denominated as a separate profession. What did the incarceration of violent human beings have to do with misleading statements in a stock prospectus? What did murder have to do with copyright and intellectual property analysis of Anthrax Avenger?

Here he was trying to be a criminal lawyer, and he couldn't even find his client. The game was too tough, and there were no Options or Customize or Settings or Properties menus to pull down and select a preferable state of affairs.

He implored Ms. Microsoft Hearts with a desperate look.

"Bye," she said, without looking up from Terri's two-of-clubs lead.

His shoulders sagged on the way back out to his Honda. Highway 40 was jammed—his car was stuck in traffic, his thoughts mired in ennui laced with anxiety. He called in to check voice mail and found a message from Myrna Schweich, defense lawyer and criminal-law big sister.

"How's the town's favorite hate criminal? Sorry to cut you off the other day. It was an emergency. *Was* an emergency, is right. I told my guy to stay in jail. He said my job was to get him out of jail, and he fired me. He hired another lawyer, who got him out of jail. Now? He's dead. So, I have time. Mary Whitlow's rape-slash-affair sounds funnier every time I read it. Call me."

Watson tried her on the communicator and got a busy signal, which meant she had two lines going at once and her receptionist was on the third one. Harper's phone call had put the fear of the federal government in him. He was scheduled to publicly bump heads with an Assistant United States Attorney—a seasoned pro who seemed to have both the facts and the law on his side. Meanwhile, his opponent's employer—the federal government—had somehow made off with his client. His big-firm associate's instincts told him to seek the advice of a senior partner, but that would lead to Arthur, a guilty plea for Whitlow, and life in prison for both of them, though Watson's would be the figurative prison of conscience.

So far, the only person on Watson's side was a loopy, luscious brain scientist into monkey sex and neuro–hand jobs. His Honda crept forward in a continental drift of traffic until he was looking at the Clayton exit, the same one he used to take to get to . . . Myrna Schweich! Criminal-law big sister. She was right there! All he had to do was pull off and go see her. He was due at Arthur's, but if he stayed on 40, it would take him an hour to get downtown anyway. Why not jump off for a consult, and take another route downtown?

Her office was in a plain, rectangular two-story in Clayton that housed dentists' offices, small-time collection agencies, and a mishmash of solo practitioners who shared a pool of receptionists and secretaries. Watson said hi to Tilly, Myrna's receptionist, who called Myrna and waved him on back to his sentimental haunt, the office where he had written his first appellate brief.

"Lawyers for hate criminals!" she said. "Joey, we miss you."

Myrna Schweich tipped back in a swivel chair and tried to put her Nikes up on her desk, but her legs were too short, so she opened a lower desk drawer and propped them there instead. A lavender headband pulled her orange hair back and framed a faceful of freckles. She had a child-size mouth lipsticked in an Urban Decay hue somewhere between bruise violet and black bile. Black harem pants hung off of her legs, and her black T-shirt had white block letters above and below her breasts that said: FUCK ART, LET'S DANCE.

"So? You won't work for me, because the wife wants the big bucks. Now you come crawling in here on your hands and knees for advice? How's the money downtown? The money's good, but it costs a lot, right? Didn't I tell you?"

She had the criminal lawyer's knack for reading the mind's construction in the face; she already knew why he had come.

"Debt is my gestalt," he said. "My worldview, my hierarchy of need, my reason to be. Making more money doesn't help. It gets spent. I have a bonus coming up. Spent."

"I know some great personal bankruptcy lawyers," she said. "I think you need one of those financial psychologists."

After she heard the blow-by-blow of Harper's phone call, she took a pull on a mid-morning Heineken, then fished a cigarette loose from a pack of Gitanes and pushed it across her desk at him. She picked up a small ceramic skull from her desktop and flicked a dial in the socket where the nose belonged. A tiny blue flame appeared at the apex of the skull. She touched it to her Gitane and puffed.

"It won't comfort you to know this," she said, "but I routinely kick Harper's ass all over federal district court, and I could do so even if I was legless and strapped in a wheelchair."

His eyes brightened. "Do you want the case?"

Her orange eyebrows almost crossed. "For no pay? Joey, we were just talking about money. Besides, when the accused hires a great criminal lawyer, people think, 'Hey, he must *need* a great criminal lawyer.' "

She handed him a sweating Heineken, pushed the Gitanes at him again, and slid the skull over to his side of the desk. Her fingernails were painted black and spiculed with raised white spots. He noticed molded lettering forming a semicircle around the butane spout on the skull: SMOKING GAVE ME CANCER it said.

She exhaled luxuriously and noticed him looking at her nails, her T-shirt, her bruise-colored lipstick, her Heineken. "Didn't get home last night," she said, lifting her eyebrows at the memory of a story that was too long to tell. "Cops on horseback herded us out of Laclede's Landing at three A.M. Mufugly and bent-over. I was maced. I'm a member of the bar, and I was maced while entertaining paying clients.

"Look at me," she said, touching her fingertips to her shoulders, on either side of FUCK ART, "I'm five feet in heels. Do they need to mace me? This is what, Tiananmen Square? I am who, Rodney King on PCP? I've cross-examined half of those cops in court—that's why they do it. Get me some white-collar perpetrators who play golf at Bellerive Country Club, wouldya?"

"I'm on my way back downtown," he said. "Yesterday, I went to the brain place, and I have a neuro doctor looking for a mental defect."

"That's good," she said bobbing her head. "I suspected a mental defect all along. That would explain why you went to a place like Stern, Pale. You have a mental defect. I knew it."

"I wouldn't point fingers at mental defects," said Watson, "especially if I had black nail polish. Anyway, so then I went to see my client and he's not there. He's gone, I guess. Or not gone—he's been 'turned over to the Marshals Service,' " he said, mimicking the Microsoft Hearts player.

"They are moving him," said Myrna. "Maybe into administrative confinement. Maybe for medical treatment. Maybe a different prison. Wait twenty-four hours, then they'll tell you." She fanned the back of her right hand, buffed the black nails on her T-shirt, and glanced at her watch. "Cultivate the forensic psycho-neuro babe, especially if, as you say, she's free. But I'd be more worried about getting some standard, Ivy League headshrinkers and a good investigator. You got an investigator?"

"You mean, like a private detective?" said Watson, thinking, *How dramatic, how TV, how movie!* "You mean, Jack Nicholson?" he asked. "Jay Gittes in Chinatown?"

"Holy fuck," she said. "This is the legal equivalent of ER. Legal triage." She pulled a marker out of her pen cup and handed it to him. "Write H-E-L-P on your forehead, wouldya? You go off and draft up some fancy motions for Judge Stang on your computer about how people have a compelling, fundamental, constitutional right to commit hate crimes in their bedrooms, and I'll get you an investigator. This ain't moot court, Maynard. It's a fucking trial. Judge Stang is the Emperor Nero, Mike Harper's the lion, and you and your little bigot buddy are beef-tenderized Christians. You can borrow my investigator. The court will reimburse you for up to twenty hours at sixty dollars per under the local rules. It's a Sixth Amendment thing. I'll put him on the ambulance attendants and the neighbors. What about the CID boys first on the scene? Who were they?"

"CID?" asked Watson.

"Criminal Investigation Division," said Myrna, barely suppressing exasperation. "It's an army base in southern Missouri, right? Those guys see Jimmy Hoffa riding Halley's Comet before they see a murder crime scene. My guess is a couple of nineteen-year-old MPs walked all over the place picking up bloody murder weapons and wiping their fingers on the gal's lingerie before a staff sergeant got there."

"OK," said Watson. "CID. Anybody else?"

"Witnesses? Neighbors? EMTs? Coroners?"

"Wait," said Watson. "Wait. Whitlow wanted me to talk to a neighbor. Hold it." He pulled a folder out of his briefcase and finger-walked through manilas and sheets of paper printed from his laptop. "Lucy Martinez. Neighbor, two doors down. He wanted me to talk to her and find out about one of his friends getting his car out of the tow lot. Some guy named Buck?"

"Buck?" asked Myrna. She sounded concerned and then pretended she wasn't. "What else do we know about Buck?"

"Some friend of his. They belong to a club." He watched her tend to the ash on her cigarette. "Why?"

"No reason," she said quickly. "Just sounded funny. I mean, why is a guy facing down the death penalty worrying about his car getting towed?"

"Well," said Watson, "he doesn't care about his car anymore, because this Buck fella apparently found some money."

"Really," she said.

"So maybe he'll hire himself a lawyer. But, I don't think he understands how much money would be involved."

"And you have to act like a good lawyer until you're off the case," she said.

"Right," said Watson. "So, what should I do?"

She handed him a pencil and a legal pad.

"You need facts. You need the FBI Form 302s. Those are field reports the FBI agents file after they interview witnesses. You need the MPs' field reports. You need reports from coroners, medical examiners, rape trauma personnel, autopsies, ballistic reports. Make sure you get both the emergency room intake on Mary Whitlow and the rape trauma unit's records. The ER docs usually think she was asking for it, or she wanted it, and the rape trauma gals think that any sex beyond hand-holding with a male is rape.

"Does the file presently contain any statements from the EMTs or ambulance attendants? Lesson one: Ambulance attendants are keen, dispassionate observers of victims, perpetrators, and crime scenes. The best and sometimes the first witnesses to arrive. Plus they are immune to the horror that obscures the vision of your average witness to mayhem, mutilation, and death. Nothing fazes them. Everybody else is throwing up, and the ambulance attendants are noticing things. 'Hey, Billy Bob, look at that, his pants are off and his dick is over there under the washing machine. What'd she use to hack that off?'

"Who collected the evidence? Whose names are on the little labels and whose names are on the reports? Usually, four or five klutzes collect the evidence, and the smart guy who can keep his stories straight signs the reports. That way, instead of having four iffy witnesses for the government, they have one handsome college graduate who keeps his stories straight and can do five trials a day without breathing hard. We want the iffy guys. Who cleaned up after the cops turned the crime scene back over to the base personnel? Housekeeping, janitors, environmental engineers? Whatever the army calls them, we want to talk to them."

Watson scribbled furiously, pausing only for swigs of Heineken.

"You can have the investigator do most of it. But you'll use up your pro bono allowance pretty quick."

Two trills sounded on Myrna's phone.

"But you need some good evidence to put shock collars on those fucking government lawyers. When they attack, you want to pull out stuff that makes them turn around three times and piss on themselves." She glanced down at a caller ID readout and picked up.

"Hi, sweetheart. No, but Mommy will be home tonight. And I'll bring some ice cream, too. I love you, too. Is Nana taking you to the playground? That's a good girl. Mommy had to work last night, helping people with lots of problems. Well, actually, people who used to have lots of problems until I helped them, but now I still need to talk to them in case they ever have lots of problems again. You are a precious little angel from heaven. I love you too. Bye."

She hung up the phone.

"My investigator normally gets eighty an hour and is worth every penny of it. His name is Dirt."

"Dirt?"

"He brings me the dirt. He says I treat him like dirt, he's cheaper than dirt, and so on and so forth. Dirt is good. A superior investigator. As I said, the court will cover sixty an hour up to I think, twenty hours," Myrna said thoughtfully and then nodded. "I'll make the rest up to him somehow." She smiled. "And you? Maybe someday, you can make it up to me, huh?"

"That's the other thing," said Watson. "Now Whitlow says he might have some money, but he thinks he can use me as a free, appointed lawyer, while he spends the money on experts and investigators. I told him he can't do that."

"Sounds like a smart fella anyway," she said. "I wouldn't worry about him having money until somebody actually shows up with a cashier's check. If that happens, take it from there."

"Anything else, boss?" he asked.

"The wife," she said.

Watson's thoughts immediately went to the night before. Quasi-adultery. He had semi-betrayed his wife, the mother of their children. He was the male equivalent of a demi-vierge, a girl or woman who engages in lewdness and promiscuous petting but retains her virginity.

"Sandra wants me to get rid of the case," he said. "She and Arthur could move in together. Then I guess they could be Mom and Dad and tell me what to do with even more authority."

"Not *your* wife," she said, smirking. "*His* wife. Your *client's* wife." She fetched another Gitane out of the pack and lit it with the Yorick's skull cigarette lighter. She kicked her stubby legs back up onto the desk drawer, puffed on the Gitane, and ruminated.

"OK," she said. "At the scene, wifey says she was being acquaintance-raped and her husband killed the aggressor. By the time she gets to the rape trauma unit, her story changes. Why? Because her husband threatened her and made her tell a lie at the scene? Maybe. But she also knows that if it's a rape, they are going to be wanting samples of semen, hair, fibers, blood, looking for tissue trauma. Maybe she realizes they ain't gonna find any semen or hair or fibers or tissue trauma on her, so she changes her story. Now it's an affair, but they hadn't done anything yet, they were just getting ready to do it when Barney Bigot arrived."

"That's not all," said Watson. "Harper claims he's sending me printouts from the victim's TDD. It's a keyboarding device deaf people use to type back and forth on the phone. In her last message to the victim, she said something like, 'I just want us to be alone together,' and that James would be away in Nevada."

"No shit?" asked Myrna. "Looks like old James missed his plane to Nevada and ended up one-way death row." She puffed again. "I don't know," she mused. "We've established one thing. Mary Whitlow knows how to lie. She's done it at least once, and was good at it when she had to be. Let's see what Dirt turns up for you."

Back at the office, Watson dialed Arthur and got his secretary, Marcia. "Is he busy?" he asked, insinuating himself into her good graces with a conspiratorial whisper.

"Depends," she said. "Do you want him to be busy?"

"Thanks," said Watson. "You're my witness. I called."

More mail. He was encouraged to discover that not all the citizens of St. Louis thought he was a scumbag lawyer whose wits were livened up only by money and publicity. He had at least one fan:

Dear Mr. Watson:

I am sure that a lot of people are attacking you for the important work you are doing defending Mr. James Whitlow against the federal government's so-called hate crime laws. You and they should know that important scientific studies have shown that the blacks experience profound mental confusion once they travel more than ten or twenty degrees north of the equator, because the dramatic alteration in the earth's polarity disturbs the magnetic properties of certain important cellular components of their brains.

And here we are at 35 degrees north? What do you expect but the kind of thing where a black thinks he can sleep with a married white woman just because she is mentally or emotionally weak at the moment?

If you have misgivings about what you are doing, you should know that at least one person with a very high IQ who has studied the matter carefully agrees with what you are doing and prays for you every day.

Yours Truly,

Kyle Whitcomb, M.A. Genetics,
hybrid race expert

The tiny comfort of having at least one patently demented supporter was dashed by letter number two. Must they arrive in pairs? Like animals entering the ruptured ark of the career he was trying to build?

Dear Attorney Joseph:

It seems that you are that unbearable whiteness of being evil. You are cold, Northern, white, and have no humanity or anything resembling human feeling. Greek, white men stole philosophy, reason, and mathematics from the Egyptians, and then perverted these native African sciences and used them to design the slave trade and gas chambers. Maybe we need a better missile system with more big, white penises pointing skyward? And somebody like you to defend the company who erects them?

Finally it is the lynchee's turn to savor the administration of justice.

Adam Africa
O'Fallon, Missouri

He put in a call to the Marshals Service and left a message for a return call. He logged on, clicked an icon to dial up the firm's Internet provider, and summoned two search engines, both of them at least five times more powerful than the firm-approved stuff the other lawyers used. They appeared as graphical renditions of robot spiders, with bellies containing double rows of blank slots for entering search terms. He named one spider Rachel and began entering text strings in the slots: *Rachel Palmquist, neuroscience, Psychon Project, Gage Institute, violence, criminal, brain, forensic, neuropsychology, neuropsychiatry, scanning.* He programmed it for a search of the Web, the WELL, ECHO, Usenet, FidoNet, BITNET, even AOL and CompuServe. He told them to assimilate and acquire lesser search engines and in turn dispatch those engine-applets abroad on the Net to gather and winnow according to the same subordinate search-term equations. In a few minutes, the search engines would return with an achieved target number of hits. He named the other spider Hate, opened its belly of skeletal search slots and entered *hate speech, free speech, First Amendment, bias crime, penalty enhance!, case title (Wisconsin & Mitchell), federal death penalty.* He'd already scoured Westlaw with these terms and found a boatload of law review topics and cases, the usual heat and light of an exploding First Amendment issue. Now he needed to know the media perceptions of these issues, the political ramifications of laws he had not even known about a week ago.

So far, most of his research was on the different kinds of hate crime statutes: how they worked, whether they unconstitutionally constrained free speech or thought, whether they were so vague they allowed prosecutors unbridled discretion to determine whose crimes were accompanied by hate or bias and whose weren't. The statutes provided extra penalties if it could be shown that the defendant intentionally selected a victim because of the victim's race, color, religion, ancestry, national origin, disability, or sexual orientation. It was left to the courts to sort out how one went about proving a person committed a crime because of the victim's race, or the perpetrator's racism.

Symbols, remarks, gang signs, associations, and—uh-oh!—tattoos made up the bulk of the evidence in these cases, which was why the First Amendment was usually the first line of defense. Did Whitlow have a First Amendment right to use the n-word while shooting an African-American? No. But it was possibly unconstitutional for the government to introduce evidence of his associations, beliefs, reading material, even his tattoo. Because these, unlike the speech that occurred at the scene, were arguably protected by the First Amendment and the freedoms of association.

As minority groups were painfully aware, the same laws, ostensibly passed to protect them, had also been used against them. A study by Klanwatch had shown nearly half of the racially motivated murders over a three-year period were committed by blacks, who made up 12 percent of the population—a statistic one was not likely to see in an article about Whitlow in the *Post-Dispatch*. Blacks probably don't commit more hate crimes than whites, but blacks get charged more often with hate crimes by police and prosecutors who decide what is or isn't a hate crime.

The early hate crime laws directly addressed the problem of hatred by trying to make it illegal to use hateful speech or commit hateful, symbolic acts—cross burning, say, or swastika painting or wearing white sheets with holes in them. The Supreme Court struck those laws down as unconstitutional, because they tried to punish speech or thought. If you painted a peace symbol on the side of a synagogue, you got a suspended sentence under the vandalism statutes; if you painted a swastika you got ten years under the hate crime statute. In the argot of First Amendment law, the early hate crime statutes were not *content* or *viewpoint neutral*. Easy call. That happened in 1993.

So instead of directly banning hateful speech and hateful acts, the state legislatures *enhanced* the penalties for crimes—trespass, defacing property, assault, murder—that seemed to be motivated by hate or that seemed to have occurred because of the victim's protected status or the perpetrator's hatefulness. Under the new statutes, hate alone was not a crime, but hate could earn you a double or triple sentence.

Many commentators argued that this was a distinction without a difference. Like punishing draft-card burners for arson. To them, the new penalty-enhancement hate laws were artful dodges around the First

Amendment, and were just another way for legislatures to punish un-popular thoughts and silence hurtful speech. As one authority, Susan Gellman, succinctly put it in the title to her law review article: "Sticks and Stones Can Put You in Jail, But Can Words Increase Your Sentence?" Others saw no constitutional problem in giving a racist killer a double sentence, in the same way society's punishment for a premeditated murder is significantly harsher than that for a murder committed by a drunk in a barroom brawl. But, some argued, proving intent is easily ac-complished by examining external acts and circumstances (did the de-fendant "lie in wait," did he plan, did he tell others what he was going to do?); proving *motive* requires a journey into the mind of the defendant (was he starving and in need of the victim's money, was he uncon-sciously attacking an authoritarian father-figure because he was abused as a child, does violence give him pleasure, did he hate the victim be-cause the victim was ugly?—OK hate, qualifying for an unenhanced penalty—or did he hate the victim because he was white?—bad hate, qualifying for an enhanced penalty).

Usually the evidence consisted of remarks made at the scene or of symbols—burning crosses, swastikas, or in at least one case, a pig's head. Watson had read about a case involving a Long Island chimney sweep who quarreled with his Jewish girlfriend, got drunk, and threw a pig's head through the plate-glass window of her Orthodox family's home on the first night of the Jewish New Year. The Nassau County Bias Crimes Unit investigated the case for over a year, until the drunk pig's-head-tossing chimney sweep turned himself in. A detective classified the prank as a hate crime because "he knew they were kosher."

He clicked on the SpiderMaster and programmed it to adjust Boolean connectors until the spiders named Hate and Rachel came back with forty quality hits apiece.

Arthur appeared at the door. *Ulp.*

"I was on my way over," said Watson.

"We're going to see Judge Stang in half an hour," he said grimly, his tone a dismal harmony of anger and . . . apprehension? "In chambers," he added importantly.

"Why are we going to see Judge Stang?" Watson asked, remaining calm, though this seemed an ill omen indeed. Even Watson knew that Judge Stang saw almost no one—certainly no lawyers—in chambers. He confined his audiences with lawyers to trials or informal matters in

open court, where he could humiliate them in front of clients and opposing counsel.

"Why are *we* going to see Judge Stang?" Arthur repeated acidly, a
reptilian glitter deep in his retinas, as if he had a couple of gleaming ser-
pents coiled up back there behind his eyes, nestled in brain tissue, flicking their tongues, poised to strike. "Probably because Judge Stang is a
medicated psychotic," he said. "I tried to make an appointment to see
him. Instead, I received a message from his clerk advising me that the
right honorable judge would not discuss matters pertaining to the case
of U.S. versus Whitlow without the attorney of record for the defendant
present." Arthur looked at him with an even more serpentine glare.
"That's you."

The spider named Rachel returned, beeped at them from the monitor,
opened her segmented belly, and displayed the hits his search request
had retrieved. The one named Hate was still out on the prowl.

"What is that?" asked Arthur, making a face at the screen. "A game?"

Watson temporized. "It's a spider," he said, at a loss for anything
more descriptive. "A search engine." How to describe the future to this
geriatric Luddite, a technological neonate. Arthur's fountain pens, his
cotton bond papers, and his Dictaphone were like war clubs in a campaign against air-launched Cruise missiles. *"What's that!?"* Watson
wanted to say. *"That's a loaded Sun Microsystems workstation cabled to a
dedicated, wide-band, fiber-optic data line, running the most recent beta version of Red HotJava (downloaded less than a week ago) and a beta version of an
agent called ArachnoManiac, which I have painstakingly tweaked to performance perfection during a series of all-nighters, so that it can venture out onto
the Internet and retrieve more and better information in four minutes than you
could find with a squadron of your two-hundred-dollar-an-hour associates in a
week."*

"It's software," said Watson respectfully. "Spiders, robots, browsers,
gophers . . . They find information on the Net or Web and bring it back
to you."

He neglected to add that it was illegal software under the technical
terms of the firm's strict network security policies. But Arthur barely
understood the difference between hardware and software, and Inspector Digit, the firm's head MIS man, was a buddy of Watson's. He was
safe, he hoped. What was an ambitious, young, techno-savvy associate
to do? Use the five-year-old brontosaurus browsers the firm supplied?

"Fascinating," Arthur said, strains of scorn and facetiousness in his voice. "Do you suppose one of these robot spiders could tell me why a talented, highly compensated young lawyer on track for partnership would ignore explicit instructions from a senior partner who controls seventy percent of his workload?"

"Arthur, I got the call yesterday. I stopped by your office and you . . . you were on the phone. And today? Ask Marcia. You were busy!"

"Why this lawyer would squander his professional talents and firm resources defending a murderer *in forma pauperis*? Why he would reject a perfectly reasonable plea offer without consulting his boss or his client?"

"I didn't reject the plea," Watson protested. "I tried to tell him about it this morning, but I—" A split-second internal debate. He was afraid to tell Arthur that he couldn't find his client, much less counsel him about a plea. "I was not able to see him. I will tell him about the offer . . ." He faded, unable to manage a convincing finish. "And what I think of it."

They looked at each other across Watson's desk.

"I've done research into this hate business," Watson said.

"I can see that," said Arthur, with a hateful look at his deskful of hate research. "Maybe this is all for the best," he said with an ophidian hiss, trying to pace, as was his custom when annoyed, forgetting he was in an associate's office, where the best he could do was turn around a few times. "If you want to represent destitute felons, it's best discovered early in your career . . . so you can find a position commensurate with your calling." He stopped marching in place and arched an eyebrow. "The public defender's office will take anyone with a pulse and a law degree. You'll make a fourth of what you draw down here." He shrugged and coughed. "But representing the kind of people you want to represent is more important than money, isn't it? I'm sure Sandra would support your decision."

A new low for the old poltroon. Dragging the wife into it. Like many fair-minded suburban homeowners, Sandra felt that society would be better off if accused murderers were quietly executed the day after being arraigned. Trials were superfluous spectacles offering guilty people the opportunity to discover technicalities and procedural infirmities, which then only served to delay the inevitable.

"Be in my office with your coat on in fifteen minutes," said Arthur and left.

Poop happens! He took a sharp breath through gritted teeth. Judge Stang, in chambers!

To laypeople, including casual litigants and *Court TV* spectators in LazyBoy recliners, judges appear as Platonic Guardians wearing black robes, throned atop burnished oak tribunals from whence they issue fiats and decrees, pardons and sentences, declaratory judgments and evidentiary rulings, in the public arena of the courtroom. Only lawyers, as a rule, go behind the scenes to enter the private offices of judges—a conference described as seeing the judge "in chambers."

Watson had no trial experience, but he'd seen enough litigation—the before and after of trial work—to know that, in chambers, judges perform the less public function of managing the giant social enterprise of criminal and civil litigation. Here, they meet with lawyers—the officers and subordinates of that enterprise. Here, remarks are generally off the record, because there is no court reporter to make a record. Oral agreements and statements of fact are, however, no less binding than the pronouncements made in open court—perhaps even more binding, because the lawyer's word and reputation are at stake, and a lawyer who lies or goes back on a deal struck in chambers commits professional suicide.

Despite the informality and the lack of a record, experienced lawyers meeting with a judge in chambers are in a state of vigilance second only to the mental red alert of opening or closing arguments to a jury. Even with less than a year's experience as squire and footman for the likes of Arthur, Watson had seen firsthand how the most casual session in chambers can produce permanent dispositive consequences for the case at bar. At any moment, the judge may frown and give you to understand that a motion to dismiss might be well received in the $5 million insurance fraud claim you are defending. He or she may banter about a prior case, with facts suspiciously similar to your own, in which the judge was outraged at the tactics employed by counsel, the same tactics you were thinking about using the first day of trial. A case that would otherwise require six months of interminable wrangling in open court— where the rules must be obeyed and the lawyers' voluminous objections recorded—can be settled in chambers in the span of a coffee break.

A scrupulous judge will not discuss the merits of a case ex parte, meaning without opposing counsel present. An unscrupulous one will force settlement by yanking a lawyer aside and delivering a blunt appraisal of a bullshit case or the invaluable information that such an appraisal was delivered to opposing counsel. Then there was Judge Stang, about as predictable as a hebephrenic in a funhouse.

He opened the spider named Rachel and read the previews of the first five hits and the accompanying term-search blurbs of disconnected text. *L.A. Times,* December 12, 1999, "Neuroscientists to Testify at Sentencing Hearing of Freeway Killer": "Dr. Palmquist and Dr. Ling, neuroscientists from the renowned Gage Institute, are expected to offer PET scans of the defendant in an attempt to prove that the defendant is incorrigibly sociopathologic, incapable of human empathy." *Hartford Courant,* May 10, 2000, "Mitigation Hearing Set for Mall Molester": "Palmquist testimony about those scans are expected to show that important connections between the defendant's frontal lobes and the limbic regions of the brain have rendered the defendant a sociopathic automaton incapable of considering the well-being of other human beings."

More mitigation and sentencing hits featuring Dr. Palmquist expounding on the incorrigibility of the criminal psychopath to be sentenced. Watson broke into a mild sweat seeing her name associated only with prosecutors and government agencies all across the country, using evidence of a mental defect not as a defense to the charged crime but as proof that any attempt at rehabilitation was pointless. He altered the weight of the term *Psychon* using a virtual sliding bar, and the sample yielded more news clips and newswire summaries. APNewswire, "Crime Commission Promises Government Action on Rising Tide of Violence": "Prominent geneticists, biologists, neuroscientists, and neuropsychologists have convened a controversial seminar on the biological and genetic aspects of violence and violent criminal behavior. . . . Dr. Rachel Palmquist, a member of what is referred to in the neuroscience community as the Gage Group, testified that violence was a biological or genetic defect, a medical problem, a symptom of a mental disorder, which could be remedied or managed with chemical therapy, or in extreme cases, invasive modification of the dysfunctional neural networks."

The signature trill of an outside call sounded from somewhere in the metropolis of stacked documents on his desk. Watson extracted the receiver from the paper canyons. "Joseph Watson," he said, eyeballing the system clock on his screen.

The Marshals Service. He got into it with a clerical type on the other end. She sounded like the sister of the woman at the Des Peres County Correctional Center. "We may not provide information for twenty-four hours once the prisoner has been turned to the Marshals Service," she said. Was he hearing pointing and clicking? Were Anna and Terri and the whole Microsoft Hearts gang at her place as well?

The other two buttons on his phone lit up. Outside calls. His information manager appeared on the screen with a double beep, identified the caller as Rachel Palmquist, MD, PhD, and presented her card file.

"I have another call," said Watson. "Could you hold for just a moment." He punched another button.

"Rachel?" he said in breathy anticipation.

"Not quite," said Arthur. "Where are you?"

"I'll be right there," said Watson, "Really, I'm coming. I think Doctor Palmquist is waiting on my other line." He felt his armpits turn into two small saunas as he pressed another blinking button.

"Rachel?" said Watson.

"Can't talk long," she said. "I thought we'd schedule a session comparing your response patterns with Cham's. Also, in order to reduce signal-to-noise ratios, I need to be able to average a statistically significant number of . . . events, like the event we captured under the MEG. I'll be blunt, I need more data. Let's rig up another chair for you right next to his and fit you out with a headful of electrodes like his and a console with buttons and so on. And maybe a mate of your choice in the other chair. How about tomorrow afternoon? Saturday. Busy?"

Watson looked up and saw Arthur in his trench coat, frowning at him from his open door.

"Three o'clock," said Watson. "We need to talk about Whitlow."

"I know," she said. "Now the prosecution wants him. We'll talk tomorrow. Bye."

"What?" he said, and heard her click sound in his ear.

The blinking light on the line to the Marshals Service went out.

"Let's go," said Arthur.

CHAPTER 12

Entering chambers for the first time, a young lawyer may find the chatty relaxed atmosphere of a den or family room, complete with a set of stuffed chairs, an ottoman, a coffee table, and sometimes even coffee. More often, the lawyer finds an interior design favored by dictators, as exemplified by Mussolini, whose office was arranged so that a visitor walked across a cavernous, formal room and shrank like Alice in Wonderland, while approaching a huge desk on a riser with a stout, powerful person behind it and two hard-back chairs in front for squirming supplicants.

In chambers, judges become more like people—formal or informal, autocratic or friendly, morose or cheerful, Type A or Type B—with one important difference: No matter what their personality, they retain the same almost superhuman power over careers and clients. In chambers, the lawyers may feel they are having an after-dinner conversation with the judge about their case, or they may sustain the intense scrutiny one receives when applying for a salaried position or a large, unsecured loan. Most lawyers endure these tolerably stressful sessions, never wondering about the resonance of the expression "judge's chambers."

Visitors to Federal District Judge Whittaker J. Stang's chambers, however, formulated their own adrenaline-induced, overwrought notions about the origin of the terminology, because they were unceremoniously introduced to a lawyer's chamber of horrors run by a quixotic despot who seemed to take infinite pleasure in administering random, exquisitely painful shocks of professional anxiety to the legal creatures who had been summoned into his domain. For lawyers, Judge Stang's chambers were of the gas and torture variety.

Arthur and Watson cooled their heels in the outer office, listening to Judge Stang shout orders to his secretary concerning the optimum strength and temperature of the tea she was brewing in a kitchenette to the rear. The two lawyers had just settled in on a cracked leather sofa with a flaking finish and torn seams when the voice of justice boomed from within, bringing them to their feet, where they stood at attention, even though the judge couldn't see them.

"Ida?" he yelled. "If those two-legged rodents from that big-firm outfit ever get here, MAKE THEM WAIT, you hear me? Nothing but a bunch of shallow, venal, overpaid shirkers. Big-firm hotshots. The associates make more than I do—for what? Legal research. Pah. And the money-bag partners use litigation for everything except dispute resolution: publicity, vanity, revenue. If I could personally execute a few of them with a sidearm, I'd feel so much better about myself and my work."

Then there was silence, punctuated only by the crack of a match being struck, the hiss of sulfur burning, and the soft clink of the burnt stick falling into an ashtray, followed by the aroma of cigar smoke.

After a few minutes, a stooped grimalkin in a floral print dress, who looked as if she had been serving tea to Judge Stang since the Missouri Compromise, emerged from the kitchenette. The bent fingers of her left hand held a wavering saucer and cup, while her right clasped the handle of a four-footed cane. Her frail skull supported a swollen wreath of silver braids and ornate combs encrusted with verdigris. Watson recognized a scent and couldn't place it, until his olfactory lobe did a neural network search, found a matching trace, and disinterred a memory from his nonage: his great-grandma bowing over stoppered bottles and powder puffs at her dressing table saying, "That's lavender water, Joey." So it was, and Ida probably had the last bottle of lavender water in the Western world.

"This way, boys," she said, giving Arthur a second look. "Arty Mahoney?" she croaked, pointing at him with a hoist of her cane, swags of mottled skin swaying from the bones of her arm, her eyes bright with memory.

"How nice to see you, Ida," said Arthur graciously.

"You boys are lucky lawyers today," she whispered hoarsely and winked. "The judge is in very high spirits. His psychiatrists have formally advised the Eighth Circuit's Investigative Judicial Council that he is not legally insane and therefore is not an impediment to the effective administration of justice."

"That's always so good to hear," said Arthur warmly.

"We're all happy for him," said Ida. "The doctors say it's nothing but a few run-of-the-mill, garden-variety, full-blown, chronic, severe personality disorders. Nothing near what those cry-baby lawyers who complained about him would need to get the right honorable judge off the bench."

"Thank God," said Arthur.

"Do tell," Ida concurred. "Our prayers were answered."

She motioned for them to follow her into the inner sanctums, so they waddled in tiny penguin steps behind her as she planted her orthopedic cane and took two steps, planted again and took another step. . . .

"Judge Whittaker J. Stang," she complained, as she at long last came alongside his desk, "you did not tell me that Arty Mahoney was coming to see us. Arty, why, we haven't seen you since I don't know when?"

Slumped in a high-backed red leather recliner and turned sideways behind a huge, battered wooden desk, Judge Stang looked smaller and thinner than when Watson last quaked in the shadow of judicial dominion at informal matters. The judge leaned back and puffed on a nine-inch Davidoff cigar, befogging the confines of a room in a building where smoking was prohibited by federal law.

Another scent touched off memories from Watson's childhood. Wildroot. Grandpa Watson's favorite hair tonic. He detected the telltale sheen on the judge's gray wisps, the slicked and pasted strands across his baldness. The judge wore a clean, threadbare coat, a starched white shirt, and a burgundy tie with faded heraldic imagery. A pair of reading glasses sat on the tip of his nose, through which he perused the contents of the *River City News*—the hate crime edition.

Watson grew banjo eyes at the sight of the familiar headline.

"Maybe you don't know when we last saw Mr. Mahoney," Judge Stang grumbled, without looking up from his reading, "but I do. It was that asinine antitrust litigation we all made ourselves sick on for nine months back in 1989, only to have counselor Mahoney roll over and play dead on the courthouse steps instead of finishing the goddamn trial. Pah!"

"Good morning, Judge," said Arthur.

"Settle the case, try the case, I don't care," Judge Stang groused; the swivel mechanism of his ancient chair squealed as he turned in it. "But don't reject a settlement offer and then take the very same offer after two years of discovery and ten days of trial in my courtroom!" The judge slammed his desk drawer closed in a fit of fresh anger, as if the incident had happened yesterday, instead of ten plus years ago.

"You did the same thing back when I was trying to teach you how to be a prosecutor. Remember that racketeering fiasco? Those Lebanese Mafia hoodlums got the best of you. Not once. Twice!"

"Judge," sighed Arthur, "we've been over this before."

"Not over," snapped Judge Stang. "Under. We've been under it. Like a steaming turd from a jackass we were under it! Over it? Maybe you got over it."

Arthur turned around several times looking for a chair to sit in, until he realized there weren't any.

"Judge," said Arthur, "we are here . . . Actually, Judge, are there chairs handy?"

"No chairs," said Judge Stang. "Lawyers talk less when they're forced to appear before me without a chair to sit in or a podium to hide behind. And whenever lawyers talk less, justice proceeds apace. State your business. And be brief."

"Yes, Judge," said Arthur. "I—"

"Meat, pith, marrow," interjected the judge, peering at them through wraiths of drifting blue cigar smoke. "Serve the blubber and bombast up to some other minion of the public weal."

"Yes, Judge," Arthur agreed.

Ida bowed over the worktable and rattled the cup on its saucer as she lowered it toward Judge Stang's elbow.

"Don't spill it!" he barked, which touched off intention tremors in the old woman's limbs and heavy seas within the cup as she placed the clanking ensemble onto his desktop.

Arthur began, "Judge, we are here—"

"Gist without jibber jabber," snapped the judge. "Concision the first order of business. Don't squander the court's patience puffing your cheeks up on stately bombast and lofty fustian. Speak plainly! If you can't do that, go on and take one of those talking time-and-temperature elevators upstairs to the Parthenon where the Eighth Circuit sits on their regal behinds listening to oral arguments. Take your prolix prattle and your supersophistical spew and sling it around up there for a while. You hear me?"

"Your Honor," said Arthur firmly, "I—"

"Nothing long is ever pleasing," observed the judge. "Brevity is the soul of wit, the sine qua non of lingerie, the judicious use of words that cover more ground than they occupy. My kingdom for less discourse. On with it, sir. Take the short, straight path. Once more into the speech."

"I'm trying, Judge," Arthur said tersely.

"Trying won't do it, Counselor," shouted the judge, a vein swelling in the hollow of his ancient temple. "You're too old to practice law, it's time to get it right."

The two old gents went on fencing and fisticuffing with lawyerly effusions, while Watson took a look around Judge Stang's brand-new sunny, modern, spacious chambers on the twenty-eighth floor of the Courthouse of the Future. It looked like a pod in an orbiting space station that had been incongruously stuffed with memorabilia and curiosa—circa New Deal—the court's personal effects brought over intact from the old federal building. Next to the judge's scarred wooden desk was a trendy, sweeping marble arc of a desk that came with the building and now served as storage space for two huge computer monitors that were dark and silent. Alongside were two unplugged minitower Ultra Pentium computers, which the judge used as bookends for a multivolume set of Wright, Miller, and Kane, *Federal Practice and Procedure,* bent and battered, in leather covers worn smooth and slick with oil from human hands. Disintegrating supplements, which had probably come in before the McCarthy Hearings, were crumbling into a dusty patina on the marble desktop. One of the minitowers' CD-ROM disk trays was open, providing a nice fit for an extra canister of cigars.

The judge lifted the floral-embossed cup, blew once across the rim, dispatched the tea in a single gulp, then delicately sipped on his cigar.

Arthur saw his chance and filled the hiatus with a complete sentence. "Judge, we're here on the matter of U.S. versus Whitlow, a federal murder case, in which you've appointed my first-year associate, Joseph Watson, here, to represent a hate criminal."

Watson felt the lawyer's instinct to speak up for his client, but he knew a single word from him in Arthur's attenuated state would result in instant termination and the ensuing Hell to pay at home. On the other hand (it occurred to him for just an instant), imagine the heroic tale he could tell to Rachel Palmquist? How he'd sacrificed his career to save their case? But even more than a desire to impress the good doctor, he was developing the advocate's irrational, obsessive concern for his client, James Whitlow—the headstrong, wayward, strapping bigot, who didn't know any better and needed looking after.

"That's right," said Judge Stang. "I appointed him, fully expecting to be impressed by his performance, which is so far lacking." The judge turned a penetrating stare on Watson, smoke and wrath bloodying the whites of his eyes. "Where's my chewed two-by-four sawdust, boy?"

Watson had put the wood in a file cabinet, never dreaming he would actually have to . . .

"Judge," said Arthur with a feigned cough that landed somewhere between indulgence and impatience, "we are all well acquainted with the court's redoubtable, often effective theatrics used to motivate lawyers in performing the court's business, but I hope we are entitled to assume that this charade with the piece of wood was a symbolic gesture. I mean, seriously, Judge, you're— Surely the court did not actually, er, I don't mean to suggest . . . I'm asking the court to reconsider its treatment and not inflict such an indignity on a young lawyer, newly admitted to the practice. It's inconsistent with Your Honor's impartiality and unbecoming of the high standards of jurisprudence the lawyers of this district have come to expect from this court."

Judge Stang took another puff and swiveled in his chair, turning away from the lawyers and toward his view of downtown St. Louis and the Mississippi River. "You're right, it is unbecoming."

"I thought you'd agree," said Arthur modestly. "If nothing else, it creates the appearance of impropriety."

"It's inconsistent with impartiality," repeated the judge, waving smoke away from his face, "and it's the appearance of impropriety, or however you put it."

"That's right, Judge," said Arthur. "It's unduly harsh."

"The court is persuaded by the arguments of counsel. Upon reconsideration, I hereby order *you* to chew the lumber into sawdust. You're probably the one who put the lad up to that spurious motion to withdraw."

Arthur set his briefcase down in lieu of sitting or pacing. "Notwithstanding the question of the court's power to order such a thing," said Arthur, "I must—"

"I've got power, and you've got money," said the judge, still turned away from the lawyers, as if he were entertaining call-in questions on talk radio. "I admit I don't know the answer to your not withstood question, but I can settle it for you in two shakes."

He tapped the cigar on a stone ashtray the size of a dinner plate. "Ida? Send one of the girls in."

"Judge," stammered Arthur, "th-this is really a peripheral matter. W-We didn't come here to—"

Watson winced, watching his superior, one of the most powerful partners in his firm, chastened into fawning obeisance by the absolute power of a federal district court judge. *Arthur had stuttered,* Watson realized in that amazed state in which one perceives another, heretofore unimagined dimension to human affairs. After watching his boss smoothly and seamlessly manage global conference telephone calls and client meetings, preside over internecine, intrafirm feuds among partners of differing ranks, quell the malpractice insurance crisis, manage in-house counsel from the firm's number one client, play opposing counsel like Gameboys— Could it be that after all those dazzling, clutch performances, Arthur Mahoney was afraid of a mere judge?

At the firm, the partners spoke dismissively of Judge Stang—a carbon-dated crackpot whom fate, or more likely good political fortune, had appointed to a lifelong career. Watson suddenly realized the obvious: No matter how many research memos, motions, discovery requests, posturings, settlement demands, and correspondence were created to obstruct and delay other parties in their quest for justice, litigators were ultimately at the total mercy of judges. The trace of apprehension Watson had detected in Arthur back at the office had now swelled into outright fear.

"Good morning, Judge," said one of Judge Stang's clerks—the blonde—whom Watson recognized from the first day at informal matters when he had made his fateful motion seeking to withdraw from the case. She was friendly, fresh, bright, in a short suit and an ecru silk blouse, a burgundy scarf knotted and spread like a bow on a basket of fruit.

The judge continued staring out his window, so the clerk made her way around the desk and stood alongside.

"I think I asked you and the other girl to do some research on this lumber question that came up about a week ago in our little murder case, and whether it was something I was able to do or not."

"Yes, Judge," she said cheerfully, "we carefully looked at the issue, exactly as you formulated it, and our answer is no."

"You see, Judge," said Arthur politely. "It's just not in keeping with the decorum of the . . ."

"No?" interrupted the judge, beaming at his clerk. "That's excellent. Fine work, indeed. No. That's what I thought."

"No?" said Arthur, looking from the back of the judge's head to the clerk with a puzzled expression.

"That's correct," said the clerk. She opened a leather folio and peeled back three or four pages. "The precise issue as formulated by the judge was: Is it a felony criminal offense for a federal district court judge, pursuant to the court's discretionary and local-rule-making authority, to discipline one of its officers by instructing him or her to chew a not unreasonable length of unsoiled, untreated, nontoxic lumber into sawdust? Our answer is: No, we could find no case law or statutory language that would suggest such an action could be considered a felony criminal offense under current law. The judge specifically instructed us not to look at the question of whether such an order was an abuse of the court's discretion, beyond the disciplinary powers of the court, or subject to reversal on appeal."

Arthur hung his head and sighed.

"So, I am correct in assuming that it is not a felony criminal offense if I order Mr. Mahoney here to chew a length of two-by-four into sawdust? Is it a high crime or misdemeanor?"

"We searched the on-line services," said the blonde pertly, "and there are no reported cases of a judge being charged with a felony or a misdemeanor for ordering a lawyer to chew a piece of wood into sawdust."

"There you have it," said the judge, still looking out the window. "Follow instructions, and no one will have to know about your contempt of court or the ensuing penalty. If you want to challenge me on it, you'll have to do so in open court—which is your right." He tapped a ring of ash off the cigar. "It won't be the first time I've watched a lawyer drown in the gulf of his own folly."

Arthur froze like a pointing hound and stared helplessly while the judge said, "Thank you, dear," to his clerk and then surveyed his desktop in search of new business.

"Oh, it's my pleasure," the clerk replied. "Judge, I might also mention that the Assistant United States Attorney in this case has filed the motion he spoke to you about yesterday. We thought perhaps you and the lawyers might care to discuss it before they leave. I believe the prosecution was seeking a physical and mental examination of the defendant pursuant to Rule Twelve."

She leaned over the two dead minitower computers and handed the judge a document, then turned and held a copy out midway between Watson and Arthur. Watson took a step forward and extended his hand; Arthur cut him off and seized the document.

"Just what the Hell is the Psychon Project anyway?" asked the judge. "They've run four or five of these stiffs up to Minnesota, and then they come back in here claiming the defendants are congenital racist, psychopathic hate killers who should be put away for life. It's a new one on me. It used to be that a mental defect meant you were *not* guilty. Now, they've turned it upside down. Now if you're brain-damaged or crazy, it just means you were probably crazy enough to kill somebody, and what's more, crazy enough to do it again."

Watson froze and then looked over Arthur's shoulder.

"And as long as we are on the subject," growled the judge, "I might as well tell you boys that I had a little ex parte with the U.S. Attorney on this case the other day. Whenever I do that, I make sure and keep things fair by having another little ex parte with the other side, and that way, when you put the two ex partes together, they make up what I call an 'in wholé,' and nobody can complain. Can they, Mr. Mahoney?"

"Judge, we would have no complaint about anything that leads to a speedy resolution of this matter, so we can extricate my associate, Mr. Watson, from a case he is clearly not qualified to defend."

"I'll worry about who's qualified," said the judge. "Mr. Watson, were you by any chance planning to assert a mental defect or disease, any medical or psychiatric condition as a defense in this action? Because if you are, we can transport this fellow to the federal hospital up there at Mayo's and satisfy you and the prosecutor in one stroke. It's the best way I know of to get free medical testing for an indigent client. Of course, the prosecutor has moved first and made sure that he'll get to see everything too, and most of the doctors at these federal medical centers are government whores as you probably know. So you run the risk that the results may not be favorable to your client. There's every chance that they'll come back saying he knew exactly what he was doing and that he's as sane as you and me."

Arthur abruptly turned aside and coughed.

"Something stuck in your craw, Mr. Mahoney?"

"No, Judge," gasped Arthur, "Excuse me, I just—"

"So," said the judge, "if you were maybe thinking about filing a motion under seal to have this man sent to a government facility without telling the prosecutor what you're up to, that chance is gone. Whatever they do up there will be common knowledge. I told the prosecutor as much yesterday."

The judge picked up his empty teacup and stared into it with a sour look.

"Do you have any objection to having medical and psychiatric examinations of your client done?"

Watson glanced sideways at Arthur. "In fact, Judge, I am finishing a Rule 12.2 motion notifying the court that we may assert a mental defect as a defense at trial," he said. "At a minimum, I would be seeking the court's permission for a medical examination to determine if the defendant's history of neurological disease could have contributed in whole or in part to his alleged impulsive behavior."

"Consider him shipped," said Judge Stang. "In fact, I issued the order yesterday, and my guess is he's gone by now. Let's get all this mental crap over with, and then I'll tell the lawyers what kind of medical evidence I'm going to let the jury hear."

"Just one other thing," said Watson. "You said the prosecutor gets to see everything that comes back from Mayo's. What if, in addition to the Mayo's testing, we consult our own expert—our own neuroscientist or neuropsychologist?"

"That typically costs money," said the judge. "Under the Criminal Justice Act, I can give you a free trip to Mayo's. I can't pay federal marshals to escort your boy around town until he finds a shrink who understands him and then write more checks to cover his medical expenses."

"The fees are not yet an issue," said Watson. "But I do have one other concern—what happens if we consult the expert of our choice, and that expert renders an opinion we don't like? Is the government entitled to discover that expert's opinion, even if we don't call him . . . or her?" he added, checking Arthur with a sideways glance.

The judge swiveled back around and looked at Arthur Mahoney for what seemed to be the first time during their meeting. "See what happens when a lawyer is an advocate, instead of a shirker?" he asked with a grin.

"My concern also lies with the client," Arthur protested. "I don't like Mr. Watson's chances in a murder trial, especially since he's never even seen a jury trial, much less conducted one."

The judge turned back to Watson. "Hot topic, Mr. Watson. You'll find a lot of commentary in the law journals about what happens when the psychiatrist you consult formulates an opinion you don't want anyone to know about."

"I already found them," said Watson. "They came out after the Supreme Court's opinion in Ake versus Oklahoma, which guarantees criminal defendants the right to expert psychiatric assistance. But the circuits are split on the question of what happens when the expert you've consulted—an expert the prosecution knows about—renders an opinion that is helpful to the government rather than to the defense. And the Eighth Circuit hasn't addressed the issue yet."

"Don't worry about them," said the judge with a grimace. "The Eighth Circuit can fuck themselves with a sixpenny nail." He swiveled back toward his clerk. "Sweetheart?" he said, and handed his clerk the prosecutor's motion. "Stamp my signature on that and any other papers we need to get our hate killer shipped off to the medical center for federal prisoners up there in Mayo's."

"Yes, Judge," said the clerk.

"Oh, yes," said the judge. "Now, as we all know, it would be inappropriate for me to give Mr. Watson, here, my opinion about any prospective motion he or the government might file in this case, so would you dig up that unpublished opinion of ours in that case we had last year where the government came in and tried to get their hands on the written report of a nontestifying psychiatrist consulted by the defense. If memory serves it was that soft-spoken young fella who showed up in the Federal Express office asking for a box to mail an Uzi to his brother in Philadelphia."

"I remember, Judge," said the clerk. "I wrote . . . er, ah, I helped write the court's order and opinion."

"If I'm remembering," said the judge, "the defense consulted three psychiatrists—the first one said the defendant was sane, the second one said he was insane, and the third one said I was insane. The defense announced they intended to call psychiatrist number two at trial, and the government filed a motion seeking to compel disclosure of the reports from numbers one and three. And what did we say?"

The clerk smiled. "Is the court asking me for the wording of the court's written opinion, or the wording of the court's oral opinion?"

"Brevity," said the judge. "Make it oral."

The clerk nodded and pleasantly announced, "The court's oral opinion denying the prosecutor's motion to discover and subpoena the nontestifying psychiatrists consulted by the defense was"—she straightened her back and lowered her voice slightly—" 'Tell that government lawyer to go fuck himself with a tenpenny nail.' "

The clerk smiled, the judge nodded approvingly, and Arthur passed Watson a baleful glance through the haze of cigar smoke.

"Thank you, Kendra, dear," said the judge. "That will be all for now. Give Mr. Watson, here, a copy of the court's written opinion explaining how the reports of the nontestifying psychiatrists consulted by the defense in a criminal trial are protected by the work product doctrine and therefore the government can't have them."

"Your Honor," interrupted Arthur. "If I may, the court has appointed a recent law school graduate with no trial experience to defend a high-profile, controversial murder case in which the government is seeking the death penalty. I fail to see . . ."

The judge ignored Arthur and swiveled away to look again on his generous view of downtown St. Louis and the Mississippi River, the barges plowing through dappled waves, the bridges gleaming in the sun. He fetched a ring of keys from his desk drawer, selected one, and used it to gouge wax out of his ear. He examined the sample, wiped the key on his sock, and mused aloud. "I don't care if Frank Donahue runs for the Senate, but if he tries to do it in my courtroom I'll fix him like a bitch in heat."

Arthur cleared his throat. "I appreciate the court's concern with the political vicissitudes of the community, but I confess that I'm not understanding the court's reasoning here," he said in a tone that imperceptibly suggested the court was incapable of reason.

"Why would you?" the judge smiled, still staring out the window. "The court's reasoning is beyond your abbreviated mental faculties."

"This case—" began Arthur.

"Is excrement," said the judge. "It's the kind of crap you used to go in for back when we were in Tom McGrath's office. I've read the statute,

I've read the charges, I've read the newspapers, and I keep running across two words that give me a lot of trouble. Two words I come across a lot in tort law, in the stock market, in metaphysics, in politics, when I go to see my doctor about my failing health, and when I try to figure out my wife's heartburn. She'll eat nachos with hot pepper salsa and avocados, taco salad with Tabasco, jalapeno dip, chili rellenos, then she'll drink a pot of coffee while nibbling on Godiva chocolates, and later that night she'll wake me up and tell me it's my excessive drinking that gives her heartburn."

Arthur gave Watson a look that said, *You see? Rabid psychosis.*

"Two words," said Judge Stang. "I don't suppose either of you two learned, overcompensated legal paragons might know what those two words are?"

"Because of," said Watson quietly.

Arthur's head did not move, but Watson could see his hackles bristle and the muscles stiffen at the back of his neck, as if he were just learning how to wiggle his ears.

"There," whispered Judge Stang with a hiss of satisfaction. He swiveled around in his chair and lifted a crooked finger, pointing it at Watson—a teacher beaming with pride at a well-schooled protégé. "That's my boy. *Because of.*" His eyes flashed back to Arthur. "So far, I've got one lawyer thinking about the client."

A muscle twitched at the corner of Arthur's lip. Watson realized that their master-servant relationship had just become a triangle, with a lunatic federal judge grinning at both of them from the other apex, a Third Column, threatening either or both.

"This new-fangled hate guideline says I got to increase this dumb fuck's sentence by six levels if he intentionally selected his victim *because of* race or disability."

"Judge, we did not come here to discuss causation," Arthur began.

Judge Stang turned back to his picture-window view of the river, tipped back in his recliner, and kicked his legs up onto the marble desktop, placing his feet directly in front of a dead computer monitor. He set the cigar in his teeth and clasped his hands behind his head.

"There's a two-hundred-thousand-dollar house standing in a dry forest, Mr. Mahoney," said Judge Stang, gazing out the window again and musing through wisps of cigar smoke. "Lightning strikes a hundred yards due west of the house and starts a fire. A hundred yards due east of the same house, in the same forest, a man negligently discards a cigarette and starts another fire. The two fires converge into one fire and then consume the house. The fire chiefs agree that either fire alone would have destroyed the house. The owner of the house brings a cause of action seeking two hundred thousand dollars in damages against the cigarette smoker for negligence. What result?"

Arthur heaved another sigh of exasperation. "I confess I don't remember, Judge."

"Tricky business, causation," said the judge. "Very tricky. Take the fire. A trial about something as big as the great outdoors, as plain as two forest fires, and as simple as a civil action for negligence. But simple it ain't. Now, what do you suppose would happen if I tried to conduct a trial about two fires that tore through some delinquent psycho punk's brain and made him shoot somebody? Are we going to impanel a jury to inquire after just what kind of hate this degenerate had running around inside his head? And after we identify all the warped, deviant varietals of hatred, some drug-induced, maybe some abuse-induced, maybe some booze-induced, maybe some induced by—don't say it! *Prejudice!* Maybe some induced by being a hot-blooded John Trot who wipes before he shits himself— After we hear about all of that, then we'll ask the jury which kind of hate made him pull the trigger? Not in my courtroom. Not if I can help it."

"Surely the court is aware of the epidemic of hate crimes sweeping the nation," Mahoney said. "Society is entitled to impose penalties for crimes motivated by hatred of protected groups over and above crimes inspired by other less socially deleterious motives."

"Pish," said Judge Stang, picking a shred of tobacco from between his teeth. "You want to make hatred illegal? I've sat up here for fifty years and seen nothing but hatred. Everybody they drag in here is full of it, them that's doing the prosecuting is full of it, I'm full of it, you're full of it, and now what? You want to make certain varieties illegal? What are we going to do? Get some samples of hate and send them off to the forensic lab? See what kind we're dealing with?"

The judge struck another match. "That's well and good, until they make it illegal to hate hate criminals. Then what?"

"Eh-uh, Judge," stammered Arthur, "I still don't quite understand what all this has to do with appointing my associate, Mr. Watson, here, when he has no experience in criminal law, no trial experience, barely any legal experience."

"The court doesn't have to worry about two fires burning in your brain, Mr. Mahoney," said the judge. "There's nothing there but a consuming passion to avoid lost revenue and unbillable associate hours."

Arthur's back arched. "The court is exceeding the bounds of—"

"Mr. Watson, here, wrote an excellent article on this national mania for punishing hatred and the obvious constitutional infirmities associated with these overreaching, well-intentioned statutes," Judge Stang casually interjected. "I read it. I liked it." Watson's lungs swelled with pride. "Come on, Mahoney. You get your pick of the racehorses over there. The boy's savvy, and that's why you hired him. I'll bet he had five or ten other offers to pick from. Being young and foolish, he took yours, because you pay the most. Now, between him and my clerks, we'll find plenty of case law to support my conclusion that this piece of crap Frank Donahue is calling a hate crime is nothing more than a Senate bid. The U.S. Attorney will appeal my dismissal of his hate crime charges, and if he does, I may get reversed by those disembodied legal gods who frolic around up there in the Eighth Circuit's version of Mount Olympus. And if the deities reverse me, the case will be sent back for trial. At trial, young Mr. Watson here will get his head handed to him on a platter and the jury may even send his client to the injection room. Whereupon, the defendant will find another lawyer and file a motion claiming ineffective assistance of counsel because a psychotic old federal district judge appointed a know-nothing greenhorn to a death-penalty case. The long and short of it? I get a shot at Frank Donahue coming, and another one at him going."

Arthur smiled bitterly.

"The Eighth Circuit can reverse me to Hell and gone," said the judge, smoke stinging his eyes into a squint, "they can mandamus my ass from backbone to breakfast, but no white-trash punk is leaving my courtroom for the graveyard just because Frank Donahue wants to be senator."

"Yes, Judge," said Arthur, "I understand."

"You don't understand," said the judge, "and I don't care."

Watson held his breath and waited, prepared for another twenty minutes of verbal blunderbussing on the issue of whether Arthur understood, and was relieved to see his boss pick up his briefcase in apparent capitulation.

"I'm a judge," said Judge Stang, looking first at Watson and then at Arthur over his reading glasses. "I take each lawyer, each litigant, each defendant, the way I find them, and then I do my job. I try to be fair."

"Yes, Judge," sighed Arthur.

"That's why I don't want to see you in here again unless you have exactly twenty-four and one half ounces of chewed sawdust in an appropriate receptacle. Chewed, you hear me? I'll send it over to forensics for saliva analysis if I have to. Don't make me do that!"

"Will that be all, Judge?" Arthur asked tersely.

"And you," said Judge Stang, shifting to Watson. "Motions. Good ones! Lots of evidentiary theory. Because when I grant them, the prosecutors are going to take you straight upstairs on an expedited, interlocutory appeal to the divinities in the Eighth Circuit. Once you get there, you can't argue anything that you didn't raise in your pretrial motions, so make sure it's all there and well done, understand?"

"Yes, Judge," said Watson.

"The primal eldest curse in my courtroom is to show up unprepared," Judge Stang said. "When lawyers show up unprepared, I don't quit abusing them until I am certain that they will leave my courtroom and promptly take their own lives. The next time they even *think* about coming to my courtroom without being thoroughly prepared, they fall on their knees and retch at the memory of what I did to them the last time."

The judge removed his reading glasses and rubbed the bridge of his nose with his gnarled fingers. "You seem like a steady fellow, and you do good work. But I want to be *absolutely sure* we skip that first step with you. Don't show up in my courtroom or file any papers in this case unless they are the very best you can do. Understand me? Short, accurate, unassailable memoranda applying controlling law to the facts of your case. Got it? I've read your writing. You have talent. That puts you about a tenth of the way there. The rest is work. Go do it."

CHAPTER 13

The talking time-and-temperature elevators took them to the lobby, where Arthur wordlessly led the way to the parking garage. Watson glanced sideways as far as he dared, scanning his boss's face for any sign of anger or danger—a clenched jaw, a baleful eye, another snakish hiss. Instead, as they approached the snack bar and newsstand on the first floor, Arthur motioned toward the glass door and smiled.

"Some refreshments, Joe?" he said cordially. "Judge Stang's dry sense of humor can parch a fellow's throat, don't you think?"

"No kidding." Watson's obliging chuckle did nothing to dispel his uneasiness. He was in for it. It was only a matter of time.

Inside, Arthur selected a caffeine-free Diet Coke, and Watson went for a regular. The cashier was settled on a stool behind the counter, his fingertips skimming a page of Braille. A long white cane leaned against the wall behind him.

When Arthur placed the sodas on the counter, the man said, "Good afternoon, gentlemen."

"Good afternoon," said Arthur. "Two sodas, please. I'll get them both."

The man punched buttons on the register keypad, took a five-dollar bill from Arthur and slid it into a tray device. A tone sounded and

Arthur's change arrived in a metal dish attached to the cash register. The cashier handed him the bills.

"Thanks," said Watson, following Arthur out to the bank of elevators.

"Bit of history for you," said Arthur pleasantly as they waited to ride down to the parking garage. "The commissary here in the federal building has hired the blind for years. It's a tradition going back long before the Americans with Disabilities Act. Most of them are still trained to detect counterfeit money by touch alone. Of course now the infrared scanners tell them whether the bill is genuine and its amount."

"Wow," said Watson, alarmed because Arthur was deliberately not mentioning the humiliating dressing-down he'd just received from Ivan.

"Just a dollop of courthouse history from an old prosecutor," said Arthur warmly.

"Yeah," said Watson. "Thanks. That's so interesting." Should he say something lame, like, "Boy, how about that Judge Stang?" Maybe Arthur was saving it for the privacy of the car?

Another wordless walk across Red Level Five in the parking garage of the Courthouse of the Future. Arthur flicked his remote, the car doors unlocked with a thunk, and the two lawyers reensconced themselves in the sumptuous beige interior of a black BMW 890il, Arthur's "summer car," which he drove when he wasn't driving his "all-weather car," a Toyota Land Cruiser. Watson smelled new-car leather and sensed another discomfiting silence, until his boss spun the ignition and summoned the muffled purr of eight cylinders, 240 horses, and a Mozart string quartet in C Major. Digital readouts on the instrument panel advised them of time, temperature, remaining gas mileage, date of last service, date of next service . . .

"I had another call from Ben Verucca at Subliminal Solutions," said Arthur. He peeled two crispy Abe Lincolns from his vest pocket wallet and passed them to an attendant in the booth without looking at her, then drove off, while Watson calculated the change he'd left behind.

Watson glanced sideways again. He checked Arthur's knuckles to see if they were perhaps white and squeaking on the leather steering wheel. Instead, he saw his boss looking calm, confident, resolutely proceeding to the next client matter, leaving the recent judicial misadventure behind them, moving on to more important tasks looming on their shared professional horizons.

"Greek SlaughterHouse?" said Watson, grateful for another momentary reprieve, still anxiously pondering the nature of the ultimate retribution.

"Tower of Torture version 4.0," said Arthur. "Ben has some questions, and he thought your background might be helpful."

Coded language, and Watson knew it. If Watson said, "My background?" Arthur would pretend he was talking about his background on Tower of Torture 3.11 and its related patent and trademark issues. But Arthur and Ben Verucca were really talking about Watson's background as a sometime Catholic and the issues pertaining to Subliminal Solutions's recent top-secret efforts to facilitate another sighting of the Blessed Virgin Mary in the newest version of Tower of Torture—subliminal incentives to achieve the kind of wild sales precipitated by the first sighting.

Expecting the first order of business to be Judge Stang's gruesome interrogation in chambers, Watson was getting topics mixed up in his overwrought imagination: Judge Stang appeared in a multimedia version of judicial chambers—gas, torture, death—dressed in black with an executioner's mask, putting hapless lawyers into the spiked interiors of the Iron Maiden of Nuremberg, or crumpling them up in the mangling irons of a Scavenger's Daughter. Judge Stang as Death's Blacksmith, pumping the bellows and fanning the coals under the Sicilian Bull of Phalaris, where Watson would soon be roasting and making the pipes sing with the burlesque bellowing of the bronze bull. He started in on a Hail Mary.

"What was the message the, uh, Virgin gave at the first sighting?" asked Arthur.

A pro forma request. The entire multimedia gaming industry knew the message by heart. But he repeated it aloud, for his employer's benefit—anything to forestall the accusation of disloyalty before the throne of Judge Stang. "I think the final consensus was that she said: 'We love you. My Son is very proud of you. Thank you for trying so hard to be good. Hope to see you soon. Love, Mary.' "

"Yes," said Arthur. "Very close to the reports I remember receiving. Good."

"Yes," said Watson.

They drove another block or two, while Watson murmurously hummed Mozart and awaited the flourish of the switch in the woodshed.

Arthur pressed a stylish little console button and skipped a track ahead on old Wolfgang. "Ben was wondering, speculating really, about what would happen if the Blessed Virgin Mary appeared again, for whatever reason, in Tower of Torture 4.0," said Arthur. "Spontaneously, of course," he added, "like the last one. But Ben was wondering out loud about what would happen if the Virgin's message was more . . . dramatic?"

"A dramatic Virgin Mary?"

"Yes, livelier. More than a predictable expression of maternal love. What if some gamers claimed to be healed of certain afflictions, for instance? It's the Catholic matters Ben needs help on. He heard something about blind or specially abled individuals being cured because they bathed in magic cisterns or drank from springs that welled up in the spots where the Blessed Virgin appeared."

"Lourdes," said Watson.

"Yes," said Arthur. "What would be the effect of something like that?"

"On the screen?" Watson asked incredulously.

"Leave that to the programmers," he said. "I mean, it's academic, of course. Obviously, no earthly person can predict what she will do if she appears again. But what if her message was somewhat more ominous, on the order of a dark warning issued to the sinful human race. What if she told everyone to shape up quick or the Four Horsemen of the Apocalypse are going to tear through town mowing down children with scythes and reaping hooks and sprinkling fatal virus dust everywhere? Would that stimulate more interest in the product? Ben was wondering what your thoughts would be, given your background and your . . . product expertise."

"Uh," said Watson.

"Maybe you could do a short memo on the other appearances. Lourdes, right?" said Arthur, proud of his memory and his knowledge of off-beat religions like Catholicism. "And Ben mentioned Fatima? Guadalupe? Aren't there several?"

While his boss volubly mispronounced renowned Catholic shrines, Watson winced and thought better of correcting him.

"You could maybe summarize what happened at each sighting: What the, uh, Virgin said. What was actually seen by the witnesses. Maybe something more dramatic, or confrontational? Shape up, or eternal damnation? The world destroyed by fire in fulfillment of the Scriptures?"

"Sure," said Watson.

"Tonight," said Arthur, "or tomorrow morning, if you can manage."

"DOT trucking industry regulations," said Watson. "They're due." He held his breath. Truth be told, they were due this morning, which Arthur would either remember now or later, when he looked at his calendar back at the office.

"Not a problem," said Arthur. He gently picked up the phone from the walnut console and pushed a speed-dial sequence. He asked for Geoff Wilke, in-house counsel at Biggs Trucking, and advised Geoff that some of the new administrative guidelines required careful consideration and an amendment to the original summary of DOT regs. Arthur would personally deliver the file on Monday with Nancy Slattery, who had assumed responsibility for the project.

Watson listened so closely, he felt like voice recognition technology analyzing the stress patterns in Arthur's voice. Still no trace of anger or impatience.

When Arthur hung up, Watson said, "I'm sorry, Arthur. I owed you that memo. I haven't forgotten about it. I just . . ."

"You're overwhelmed," said Arthur.

Watson searched his boss's face for signs of irony, finding only genuine concern.

"You had no idea we would be seeing Judge Stang in chambers. Then you had to try to find your client. And the memo? Don't worry," said Arthur. "Part of my job is managing associates. I saw it all coming this morning. Nancy will take care of it."

If Watson wasn't mistaken, Watson's attempts to find Whitlow had not come up in Judge Stang's chambers.

"How did you know I was looking for my client?"

"I talked to Mr. Harper in the U.S. Attorney's office and to Dr. Palmquist," said Arthur patiently. "Mr. Whitlow is on his way to the federal medical center at Rochester, Minnesota."

"Thanks," said Watson uneasily, "I appreciate that."

He tried to feel relieved. Maybe Arthur was remembering his days as an overworked associate. Wrong again—Arthur had gone directly from prosecutor to Stern, Pale partner and had never labored in associate limbo. How to test the sore spot of the morning's events in Judge Stang's chambers?

"And as for our little to-do this morning with the right honorable Judge Stang," said Arthur, "don't worry. You did the correct thing by patronizing him. After all, he is the ultimate boss. I hope you live long enough to see a demented colleague appointed to the federal bench because he happens to drink with the right senator, and then spend the rest of your career suffering his overweening abuses. Do you know what separates him from the people he sends to prison every day?" he asked.

"What?" asked Watson.

"Medication," said Arthur, with a scowl and a sigh. "Ah, well," he said with a 'reassuring smile. "That's that. You know," he added warmly, "it's almost impossible to find time to talk about all the matters we need to go over. Are you in tomorrow?"

"Saturday?" said Watson. "I was going to come in and go through the mail and prepare some of my motions in the Whitlow case."

"Great," said Arthur. "We'll chat then."

Back in his office, Watson programmed and dispatched a couple more spiders to find information about appearances by the Blessed Virgin Mary. He sent another one out to find media hits on Judge Whittaker J. Stang. Then a separate Westlaw search summarizing every criminal case originating in Stang's court from which an appeal had been taken. He did a separate search to find any opinion written by Stang mentioning the First Amendment, federal sentencing enhancements, or hate crimes. Then he retrieved hits collected by the spiders named Hate and Rachel and scanned them in the filter index.

Journal of Forensic Psychology, August 1998: "Congress approved funding for a variety of research initiatives to determine the biological and genetic causes of violence under the umbrella term Psychon Project. Instead of studying the usual social or demographic roots of criminal behavior, Psychon task force researchers were charged with finding reliable methods of diagnosing and treating various criminal pathologies using a medical model."

Forensic Neurosciences Digest, June 1999: "Neuroscience can now identify, with a reasonable degree of medical certainty, the psychobiology of the violent offender. The database and recurrent network search technologies developed by the Psychon Project in the decade of the brain allow parole boards and sentencing judges to predict with reasonable accuracy the likelihood that an individual defendant will prove to be a repeat offender."

British Journal of Experimental Neuroscience, January 2001: "Dr. Rachel Palmquist, a Gage Institute neuroscientist, participated in a press conference here after the fourth annual meeting of the umbrella research group called the Psychon Project. . . . 'It is now possible to breed violent species of mice, for instance, or administer hormones or neurochemicals that mimic the neurobiology of violence in an otherwise healthy animal. It is possible to raise an animal in a threatening, hostile environment where the organism is continually and violently attacked. The brain of that animal is different, chemically, structurally, neurologically from the brains of rats used as controls. That's established. We're now investigating the very real possibility that we can repair or ablate those circuits which predispose an animal to violence, or other impulsive, pathological social behaviors.' "

St. Louis Post-Dispatch, "Palmquist, Gage Neuroscience Group to Head Biology, Genetics Task Force on Violent Crime," March 3, 2001: " 'People get squeamish about mind control only because they don't realize their mind is being controlled every second—it's just a matter of who's in charge. You're free to be in charge of your own neural circuits as long as they don't malfunction and issue instructions to the rest of you to visit the shopping center with an automatic weapon. When that happens, it's time for medicine to intervene to repair or alleviate the pathology.' "

For being a recluse, Judge Stang still managed to show up in plenty of media hits commemorating banquets and bar association conferences honoring him for eons of service in the federal courts. He was usually pictured with a scowl on his face, standing between two beaming luminaries of the bar. A slew of clippings and photos were from the days when he presided over the Lebanese Mafia trials in the eighties. Judge Stang with Supreme Court Chief Justice Earl Warren, another with Warren Burger, and later, William Rehnquist. The keyword *Spence* caught Watson's eye, and when he opened the hit he felt a tingle: Judge Stang shaking hands with one of Watson's heroes from his law school days, Gerry Spence, at Gerry Spence's summer clinic in Wyoming—the only photo Watson could find where the judge looked to be on the verge of actually smiling.

Chapter 14

Watson came home early—7:00 P.M.—almost a record! But the Memsahib was not happy about the events in Judge Stang's chamber; even Watson's selective narrative was too much for her. She quickly grasped the essentials: that the murder case had not gone away, and that Arthur was possibly displeased—never mind Judge Stang's tributes to her husband's lawyering skills.

"I'm really worried about you and Arthur," she said, her eyes watering into the telltale, pink-rimmed look, serving notice that he was failing in his vocation to keep her and the kids happy and secure.

He tried plying her with extra wine, but she wasn't interested. And later, just before bed, he heard her say his name while she was talking to her mother on the phone in the bedroom. When he tiptoed closer to the door, she paused, then changed the subject to Benjy's ear infections. He felt a tingle of dread and wondered if she already sensed his budding infidelity. Maybe she didn't consciously know it yet, and she was displacing her forebodings onto the subject of his alleged disloyalty to Stern, Pale. A system monitor must have tripped somewhere in her subconscious, prompting her to call home for help. He was convinced that she was overdoing things by going outside of their marriage for assistance. She apparently had a different opinion.

Maybe Watson had crossed some kind of line, and had simply lulled himself into believing he could never get in trouble serving the will of the mighty Whittaker J. Stang (a guy who hung out with the likes of Gerry Spence!) and the Code of Professional Responsibility. Arthur couldn't publicly fire him for doing his duty to an appointed client: The scandal would humiliate Stern, Pale and impugn the firm's standing as officers of the court, as model citizens, as members of the bar. No, the worst Arthur could do would be a couple of mediocre annual performance reviews on other subjects, like quality of work or billable hours. After about a year, the firm would suggest he start looking elsewhere, at which point he would look elsewhere and perhaps leave. In short, no immediate threat on the career horizon, and the long-term consequences were too insubstantial.

And in the meantime, what if he was able to manage a dismissal of a few of those charges against Whitlow? The possibility was not remote after the recent session before the judge. Big plume for his lawyer cap, whether Stern, Pale liked it or not. Federal judges sit up and notice criminal defense victories, especially if an appointed lawyer or a public defender manages to pull one out of the hat.

Time to hang his Clarence Darrow quote on the wall of his office at Stern, Pale, he decided. He would take it with him when he went in tomorrow. He retrieved it from his quote database on the notebook, where he often foraged for telling points to add to his memos or briefs.

In 1902 the warden of the Cook County jail in Chicago invited Clarence Darrow to speak to the inmates of the jail. Darrow accepted and gave the prisoners one of his many famous speeches. Watson had found the speech in *Attorney for the Damned: Clarence Darrow in the Courtroom*, edited by Arthur Weinberg, where the whole thing ran to twelve pages, from which Watson had clipped inspirational excerpts into his computer database, including the following:

> When your case gets into court it will make little difference whether you are guilty or innocent, but it's better if you have a smart lawyer. And you cannot have a smart lawyer unless you have money. First and last it's a question of money. Those men who own the earth make the laws to protect what they have. They fix up a sort of fence or pen around what they have, and they fix the law so the fellow on the outside cannot get in. The laws are really

organized for the protection of the men who rule the world. They were never organized or enforced to do justice. We have no system for doing justice . . .

Take the poorest person in this room. If the community had provided a system of doing justice, the poorest person in this room would have as good a lawyer as the richest, would he not? When you went into court you would have just as long a trial and just as fair a trial as the richest person in Chicago. Your case would not be tried in fifteen or twenty minutes, whereas it would take fifteen days to get through with a rich man's case.

Poor Darrow. Fifteen days would barely suffice to argue a motion to suppress on behalf of O.J. or Claus Von Bülow. And trials?

What about the infamous Rutger Lupine sexual harassment case? The trial took twenty-two months, gavel to gavel, beginning in the latter half of 1999 and ending in mid-2001—the case of a wealthy bisexual and transsexual sex criminal, whose mixed race, ancestry, and nationality, as well as his/her promiscuous conversion to twelve of the world's leading religions, arguably immunized him/her against all charges of committing hate crimes against others because of their race, religion, ancestry, gender, age, sexual orientation, and disability. Lupine's defense that he/she himself/herself was a member of every protected group he/she was charged with discriminating against ultimately failed, and he/she was convicted of nineteen separate counts of verbal assault with a gender-based assumption, and fourteen separate counts of felonious, hostile-environment harassment intended to subordinate and degrade people of different abilities, religions, ancestries, genders, and sexual orientations. The case swelled up bigger than a day-care kid-sex scandal when a search of Lupine's sector housing turned up a cybersex machine, complete with a tactile bodysuit, customized female pelvic unit, virtual reality helmet, teledildonic gloves, and fiber-optic cables rigging the whole thing to a network array of central processing units. He was wired for interaction with legally obscene, CDA-prohibited pornographic software or for cybersex with virtual representations of other sex criminals who were bold enough to go on-line looking for felonious teledildonic sex. All of which added up to another forty-nine separate violations of the Communications Decency Act, with a minimum ten-year sentence under the 2001 amendments.

Fifteen days to get through with a rich man's case, Mr. Darrow? Try fifteen months, at least, for a criminal in the upper tax brackets, like O.J. or Lupine.

Of his own career, Darrow had written in his autobiography: "I was dealing with life, with its fears, its aspirations and despairs. With me it was going to the foundation of motive and conduct and adjustments for human beings, instead of blindly talking hatred and vengeance and that subtle, indefinable quality that men call 'justice' and of which nothing really is known."

From the same volume came a quote Watson had retrieved after he had been named Whitlow's court-appointed lawyer. He blocked and copied it for his brief on Whitlow's behalf to the Eighth Circuit, should that great day ever come: "There is no such crime as a crime of thought; there are only crimes of action." Darrow told juries, "I am not bound to believe them right in order to take their case, and you are not bound to believe them right in order to find them not guilty."

Watson felt Darrow's righteous glee at disrupting the normal equation of federal justice: Provide a smart lawyer at no cost and upset the handcart of "justice," normally defined by well-funded government lawyers and rich defendants with cash.

Next morning, he woke up early and resolved to do penance. He would stay home—at least until ten or ten-thirty—before going in to see Arthur. He would fix the training wheels on Sheila's bike, push Benjy in the swing, show his wife he was a good father, as well as a provider.

He strolled outside to get the morning paper and take in his corner of the world. Sandra's eye was infallible. A year ago, when they'd bought the house in Ladue, she'd described the suburb as "perfect." It was. No Bosnian Serbs lived in Ladue. No Chernobylian nuclear accidents. No West Bank. No Hutus or Tutsis. No drug cartels, no Somalian or Liberian warlords. No reactor waste reprocessing facilities. No death camps or euthanasia hostels for limiting federal entitlements to the elderly. Small, upscale, yet affordable—barely, on a Stern, Pale associate's salary—it had charm and, yes, excellent schools. The schools were so good, they gave honorary degrees to the parents willing to pay the property taxes necessary for their children to obtain the very best education.

On warm summer evenings, Joe and Sandra and the other parents set up lawn chairs anywhere but on the flawless green lawns and watched as the kids left their high-resolution video monitors and surround-sound home entertainment centers (without being told!) and emerged, blinking, into the waning sunlight of Planet Earth, complaining about the smell of dirt. These kids had all been held back a year or two to ensure academic dominance. They could go a hundred yards or even more away from home on their own, because they were medicated and xenophobic, trained to spot the trademark disarming smiles of strangers and other pathological serial killers.

"Come here, little girl," spoken by an adult male in Ladue, was good for life in prison. Family values were in such abundance, they were strewn everywhere, and you needed a shovel and an old black yardman named Willy to help you gather them all up.

Later in the morning, Watson fixed Sheila's training wheels. He rolled a big plastic ball in the yard with Benjy, who was just learning to pull himself up on it and fall over. Fifteen or twenty minutes at least of uninterrupted quality time. *This is life*, he thought, *just being. Just sharing. It's so simple.*

His buddy, Andy Harmon, who lived across the street, came out in his bathrobe to get his paper.

"Hi, Andy," Watson gushed, craving companionship, regretting his enforced absence from the human race.

"Hi, Joe," said Andy.

And Joe thought, *What a great guy!* Andy was the North Star, fire in the hearth, salt of the earth, heart of hearts. Andy had bought his house twenty years ago, when nice people could still afford to buy in the neighborhood. Now he was an affable part-time plumber surrounded by anal-retentive litigators and litigious gastroenterologists.

"Joe," hollered Andy. "I'm hankering for a little hate crime tonight. If I get caught, will you be my lawyer?" He slapped his thigh, hee-hawed, and went back inside.

Flowers were up, trees full-blown with leaves, new grass, the smell of humus and the promise of seeds. A beautiful June morning . . . until the Saturday morning lawn services began arriving. White pickup trucks with orange hoses wound around yellow tubs full of chlordane. Tankers filled with Dursban and Dylox, Diazinon Ultra and Dacthal. All dedicated to maintaining the sort of lawns you find in perfect neighborhoods.

Choirs of birds thronged the trees, the wind soughed in taped saplings—newly leafed red maples, pin oaks, lindens, dogwoods—bees bombinated, children laughed, wind chimes tinkled—none of which could be heard over the snarl and roar of lawn mowers, chain saws, leaf blowers, hedge trimmers, weed whackers, and tree-fogging equipment.

BCL, Inc.—Better Chemical Lawns—pulled up next door, where the widow Oma Hodgkins was outside supervising the weekly administration of herbicides and insecticides. A hooded toxicologist in a disposable jumpsuit, rubber gloves, and goggles started the compressor on the tank truck. Watson decided to get the kids inside, then maybe head downtown to the office for a little peace and quiet and some filtered air, but then he looked up at the wrong time, in the wrong direction, and saw Oma, and she was waving him over to meet her at the property line.

Almost bald, she had long, thin, silver chemotherapy tufts of hair on a speckled scalp. Four years ago, she'd lost her husband, Irv, to cancer. Shortly thereafter, two family dogs developed strange lymphomas and expired despite a king's ransom in canine chemotherapy. The daughter, Uma Hodgkins, succumbed to a chronic skin disorder that had been written up in international medical journals. When dog number three developed mange and autoimmune anomalies, Oma concluded that she didn't need an epidemiologist from the Centers for Disease Control to tell her this cancer cluster was no coincidence. She did her own research, talked to several doctors and lawyers, and then identified the culprit: electromagnetic fields from high-tension power lines six blocks away. She kept expounding about how she had found a neighborhood association of like-minded citizens who were contemplating class action litigation against Union Electric, and Joe could tell she was offended when he didn't beg for the chance to represent them.

"Nice morning, isn't it, Joe?" she said, inhaling a rainbow mist of heptachlor droplets from the tree sprayer.

She usually led off with one token pleasantry before getting down to business and insinuating that the entire neighborhood would be better off if Watson took better care of his lawn. She didn't have the gumption to confess that she had petitioned the neighborhood association to hire a lawn service and add the bill to his share of the common fees; he had heard about it from Andy.

"Just talked with the lawn man," said Oma. "He says those grubs of yours are going to spread. He said the neighborhood should coordinate applications so we can kill them all at once. Otherwise," she said, with an earnestness she'd probably acquired from her oncologist, "the grubs will spread."

Watson had never heard of grubs until he'd moved into Ladue, where grubs were not only common lawn pests but, if left untreated, were also a reliable indication of poor moral character and a lack of family values.

"I'll tell Sandra about it," he said.

"I saw your name in the paper," said Oma. "Now you're a criminal lawyer." She lifted an eyebrow and looked at the spurge and kudzu trellising around his ankles and the discolored spots caused by fairy ring fungus, brown patch, and black smut—lethal fungi she had delighted in naming aloud for his edification, back when he'd first moved in and received remedial lawn lessons from her.

"Oh well," she said, a toss of her head eloquently expressing her opinion that his new hobby of defending murderers was no surprise to her: First, spurge and grubs go unattended. Then, you get brown patch and dollar spot. Next, you start defending murderers. Pretty soon, you'll probably ignore your own children because you're off somewhere exposing yourself to fatal viruses by indulging in wanton, extramarital coupling.

"I know," she said sadly, "that you don't have a feeling for lawns."

"I don't," said Joe, avoiding eye contact, temporarily ashamed of his congenital indifference to grass, trying to remain her friend and neighbor.

"No oceans out here," she said, looking out over the nonhorizon of the minimall. "No endless blue sea melting into the blue eye of God. No vistas. The city lights take away the night sky. We have nothing to measure mortal human beings against. I want a lawn where the green is so deep, it goes on forever. Infinite green is what I want."

"It is a beautiful lawn," said Watson. "You've really taken care of it, and it shows."

"You know," said Oma, "my mother always said you can tell a lot about a family by the look of their lawn." Then she looked up suddenly and asked, as if the idea had just occurred to her, "You want my man to leave you an estimate?"

"I'll talk to Sandra about it," he said, backing away as the tanker's pressure relief valves spumed forth a blossoming mushroom cloud of chlordane.

Lawn veneration was also disrupting his interior home life. Hannibal and Lilith—big, muscular mongrels from the pound—were roaming inside. The lawn had just been seeded, and Sandra didn't want them trampling and digging in the yard. Plausible, he thought, but that didn't stop her from relishing the way the dogs set her husband's teeth on edge. The dogs nipped and chased each other, claws scrabbling across the tiles, gouts of fur floating in their wake, low-throated growls. Baseline, routine hostility, punctuated by attack-level snarls.

Sheila and Benjy sensed the escalating canine brawl. They stood on chairs, covered their ears, and shrieked, "THE DOGS ARE GOING TO KILL EACH OTHER AGAIN!"

Hannibal and Lilith erupted in a full-blown snarling, barking mêlée. Sandra, who had zero patience for disobedience or misbehavior from the children, always serenely insisted that the dogs were "fine" whenever Watson threatened to club them with a fireplace tool or pitch them out into a blizzard.

Domestic volatility. His home page was in shambles, under construction, corrupted. Maybe he needed to install one of those decibel meters they use during ball games. He could hang it on the wall and mark everything above 90 decibels in fire-engine red. And when they all started screaming, he could watch the needle ascend into the red and shout "QUIET!" and point to it as an objective measure that there was too much noise.

Home life was too fraught with emotional trauma, uncertainty, domestic peril, daily catastrophes—all impossible to guard against via proper system maintenance. Hard drive failure was easy to guard against. Just maintain meticulous and thorough backups. Keep mirror images of the logical drive on a separate removable device. But how to run an uninstall or debug utility on the wife? Defrag and reformat your kid's brain? PKZIP the two dog files and archive them in remote sectors of his hard drive, eliminate their presence on his personalized desktop, while allowing other family members access to them by way of multitasking, elsewhere, off in some other window, far from his? If only he could chart Sandra's moods as easily and precisely as he could follow the movement of Cisco and Sun Microsystem stock options.

Someone should see the Creator about averaging out some of the highs and lows in life's emotional performance profiles. Wait. How about just taking out the lows? Less depression, more elation. Or maybe make lows more bearable with safe, organic pills of some kind? But without lows would the highs then be, relatively speaking, lower? Is it like the stock market? Eliminate lows and there goes half of the buy-low–sell-high equation? Investors would have to make do with buy high, sell higher—which would perhaps be only half as gratifying?

As the dogs reached another crescendo of barking, he drowned out the bedlam by turning on the garbage disposal, which shook the whole house with an explosive sound of glass or metal.

"WHO PUT SILVERWARE IN THE GARBAGE DISPOSAL?"

He cut off the machine, put his hand into the maw, and shredded his fingers on the shards of a jelly jar glass. The sight of copious bleeding inspired gasps and a moment of silence from his family, long enough for them to ascertain that all of his fingers were still there, whereupon they went back to fighting with each other and screaming at the dogs.

Watson wrapped his hand in a floral dish towel, went out to the garage, brought in a five-horsepower Shop-Vac, and suctioned the glass out of the disposal. He let the deafening roar wash over him like warm water, and watched the domestic chaos happening like a silent movie on the other side of the noise.

"Do you have any money?" Sandra mouthed over the blast.

He lip-read the communication perfectly, so he screamed, "WHAT?"

She stooped over the Shop-Vac and switched it off.

"I drove all the way to the ATM for insufficient funds," she said. "Then I went to the store anyway. Six other people were standing behind me, the kids are with me, the household supplies are in eight bags, and the cashier tells me that both of our credit cards have been rejected. Both over the limit. Do we need to talk about money?"

He could feel the subtext straining to assert itself, and it struck terror into his professional heart: *If we need more money, I could go back to the accounting firm, and you could stay home more. You could fall off partnership track, and spend time dipping milquetoast with the kids, while the other guys in the firm would be downtown working, eating your lunch, racking up billable hours, and snickering at your professional impotence.*

He put his fingertips to his temples. "Uh, I have an idea. Let's wait until after my appointed case goes away, and then we'll talk. How's that?"

She held off giving him a look.

"I'll get some extra money to get us through this," he said. "It's temporary. Bonuses are due. I've got a good one coming." He could go to Arthur, the alpha male, and ask him for an early disbursement.

"The four-wheel drive needs service," she said.

"Runs great," said Watson. "Don't service it."

"The CD player skips on rough pavement. Sheila broke the cruise control. The memory settings for the custom seat position erase themselves on start-up. We owe taxes and fees for the auto license renewal. Sheila can't ride her bike in that driveway without falling over. Nobody else in the whole neighborhood has a gravel driveway."

"We are bleeding money," he said, showing her the fisted, bloody towel. "The car payments. The loan payments. The real estate taxes. I load my financial software, I get short of breath. We are headed for shock due to loss of blood volume. My bonus will be ten grand. That'll get the driveway paved and keep us out of Chapter Seven until after Christmas."

"If we need money, I could . . ."

"Aaagh!" Watson screamed. "Two more months. Two months! That's all I ask. Then we'll decide what to do."

Hannibal bit Lilith. Lilith skirted Sheila in an evasive maneuver. She was between them.

"Sheila," said Watson.

Hannibal barked and lunged. Lilith growled and snapped. Hannibal bit Sheila.

Watson took two bounds across the kitchen, where he kicked both dogs and sent them skidding across the floor on their scrabbling claws. Sheila's face turned purple in a soundless, terrified windup to a scream. She held her hand out and watched the white dents in her skin turn blue, and then darken with blood.

He was suddenly calm, as if fuses or circuit breakers had melted somewhere in his overloaded nervous system. He saw himself, a stock character in a modern travesty. He carried his shrieking daughter to the sink and put her hand under running water. Sandra handed him disinfectant soap. He cleansed the wounds while she cooed soothingly into Sheila's ear. He carried Sheila to the family room and put *The Lion King* on the VCR, something stately and patriarchal to calm her.

He ran upstairs to the little alcove off the bedroom that he used as a makeshift office at home. He switched on the subnotebook to print the Clarence Darrow quote before going into work. He watched the stylish operating system logo dancing with animated little Java applets come onto the screen. Very snazzola. He raised his coffee cup and sipped, put his fingers on the keypad, and looked back at the screen, expecting to see his carefully configured, colorful, efficient, tweaked-to-optimum-performance desktop, and instead saw a mask of death. A black screen with white letters:

*FATAL UNRECOVERABLE ERROR!!! PERMANENT CORRUP-
TION IN THE OPERATING SYSTEM KERNEL. THE SYSTEM IS
UNSTABLE AT THIS TIME. ONE OR MORE SYSTEM COMPO-
NENTS HAVE FAILED. DATA LOSS PROBABLE. SYSTEM-WIDE
CORRUPTION DETECTED AT KERNEL LEVEL. SHUT DOWN
THE SYSTEM AND CONTACT QUALIFIED SERVICE PERSON-
NEL.*

On another day, he would have screamed an obscenity aloud. But this message was so grave and so ominous and had appeared at such a juncture of personal and professional upheavals that it filled him with dread and darkest foreboding, like those breaches of nature attending the death of kings in Shakespeare's plays. He did not fear for his data or his desktop or his programs—he was Mr. Backup and made daily incrementals and weekly fulls. Instead he feared for his life, his mental health, his marriage, his children, his very being. Suddenly, all of nature, all of reality, seemed a seamless web of psychic and physical events.

His undergraduate flirtation with anthropology asserted itself again. He was swept up in the same fearful, troubling events—disorder, domestic discord—that have plagued men and women in all cultures for centuries. The houseplants were probably dying. Ball lightning and prodigies would appear in tonight's firmament. All caused by adultery. But this was the modern world, wasn't it? Adultery couldn't corrupt his hard drive, could it? Disrupt the kernel of his operating system?

He'd once done a paper on various tribes in Borneo for his anthropology professor at Ignatius University. He reached up and pulled down his abridged version of Frazer's *Golden Bough* from his bookshelf over the desk and went in search of some Borneo authority for the proposition that adultery was a modern, Western crime, a transgression added only recently in human evolutionary time, probably caused by overdeveloped property instincts and the sexual possessiveness of males in developed nations. Incest he knew was almost always taboo, but he could not remember how the tribes of Borneo had felt about simple adultery, for instance with a beautiful brain scientist.

The index led him to the Kayans, a tribe in the interior of Borneo, who seemed unwilling to support his theory. According to Frazer, the Kayans believe that adultery is punished by the spirits, who visit the whole tribe with failure of the crops and other misfortunes. He read the passage, vividly imagining himself and Rachel Palmquist called to task for exposing their village to the wrath of nature gods:

> Hence in order to avert these calamities from the innocent members of the tribe, the two culprits, with all their possessions, are put in quarantine on a gravel bank in the middle of the river; then in order thoroughly to disinfect them, pigs and fowls are killed, and with the blood priestesses smear the property of the guilty pair. Finally the two are set on a raft, with sixteen eggs, and allowed to drift down the stream.

CHAPTER 15

Saturday morning. Face time for Stern, Palers. Watson took a stroll and said hi to litigation partners. Then he printed his Darrow quote from a backup file and hung it on his bulletin board. He listened to his voice mail: routine discovery matters; firm luncheons; departmental meetings; then a woman's voice, hoarse, slurring and drawling in an Ozark twang . . .

"Mr. Watson? If they give me the right Watson that is James Whitlow's lawyer? If it's against the law for me to call you, I guess I'll get sued or arrested." She was drunk, or medicated, and he thought he heard someone—a man? Two men?—talking in the background. "But anyways, this is Mary Whitlow, and I need for you to tell my husband, the murderer, that we are both going to be dead if he don't give back what he took. They don't believe the story that he's got Buck spreadin' around that I hid it somewheres. They know it's him that took it. Des Peres County jail ain't going to protect him. They got people in there who can kill him six ways to Sunday and not get caught. Don't call me, Mr. Watson. I will call you from a pay phone. Tell fuckbrain that they know it's him who took it, and they will kill him if he don't give it back."

Watson replayed the message. Time-stamped at 1:34 A.M., with traffic noise in the background. *I need for you to tell my husband, the murderer, that we are both going to be dead if he don't give back what he took. . . . Des Peres County jail ain't going to protect him. They got people in there who can kill him six ways to Sunday and not get caught."*

He wanted to start making the phone calls necessary to find his client in Minnesota, but Arthur would be coming around, his patience exhausted, looking for him and the rush project for Ben Verucca. So Watson hunkered down over his monitor and wrote and then proofread his memo on appearances of the Blessed Virgin Mary, a tight, well-crafted piece he hoped would palliate Arthur's Whitlow-induced irritations. The memo included bulleted summaries of Fatima; Lourdes; Guadalupe; the tears of blood from the Little Madonna of Civitavecchia; weeping statues in County Wicklow, Ireland; a wooden Madonna at a convent in Akita, Japan. But the body of the memo dealt with an amped-up, gnarly rendition of the alleged appearance of the Blessed Virgin Mary at Medjugorje, Bosnia and Herzegovina, June 24, 1981, on Apparition Hill. Six local children reported that the Virgin had appeared and revealed images of Heaven and Hell, messages pertaining to world events, and instructions that pilgrims and believers should pray for peace.

In his memo, Watson suggested that if the Virgin were to make another spontaneous appearance in a Subliminal Solutions product, the multimedia presentation could include some 3-D graphics in 65,000 colors of infernal torments and carnal delights, followed by some carnal torments and infernal delights, perhaps dwelling somewhat on selected, worldly, dissolute, sensual enchantments, before portraying the wages of sin in the form of graphic, Inferno-type violence, followed by a proclamation that the civil war of the 1990s in Bosnia had occurred because the world had disregarded Mary's messages. Could the Virgin be demanding and avenging? A goddess of love and war, like Ishtar? A shapely, sex-charged Valkyrie? A voluptuous houri with an hourglass figure? Maybe she could be a goddess for the new millennium—empowered, assertive, ready to break through celestial glass ceilings in Olympus, Heaven, Valhalla? Could her multimedia persona (if it appeared) achieve self-actualization, autonomy, and equality rights? Could she exercise power—compassionate, maternal, divine, omniscient—exceeding the cliché brutishness of the male gods? High concept publicity and marketing hook here. She could be the antidote to Barbie. Instead of starving themselves to perfection, women everywhere could be bulking up to achieve the Virgin Mary's new, heroic proportions, roaring with godlike self-esteem and liberated sexual appetites. A Venus of Willendorf after six months on StairMaster and NordicTrack. That's it! A Norse goddess on NordicTrack 2000! All of which might fold into the industry push to establish a female niche in the largely male multimedia gaming market.

It was quick and slightly dirty, but that's what the boss had ordered. Now, he thought to himself, after despoiling the religion of his youth, he could get back to work drafting a fusillade of motions to rain down on the head of Mr. Harper, his opponent in U.S. v. Whitlow.

"Courier envelope, sir," said one of the messengers from Office Services. A sporty youth in a tie and white shirt handed Watson a bulky rip-stop envelope from the mail delivery cart.

"Thanks," said Watson, puzzled because the package felt lumpy—clearly not the usual documents.

No return address. He couldn't tear it open, so he moved stacks of documents around until he excavated a long-lost pair of scissors from beneath hate crime research strata on his desktop. The first slice released a puff of air from inside the pouch. He smelled it before he saw it: Money. A stack of bills thicker than his fist, five bundles of twenties bound together in a bale with thick brown rubber bands.

He dropped it on his desk and saw someone walk by in the hallway. He dodged around the end of his computer table and soundlessly closed the door to his office, then ran back, planting a clenched fist on his sternum to suppress a string of breathless arrhythmias. He caught his wind and stared at a very fat stack of twenty-dollar bills, which was so far nicely complementing his haphazard office decor.

He shook the floppy envelope, and a note typed on plain white stationery fell out:

PRIVILEGED COMMUNICATION

ATTORNEY-CLIENT PRIVILEGE, WORK PRODUCT

TO: Joseph Watson, attorney for James Whitlow.

Retainer, fees, expenses, however you want to do it. We suggest independent medicals, because he has been shipped up to the federal whores in Rochester.

When this runs out, tell our client by phone that Dr. Green's fees are too high. He'll know what you mean, and we'll send more. Cost is not the concern. Results are.

Don't discuss the case or payment arrangements by phone. Psychon tapes calls.

I'll be in touch,

Buck's Lawyer

Tell our client? Part of him resisted even touching the money. Can they dust money for fingerprints or do DNA tests? Another part felt the need to know the amount in question before he could adequately address the moral and legal questions chasing each other's tails inside his skull. He fanned one of the bundles and started counting, entering a trance as he watched twenties swarming through his fingertips.

Buck's lawyer was familiar with the IRS reporting requirements: 499 twenty-dollar bills, $9,980.00. Cash. Buck's lawyer? Was he really a lawyer? Was Buck really a person? A former prisoner?

A soft tap on his door. "Joe?"

Arthur's voice!

Watson rubber-banded unbundled stacks of newly counted cash and dropped them and the note in his satchel-type briefcase and toed it under his desk.

"Yeah?" said Joe. "Arthur? Good morning. Come on in. Sorry, I shut . . ."

Arthur opened the door wide enough to admit his head and smiled.

"I was hoping to transmit the Virgin Mary memo to Ben Verucca, and then come back for a . . . chat?" he said, a peculiar smile distending the corners of his mouth.

"Sure," said Watson. "I'm just finishing it."

Another tenuous smile made Watson tingle. Was Arthur behaving strangely? Or had cash-money paranoia infected his perceptions of others?

"Is it anywhere close?" he urged. "Handwritten edits are OK. I'll just have Marcia put them in before she sends it. She comes in on Saturdays to help me out."

Watson grabbed the Virgin Mary memo. "Just a few pencil edits," he said.

"That's fine," said Arthur, stepping all the way into Watson's office and taking the memo.

When the door swung open, Watson saw a small crowd standing behind Arthur—the head of information systems, Inspector Digit; Drath Bludsole, domestic relations specialist and junior partner in charge of associate evaluations; a security guard? Why were they here? The smile left Arthur's face.

"What . . . ?" began Watson, feeling blood throb in his head, synched to a sudden rhythmic squirming in his chest. Was the money traced?

"I wish I could be sorry, Joe," said Arthur solemnly. "You know better."

"Better?" said Watson, giving the briefcase another shoe shove. "I don't . . ."

"Loading third-party software on the firm's computer local-area networks is a terminating offense," Arthur said gravely. "You know that. You know the dangers. The viruses, the firewall hazards, the threat to sensitive client information, and the compromised integrity of our systems and networks. It's part of every associate's orientation. It's written bold in the personnel manuals."

Inspector Digit had a floppy disk in hand. He kept looking at it, instead of looking at Watson's face.

Watson's skin burned, a surge of nausea making it even harder to breathe. "This is about software?" he hissed sarcastically. "Software, Arthur? This is my appointed case. This is Judge Stang, right? Software?"

Arthur managed a convincingly flabbergasted sag to his face and looked back over his shoulder at Inspector Digit and Drath Bludsole. Bludsole and Arthur shrugged their shoulders and tossed their heads. *Not the first associate with a noggin full of loopy ideas,* they seemed to be thinking.

"What could this possibly have to do with your appointed case or Judge Stang?" asked Arthur. "Loading third-party software onto the firm network is a terminating offense. Every employee in the firm knows that." He turned to Inspector Digit, then back to Watson. "Certainly every lawyer, especially those with computer backgrounds."

"Horseshit from a bull," said Watson. "We beta test, and he knows it." He still hadn't managed to goad Digit into actual eye contact. "And you know it too." Watson glared at his boss.

Arthur must have practiced in front of the mirror last night, because he assembled his features into yet another amazed look. "*We?* You mean, there are other associates who have endangered the firm's information systems and compromised confidential client files with unapproved software? I find that hard to believe. But if that is so, we'll scan their PCs after we leave here, and they will be terminated. Today."

Digit shuffled his feet. Arthur showed Watson his courtroom, game face. "But we need names," he added grimly, "or else we're forced to assume that this is another wild accusation of yours, like your notion that you are being terminated for fulfilling your obligations to a client appointed to you by the federal court."

Arthur, Digit, Drath, everybody in the room knew who the other chiphead lawyers were in the associate ranks. Gweebos. Hackers. Webheads and Westlaw geeks. The normal rules did not apply to associates with a certain level of expertise. Names would do nothing except establish Watson's willingness to squeal and take comrades with him, down in flames and out onto the street.

"I thought so," said Arthur. "You know the termination and separation drills," he said crisply. "The same ones we put in place for our employment law clients. Mr. Shannon, here, will handle security matters," he added, waving the security guard forward. "He will supervise the removal of your personal property and make certain that firm property remains. For obvious reasons you will not be allowed to access the computer systems before being escorted from the building. I'm sure we'd both prefer that there be no question of sabotage."

"Sabotage?" Watson choked.

"You may remove paper files pertaining to work you are doing for your own personal clients, but you may not remove files pertaining to firm clients. If there is a question, Officer Shannon will inspect the file, and I will resolve any doubts. Of course, you are free to take research and work product pertaining to your appointed case, which to my knowledge is your only significant personal client."

"I'm being fired for refusing to plead out my appointed case," said Watson, addressing no one in particular. "For doing what Judge Stang ordered me to do."

Arthur gave the group another astonished look. "I anticipated that you would challenge our judgment in this matter." Arthur turned to Digit and waved him forward. "The information systems people will reboot your machine and run a program that will identify and inventory all of the software in your system, registration numbers, version numbers, and a list of files altered within certain time frames."

Digit politely waited for Watson to step back. Watson toed his briefcase even further under the desk.

"Joe," said Drath, "I hope you understand the firm's position. Believe me, if this were a simple performance issue or a bad fit, we would allow you to make arrangements elsewhere and resign. But we can't tolerate an ongoing security threat."

"My bonus?" Watson asked, almost demanded.

"Termination for cause," said Drath, with a don't-blame-me shrug. "The compensation committee won't set associate bonuses until next week. At which time, you will not be a Stern, Pale employee. How could we . . . ?"

"How could you dry-fuck me?" asked Watson. "Is that what you mean?"

Digit popped the floppy disk in drive A and pushed reset. Arthur and Drath took a step out into the hallway and bowed their heads, turning to keep Watson in view.

"Sir," said the security officer, "you may remove your personal belongings from your desk."

Watson selected a brown accordion file, full of research in manila folders, clearly labeled "U.S. v. Whitlow" and coded with the case's nonbillable client numbers.

"I'm going to pack my research on the appointed case first," he announced, holding the red jacket up for Arthur and the security guard to see. Arthur nodded and continued talking with Drath.

Watson pulled the briefcase out, quickly opened it, and dropped the accordion file into the standing compartment where the wad of money was, covering the stacked bills. He calmly reached up and grabbed more folders and accordion files, displaying them briefly for the guard's approval and filling the entire compartment of the briefcase. The files stuck up a few inches higher than he liked, but the briefcase was so deep, the files were still below the dividers.

"The boys from office services have dead-file boxes out here for your personal books and belongings," Arthur said.

The security guard followed Watson over to his file cabinet. Watson retrieved Judge Stang's two-by-four from the bottom drawer and passed it out to Arthur in the hallway.

"If memory serves, this is yours, Boss."

Arthur accepted it with a grimace and gently leaned it against the wall in the hall.

The last thing Watson packed was the last thing he had printed from his desktop machine—the Darrow quote.

CHAPTER 16

Myrna picked up the bundle of bills, dropped it on her desktop, tilted her head, and listened to the thud. "All twenties?"

"All twenties," said Watson, running his fingers nervously through his hair. She seemed blasé, almost unsurprised, about the trip to Judge Stang's chambers and Joe's swift, brutal termination. He looked at her phone, wondering when and how he was going to break this to Sandra. Maybe he could write a novel in the first person, *Vexing the Memsahib.* Unemployment. *"The System Is Unstable at This Time. Abort, Retry, Ignore?"* Sandra would call in her parents, reboot him from a clean floppy, then have the in-laws debug him and scan him for boot sector viruses. "This Work-A-Daddy Unit is not functioning properly," they would say. "It's a rogue Go-Bot with fatal memory allocation errors. We need to lock out bad sectors, reformat, and update the flash BIOS. Reprogram to produce income."

Sheila and Benjy loomed onto the stage of conscience, pathetic victims in a tragedy directed by and starring cad, bounder, terminated lawyer, faithless spouse, criminal consort, and failed father Joseph Watson. His chest tightened with what, in later life, would probably be diagnosed as pre-angina. Once he withdrew all the money out of the stock funds, his kids would probably have to make do with the local community college. As for what Sandra's dad called Real Money? Nowhere in sight, except what R. J. Connally would maybe consider a smidgen there in front of him on Myrna's desk.

She dropped the bundle again. "Sounds like ten grand to me," she smirked through smoke. "Don't tell me. Just under ten grand, right?"

"Just under," said Watson. "Unemployment makes it seem like way over."

"They got balls as big as boulders," she said. "If Judge Stang knew that they were riding you out on a rail because of an appointed case, he'd get the whole fucking place disbarred. Maybe I'll tell him myself. Nope, I'll tell Ida. She's the best way to him. No one gets to Judge Stang except through Ida, or one of the clerks."

She dropped the sheaf of Andrew Jacksons on the desk again and listened to the thud.

"It smells like April," she sighed. "Memory and desire stirring dull debts with fresh cash. It's so fulfilling in some elemental way. Words are inadequate. Imagine you are ravenously hungry, you are parched and hornier than a three-headed iguana, and one of your clients comes in and gives you a bacon-wrapped filet, butter-soaked lobster, chilled spring water, iced chardonnay, some goopy, resiny buds of Afghani pot, and oral sex—all at once."

"What do I do with it?" asked Watson.

"Celebrate," said Myrna. "Have a few beers. Fire up a W. C. Fields–size bomber and get functionally stupid. You've escaped from the Empire's tractor beams, and your first day flying solo in the rebel sectors you pick up a client who pays in tax-free cash. You're sitting so fat you need new clothes."

"I don't have to tell the court about the money?"

The Nikes fell off the open drawer as she doubled over in a smoky coughing fit.

"The money, the fact that it exists, the fact that it was offered, the pay arrangements, the discussion of medical experts and how to compensate them—are all privileged communications from your client and his lawyer. If the attorney or the client is dumb enough to *share* the privileged communication with a third party, like a judge, the privilege is destroyed. Do you want to rephrase your question, Counselor?"

"What do I do?" asked Watson.

"Take the money and enter your appearance with the court as retained counsel," she said. "Let me put it another way: Stop being a paralegal, an amanuensis, a famulus and factotum, a water boy, utility knife, and all-purpose hand tool for some mugwump partner, and start being a lawyer. Somebody just parked a sledful of cash on your desk. They want to hire you. Do you want to work?"

Watson stood and paced, displaying behavior imprinted during his duckling days of following Arthur around. "I don't have a job. No office. My shit is stacked in boxes in the back of the Honda. I lost my bonus and the firm-issued computer. I got a tin lizzie Pentium at home with a one-gig hard drive and a 14.4 modem in it. It barely runs Reader Rabbit for DOS, let alone Westlaw. What do I do? Crank up the kids' printer and file dot-matrix memoranda in federal court?"

Myrna tapped a finger on her cigarette. "Give me three hundred bucks a month and you can have the spare room next door. Take three or four grand and go buy a fucking computer if it makes you feel better. Money has appeared. I could even help you. We could be partners," she offered, and when he looked up quickly, "on a case-by-case basis, of course, meaning, on this case, for starters."

"Really?" he asked. The first sign of reinforcements filled him with joy. "You'd help me?"

"Sure," she said, "I charge by the hour. Three hundred in court. Two hundred out of court. And don't forget Dirt," she added, patting a folder on her desk. "He's been busy. Doing great work, too."

She watched him doing math in his head, then she touched the bundle of bills.

"I have a feeling more of this will show up soon," she said. "On this side of the law, people don't say things like . . . How did they put it?" She fingered the note from Buck's lawyer, drew it over to her side of the desk, and read from it. " 'Cost is not the concern. Results are.' That's succinct. I like that."

"So," said Joe, "then you would try the case?"

"Too early to decide that," she said. "You go draft up some quality motions and memos for Judge Stang, I'll get ready for a fucking trial. But if anybody asks," she warned, "you came to me, right? I am helping you because you asked me to."

"OK," said Joe, uncertainly. He parted his lips to ask who might ask about that and why it would be important.

"Partners on the Whitlow case?" she asked, holding up her half of a high five.

"Partners," he said with a swat.

"OK. Listen up," she said, handing him a yellow legal pad and a pencil. "Take notes." Then she sat up and smiled big. "Stop being a lawyer, and start being a paralegal, an amanuensis, a famulus and factotum, a water boy, utility knife, and all-purpose hand tool for me, a mugwump partner."

She puffed up her chest, made her neck disappear into the sweatshirt she was wearing by raising her shoulders up to her ears, lowered her voice, and held forth after the fashion of Rumpole of the Bailey or some other bewigged English barrister.

"Take a fucking memo," she said. "You need to talk to the wife," she said. "Did you talk to your wifey person yet?"

"My wife?" asked Watson, understandably still preoccupied with his own domestic situation.

"His, not yours," said Myrna. "Fuck me naked running through a briar patch. Nobody's talked to the defendant's wife yet? Maybe I should talk to her. Mary Whitlow is not just the linchpin, she's the only pin. The only other person to leave the room alive."

"They gave me her statements," said Watson. "I thought it was like civil litigation, where you can't talk to the other side's witnesses unless you depose them with both lawyers present. But this morning, or last night I guess, she left me a message on my machine at work."

"She called you?" Myrna asked, sitting up and peering intently into his eyes. "What did she say?"

"Something about how she and her murdering husband would both be dead, if he didn't give back what he took. She kept talking about 'they' this and 'they' that were gonna kill them. She sounded drunk or on pills or something."

"What else?" Myrna probed. "Did she say anything about Buck? Like, 'Where is Buck?' "

Her familiar reference to Buck gave him pause. She kept talking, as if she had detected him noticing.

"I mean, you were saying all about how Whitlow was so wound up about this Buck fellow and getting his car back and all. So it occurred to me, maybe Mary knows this Buck guy and maybe she had something to say about him."

"She said something like, 'They don't believe the story that Buck is spreadin' around that I hid it somewheres.' But I don't know what *it* is, or what Buck has to do with *it*. And, no, she didn't say where or who Buck is."

"How about the crime scene? Been there?"

Watson gestured helplessly. "I guess I was just focusing on the motions in limine," he explained, "and the constitutional issues, the mental defect. I kind of assumed he did it. I was just trying to get rid of the hate charges."

"Noble aspiration," she said. "But what did I tell you?" she demanded. "It doesn't matter if he did it. Nothing matters . . ."

"Except making the government do their job and prove up their bullshit case," said Watson.

"Exactly," she said. "We don't know where the sun rises, unless the government proves it to us with experts. I wasn't there when the hearing-impaired African-American was date-raping the defendant's lawfully wedded wife. I'm betting you weren't there, but feel free to confide in me." She tagged him with a nod of her head. "OK, we weren't there. Now, Judge Stang more than likely didn't do it. The jurors probably weren't there—although anything's possible. On the first day of trial, we know one fundamental human truth: that everyone is a liar. The MPs and the CID boys are liars. The feds are liars. The U.S. Attorney is a brazen-faced varlet with a forklift for a tongue. Your client would make Scheherazade and the Arabian Nights sound like Mother Teresa on the witness stand if he could never hear the word *death* again. We know what the government proves in court. Even that ain't true, unless twelve Kmart checkout clerks say it's so. Until that happens, Whitlow was in the bathroom telling rosary beads and heard about the murder after he finished the Five Glorious Mysteries."

"But who is Buck's lawyer?" asked Watson.

"Fuck Buck's lawyer," said Myrna. "The government and the bad guys are always wanting to know who's paying whose lawyer and who's representing whom. So in the criminal defense bar, we stick together, and we don't tell them shit. Even if I knew, I couldn't tell ya. And as long as Buck's fucking lawyer pays cash retainers, we don't care who he is."

Watson took a deep breath. He wanted to feel liberated, drunk with joy at the prospect of being his own boss. Self-governance. "He could be a wise king ruling the spirited commonwealth of himself." But instead, he felt naked and vulnerable, expelled from the mighty tribe that had nourished and protected him, brought him of age . . . and cast him out. Could he make a go of it on his own?

He looked at Myrna's office chair—stuffed polyester on a plastic frame, with one knob under the seat for adjusting height. The chair he'd left behind at Stern, Pale was high-end, ergonomically designed, adjustable to the tune of three levers and two knobs, and it had buttery cordovan leather stuffed in all the right places, with adjustable pneumatic lumbar support. He was accustomed to free food, club memberships, Cardinal baseball and Blues hockey tickets, health and life insurance, a pension fund—anything to make him more comfortable in that ergonomically designed chair he sat in for sixty-five hours a week producing legal work product. It paid well, and it was clean work, no heavy lifting. Myrna, by contrast, looked like she spent maybe an hour or so a day in this ready-made chair—the rest of the time she was running around intimidating opposing counsel and bullying criminals into behaving themselves long enough for her to get them off and cash their checks.

"Well," she said, "I don't see too many choices. Either way, you're stuck with the case. I suppose you could move to withdraw because you've been fired. You could pretend Judge Stang might care about that shit, but he won't. So why not get paid for your trouble?"

"Judge Stang will never let me out," said Watson. "I had a Jesuit Latin teacher who was just like him. Don't bother looking it up—Judge Stang was a graduate of Ignatius High, class of 1943, he comes from a long line of intellectual taskmasters. Instead of translating Caesar's *Gallic Wars*, I'll be defending James Whitlow. It's all writ in the seeds of time. I'll bet he picked me because I went to Ignatius High and Ignatius University Law School. Piss on the law review article—he found out I was into intellectual bondage and discipline at the hands of religious authorities. Instead of homework, the court has ordered me to produce flawless memoranda. Instead of going to class, I will attend a pretrial motions conference, where I will know more about the law of my case than anyone else in the room. If I fail, I will be arraigned, bound naked, and lashed to the podium, where in proceedings open to the public, Judge Stang will skillfully interrogate me and display my profound ignorance to the legal community and any major media he lets in for the show."

Myrna grinned and wiped her mouth with the back of her hand. "You were in chambers," she said. "You know the man. Your terror is palpable. You bear the trademark wounds of profound psychological Stang abuse. You're a member of an elite. Correct. He will never let you out. And multiply that *never* by ten once you enter your appearance as retained counsel. After that, the case is yours, appeals and all. So, if I were you, I'd tell your client that Dr. Green's fees are already way high."

"You mean, now?" said Watson. "Dr. Green's fees are too high now?"

Myrna upended a Heineken, managing to guzzle and nod at the same time. "Way high. Tell him you've been laid off, money is tight, and Dr. Green's fees are too high." She belched with unabashed exuberance and thumped the bundle of money. "I betcha another one of these will show up," she said. "Enter your appearance. You handle pretrial and any appeals. If he goes to trial, I'll corral twelve sheep in the jury box and put the dead, hearing-impaired African-American on trial for rape. Before it's over, we'll have Mike Harper barking like a trained seal in front of Judge Stang."

"But why do these people want to hire me?" asked Watson.

Myrna stopped smiling. "That's a tough one," she said. "Maybe somebody knows somebody who knows somebody who works for Judge Stang. Maybe not." She shrugged. "You have the writing credentials. It's federal court, where all pretrial motions are submitted in writing only with supporting memoranda. No state court chicanery and oral bombast. You could make a lot of work and trouble for the U.S. Attorney by filing paper blizzards on the constitutional issues."

She was right. He'd forgotten that all pretrial motions happen on paper in federal court. And if the arguments happened on paper, he was confident he would be the equal of any government lawyer.

"The first three, four weeks will be all researching and writing legal memos," he said, thinking aloud. "That means I could beat up Harper real good before we even got to trial. That means, I could even kick your ass," he said.

"Watch it, small one," she said. "I'll grant you the writing edge, but eventually we'd probably have a little something called a trial, where I think you'd be a soft-shell crab on my plate."

"And after trial," he said, egging her on. "After trial, then?"

"Then what?" she asked irritably.

"Then I could take you or Harper up on appeal where I could write an appellate brief that would embarrass either one of you."

"Christ," she said. "I'm creating a monster here. Don't get adversarial with me, Bub. There's no need for that. We can help each other. I won't leave you alone out there," she promised, dropping the butt of her Gitane into an empty Heineken bottle. She fetched more beers from the fridge, popped the tops with a Swiss Army knife, and handed him one.

"So if you're in for the long haul," she said, reaching for the short stack of manilas she'd patted affectionately at least twice, "I have tons of good news from the dirty side of the world."

"Your investigator?"

"*Our* investigator. Dirt. We hired him—what? Forty-eight hours ago? He's already bringing it in on a silver platter, and the wife is stinking up the place."

"Mary Whitlow?" asked Watson, finally subduing the Sandra reflex.

"Mrs. Whitlow reeks," said Myrna. "Everything I hear about her has that certain odor. The liar aroma. Feculence. Listen to this. Where are my notes?" She grabbed a pad out of her briefcase and flipped pages, then flipped open one of the manilas.

"Here we go. First, the dead black dude. He's her sign language instructor, right? She's been taking sign language lessons for almost a year, because she wants to talk to her son, little seven-year-old Charlie Whitlow . . . Guess what? The deaf kid spends nine months of the year in the residential school up in Fulton, Missouri. He comes home for the summers and stays with grandma, because, according to neighbor Hilda Pence, 'The home situation is not good.' According to three different neighbors and two of the kid's teachers, Mary Whitlow doesn't know *any* sign language."

Memories tingled and attempted to surface. Whitlow had told him that Mary didn't know sign language: "*I seen in the paper where she's supposedly the queen of sign language now.*"

"That's what Whitlow told me," said Watson. "But if she doesn't know sign language, and she's not learning sign language . . ." A half-formed thought was aborted by Myrna's chatter.

"Stinky, stinky, stinky," said Myrna. "And the dead usually smell worse than anybody. The deceased black sign language instructor is a deaf poet—a black William Blake, right? A Johnny Appleseed of Technology for the Disabled. He lives in Webster Groves. It ain't silver-spoon Ladue, but it ain't North St. Louis, either. Home, above average. Assessed value, a hundred and fifty grand. Maybe he got a deal on it. But listen to this. His ma holds a note on a Gulf Shores condo to the tune of four hundred grand, and guess who was making cash payments on the note? The deaf poet, who was doing very well at something and trying to hide it. Just what, we don't know yet, but something tells me it ain't cattle futures.

"He worked at Acrobat Printing, some high-end computer graphics and copying joint. And guess who else worked there? Mary Whitlow. OK, according to his paycheck deposits, he was making like thirty-five grand at Acrobat. He volunteered at the Center for Deaf Awareness and Technology for the Deaf and sold Voice Transcription Devices, those gadgets that display spoken words, but that was for nonprofit, right? He sold his own computer-generated artistically engraved poetry pamphlets. Good enough. Let's go mad-cow and figure he made ten grand selling those. Where'd the rest of the cash come from? No money on his folks' side. He was divorced, paid alimony and child support on two kids by a previous marriage. And, he had a record. For what, we don't know yet. Dirt will find out."

Watson imagined Mary Whitlow and the black William Blake sitting in her house. *If she didn't know sign language then how would they—?*

Myrna shook cigarette number two out of its sky-blue Gitane packaging and again interrupted his thoughts. "Let's do some event reconstruction. Wifey supposedly sends her black boyfriend a message on a— What's it called? T-what?"

"TDD," said Watson. "It's how deaf people type back and forth on the phone."

"OK, she sends a love letter on the TDD," said Myrna, "telling her boyfriend that her husband will be out of town and she can't wait to see him. Day of the murder, she calls MP headquarters at Fort Fuckup and says her husband just shot a man who was trying to rape her. When the MPs arrive on the scene, she fills out the story a little and so does Barney Bigot. She's having one of those sign language lessons that don't seem to do any good, and her instructor gets frisky on her, chases her into the bedroom, and tries to rape her. Her husband just happens to be walking in the door, hears her cries for help, gets his gun, and shoots the black, deaf guy before he can rape her. OK, the teenage MPs take that all down, call it in to headquarters, and get told to transport her to the emergency room, where a rape trauma team is coming in to see her.

"The MPs pack wifey off to the ER. She rides all the way to the ER, where she changes her story. She wasn't being raped. Now we get the affair story. But watch this. We get three accounts. Version one: As the male ER nurse reports it to the MPs, 'The patient stated that she was having an affair and was hiding it from her husband, who came home and killed her boyfriend.' "

Myrna puffed twice. "See the n-word in there anywhere?" she asked, shaking her head. "Maybe the ER nurse was being delicate?"

She flipped two pages. "Now, in the ER, the MP interviews her again, this time about what *really* happened. Now we get a more detailed version of the affair story. "The victim told Officer Nance, 'I was with my boyfriend. I was getting ready to go down on him. His pants were unzipped. My husband came home and shot him. He made me call the police and tell them it was a rape.' "

She looked up from her page. "Need I repeat?" she asked. "Nigger this? Deaf that? N-O. In fact," said Myrna, licking her fingers and flipping pages, "we hear nothing about niggers until the FBI field officers get out there and talk to Mary, at which point the stuff reads like *Mississippi Burning* and we got niggers till Hell won't have any more.

"The FBI version is that she and the sign language instructor were practicing extreme sign language, I guess, when Daddy comes home early from work. Daddy talks hate talk." Myrna theatrically lowered her voice, and posed like an actor reading from a script. " 'Looks like I'm gonna shoot me a deaf nigger, I need three signs or whatever. I need dead, I need deaf, I need nigger most of all.' *Bang!* Shoots him, points the gun at the wife and says, 'I ain't gonna be backdoored by no nigger. You call the cops and tell them I found this piece-of-shit nigger raping you and I killed him.' She does what she's told and lies. Hate crime USA, right?"

Myrna held out a half-inch ash on her cigarette and looked about the room in desperation. "Where's my ashtray?"

"Here," said Watson, pushing another green bottle at her.

"You've just been introduced to what the FBI calls 'careful interviewing techniques' designed to uncover any possible racial, ethnic, handicap, gender, or vulnerable victim characteristics that may have motivated a crime. To unsophisticated locals, the crime is a crime, but if you ask the right questions . . . lo and behold, out of the mists of human depravity, a hate crime appears. These guys know employment when they see it. The possibilities are endless. Hate could mean more business for them than crack cocaine. After all, hate is everywhere, and it's free!"

Myrna irritably dashed ashes into the green bottle. "Now, why does wifey ride all the way to the emergency room before she tells a male nurse what really happened?"

"Why?" said Watson.

"Did you look at the MP reports?" asked Myrna. "She's in the back of the car for fifteen minutes during the drive to the emergency room, and the whole way, she ain't talking. She says nothing."

"Maybe she was scared," said Watson.

"Maybe she was," said Myrna. "Which would make me think she would want her racist, murdering husband arrested as soon as possible. If she keeps telling the rape story, he ain't gonna get arrested, might even slip away the minute they let him out of their sight. If she tells the I-was-having-an-affair-and-he-killed-my-boyfriend story, he gets arrested like right now for murder."

"OK," said Watson.

"Maybe this is one of those hate marriages. He hates niggers. She hates him. He hates her. Racist husband comes home and finds her smiling at the ceiling over a black man's shoulder. So, he pulls out his gun and shoots her paramour in the chest? I can see that part, I guess. Now, keep in mind we're allegedly dealing with Mr. Hot Blood, Mr. Mental Defect, who shoots the black dude but suddenly regains control and does not shoot his wife who was in bed with a black? Ladies and gentlemen of the minimum wage, he did not kill his wife because he wants to get to know her better, now that she's been sleeping with African-Americans. And he also carefully leaves a witness—one who hates him—behind to tell the story of how he called a deaf guy a nigger and shot him in the chest? Why not shoot her and say he couldn't get a clear shot at the rape-mongering darky? Better, shoot her and then claim the gentleman of color and colorful leisure shot her before he could save her?"

Watson scribbled furiously and tried to keep up with her.

"I can smell her. Barney Bigot's rape story is better, but if you ask me he's also a person of odor. I digress, let's smell them one at a time.

"Once the cops get there, why does Mrs. W. wait so long before she tells them what really happened? Scared? Maybe. But what if she doesn't want to have it out—her word against his—right there at the scene? With all that fresh evidence and plenty of handy storytelling props? What if there's another story neither one of them wants told? There's the rape story, there's the discovered affair and the crime of passion story—what if there's another story? A story her hotheaded husband might have hollered out at the top of his lungs if he saw her suddenly doubling back on him?"

"Wow," said Watson.

"OK, but your boy is stinky-poo, too. His story is, he shows up at home just in time to kill a black who was getting ready to rape his wife. It happens, I guess. But where's the gun come from? According to her, he kept the gun in his car. OK, so he comes in the house and sees or hears his wife being raped by a black man. So then what? He says, 'I know, I'll go back out to the car and get my gun so I can shoot this nigger. Maybe I'll get back in time to kill him before he actually rapes my wife'?"

She paced and shook out a third Gitane. "Even if the gun is hidden in the house, it's still too neat. His wife is screaming for help, being assaulted by a black rapist, so you, a white racist, calmly pause to locate a weapon—which may or may not be loaded—somewhere else in the house? Then you walk in the room and shoot the interloper just as he's taking down his pants? What is this, a fucking movie? Mr. Hot Blood would pick up a bedside lamp or a chair and beat the fucker senseless, then he'd go get the gun and shoot him in the head, not in the chest.

"Back to the MP reports. The black William Blake is in bed with his trousers half off and big ugly hole in his chest. The bed is unmade and full of blood, but otherwise, the place looks like home sweet home.

"Where's the mess? Wifey is not torn up, beat up, dirty? She hasn't been raped. No semen, no tissue trauma, no fiber or hair business on her. So, we know he's got to be taking those pants off, not putting them back on. She's wearing blue jeans and a T-shirt. First, let's say he was raping her. All of her clothes are on. OK, so he chases her around the place without knocking anything over. He gets her down on the bed without hitting her or tearing off any of her clothes or ripping out her hair. And then what? He lets go of her and drops his trousers? What's he gonna do, fuck a hole in her blue jeans? But before he can do that, he looks up and *blammo*, right in the chest? Maybe. Too movie for me. And again, no mess.

"In my opinion," she said, "we got two liars and a dead criminal. And I saved the best for last." She flipped another a page. "What did I tell you? The ambulance attendant, Billy Ray Willard, went out with our hero, Dirt, for a couple of beers after doing a night shift. Guess what? Billy Ray saw the same nursery monitor we heard about in the MP's report. Remember the nursery monitor?"

"Uh," said Watson. "Yeah. In the MP report. You said she was probably running a day care."

"Wrong!" she said. "I told you to find out about it. But you didn't. You went off to read hate crime cases, instead. Well, Billy Ray has two kids of his own and a nursery monitor. And he thought it was kinda funny that the transmitter unit was in the living room. I mean, usually you put the transmitter in the kid's room and the receiver in the kitchen or the backyard or whatever, right? So, Billy Ray thought there might be a baby unattended somewhere in the house, so he went and explored. No baby, and, no receiving unit. What good is half of a nursery monitor?"

Watson shrugged.

"Better question," she said. "Where's the other half?"

She pulled two more Heinekens out from under her desk. "Last of the Heinies, Buckaroo." She took a long swig, wiped her bluish lips with the back of her hand, and said, "Next week, I'll dress up in my pink frock, put a bow in my hair, and pay Mary Whitlow a visit. See if I can find out what is missing that is going to get them both killed."

Watson accepted Heineken number two and looked over his notes, which were beginning to swim slightly under his gaze.

"Hey," she said, "when we finish all this heavy, Sherlock Holmes–type mental labor, maybe we should go see that room you're renting next door? Best thing about it is a ventilation fan in the shitter, and I think I saw W. C. Fields in there needing some help with a big Rastafarian bomber of Jamaican tobacco. Maybe old W.C. will give us a hand moving your stuff in?"

CHAPTER 17

He stood outside Myrna's place with a redoubtable buzz on, trying to remember which key would get him back into his Honda, because his keyless entry wouldn't work, or maybe he was pushing the wrong button. *Lock? Unlock? Am I pointing it in the right direction?*

He stashed the money from Buck's lawyer in the trunk of his Honda. Two choices: go home and tell Sandra how he had been fired and lost his bonus because he ignored his boss's advice and became obsessed with the defense of a murderer; or go to the Gage Institute and tell his secret goddess of brain science how he had sacrificed an annual salary of a hundred and five grand, plus bonuses, just so he could preserve their professional alliance and zealously defend their client. Let's see.

He'd carried all of his boxes inside and stacked them in what he was trying to think of as his office—a hundred-square-foot box with a single sash window opening onto a view of an alley and a swath of high-tension power lines. He had forgotten a dead-file box in the passenger's seat. It was open and overflowing with accoutrements from his dismantled desktop: a gargoyle pen cup; paperweights commemorating indentured servitude to the law journal; a trackball; a framed photo of his wife and kids, which he retrieved and examined through the fog left by Myrna's recreational substances.

The photo was of Sandra, smiling, stooping behind Sheila and Benjy, gathering them in her arms during an outing at the zoo. Summer foliage dappled shadows on their carefree and happy faces—faces as distant as stars whose light was just now arriving, bringing images of events from long ago and far away. Back in those days, Papa was downtown being a working fool of a lawyer, shrewdly discerning important similarities between CarnageMaster and Greek SlaughterHouse, similarities that would eventually materialize into patent, copyright, and trademark infringement claims and defenses, claims and defenses that would protect the profits of Subliminal Solutions Multimedia, Anomie Enterprises, and Abulia Systems and create fees for Stern, Pale and pay tuition into Sheila's and Benjy's college funds and the elusive goal of seed money.

And these days? These days Papa was busy defending a murderer and trampling on domestic bliss, blinded by science, and risking everything for the chance to make the two-backed beast with the Venus of neuroscience and easy virtue.

Remorse for infidelity is such a cliché it is almost impossible to feel it. The brain probably contrives to deny such sentiments because it doesn't want to admit it isn't capable of something more original. Here he was, feeling an obligatory compunction for even contemplating infidelity—while savoring fond memories of Aphrodite, M.D., and her magic, neuroscientific manual labor.

Until about a week ago, Watson was pretty sure that sexual attraction was touched off by various hormones and enzymes, glandular secretions operating on other glands, and so on down the nervous system line. Not anymore. Fleeting animal magnetism this wasn't. Only humans save up the erotic cravings of a thousand frustrated nights and focus them on a single being. Did Cham feel the same tingle in his ganglions, the changes in blood pH caused by testosterone or prostaglandins?

Watson was something more than Cham—and he would look into believing that someday, when he could set aside some time for self-delusion—but for now, he thought it best to call home and buy time, while he tended to the many subcompartments of his fragmenting self.

He reached for his communicator, then stopped: No car phone. He was solo, adrift in radio silence, cut off from the human race. He could go places, he suddenly realized, and no one would have any way of reaching him. Stern, Pale code signals were probably passing through

the atmosphere all around him, and he was deaf to their Orange cries
for Westlaw help. Blissful liberation.

He found a pay phone, marveling that Southwestern Bell still made
them, then rifled the Honda's ashtray for the necessary coins.

"San?" he said, into a filthy, gum-encrusted mouthpiece, affecting the
urgency of a routine, something's-come-up call. The plate-glass panes
were smeared with spit and gum on the inside, salt and street slop on
the outside. He choked on fumes from the catalytic converters of passing cars.

"I called Mom and Dad this afternoon," she said. "They agree that I
need to get the children out of the house."

Anxiety became panic. He hadn't even told her anything yet, and she
was already moving the kids out. *THE SYSTEM IS UNSTABLE AT THIS
TIME.*

"What happened?" he pleaded, which, in BeastMaster language,
translated as: "Which of the creatures I let off the leash now and then
has been found out?"

"I was in the laundry room, so I didn't hear the phone ring." Her
voice shook, as if she was only now gaining enough self-control to talk.
"I came into the kitchen, and the kids were talking on the phone." Her
sobbing was causing distortion on the line. "So I said, 'Who is that?
Sheila, honey, who are you talking to?' "

A woman! he thought. He was late! *FATAL UNRECOVERABLE
ERROR!!! PERMANENT CORRUPTION IN THE OPERATING SYS-
TEM KERNEL.* He had told Rachel he would be there at three! He frantically pulled his sleeve back from his watch. It was four-thirty! She
probably called the firm. And then she . . . He could almost hear Sheila's
tiny, pure voice, "It's a friend of Daddy's, Mom. She has pictures of his
brain squirting magnetism. A lady wants to talk to Papa." Worst fears
swooped in like ravens filling gnarled limbs in the blasted heath of his
conscience. He was consumed by shame, choking on self-loathing,
drowning in self-abasement . . . But hold on, just what did she have on
him?

"Your daughter was talking to a murderer on our phone. A hate
killer! Exchanging pleasantries with a convict. He asked Sheila if she
was in kindergarten."

"Oh, God," sighed Watson, trying not to sound relieved. "You mean,
Whitlow? This is only Whitlow?"

"Only?" she cried. "Your child was talking to a racist murderer on the phone! HE WAS TALKING TO HER! DO YOU UNDERSTAND?"

"No one else called?" he asked, unable to believe his good fortune. Adultery, betrayal, brain sex, unemployment, failure as father and provider—those hadn't even come up. So far, he was headed only for a guilty plea and a suspended sentence for consorting with a murderer.

"San, I'm sorry," he said, stepping into his socially responsible role of protecting the rights of the wrongfully accused—well, OK, at least partly wrongfully accused. "I didn't give him the phone number. He must have called information. I voted for not listing it, remember? You listed it, which means Better Chemical Lawns, James Whitlow, and Saddam Hussein can get it whenever they get the urge to chat."

"When I listed it," she hissed, "my husband was a corporate attorney. I don't want to be married to a criminal lawyer. I don't like criminals or their lawyers! Sheila said that he kept telling her what a nice little girl she was. For all I know this animal is not only a killer but a child molester, too!"

"San, he's in jail looking at a life sentence. I think we're safe."

"Unless you get him off!"

He suddenly saw himself appearing before Judge Stang at informal matters. Motion to Withdraw due to Loss of Consortium. See attached affidavit of Sandra Connally Watson (paragraph 7) in which she states: "I cannot touch a person who has been in the same room with a murderer."

"I took the phone away from Sheila," she continued, "and this . . . convict tells me that he can't reach you at the firm because the switchboard says you don't work there anymore. He gives me the number for something called the CIU—the Criminally Insane Unit—at a federal medical center in Minnesota and says he needs to talk to you."

"Oh," he said. "He left a number? What is it?"

"Call the switchboard," she said. "I was not about to encourage him by *taking a message*. The man is a murderer! Did you get fired?"

"Arthur stabbed me in the back with a piece of software because of my appointed case," he said. "Don't worry. I may be able to sue the firm for damages. They can't fire me for obeying a federal district court judge. I was framed. I was set up."

"Since when can you sue them? When you were defending corporate employers you always told me that at-will employees have three rights:

the right to get fired, the right to stay fired, and the right to have their wrongful termination cases thrown out of court. *Don't worry?* We have no money. You have no job. Don't worry? Three years of law school gone!"

"I got the bonus," he lied. The prevarication was sudden, effortless, popped out before he had time to stop it. One of those automatic parallel processes he'd been learning about. "The bonus will hold us for a while," he said. "And I picked up a paying client through Myrna Schweich. Remember Myrna Schweich? I did research for her in law school."

"That punk-rock criminal lawyer?"

"She's not— She's a very well-respected attorney."

"When I saw her, she had a cropped Nine Inch Nails T-shirt, body piercings, and purple lipstick."

"She's . . . That's her act. Trappings for her clients."

"I DON'T LIKE CRIMINAL LAWYERS!" A full-throated hue and cry, her tongue a lash on his back. He had a sudden hankering to meet some dwarves up in the Catskills for a few fingers of grog and a game of ninepin, followed by a nice twenty-year nap.

When she regained control, she said, "The kids will be staying at my folks' house until criminals and criminal lawyers are out of our lives."

What could he say to that? *Don't do that, honey. I think early exposure to criminals and the lawyers who represent them is an important civics lesson.*

"This will all be over in a couple months," he said. "I promise. I have to meet with the medical experts pretty intensively for the next week or so. The scanning and the neurological tests are very high tech. I have to explain them to the court and to my client. I need to . . . We have an investigator now. And money. The client has collected a retainer from family and friends."

"I thought Arthur told you to get rid of the case, or plead guilty? What if you got rid of it—would Arthur give you your job back?"

"Sandra, I can't plead a guy to life in prison, just to keep my job. That's unethical." *Nothing like murder or adultery,* he thought, *but ethically questionable, to be sure.*

"We'll be at Mom and Dad's," she said, and hung up.

Was she bluffing? What hope would he have of reasoning with a person who was moving out over a phone call from a client? Besides, if Mary Whitlow was telling the truth, "they" were going to kill his client, probably information he should pass along as soon as possible. He could go home later and throw himself on the floor of her temple, do penance, make amends.

He fed more coins into the antique phone and called his former employer. A Stern, Pale receptionist cheerfully and professionally gave him the phone number James Whitlow had left for him. Without overtly referring to the unsavory topic of his abrupt termination, she asked for a forwarding address and phone. Watson fished Myrna Schweich's card out of his pants pocket and read it to her.

"Good," she said, "because we have a package here for you. Do you want me to hold it for you or forward it by mail?"

"Does it have a return address?" he asked, holding his breath, wondering just for a moment if Buck's lawyer had thoughtfully anticipated his request.

"Yes it does," she said. "Michael Harper, Esquire. Office of the United States Attorney."

"Oh," he said. "OK. Yeah. Please, just forward it to me at Myrna Schweich's office."

He charged the call to Whitlow on his firm calling card out of spite. Federal medical center personnel told him that Whitlow was in a holding cell down in Radiology, and forwarded his call. He listened to a recorded message about how he should help safeguard our country's future by investing in United States Savings Bonds.

He felt joy and relief at the sound of his client's voice. The accused was safe and unharmed.

"James?" said Watson.

"You saved my life, lawyer," said Whitlow.

"I . . . did," said Watson, flattening the intonation, so that it came out a statement, instead of the intended question.

"The brothers were coming for me. I'd be fucked in the ass and picking up pieces of my skull if you hadn'ta got me outta Des Peres. And if the coloreds wouldn'ta got me, these other ugly white motherfuckers would have. Open season on me. How'd you do it? How'd you get me out?"

"I . . . just . . . Well, the testing," said Watson. "We needed to do the testing, right? So I got the government to sign on to that, and then—"

"You saved my Christian fucking neck, lawyer," he said. "The block captain on the midnights was a huge . . . uh . . . Afro-American from Mississippi. Somebody told him about the tattoo. I woke up at three A.M. and he was standing over me, looking at it with a flashlight. He says,

'Friday nights ain't nobody down in that cell block station after lockup 'cept me.' Then he says out loud, 'Any a you niggers read the newspapers 'bout this white piece of shit we got in here with us?' And the whole block breaks out whooping and crawling up and down the bars like a bunch of . . . well, like Afro-Americans sometimes do. And then he puts his flashlight under his face, like a boot camp drill sergeant, and he says, 'Friday night, motherfucker. Midnight.' "

"A guard threatened you?" asked Watson. "A prison employee?"

"Threatened me?" yelled Whitlow. "No threat about it. Fucking *kill* me was what he had in mind. I'da been dead last night at midnight if you hadn'ta got me outta there."

"I did what I could," said Watson, so professionally that he almost convinced himself he'd had something to do with it. "Now listen to me. You're in a government facility. You're being tested by doctors and psychologists who work for the government. We'll get the raw data back here by computer right away, but I need to have experts analyze the stuff and keep the government honest. I was fired from the big firm for putting too much time in on this case. So Dr. Green's fees are already too high, and I want to make sure we have all the experts we need. And I need to work on your case only, without worrying about working for other clients."

"You done me right," said Whitlow. "You won't be sorry for sticking with me, Joe."

"Yeah," said Watson, "I don't want to be sorry. And your wife tried to call me. She left me a message. She kept talking about somebody 'they,' and that 'they' would kill both of you unless you gave back something you took."

"Well, no shit!" he whispered hoarsely. "Tell her *no fucking shit* they will kill us. Who does she think she is fucking with? They'll kill her first, which is OK by me! And me? I'm lookin' at death row here. Everybody wants to kill me! She gonna scare me with that?"

"Who is they and what is it that she says you took?" asked Watson. "And is it related to the charges here? Or your defense?"

"No," he said savagely. "Completely unrelated. Got nothing to do with nothing. *She's the cunt who is trying to kill me!*"

"Easy," said Watson. "Let's wait and talk when we get together again."

"I'm staying *here*," said Whitlow. "Just tell me what I got to do to stay here or go to another jail hospital. If I go back to a Missouri jail, I die. Understand?"

"I'll talk to the doctors," said Watson, "or the judge. I'll see what I can do."

"Good," said Whitlow. "And when you talk to them, ask them what they are doing to me up here. I'm gettin' put into X-ray machines and scanners," said Whitlow. "They're showing me pictures of nig— of Afro-Americans. I'm looking at words and puzzles. They show me pictures while I'm in a X-ray machine and ask me to tell stories about what I'm seeing. They put wires and patches all over me, then they put my head inside these big metal donuts and show me pictures of snakes and wars and mothers holding their kids. It's some weird psycho-shit they are doing on me. I don't like it."

"Take the tests," said Watson. "We need the data. I'll talk to the doctors about keeping you out of Missouri for as long as possible. But, I mean, sooner or later, you gotta come back for trial. Right?"

"Ain't they got a brain hospital back there?" Whitlow whined. "Like this one? And maybe they could post some big, white guards outside the door. Ah, never mind," he said. "Cunt! This nigger stuff was not supposed to come up. It's a big fuck in the ass, with her in charge. She's fucking me good! This was not the plan."

"What plan?" asked Watson.

He heard a hissing sigh on the other end.

"Never mind," he said. "Just tell me if she says any more shit to the newspapers or to the government about me hating niggers."

"She—" began Watson.

"I didn't say 'nigger,' " said Whitlow. "She said 'nigger,' OK? I ain't stupid enough to say 'nigger' in front of a cop. That's her saying it. Not me."

"You didn't use the word *nigger*?"

"What?" he asked. "You mean ever?"

The sound of a metal door slamming came over the line. Men talking.

"Look," said Whitlow, "the guard's sticking his face in here sayin' I got to get off so they can put my head in another scanning machine. What are they looking for? You find that out, and we'll take care of Dr. Green's fees."

CHAPTER 18

H e grabbed a wad of Buck's lawyer's money out of the trunk of the Honda and bought a fat red rose with petals as big as tongues, and a thirty-dollar French red (plastic corkscrew included) at the wine store next to the florist. Loose and dangerous living. Most guys fuck up either their home lives or their careers, not both at once. He felt himself slipping into the daredevil, nothing-left-to-lose zone, conveniently omitting Sheila and Benjy from the equation, probably because of the bomber he smoked with Myrna Schweich, which had settled like a fog over whatever he had been thinking about . . . something about the children?

He called the institute and apologized to her voice mail for being late, then paused and added, "I'm on my way."

A disinterested observer would probably conclude that it was all Sandra's fault, right? Hauling their kids out of the house? Calling up the in-law calvary? Decrying his career choices? Siding with Arthur and alienating his affections? Driving him into the arms of a neuroscientist in waiting?

As he parked the Honda and floated into the Gage Institute, he had constructed a plausible tissue of explanations he could live with long enough to put himself in charm's way. The rose and booze were business gifts, not tokens of affection. Where was he supposed to go? To San-dra's folks' house? Too many fires to put out, too many guns going off. Triage. First things first. Namely get the appointed case under control, then his career, then the good provider could go home on his hands and knees and promise to be a sensitive, quality-time parent from there on out. If he begged for a reprieve prematurely, he then would have to head right back out the door to save his criminal and chase his neuroscientist, and the domestic turmoil would begin again.

The lobby was empty, except for her and her true smile.

"You look somewhat merrily deranged," she said. "Alcohol? Drugs? I smell something."

"How about termination?" he asked. "Can you smell that?"

Up in her office, they leaned together over one of her worktables. Homer would have admired Watson's tale of his last stand against the evil Arthur—armor ringing around foes, insults given and taken, honor compromised, cloven helmets, parting oaths. Next, breathless updates on Whitlow and his journey to Rochester. She had inside Psychon dope, he had Judge Stang stories to tell. He told her about his new office next door to Myrna, how Sandra had found Sheila and Benjy on the phone with Whitlow.

The anecdotal reappearance of the children gave momentary pause. She tapped on the worktable with a Gage Institute pencil embellished with the NIH Decade of the Brain logo, then pulled a paper out of Whit-low's file and read it.

" 'The personality profiles on Mr. Whitlow show repetitive, destruc-tive behaviors characterized by impulsivity, intense emotional arousal, self-stimulation, lack of self-control. He does not appreciate the ethical implications of his own behavior.' "

Her office door was open, and they heard some other obsessed, dili-gent, late-night-Saturday neuroscientist close a door down the hall. Footsteps, faint at first, grew louder, approaching. She twirled the shaft of the pencil between her pursed lips, then glanced up and noticed him watching her mouth. Time's winged chariot stopped; only the footsteps drew nearer. His mouth fell open. She touched her breast through her lab coat, right under the badge that said LEVEL 5 CLEARANCE, PSYCHON PROJECT. His eyes dropped to where her fingers had been, the echoing footfalls grew louder, she pulled a stray ringlet behind her ear and re-sumed talking.

"For a jury instruction on antisocial personalities, I like *The Merck*

Manual. It's mainstream and unobjectionable." She pulled a sheet of paper out of a folder and read aloud again: " 'This personality type often is associated with a history of alcoholism, drug addiction, imprisonment, occupational failure, sexual deviation, or promiscuity.' "

She smiled and rubbed her legs together, the swish of her hose sending synaptic brushfire through his nervous system.

The approaching steps paused, and Watson heard another door close.

Then he felt the outside of her ankle slide up the inside of his leg and the nylon arch of her foot wrap itself deftly around his erection.

"Goodnight, Dr. Palmquist," said a male voice softly in the hall, passing by without stopping.

"Goodnight," she called briskly, the voice of science, reading from her paper. While her warm foot prodded under the table, she gave him the business end of her voice: " 'These persons are impulsive, irresponsible, amoral, and unable to forgo immediate gratification. They cannot form sustained affectionate relationships with others, but their charm and plausibility may be highly developed and skillfully used for their own ends. They tolerate frustration poorly, and opposition is likely to elicit hostility, aggression, or serious violence. Their antisocial behavior shows little foresight and is not associated with remorse or guilt, since these people seem to have a keen capacity for rationalizing and for blaming their irresponsible behavior on others.' "

A door opened somewhere down at the opposite end of the hallway, and closed. Silence. They stared into each other's eyes across the table.

"I have a keen capacity for rationalizing and for blaming my irresponsible behavior on others," he said. "This is all your fault. None of this was my idea."

They met halfway across the table, grabbing at each other's body parts through their clothing. He opened her lab coat, unbuttoned the blouse, pulled frantically at a pewter-colored, strapless underwire bra.

She froze in mid–heavy breath. "We need to go somewhere," she said. "Now."

Watson smoothed shirt flaps over the rise in his pants while she made herself presentable for the journey. The hallways were dark, lit only by utility lights and exit signs.

"Where are we going?" he whispered.

"The storage room," she said. "Behind the primate labs."

Downstairs, they nervously searched the high-ceilinged lab for signs of human beings and crept among the cages, making their way to the back of the lab. She opened a heavy steel door, then slammed and locked it behind them and cut the lights, leaving only glowing yellow horizontal bars streaming in through the ventilation slots from the primate labs. They pulled at each other's clothes again and sank slowly onto a padded mat.

She straddled him and prepared to make the necessary port connections, male and female adapters ready, I/O enabled, server/client, master/slave. Just a couple of high-end biological machines preparing to hot-dock with cable modems and access each other's front-end processors.

Over the low roar of ventilation fans from the next room, Watson could hear the ululations of macaques, baboons, chimps, and vervets shrieking and catcalling as if they knew exactly where their betters had headed. Elsa and Cham were their neighbors, and the whole primate community was having a real howl fest over the arrival of this new hairless species who had to put on airs and reproduce in private.

She dismounted and used his chest as a pillow, panting softly against his sternum. "Let's suffer for a minute."

She sat back on smooth oval haunches and swayed slightly. He had been lip-biting and sucking through the pewter lace, which looked frilly and fragile as ashes and had somehow survived mutual disrobing. She reared back, freeing her hands, grasping the underwires and undoing the front clasp, so he could have at his two globular obsessions.

Her scents, her perfume, mingled with the ancestral odors wafting in from the primate labs—the reek of monkey urine and the ripe aroma of fermenting banana peels. Water trickled through troughs and drains leading from the hosed-down cages. For just a moment, he was able to see Palmquist as nothing more than a really smart animal. Her odors, her breathing, stray moans, soft grunts of pleasure. A certain avidity or concupiscence, which aroused him at first then put him off when it acquired the ardor of selfish aggression.

This is the way it happens, he thought, momentarily having an out-of-body view of two primates grappling and clawing at each other. *Put yourself in a certain circumstance, then a spark touches off combustible passions.*

The adultery nightmares would be true from now on. *"Are you ready to be faithful to one woman?"* His father would have his answer now. *"I had sunk to the state of a beast that licks his chaps after meat."* More monkey calls from the next room. He was sure he picked out Cham's voice, howling, even though his head was immobilized in its crown vise "I know you, Watson!" he was saying in monkey talk.

He felt a chill spread inward from his extremities. He would live the rest of his life inside this very small braincase, behind two eyes, where he would never be able to escape self-loathing inspired by what he was about to do. He had a sudden desire to wait just a minute or two. See if he could recapture the reckless abandon that had brought him here in the first place.

She sensed something was wrong and energetically headed south to remedy the situation.

"Momentary systems failure," he warned. "I need to think for a minute."

"He's thinking again," she said. "And I don't have my equipment down here. Where's a gal's functional MRI scanner and CRAY T3E supercomputer when she needs it?"

She settled herself alongside him and touched her head to his.

"Why?" he said into a clump of dark, fragrant, damp tresses just behind her ear. "This never happened before."

"Somehow that makes me feel worse," she said.

"I mean," he protested, "I normally don't think about it while I'm doing it. But this time, I'm asking myself—"

"This'll be good," she murmured into his chest, "especially if you're looking for an answer anywhere above the waist or outside the septal pleasure centers."

"Well," he said. "I mean . . . Why?"

She sighed and laughed into his flesh. "I think we will have an easier time figuring out why Mr. Whitlow shot the hearing-impaired African-American. I think you're trying to commit a hate crime against your wife, but your central nervous system lost its, uh, nerve at the last minute."

"But I—"

"What I'd really like to do is get some films for my graduate students: 'Class, these are PET scan images of a male brain examining itself, doing system diagnostics on the components in charge of its libido. Notice the well-developed neural networks for self-deception, denial, repression, and sublimation. Notice the circuitry laid down by therapeutic remorse and crabbed rationalizations.' "

"Knock it off," said Watson. "I changed my mind. I think we better just get to work."

"That's right," she said. "We're supposed to be building a neuropsychological defense so we can save the life of a hate killer and help him get out of jail sooner. It's important, urgent work for the higher good, but I think we are entitled to a break now and then."

"And I should be . . ."

"You should be home helping the wife put the kids to bed. But you're not." She lifted herself onto an elbow and looked at him. "You're here with these," she said, cupping her breasts in the palms of her hands and holding them out to him. "Another stone Pavlovian breast man," she said. "I keep hearing about these ass men," she complained, "but I've never met one."

She settled back onto his chest and giggled.

She managed to be frivolous and relentlessly scientific at the same time. The day's tumultuous events had left him craving human affection. He had wanted her badly, and then raw guilt—not virtue!—had intervened. He'd brought her gifts celebrating her grant proposal—couldn't she indulge him an episode of soul searching?

He was risking his marriage, his children, his peace of mind—all for his first adventure in adultery, which so far felt morally monumental, something she failed to appreciate. He needed some grand passion to blame for his behavior, or at least explain it; but she was not cooperating.

"It's easy for you," he said. "You're not married, you don't have kids."

"Nope," she said. "Tried that. Failed before making it to the kid part. Now it's too late. Kids would be like kryptonite to my career."

"Maybe I'm heading for divorce," he said.

"Whoa, Bud," she said. "Don't leave that baby on my doorstep. Keep this in perspective. I have a better question for you. Why are you asking your brain to explain itself? Don't let me discourage you from trying. Neuroscientists find these performances infinitely amusing."

"So," he asked, disgust creeping into his voice. " 'The unexamined life is not worth living.' That was just the brain of Socrates giving off static? Self-examination is, what? Impossible?"

"Not impossible," she sighed, "so much as completely unreliable. You're asking a biological machine to step aside from itself and give an objective assessment of its operations. If you were the HAL 9000 series in *2001*, you'd patiently explain to me and astronaut Dave and your wife how you've got to do what's best for the mission. But really, you're doing what's best for HAL."

"What about—?" he began and trailed off. "How shall I say this—"

"I think the concept you're after is called free will," she said. "No, wait, you and Whitlow are both Catholic boys, been with the Jesuits. It's the soul you want to know about? Right?" Her tone of voice suggested nothing could be more prosaic and unimaginative.

"Yeah," said Watson.

"Dualism, remember?" she said. "Ghost in the machine. You want to say that the Material Girl has a spirit inside of her brain, which somehow hovers around in there but also issues commands and supplies thoughts to the brain. Am I right?"

"I guess," said Watson, unable to come up with a plausible objection to the straw man under construction.

"About the only thing most neuroscientists can agree on is that this soul of yours is an untenable hypothesis. I can think of five or ten good arguments against it, but let's use a simple one for starters. In *Consciousness Explained*, Dan Dennett uses the analogy of a cartoon featuring Casper the Friendly Ghost. You want to say you have a soul which is immaterial, not physical, made of some spooky ectoplasm that evaporates when you die and drifts off to heaven. Have it your way. You have a spirit that isn't made of atoms or electrons or molecules because it is intangible."

"OK," said Watson.

"As a brain scientist, I need to know where this intangible soul hooks up with brain tissue. Does it hook up with the dendrons? Is there a synaptic interface where soul meets neuron? Is it somewhere in the anterior cingulate sulcus, because that part of your brain lights up under the PET scanner or the fMRI when you're wrestling with moral problems? How does something that is immaterial act upon a material brain? Kids never ask: How is it that Casper glides through walls and floats through trees but can still catch falling objects or tap somebody on the shoulder? Is Casper an insubstantial ghost, or a physical entity who can bring you a toy? How does that work? Is the soul something less than vapor? Or can it actually block the neural impulse to open your fly or pull the trigger?

Watson ransacked his brain for adages interred long ago with the memories of decrepit nuns—they had soothing voices, cool, chalk-dusted hands, and white, smooth faces framed by black-and-white veils.

"OK, forget soul, then," Watson said. "The law assumes your mind is in charge of your body and it holds you responsible for your behavior."

"Free will," she said. "That's where you should have started."

"OK, then. Free will."

"Ladies and gentlemen of the jury," she said in a mocking tone, "the defendant's bigoted brain is inhabited by an essentially benevolent spirit called free will which failed to properly interact with the other components of the mind-brain continuum, causing a temporary lapse, a corruption of somatic-marker signaling, during which time a .357 magnum appeared at hand and bullets were discharged."

"We don't even have free will?"

"Folk psychology again," she said. "It's a nice fiction. Perhaps a necessary fiction—that a certain part of your consciousness can stand aside from itself, assess and control its own performance. But a brain is a symphony orchestra with no conductor. Right now we're hearing an oboe or maybe a piccolo make an inquisitive flourish of self-examination while the rest of the instruments are off soaring in a different crescendo. What's left of you is an extremely complex balance of competing wet biological parallel processors in that electrochemical batch of elbow macaroni fermenting between your ears, which is ultimately in charge of your body, but by definition cannot be in charge of itself."

"But—"

"There must be something more," she said mockingly. "There is. Survival and fitness. And after that, there is only pleasure. It shows up on an EEG as big delta waves on the lead to the septal electrode.

"The brain is notoriously bad at explaining itself. It's not to be trusted. When it lacks important information, it makes up stuff until it has a narrative. Survival often requires that it quickly, instantaneously, make sense of the body and the environment—even if it must confabulate to achieve a cohesive narrative. Phantom limbs, hallucinations, suppressed memories, false memories, false perceptions, rationalizations—anything to fill in the gaps.

"You've heard all about left brain and right brain? Sometimes to cure severe epilepsy, a neurosurgeon cuts the cable that connects them—the corpus callosum. And then, in essence, you have two separate brains, yes? And what, two souls? Or are you going to tell me that there is only one intangible soul or executive free will and it 'resides' on the left side with the language centers? On the right side with spatial perception? Meaning it can't talk?"

"I didn't say it couldn't talk," he protested. "I'm saying it's a mystery."

"Neurochemical mysteries, maybe," she scoffed, "which split brains, damaged brains, really smart brains all feel compelled to explain." She rolled her head back for a look into his eyes. "There is almost always some explanation, isn't there? The brain almost never says, 'I don't know,' when asked about its own perceptions. I've seen stroke patients insist that their hemi-paralysis is purely voluntary, and they'll get around to moving that other half of themselves as soon as they are in the mood. It's called anosognosia—the vehement denial of paralysis seen in some patients who suffer strokes on the right sides of their brains.

"So," he said uncertainly, "I should give up trying to explain myself. Worrying is just my limbics malfunctioning?"

"Actually, anxiety activity occurs more often in the paralimbic belt, the insular cortex, the posterior orbitofrontal cortex, the anterior cingulate cortex, and the anterior temporal cortex. But go ahead, worry some more, if you want. I just wish I could get some films of it. Have you ever had a serotonin level done?"

"No," he said, almost annoyed.

"Serotonin acts as a brake on violent impulses in the brain. Low serotonin levels in humans are also highly predictive of impulsivity and violence, the sorts of things your client goes in for. Your level is probably also relatively low at the moment, because you've just been fired by an alpha male. You are ready to take risks."

"So when I say, 'Fuck Arthur,' that's low serotonin talking," he said.

She laughed. "Another neuroscientist called the brain a loose confederation of neural systems," she continued. "People vary in their ability to achieve unity among the competing factions. Ask an alcoholic, 'How much do you drink?' Or ask a guy, 'Hey, why do you cheat on your wife?' and watch the many-chambered self swing into action. The brain will acquit itself. It will offer plausible denials, explanations, excuses, and promises. It will lash out in anger, make exceptions for itself, deny any data that does not comport with its view of itself, even pour itself a drink to help figure things out.

"Speaking of which," she said, crawling off of him and reaching for the bottle of wine he'd brought her. She found her lab coat and fished a book of matches from the pocket, struck a match and lit a Bunsen burner. Watson found the plastic corkscrew, tore the foil, and opened the wine. She poured two healthy servings into Gage Institute plastic cups. Then they crawled together in the penumbra of a blue tongue of light from the hissing burner she'd rigged up—the lab equivalent of a hearth—which cast deep, blue-black shadows in the curves and hollows of her marvelous skin.

Watson wondered if he might take another run at her but was afraid he would only embarrass himself again on the threshold of adultery, succumb to phantoms prefigured in nightmares and the circuit breakers and system BIOS interrupts installed by nuns, which locked up instead of processing urges to break the Seventh Commandment.

"Cheers," she said, touching her cup to his and studying the NIH logo on the side. "We will now asphyxiate neurons by drinking fine French wine from Decade of the Brain cups."

She curled up in the inverted V of his arm and torso. She set the rose he'd given her on his chest and started plucking petals off one by one.

"He hated him," she said, "he hated him not. He hated him. He hated him not. He hated him. . . . Just what sort of professional alliance do we have here?"

He watched the fan spinning overhead, sipped from his cup, and considered his place in the universe.

"So, I won't ask if you're religious," he said. "You don't believe in . . . higher beings, or whatever."

"You mean, does God exist?" she laughed. "Can't we skip the petty shit and go straight to the big questions?" She sipped and licked a stray drop from the lip of the cup. "As a scientist, I pay God the highest professional compliment—I spend my life studying His work and I never concern myself with His personal qualities. Instead, I trust myself, and I ask myself: 'Do I seem to have a soul?' And so far, based on what neuroscience has taught me about the human brain, my answer is no, I do not have a soul."

Watson drank and studied her half-lit curves swelling voluptuously out of the shadows. He wondered if he could shed his soul as easily as an old T-shirt, lose the capacity for guilt and self-doubt, stop worrying about adultery, and get on with the business of propagating the species. After that, he could return to his most recent chosen profession: defending murderers.

"Just how do a hundred billion neurons cooperate to produce the interior life of the mind?" she asked. "We don't know yet. But when the explanation comes, I assure you the pure science of it will be more magnificent than any soul." She held her cup to his lips. "Besides, biology is more fun. Remember the MEG—the magnetoencephalography?"

"How could I forget?"

"OK, that device—the hair dryer—was *recording* magnetic fields from your brain. But we use another device to *create* magnetic fields, and we can aim them into your brain, use them to stimulate areas of the brain, produce or mimic cerebral activity, noninvasively."

"So," he said.

"So," she said mischievously, "I aim my MEG stimulator at your lateral hypothalamus, and just when you start having an orgasm, I blast your limbics with a powerful magnetic field and it touches off urges so powerful they override your moral viruses."

"Is it safe?"

"Harmless," she said. "I've done it at least a half dozen times."

Before he could think about that one, she leaned down suddenly, kissed him on the cheek, and murmured in his ear, "When we get to know each other a little better, after we reach a certain level of trust," she said, "you'll let me put a little canula down into your septal area so I can inject some acetylcholine in there while we're doing it."

"And what would that do?" he asked, suddenly aroused by her suggestive tone, but wincing at the thought of a hole being drilled in his skull.

"Oh, nothing much, really," she said with a soft chuckle. "Multiple orgasms lasting thirty or forty minutes or so. Pleasure so intense you can't stand it, and then we dial it back a notch to where you can just barely stand it. And then we do it again."

"I'll call for an appointment," he said.

She regarded her cup again and sipped. "Why go looking for a soul when simple biology makes us stand back in awe?" She curled up again in the hollow between his arm and his torso.

"I talked to Whitlow this afternoon," Watson said. "He has a lot of questions about what they are doing to him up there. He wants to know what they are looking for, and I was wondering the same thing. What are they looking for?"

She arched her neck, and her silhouette moved in the shadows cast by the Bunsen burner.

"To an extent," she said, "the government is looking for the same thing we are, and they want to make sure they get to see it first."

"Help me out," said Watson. "I guess I understand why *we* want to test him, because we are looking for a mental defect, right? Something that made him unable to control himself or appreciate the nature of his actions, right?"

"Right," she said. "But not something soft. Not abuse or Twinkies or insanity. We want something hard." She reached down between his legs.

"We want a defect we can point to on a scan or an EEG or an MEG and say, 'There it is—a structural defect in the frontal cortex, or decreased blood flow to the forebrain, which interferes with the normal mechanisms of impulse control or the ability to perform moral judgments—what you might call a *conscience*. That's tangible. We can show it to the jury. I can explain to them how decreased blood flow to the forebrain or a lesion compressing the forebrain will impair executive function."

"OK," said Watson, "we are looking for a mental defect—that's a defense, right? There's no such thing as an insanity *offense,* is there? So how will the government use this data?"

"I work for prosecutors all the time," she said. "I'm on your side this time, because I can double my exposure by taking either side of high-profile cases. Look at the underlying crime—murder. Think about this. I argue as a defense that the perpetrator has a biological or congenital defect, a structural malformation that makes him impulsive or antisocial or unable to appreciate the consequences of violence. OK, maybe the jury says, 'Yeah, the poor guy didn't know what he was doing because his brain is defective.' Or, maybe they say, 'This is voodoo science from experts paid to say this stuff and get the guy off. We don't care if he has a brain tumor, he's still guilty.' Or worse, they say, 'You know, that woman doctor is right. He's a brain-damaged psychopath. Let's put him away for life.' "

"OK," said Watson, "then we would lose."

"But we can lose twice," she said, her eyes narrowing in dark slits. "At the penalty phase, the prosecutors will remind us that he's a guy with a history of violent, impulsive behaviors. He hurt people. He painted swastikas. These days, he's using the n-word and killing a black. A jury found him guilty of manslaughter or murder. Now the judge will sentence him. And what factors does the judge consider at sentencing? Probably the number one consideration is: Will this criminal be reformed? Or will he be back as a repeat offender? Did he make a mistake? Or is this something chronic? What will the government do with all of your expert testimony about neurological defects at a sentencing hearing? Huh?"

She rose back up, astraddle his torso, and smiled down at him, waiting for him to make connections.

"Oh," said Watson.

"That's right," she said. "Now the government shows your PET scans, your MRI scans, and your expert opinions to the judge, and says, 'There's no hope of rehabilitation here, Your Honor. This is congenital. It's biological. It's structural and nothing short of psychosurgery is going to cure this animal. He is a super predator. A hate machine. An automaton without a conscience, incapable of remorse for his crimes.'"

"Eeesh," said Watson. "I never . . ."

"Think of Mr. Whitlow the way the government thinks of him, the way I think of him: He's a big mouse with an advanced brain. He's an unreasonably dangerous machine. Something has malfunctioned, causing his brain to issue socially unacceptable commands to the rest of his body. So now what? How best to remedy this essentially biological problem? Confine him? Why? So that all of his disordered mental processing will be turned inward on itself and on others with similarly disordered mental processing? Why? What a waste. It costs a lawyer's annual salary to house an inmate in a federal prison."

"What's the alternative?" asked Watson.

"Well," she said, "how about repair? Diagnose it like any other medical problem and fix it. And if they can't be repaired, donate them to science. I don't believe in the death penalty. Why punish somebody by killing them, when you can punish them by studying them, vivisecting them like guinea pigs, if necessary, to find out why they short-circuited? Killing only puts them out of their misery."

"Let's see," said Watson, his tone not entirely humorous, "I took up with you because I thought you were a defense witness. Now it sounds like you want to open my client's skull and take out the parts of his brain you don't like. Is that what the Psychon Project is all about?"

"I can't tell you about the classified aspects of the Psychon Project," she said. "We are looking for genetic, biological, environmental, medical causes of violence. The sociologists have had their day and things have only gotten worse. It's time for the biologists, the geneticists, the neuroscientists to take over."

"But repair," said Watson. "How does one repair violence?"

"The same way we repair excess stress," she said, flourishing her cup and drinking from it, "medication. The animal studies aren't classified, so I can tell you that we have created violent animals by raising them in hostile environments. And then we have repaired them, using drugs, microfine electrodes, noninvasive, pinpoint radiation via gamma knife resection. We don't have to open the animals' heads to fix them. Any more than I have to open yours to make you come."

She poured the last of the bottle into their cups, the light from the flame lambent on her skin.

"What if you could know absolutely anything about anybody who ever lived?" she whispered in his ear. "What would you want to know?"

Having come this far, Watson thought about attempting sincerity. "I guess . . . I guess, I would want to know if Jesus Christ was really God," he said, slurring his speech slightly in the throes of red wine and religious sentiment. "That would resolve more than a few major intrapsychic conflicts. It would absolve me of the rigors of faith. I could just bathe in certainty for the rest of my life and ascend into the bosom of God when I died."

"Or live life as evolution's crowning glory," she said, "and never have to waste mental energy on superstition."

"OK," he said, "I'm done. Your turn. If you could know absolutely anything about anybody who ever lived, what would you want to know?"

She swigged. "Napoleon's serotonin levels before and after Waterloo."

"And if your serotonin level is abnormal," he said, "then you're a flawed android in need of repair?"

"Well," she said, "look at the stats. Something like six percent of the criminal population commits something like seventy percent of violent crimes. Chronic recidivists. You tell me if that doesn't suggest at least a biological component?"

"And," he said, "free will, redemption, self-improvement, character building, spiritual renewal—those all go out the window."

"Look," she said, groggily snuggling again in the blue flame of the Bunsen burner, "speaking as a scientist, I don't think there's much you can do about it if you're biologically predisposed to violence or sexual misbehavior. You just have to make the best of it, and try not to get caught. The way we do."

Their heads lolled together in a doze. In the synaptic twilight of an approaching dream, Watson imagined them walking naked out of their cave at dawn and sauntering out onto a savanna on the shores of Lake Turkana, waving at Lucy, Peking Man, Piltdown Man. Watson and the boys dropped a stray wildebeest by clubbing it to death and hurling stones at it. Later that night, they asked Cham and Elsa over for dinner and introduced them to cooked meat and fermented rice.

"Hey," she murmured, rousing him from his neolithic slumber, "I think the settings on your cortical governor are too high; they're over-riding normal hypothalamic urges. Maybe I could get in there with some stereotaxic probes and tweak the options on the limbic gonkula-tor to resist guilt and release more lust."

"Soul," he said. "It's inoperable. Beyond your expertise."

CHAPTER 19

The next day he spent some of Buck's lawyer's money and bought a computer, printer, monitor, phone, and answering machine, then stayed up all night in the room he'd rented from Myrna Schweich hooking them together, creating his very own shanty on the information highway and hanging out a virtual shingle. By dawn, he was in the usual trance, worshipping a screenful of sumptuous icons on an information warrior's desktop, which bore a working resemblance to the setup he'd left at the big firm. He had his agents, browsers, spiders, and robots all reconfigured and standing by. He had purchased a worktable, a desk, two straight-back chairs—both of which were adjustable in the sense that you could tip back on two legs or scoot them forward, but neither of which had a single knob or lever for adjusting height, tilt angle, pneumatic bladder pressure, lumbar support, or any of the other features of his former chair-bound life. The only comfort this used office furniture offered was pride of ownership.

At daybreak, he went home to an empty house, showered, made a triple espresso, put on his Stern, Pale Southwick suit, his last laundered shirt, and a dark, sober tie. He tucked his leather folio in his briefcase, his graduation fountain pen in his shirt pocket, his billfold in his breast pocket—arranging power fetishes before embarking on hazardous duty.

He did the middle button of his Southwick and struck a lawyerly pose in front of that shrine of the vain: the vanity mirror. He looked into his own eyes and tried to remember how she had drunkenly described the evolution of sight after a half bottle of wine—"two brain lobes that grew out of the skull in search of light"—and here were those lobes of exposed brain, touching themselves visually. He tried to imagine himself in her terms: a selfish gene, a brain bent on maximizing its Darwinian fitness, a "big mouse," as she had described Whitlow. No soul. No ghost in the machine. Just an acquisitive piece of meat seeking sustenance, reproduction, self-replication, and perpetuation. But where were the evolutionary or neuroscientific explanations for his own behaviors? Why was he risking the gene-transmitting arrangements he'd already worked so hard to establish?

What about the airplane rule? Most moral prerogatives had their origins in collective wisdom and common sense. For instance, a human being should have but one mate if only because complexity increases the possibility of failure. A twin-engine airplane (or a twin-engine marriage) has twice as many problems as a single-engine airplane. In love, in software, in electronics, in information theory, in prayer, in recreations, and in life itself, simplicity increases robustness. First, build a really good basket, then put all your eggs in it. Why flirt with danger and complexity? It was too early in life to be craving a distraction from thoughts of his own mortality. That came later, with Porsches and hair transplants. What was driving him to the distraction of moral complexity?

And why the devotion to the plight of James Whitlow? Correction for the sake of the narrative he was compiling for himself: Whitlow was barely worth a second thought—his devotion, if any, was to Whitlow's tantalizing legal conundrums.

Maybe his brain had decided—on its own, as it were—that it was interested in the First Amendment and hate crimes. Thus, the article he had written in law school: "Are Hate Crimes Thought Crimes?" May the state give extra punishment for crimes that externally are exactly the same—a brutal rape, a murder, arson—but that the jury decides were motivated by an impure hatred of certain protected groups? Yes, the state may, said the Supreme Court, just before his article was published.

Next question: Just what sort of evidence may the jury consider in conducting an inquiry into the psyche of the accused hate killer? Was the motive racial bias? Class bias? Personality differences? Jealous rage? Most subtle of all, and the problem that was his client's problem: how to tell the difference between a bigot who happened to kill a black person, and a bigot who killed *because of* his victim's race? Call in St. Peter, Sigmund Freud, the Grand Inquisitor, and Oprah. But remember, these inquiries into the defendant's mental processes take place in a proceeding called a *trial*, where the accused has the perfect right not to utter one word.

Big puzzles, like law school exam questions—those riddles with narratives so spare they acquire the elegance of symbolic logic: D (for defendant) is a person of bigoted beliefs and associations. V (victim) is a protected minority. D tells V, "People like you make me so angry, I could just kill you." D kills V. May D be charged with a hate crime and receive a double penalty for murder? If yes, what result if D and V are both black, handicapped, Baptist, and of the same sexual orientation?

Just the kind of formalistic argument you could never make to a jury. To a jury, the difference between (1) a bigoted killer and (2) a bigoted killer momentarily not motivated by bigotry is the difference between (1) venomous hatred and (2) poisonous hostility, i.e., essentially no difference at all.

But the freedoms of speech, of thought, of association, are such powerful constitutional talismans that a skillful appellate lawyer could present Whitlow's problem in all its formal, theoretical, constitutional beauty in the court of appeals, where there are no jurors, only learned judges. A short row of figures in black gowns peering over reading glasses and across an oak tribunal, asking questions of distressed lawyers. A bunch of Pantaloons much given to slippery sophistry, abstruse abstractions, casuistic colloquies, rabbinic ratiocinations, mandarin mandamusing, and speechifying speciousness.

Questions of fact are settled in the trial court, where lawyers like Harper and Myrna cross-examine witnesses about what *really* happened. Questions of law are settled in the appellate courts, where they don't care what really happened at the crime scene or whether D (defendant) was actually driving the car when he hit P (plaintiff) and broke P's leg. Appellate judges are concerned only if the trial judge made an error of *law* before, during, or after trial. If the trial judge ruled that an unconstitutional state law was constitutional, then appellate judges are all ears. Argue bald facts and tell them that your defendant was wrongfully convicted of negligence because the plaintiff's leg was not really broken or because D was not really driving the car, and they will dismiss your appeal.

Winning Whitlow's case in the court of appeals could be just another stage in a glacial epoch of ongoing litigation. An appellate victory might simply settle the pretrial legal issues, after which Watson would be forced to descend the ladder of legal evolution and go back down to what appellate lawyers disdainfully refer to as the "trial level" or the "trial court," the land of slippery facts, where the silver-tongued, soap-opera actors and actresses known as trial lawyers sell soap and broken legs to the sheep in the cheap seats. And Watson knew what could happen to his elegant constitutional principles, even if the Eighth Circuit blessed them before trial. In the words of La Rochefoucauld, "There is nothing more horrible than the murder of a beautiful theory by a gang of brutal facts."

Let's split hairs. He was defending a bigot who was accused of a murder and a hate crime, under a statute that was probably constitutional, with evidence that was probably challengeable, such that there was a 20 or 30 percent chance that Watson could make some serious trouble for the prosecution with a few well-aimed, energetic motions, and maybe a 5 to 10 percent chance that Watson could get rid of the hate charge by keeping out enough evidence of bigotry—meaning Whitlow would do five or ten years instead of life or death—and about a .1 percent chance that he could actually get Mr. Whitlow off.

But was this mission his brain had programmed itself to accomplish worth losing his job and his marriage over? Sure, he could always hoist the buckler of duty and defend himself. He was only obeying Judge Stang and the Rules of Professional Responsibility. And Sandra? Wife, mother to their children? Sheila? Benjy? Gene packets dependent on him (and the Memsahib) for sustenance, parental instruction, and perpetuation of humankind?

He drifted into Benjy's empty room and looked at the walls festooned with Disney characters. H (husband) commits quasi-adultery against W (wife). W takes kids, K^1 & K^2, to in-laws, leaving H to stand alone in his house and wonder what made his brain malfunction and lose sight of its mission. Maybe Whitlow and Palmquist were both what psychiatrists refer to as autochthonous ideas, abnormally dominating ideas that the patient feels were thrust upon him instead of developing out of his own content of consciousness.

After a few more conflicted neuronal maneuvers, he flossed and brushed without really thinking about it and drove downtown, also without really thinking about it, because he was thinking about seeing the good Dr. Palmquist—again!—and going over the results of Whitlow's tests, which were coming in from Rochester via secure FTP tomorrow tonight.

He fed a meter outside the courthouse, found the clerk's office inside, and filed the first document printed from his new computer: "Entry of Appearance As Retained Counsel in the matter of U.S. v. Whitlow." He walked along the terraced esplanades outside the Courthouse of the Future and down flights of marble steps so splendid they would have made Nebuchadnezzar blush for his ziggurats. He turned and looked back, up at the steel, glass, and stone edifice of federal justice towering over him. Inside were twenty-six federal courtrooms abuzz with litigation, manned and womaned by stately, well-paid intellects. Words, words, words deciding important questions of federal law, like whether boys were "harassing" girls on school buses, or whether "indecent" language was being posted somewhere on the Internet, or whether some dark and deviant miscreant was slinking around in the ink of night with Macbeth's dagger, slashing the tags off federally regulated pillows and mattresses. "Stars, hide your fires / Let not light see my black and deep desires." O piteous woe! If the wounds of these gashed pillows could but speak—poor dumb mouths!—what wailing and downy gnashing and feathery cries for justice would we hear! Inside, blacks, women, old people, handicapped people, criminals, people of ethnicity, were all scrimmaging for their fair share of federal rights. O piteous woe! Place your hands in these psychic wounds and feel their pain! And Watson was now a free agent, he could be for or against those litigants and their rights, depending upon whose ox was being gored and whether his fee was being paid by the cattlemen or the slaughterhouse, the pillow manufacturers or slashers.

Such a country! And most glorious of all, the federal laws bequeathing said rights were all accompanied by opaque, voluminous regulations detailing record-keeping, timeliness, administrative procedures, filing requirements, and other stuporific snoozers so unspeakably dense, tedious, and prolix that no one in their right mind would invest the time and effort required to read and understand them, unless they were getting paid at least $150 an hour for their trouble, present company included. Enter Joseph T. Watson, a lawyer skilled in deciphering the stuporific. The Code of Federal Regulations, the Federal Register, the United States Code—it was a safe bet no mortal person had ever read them all. Even lawyers could bear only the portions retrieved by search logic.

But overshadowing this rosy lawyer's view of his future—where citizens had federally guaranteed rights to a free refill of coffee brewed at federally regulated temperatures, federally mandated extra maternity days in the hospital, steaks cooked according to FDA specifications defining what constitutes medium rare and a lawyer on retainer in case of a dispute over the bill—was the ever-present threat of nuclear war. Yes! It could wipe out everything and take society back to a time where, instead of hiring a good lawyer, disputes were settled by yelling at each other around the village fire. Then what?

He slipped into a recurring nightmarish daydream. One day in the postapocalyptic future, the few hundred or so survivors of a nuclear holocaust would gather around a bonfire in the nuclear winter and begin planning a new society. Everyone would stand and announce their names and the skills they could contribute to making a brave new world. Engineers, mechanics, carpenters, teachers. "I build houses," one would say, and another, "I fix cars." "I'm a doctor," someone else would announce. The torchlight red on his sweaty face, Watson would step forward and proclaim, "I can search ALLFEDS on Westlaw and find controlling authority for just about any legal position this side of proving the validity of a transaction secured by lunar cheese futures and acres of blue sky."

But for now, he stood outside the Courthouse of the Future, savoring the knowledge that he was an officer of the court, a real lawyer with a real client.

When he got back to Myrna's place, he had two packages waiting: one from Michael Harper, Assistant U.S. Attorney, and another lumpy ripstop envelope from the same courier service Buck's lawyer had used on the first go-around. The familiar bundles slid through his fingers and inspired a certain affection for Buck and his lawyer.

In what he was now proudly calling "my office," he felt like a real entrepreneur. Myrna said he could do traffic and a few drunk drivers for her. He knew some friends who wrote briefs for hire and needed help. Maybe he could scrounge up a few more appointed cases? Before long, he would be weaned of the gold-plated teats of the mighty Stern, Pale and making a living as a solo practitioner.

He tore open the envelope from Harper and found another affidavit field report, TDD printouts, and sheaves from some other variety of computer printouts. Transcripts of some kind?

A trilling sound interrupted his persual. His first phone call on his new line.

"Joe? Mike Harper," said the gravelly voice. "You're moving around on me. I must have called three different places. Now you're shacking up with Myrna Schweich?"

"I'm renting from her," said Watson. "I did research for her in law school."

"You went to her?" asked Harper.

"Went?" asked Watson.

Harper laughed and in an insinuating tone of voice asked, "I mean, you called her about this case? She didn't call you?"

Watson paused, wondering again why this would be of any importance, then said, "Yeah, I called her. I left Stern, Pale and I needed office space."

"Are you familiar with her client list?" said Harper. "And she gets to know them a little too well, which can be illegal in her line of work."

"Do you want to talk to her about it?" asked Watson.

Harper rasped out a few laughs. "Listen, Arthur Mahoney tells me you've gone off the deep end. You're Clarence Darrow or some damn thing and this bigot killer is Thomas Scopes. He says you've got First Amendment on the brain and you're getting ready to paper me with memos on constitutional law. Since when is the First Amendment a defense in a murder case?"

"I don't know," said Watson. "Since when do prosecutors try to execute a guy for wearing tattoos and telling racist jokes?"

"I know, I know," chuckled Harper. "He's really a good boy at heart. Anyway, before you go too far out of your way making work for me, I thought I'd let you get to know your client a little better," he said. "I sent some stuff to your old address. I wouldn't call it *Brady* material," he added with an ominous laugh. "And I threw in the TDD printouts, too." His voice assumed his Mary Whitlow falsetto. " 'I just want us to be alone together. And next week, James will be gone to Nevada. I want to see you and have you touch me with your signs.' "

"I don't have the stuff you sent yet," said Watson, paging through the materials Harper had sent him. "The people at Stern, Pale said it was sent by regular mail. You know what that means."

A silence at the other end.

"That means government employees are responsible for delivering the documents," continued Watson, "which means the documents are probably in South Dakota by now, or maybe they were sent to Mr. Whitlow by mistake. There's no telling, when the government is in charge, is there, Mr. Harper?"

"You sound like a criminal already, and it's only your second day on the job. Your boy's in Minnesota being studied like the insect he is, and I'm seriously considering those conspiracy charges I told you about. I sent you some other stuff to consider before formally rejecting our plea offer."

"What is this, a depo?" asked Watson, riffling pages, "a hearing transcript?"

"So you *do* have it," said Harper. "Kid, you break me up," he said without a trace of levity in his voice.

Brady sounded familiar, but Watson's Criminal Procedure course had happened three years ago; he'd studied the subject matter for seventy-two hours and had retained the information all the way up to the closing paragraphs of the last essay question. He opened a window to the right of his information manager, double-clicked on the Reference icon, and selected West's Guide to Legal Terms and Notable Cases. At the query prompt, he typed in *Brady* and hit return.

"You like computers so much," said the prosecutor, "and so does your client, apparently. It's a transcript from a computer Usenet group. One of those on-line bulletin board deals where like-minded people can 'meet' in virtual conference rooms and type messages to each other on their keyboards. Mr. Whitlow chats with a group of guys who call themselves the Order of the Eagles. Maybe you've heard of them? Remember the IRS agent who was splattered all over Atlanta by a car bomb a few years back? Remember when they tried to blow up the Department of Education? The Florida abortion clinics? Nice fellas. Good old boys who like to get together and talk about their feelings. Nigger jokes. Weapons and ammo recommendations. Welfare queen stories. Nigger this, nigger that. How to kill a baby killer. When your boy signs on he uses the handle Thor61. Some kind of Aryan, right-wing militia thing, I'm told. Once he gets on-line, old Thor ain't shy when it comes to expressing his feelings about African-Americans."

While Harper dressed Whitlow up in Satan's filthy colors, Watson's query was answered: "Brady materials—evidence favorable to the defense which the prosecution is obligated to turn over, even if it is not requested. From the United States Supreme Court case Brady v. Maryland, 373 U.S. 83 (1963)."

"How did you get these?" asked Watson, skimming the pages. "This is . . ." he stammered. "This is bullshit" was what he wanted to say, but instead he cast about for a plausible legal pejorative. "This is an invasion of my client's privacy," he said, somewhat tentatively. "It's an unlawful search," he added with gusto.

Harper scoffed. "Let's analyze this together." Watson could almost hear the prosecutor's tongue pushing his cheek into the phone. "We found out that your boy visits one of these on-line, right-wing, extremist Web sites. We paid a law student nerd to log on and read a transcript of computer postings that took place in a public newsgroup and were stored in an on-line Usenet library, the contents of which are accessible to anyone with a modem. Then we downloaded the transcript and printed it out, along with any other sessions featuring your client's user ID or the handle Thor61."

Watson's eye skimmed pages until he found Thor61: "And if they think Africa is such a Garden of Eden, let 'em go back there and live in banana trees with their cousins. We could have the United Nations build basketball courts all over the continent."

Harper cleared his throat. "Maybe in law school you learned some new-wave Fourth Amendment theories about how downloading a transcript from a public computer bulletin board is an illegal search. I'm just a government employee, so it's probably way over my head. Come to think of it, Judge Stang's also just a government employee, so it might be over his head, too."

Watson scanned an affidavit and fought off an attack of gooseflesh.

(14) FBI field investigators will testify that while searching the defendant's South St. Louis residence, they discovered a poster on the wall of the defendant's garage that portrayed a caricature of a black man with large lips running in the crosshairs of a gun sight.
(15) Investigating officers found fourteen copies of a text called Sole Survivor, a fictional, futuristic account of a white supremacist who escapes to Canada in the aftermath of a violent civil war that resulted in "the dark races" seizing control of the federal government. They had received information suggesting that the defendant had given the book as a gift to a number of his friends and had

recommended it as "what is going to happen to this country if the Jew media and niggers ain't stopped."

(16) Investigating officers interviewed several patrons of the Irish Bull tavern, where, less than forty-eight hours before the murder of Elvin Brawley, the defendant, James F. Whitlow, was telling racial jokes and spewing racial invective.

"You want to put jokes, posters, and library books into evidence?" asked Watson. "Maybe you should see what kind of movies he checks out from Blockbuster. Maybe you could have somebody testify that he didn't fulfill government specifications for being sufficiently moved by the Roots miniseries."

"Good idea," said Harper. "It's not the books, it's what he did with them and his accompanying comments. More conspiracy stuff. We'll get it in. Even if we have to take an interlocutory appeal to the Eighth Circuit and reverse Judge Stang to do it."

"That's it?" asked Watson, trying to sound unimpressed.

"Oh, I forgot," Harper added with a chuckle. "We're adding a charge under the new Violence Against Women Act on the strength of Mary's testimony that he threatened her with deadly force after killing her chosen heterosexual companion." Harper chortled. "Fix me up with a computer, kid. I could write a book on this one. Jury bestseller. How's this sound? 'Members of the jury, Elvin Brawley shared a language and a disability with Mary Whitlow's only son, little Charlie Whitlow, a deaf child. Elvin taught Mary Whitlow how to talk to her son using American Sign Language, the only true language of the deaf, and then he fell in love with her and her son. One day last March, that love died, when Elvin Brawley was murdered by a racist who didn't want his own son to be able to communicate with his mother using sign language.' "

"If this is what you wouldn't call Brady material," said Watson. "Where's the stuff you would call Brady material?"

A detectable pause ensued, followed quickly by a sharp laugh.

"If I had Brady I'd have to give that to you, wouldn't I?" protested Harper.

"Yes, you would," said Watson. "I guess my next question would be *when* would you give it to me? Sometime before trial, right? Like the day before?"

"This is turning into a misunderstanding," said Harper soothingly. "I didn't say I had Brady material."

"And you didn't say you don't have Brady material, am I right?"

"These are bad boys, Joe," his tone shifting from professional adversariness to avuncular concern. "You don't want to cut your baby teeth workin' for these jackals. They run guns, fraud schemes, money laundries, counterfeit rings. They got silos in southern Missouri full of explosives. Lately they've been recruiting the skinhead fringes from military bases. And if we find out your boy is a member, he may see a couple more trials after this one, or we'll amend our complaint and do them all at once."

Watson felt a chill spreading outward from a sudden attack of nausea, just as Myrna Schweich appeared at the door. She was wearing a worsted, gray, four-button wool suit, matching gray heels, nylons, fresh, tastefully sheer makeup, a silk blouse. Downright corporate.

"Can you hold a minute?" said Watson. He put his hand over the receiver. "Dr. Green's fees came in," he whispered to Myrna. "It's Harper. He says Whitlow belongs to some kind of militia." He could feel blood drain from his face.

Myrna curled her lip, then bit it thoughtfully. "What else is he telling you?"

"Order of the Eagles," he said. "Remember the Department of Education? 1999?"

"Does he have Whitlow connected to them?" A glimmer of fear appeared in her eyes, then vanished. "Solid evidence? Or is he fishing? He's fishing, goddammit!" She took the phone from him and covered the mouthpiece with her small, freckled hand.

"Does he think that I moved you over here?" she asked.

"I don't think so," said Watson. "He asked me that. I told him I came here because I did research for you and I needed office space."

"Good. Look at me," she said solemnly, grabbing him by his sober tie, pulling his head down to her level, peering up at him with a ferocious look. "No chinks in the armor. Tell him nothing. The best offense is offensiveness," she urged. "If need be, you will stand alone in a field of corpses. You'll beat him to a bloody stump with a bicycle chain in front of a federal jury unless he gives you what you want. Are you ready?"

Watson grimly nodded, and she gave the phone back to him.

"Yeah," said Watson into the receiver, "Sorry, Harper. Go ahead."

Myrna whacked her forehead with the meat of her small palm. "Not 'Sorry, Harper'!" she mouthed in a hoarse whisper. " 'Fuck you, Harper'!"

"So, what I'm saying," said Harper, "and the reason I sent you shit that I didn't have to send you, is that this guy is badder than we thought. Natural life is going to look good to him by the time this is over."

"I can't plead him to life on the present charges," said Watson. "I'm pretty sure about that."

"Pretty sure?" she groaned.

"He will not go for that."

"Not he," whispered Myrna. "*You.* You will not go for that."

"You will not . . ." said Watson. "I mean, I will not go for that. But I'll take it to him. I'll ask him."

Myrna lit up a Gitane and blew smoke in disgust. "Is he still bringing a toothless, three-legged mongrel to the dog show?" she said loud enough for Harper to hear.

Watson shrugged.

"I can't stand it anymore," she said, snatching the receiver out of Watson's hand. "Harper?" she said. "It's Myrna Schweich. Yup. Listen, other than your dick being way too small, how are ya?"

She puffed and nodded impatiently. "Yeah," she said. "Yeah. I'm corrupting youth, here. Yeah, that's right. He was a Stern, Pale choirboy counting angels on the heads of pinheaded prosecutors, and now I'm teaching him about Satan and the federal government."

She blew a big, vibrant smoke ring and then launched a small, tight one through the middle of it. "I told him what I'm telling you," she said into the receiver. "I told him that you are trying to dick him around, and nothing you're saying today is changing my mind."

She sat on Watson's worktable, held out her cigarette, searched the tabletop over her shoulder, and when she didn't see an ashtray, tapped ashes on the floor.

"OK," she said, "so you're not dicking him around, because your dick is too small. But you are trying to fuck with us, are you not? Albeit with a tiny dick?"

She winked at Watson. "I'm a what? Joe, activate the recording device. I'm a what? You're using the c-word on an open line? You, with a dick so short it pees on itself? Harper, I am alarmed, mortified, psychologically traumatized by your language. I think it comes perilously close to sexual harassment. 'Mr. Harper threatened me, Your Honor. Then he tried to use his penis as a weapon, but I was laughing too hard.' "

She tilted her head and listened some more. "Uh-huh, uh-huh," she said with a nod. "I'll tell you what his client would say. His client would say, 'Why is the Assistant United States Attorney trying to fuck us with such a tiny dick?' "

She pinned the receiver between her chin and her collarbone. "Uh-huh. Well, if we can't reach an agreement, we go to trial, right? That's not so bad for us in federal court. We gonna have plenty of whites on that jury. You wanna scare me with a black jury, you better restage your murder and have your witness change her story, for what? The third time? The fourth time? And have it happen in East St. Louis and off federal land."

She crossed her arms, blowing smoke and disgust. "Uh-huh. Uh-huh. The problem is, Harper, if we go to trial, then the whole courthouse will see how small your dick is. You got one witness and she changes her story to match her outfits. You got an inadmissible tattoo, some nigger jokes, and a dead rapist. Uh-huh, uh-huh. I gotta go," she said. "Call us back with a serious offer. And make sure you have authority, OK? I don't want to hear this runny bullshit about how you have to ask your boss or your wife first—hear me?"

She hung up and pounded the desk with her tiny, pale fist.

"Why are they such assholes?" she fumed. "They should do plastic surgery on those fuckers over there. Take their assholes and plant them right in the middle of their faces, so everybody knows what they are dealing with right up front."

Two trills. "Outside call from your daughter," said the receptionist over the intercom.

Myrna picked up. "Sweetie," she said, fluidly assuming the voice of Mommy. "Yes, I'm thinking about you, too. Make cookies with Nana and save me some, OK? OK, bye now. I won't be long. Bye."

"Order of the Eagles," said Watson, still feeling cold and a little scared.

"Militia types," said Myrna. "Aren't they the car bomb guys?"

Watson nodded. "I entered my appearance on behalf of car bombers."

"He ain't no fucking car bomber. That's Harper fishing. Besides, car bombers or no, the case is yours. And more money has arrived. Now don't freak over this militia shit. When the Democrats are in power, anybody with a gun in their house is considered militia. Remember Ruby Ridge? Rutger Lupine? How about Richard Jewell? The government's prime suspect at the Atlanta Olympics bombing? 'Sign this waiver of your rights,' they said. 'Don't worry. It's just pretend. We're making a training session video. You can star in it. It's not real. Trust us.' These Eagle Scouts or whoever could be weekend paintball warriors for all we know. Are you going to believe the government? Harper? He wanted to be a pro golfer, but he wasn't making enough money giving lessons, so he went to law school. Now he's a tanned matinee idol for a jury of TV watchers. He's a good lawyer, but he's on the job because his dad is Frank Donahue's best friend. Even if it's a real militia, these guys don't blow up the cars of criminal lawyers." She stopped and tilted her head. "Let me think." She shook her head. "No, that was some other lawyer they blew up. I don't think he was a criminal lawyer. Probably a tax lawyer."

Watson thought about going to retch somewhere in private, but fear had paralyzed him.

"Nothing to worry about," she said, sounding for a split second like she was reassuring herself, as well. "I worked for these outfits before." She glanced at him. "Maybe it was even them. Order of something? Eagle Patriots? I get them mixed up. Anyway, you do your job by making the government prove every element of their bullshit case. You get paid well, and then the next time they call, you politely and firmly tell them that you are overcommitted, and you will not be able to devote the time their case deserves. And if that doesn't work, you tell them you have untreatable, highly contagious end-stage spinal meningitis. Just don't get involved with them. Don't become their regular lawyer. Take them case by case. Professional distance," she concluded emphatically, "is the key. I get involved only with my drug clients. The nice ones."

Watson swallowed and tried to imagine what it would be like, being polite and firm and keeping his professional distance from car bombers. He barely noticed as she segued into the Whitlow case.

"Besides," she said, while fixing him with a serious look, "you're retained counsel, now. Which means there's no way out, except maybe in a box." Then she smiled. "Which is good," she said brightly, "because Dirt has been hard at work for you. He has been mingling with the unwashed masses." The corner of her mouth curled as she fingered another sheaf of her investigator's reports. "Incoming filth alert. He's been to the base at Fort Fuckup and asked the neighbors about activities in and around the Whitlow manor."

"He went to the base? Did he talk to Mary Whitlow?"

"Everybody but," she said. "Mary's hiding somewheres, and I think the government's helping her do it. But we got some Dirty notes. Filthy notes. First, your client's request for info on neighbor Lucy Martinez. Dirt says Lucy's a window watcher. Someday she'll be captain of Neighborhood Watch. She's big on parking violations—anybody parks in her spot, she calls in and gets them towed."

"That's what Whitlow said about her," Watson added, recalling his prison interview with his client, trying to rally to the role of retained counsel without fainting.

"So, Dirt asked Lucy about Elvin Brawley. What'd he look like, how often did he visit, how long did he stay?

"Lucy says, 'Sign language instructor? The deaf, colored fella? Sure, always came on foot in civilian clothes and always carried a briefcase. But he never did stay long enough for any sign language lessons, as near as we could tell. He came to the Whitlow quarters maybe four or five times. But he stayed like less than five minutes. Not long enough for sign language, or for anything else. Just came and went with a briefcase.' Confirmation on the briefcase by neighbor Hilda Pence, who saw Elvin walking down the street with it the day he died. Hilda figured it was those computer-engraved poetry pamphlets they said he sells.

"So Dirt asked Lucy if it ever looked like Mary Whitlow was having an extramarital affair. 'Not from what I seen,' says Lucy. In Lucy's opinion, hubby's the frisky one. He used to bring a pudgy, bleached blonde over from the trailer court of an afternoon when the wife was off to work at the printing plant.

"So when they first saw the black guy come around, the neighbors figured Mary knew about her husband's two-timing and was making it revenge in four-time, but here she says it again: 'He never stayed long enough for nothing like that. Either that or he was very quick. Besides, when he did come around, James Whitlow was usually sitting outside in his car smoking cigarettes and watching the house.' "

"Watching the house?" asked Watson.

"Lucy's two doors down," said Myrna, "and according to Dirt, there's only one parking stall for each housing unit. Parking is a major perk on the base, and people get ticked when somebody parks in their spot."

"The cops didn't tow it," said Watson. "That's what Buck wanted to know. Lucy had it towed."

"Twice, according to her," said Myrna, "Whitlow parked a car in her stall. Then he just set there smokin' cigarettes and looking at his own house. So one day, Lucy ran to the PX to pick up some groceries, and when she came back, there was Whitlow again, parked in her spot, sitting in a Ford smoking cigarettes. She gave him a tap on the horn and he backed out. Then guess who came out of the Whitlow unit with a briefcase?"

Watson made a face and shook his head.

"That's right," she said. "Elvin Brawley. According to Lucy, Whitlow pulled out and deliberately drove the other direction, away from his place, then came back five minutes later and parked in his own parking spot."

"Too weird," said Watson.

"The day of the murder," Myrna continued, "old Lucy was working, waiting tables at the local Perkins, probably one of the reasons the MPs never talked to her. When she comes home, she finds that car parked in her spot again, looks like the same one, even though the stall in front of Whitlow's place is open. 'Course, this time he's not in the car, he's off being charged with murder. She doesn't know that yet. She only knows there's a car in her spot again. So, first she goes in and calls the Whitlow household. No answer. Then she goes back outside and notices that the passenger side of the Taurus is unlocked, she opens it because she sees there are keys still in the ignition, and she is thinking about moving the sucker herself. She chickens out at the last minute, but guess what she sees on the dashboard?"

Watson furrowed his brow. "A car bomb?"

"Fuckin' dummy," said Myrna. "The receiving end of a Fisher-Price nursery monitor, putting out nothing but static because the MP had turned off the transmitter before he left the premises. Remember the nursery monitor?"

"He was listening to them!" said Watson.

"Sounds like a routine," she said, "with funny business going on inside, and Whitlow outside on guard, in case something goes wrong."

Watson tried to imagine why Whitlow would sit outside his own house and listen to a deaf black guy meet for five minutes with his wife. Instead of thinking about whether the Order of the Eagles was preparing an explosive accessory for his Honda, he tried to imagine what Mary Whitlow and Elvin could be doing in the Whitlow house, while James waited outside. Memories tingled and attempted to surface. Whitlow had told him that she didn't know sign language: *"I seen in the paper where she's supposedly the queen of sign language now."* So, if she doesn't know sign language, how was she talking to him? And even if she knows enough to get by, what was Whitlow listening to on the monitor? Sign language? Two people faintly scratching written notes to each other?

"Back to Dirt and Lucy. Lucy calls into base traffic and makes a big stink about not being able to park her car. The MPs call an off-base towing service to haul off the vehicle, and Lucy gets her parking space back."

"That's the car Whitlow wanted me to find out about for him," repeated Watson. "Buck was afraid to go see about getting it himself. He thought the police had towed it because of the murder."

"That's good," she said. "That's good. But, now, apprentice criminal lawyer. What do we need to know?"

Watson looked up from his pad. "We need to know what happened in the house?"

"Yeah, yeah," she said dismissively. "What else?"

"Uh," said Watson.

"The briefcase . . ." said Myrna.

"Yeah," said Watson. "We need to know what was in the briefcase Elvin carried around."

Myrna rolled her head around in a zigzag somewhere between nodding and shaking. "Yeah, I guess," she said. "But how about this: Where *is* the fucking briefcase?"

Watson stared at her and felt his eyes get bigger.

"Hilda saw Elvin carry it into the house. Elvin gets carried out of the house dead. MPs and ambulance attendants come and go. FBI come and go. Everybody writes reports. Nobody writes about a briefcase."

"You're right," said Watson.

The woman at the tow lot. He'd talked to her on the phone. Her voice sounded somewhere in the echo chamber of memory: *"Your wife was here saying she needed to get your briefcases out of the trunk because they had your credit cards and checkbook in them."*

"It's in the trunk of the car," Watson said excitedly. "The impound lot lady. She said Mary had tried to get briefcases out of the car, but they wouldn't let her at them because she didn't have title."

"You are one smart fucking lawyer," said Myrna. She fished through the pile of papers under the notes she had been reading and selected a single sheet. "Dirt," she said with a grin. "He found out where base vehicles get towed to and paid a visit to Base Towing and Impound, Bumfuck, Missouri. The night dispatcher was very nervous. No way, no how, was he going to let Dirt in to look around in any towed vehicle. The owner, a serviceman at Fort Fuckup, was coming for it next morning. Liability. Instant termination if anybody found out. The place is patrolled at night, fenced in with chain-link. No way, no how. Not even for Dirt."

Myrna puffed again. "Five twenty-dollar bills later, the night dispatcher still will not allow Dirt onto the lot, but he does agree to provide a copy of the inventory sheet, owner's name blacked out. The keys were in the vehicle at the time of towing. And whenever that happens, the entire vehicle, including the trunk, gets inventoried."

Myrna passed Watson a flimsy photocopy that said "Impound Lot Vehicle Inventory," containing two large boxed sections, one labeled "Passenger Compartment" listing everything from empty Burger King bags, one straw, two Coke cans, seventeen cigarette butts, one owner's manual, six cassette tapes, one tire gauge, one ice scraper, one Fisher-Price nursery monitor . . .

"The nursery monitor," said Watson.

"Keep reading," said Myrna.

The box below, labeled "Vehicle Trunk," listed one car jack, one tire iron, two oil rags, one rubber jug of windshield wiper fluid, one spare tire, a box of tools containing one socket wrench, etc. . . . . two locked briefcases . . .

"It's in the trunk of the car!" exclaimed Watson.

"*They* are in the trunk of the car," said Myrna. "*Two* locked briefcases. And we can't get at them. Not without going to the cops. And if we did that, I have a feeling things could get worse for the whole family. Better ask your client what he wants us to do next. He and Buck know what's in the briefcases, and they don't want us to know, I guess."

"But the cops, the MPs, they must have known the car was there. Maybe they're holding it for evidence."

"Why?" she retorted. "It ain't plated, and it's parked in front of Lucy's house, not Whitlow's. I guarantee you if that car was on homicide hold it woulda been locked up in a concrete garage and torn apart for latent prints and blood by now. Nope. They don't know about it. And if they thought the car had something to do with the murder, they'd lock it up tight and wait to see who came after it, which is what your client's buddy was worried about. But then you would be assuming that military intelligence is more than a well-known oxymoron. You would be assuming that the traffic dispatcher somehow knew that Whitlow had been sitting in that car and then communicated that information to the MPs. The right hand not knowing what the left is up to isn't enough for the government; they even have trouble keeping track of the torso in between."

Watson wanted to solve the puzzle of the briefcases. He wanted to defend his client to the best of his abilities and become a better criminal lawyer. But there was this niggling matter of car bombs. And what if Whitlow killed Elvin Brawley pursuant to his duties as an Order of the Eagles militiaman?

"Harper has transcripts of Whitlow talking about sending niggers back to Africa, and Whitlow's got a poster in his garage of a black man in a gun sight," Watson said. "I think you and Dirt better handle this thing. It's turning out to be all factual anyway. You don't need me. You take the money. I think I'll look into getting a job as a legal research and writing instructor. It pays less, but the position has nothing to do with explosive devices."

"You're going to let Harper bluff you with a pair of deuces?" she asked.

"Harper's thinking about throwing in conspiracy and a charge under the Violence Against Women Act," said Watson. "Sounds like more than deuces to me."

"He's whistling Dixie in a dark graveyard," said Myrna. "If he actually had Whitlow tied to the Order of the Eagles, he wouldn't *tell* you about it. He'd let you plead to the hate crime bullshit and then bring a new case three months before Mr. Hate was scheduled to get out on good behavior."

"Car bombers? Conspiracy? White supremacy?" said Watson. "I pass. I draw the line at terrorism and loss of innocent lives."

"Whoa, kid," said Myrna. "Don't leave me now. We got no proof of Harper's whimsical theories. I need you. I can pick at facts all day. That's my job. But the jury ain't gonna care about a couple of factual discrepancies, not if Harper can stand up and introduce evidence about how our client's name is Mr. Bigot. He lives in a bigoty house, where he reads bigot books and goes on-line to chat with bigot pals. Here, jury, listen to some of his bigoty E-mail. His kid goes to bigot deaf camp every summer and comes home happy about bigotry. He has a really excellent tattoo and knows some good nigger jokes.

"We can't have that," she said. "You haven't been there enough to know, but the n-word does not go over well in a federal courtroom. It's like hearing somebody scream 'Fuck you' at the Pontiff during High

Mass under the dome of St. Peter's in Rome. That's why O.J.'s criminal defense lawyers were hot to get it in. It works wonders. And it still works, even after O.J. Two, O.J. Three, O.J. Four, O.J. Five, Lupine Three and Four. Whether it comes in and how often is a question of law. Evidentiary theory. Legal theory. That's your job. Best for us would be for Mary Whitlow to say 'nigger' once or twice during her version, a version we promptly demolish on cross-examination. Your job is to keep the rest of it out, if you can."

CHAPTER 20

Alone in his overbought house in Ladue, Watson's dreamscapes were overrun by hooded white figures and exploding Hondas. Arthur and Judge Stang took turns inhabiting the same shrouded, authoritarian figure who scowled down from a pedestal mounted outside the gates of heaven, sometimes warning him, "This is a bad client," other times quoting aloud from the Model Rules of Professional Responsibility: "The lawyer owes the client the duty of zealous representation."

A faceless man wearing a Magritte bowler hat and a black topcoat followed him everywhere. And, of course, when Watson tried to report the stalking shadow to the police, no one could see him except Watson. "No, really, he was right there. Just now. You mean, you didn't see him?"

When the figure finally caught up with him, a voice came from the shadowy veil under the brim where a face belonged. "You owe me. You have something that belongs to me. Remember, we made a deal?"

Watson fled in terror, jumped into his Honda, turned the key in the ignition, and blew up. Coming to in an underworld clip joint, he lifted his head out of a brass spittoon and crawled up a stool to the bar. A blowsy, congenial bartender whistled a chirpy rendition of Berlioz's *Damnation of Faust* and sauntered down to ask him for his pleasure.

"You look like a single-malt man," said the bartender, grabbing a bar rag and burnishing his drinker's nose, a sunburst of exploded capillaries on a beezer glowing with the erubescence of a taillight. "How about a little conversation fluid? We age it forever down here. Royal Nepenthe, Highland Lethe, Ancient Acheron, Styx Single Cask. You name it."

"Got any Old Tantalus?" Watson asked.

The barkeep filled a tall glass full of cracked ice and set it on the bar. He hoisted a regulation red-and-yellow gasoline can with a practiced hand and filled the glass with a super-unleaded, 93-octane, twenty-five-year-old single, sherry-oak-cask special, featuring detergent additives and engine scrubbers.

He peeled a splinter off of Watson's dry bones and used it to pick his teeth.

"Nice to see you down this way," he said with a bloody-toothed smile. "You'll like it here. We got T1 trunk lines in the major metropolitan circles, and ISDN everywhere else. You'll get your machine after the trial. And guess what? No wife. No kids. No visitors from Porlock. No forced conviviality, unless you're in the mood for it. And you don't have to waste half the day being nice to people. Plenty of time to be productive and single-mindedly pursue your career. Most guys make six figures in the shade down here," he said, pushing the tall glass of iced gasoline at him. "Drink up. You'll need it to get you through the trial."

"Trial?" asked Watson.

"Yours," said the bartender and let loose gales of hearty, Satanic laughter, pointing at Watson's lap. "Your Honor, may it please the court to have admitted into the evidence of body, I mean, the body of evidence, Exhibit A: One loutish, headstrong penis, a barbarous cuntivore without a flyspeck of decency in him. The capscallion of all rapscallions. A scurvy, vermiform scug with a serpentine twinkle in his solitary eye. An orgulous Turk who strikes in the dark vaults of the flesh like a penile thunderbolt. A greedy cur seeking shadows, slick crevices, tuna fish, ecstasy, and sleep. . . ."

After two or three nightmares with similar themes, he woke up late for another appointment with Dr. Palmquist with about three hours of solid sleep under his scalp.

En route to the Gage Institute, it occurred to him that her telephone conversations of late had been decidedly less playful and more businesslike. Of course, the mouse brutality study was in full career, and according to her last E-mail, the data was coming in from Minnesota, and still more studies of Whitlow's troublesome brain were under way. Maybe Watson was jealous of the attention she was paying to Whitlow's pathologies? What about Watson's own primitive, moral superstitions—surely they were of clinical interest, at least?

In the lobby, the guard recognized him and waved him past the kiosk. Watson was becoming a regular member of the staff.

He found her in the L of her worktables, her hand on a trackball, her face bathed in the vibrant colors of a high-definition monitor, with that peculiar blend of concentration and awe—the serious user in transports of computer-induced rapture, a form of worship that explains the time-honored industry practice of referring to program objects as "icons."

"One minute," she said, lifting a finger from the trackball. She clattered some more on the keyboard, then rose from her worktables and picked up a stack of files. "Let's go down to the viewing room."

She walked briskly ahead of him, talking as they made their way down a corridor and into a room with a spacious console and thirty-two-inch high-resolution monitors.

"First, old evidence. My assistant, Heather, has been rounding up the medicals on Mr. Whitlow," she said, offering him a swivel chair next to hers.

"She found records?" asked Watson.

Rachel gave him a "You expected less?" look. "Heather's also a graduate student in forensic medicine," she said. "If a medical record exists, she finds it, and then she gets it. Medical Insurance Bureau, the life insurance databases, the medical information networks, anything . . . Name it, she gets it, whether by cajolery, by artifice, by dogged pursuit."

"She found something good?" asked Watson.

"Take a seat," said Rachel. "This is medical *Masterpiece Theater.* First, background. We found records of the initial seizure intakes down at Southwest Missouri State. Pretty ho-hum. Idiopathic seizure, followed by normal EEGs, nothing on the functional MRI scan, medication to control the seizures, seizure-free for a period of time. Can't tell from the old records whether he's a druggie or a boozer. He refused a urinalysis once when applying for a night-shift position as a computer maintenance technician. Couple bouts of some back trouble, blah, blah."

"No other seizures, after the ones in college?" asked Watson.

"Probably not," she said. "But it may not matter once you get a look at what else Heather came up with."

"A mental defect or disease?" he said eagerly. "A hard one?"

"Easy, sport," she said. "An HMO on South Grand had some recent records, and they had forwarded others to another HMO out in Festus, Missouri, because patient Whitlow changed jobs and insurance companies. When we faxed the release out there, they sent back records, current, right up to the week before the murder."

"Really?" said Watson, his eyes widening.

"Really," she said, "and like you, I thought—how perfect!—he sees a doctor a week before the murder to get his seizure medication adjusted, the med change results in untoward psychological repercussions. *Bam!* Impulsive behavior, in the form of a murder, happens. Neurochemical defect."

"Something like that," said Watson.

"Well," she sighed. "Nothing like that. VD is more like it. Gram-stained smears positive for gonorrhea. And the next question out of the noble Mr. Whitlow's mouth, one week before the murders, according to the nurse's notes is—'I ain't gonna have to tell my wife about this, am I?' "

Watson recalled his interview with Whitlow and the prisoner's irritable plea, "*I gotta piss again! . . . That's some other medicine I'm needing. . . . It's personal.*" And Whitlow's phone message, the one Watson had listened to when he'd called into his office voice mail the day he'd met Rachel Palmquist: "*They said something about could they get the medical records from the doctor who prescribed the medicine for the infection . . . before I was in jail. . . . I don't think they should have those because that is private shit. So can we just tell them no?*"

"The piss infection," said Watson. "He was taking meds for what he called a 'piss infection.' "

"That's one way to describe it," she said. "All of which would be neither here nor there," she added, "except for what Heather coyly refers to as a careless mistake in the transmission of medical records. The HMO in Festus sent not just James Whitlow's records, but family medical."

"Family?" asked Watson.

"That's right," she said. "Hers, his, little Charlie's, the whole Whitlow clan. It's what happens when you pay your medical records personnel minimum wage. It makes them careless and more susceptible to a skillful insinuation from someone like Heather that the authorization and release is for family medical, rather than for an individual patient. It helps, especially when we are looking for genetic markers."

She sorted clamped bundles of medical records. "So your client goes in on Monday complaining that he is," she read from a page, "as he describes it, 'pissing battery acid,' and wondering if he has to tell his wife about a little bout of Cupid's itch." She put one set of papers aside and picked up another.

"Guess who comes in to the same HMO on Friday—one week before the murder?" she asked, looking at him over her glasses.

"No," he said.

"Yes. Mary Whitlow, complaining of irritation, burning on urination, and purulent discharge."

Watson screwed up his face. "He told her?"

"He didn't tell her," she said, then read from the records. " 'When informed of her diagnosis, patient became angry and extremely upset. She accused the medical staff of misdiagnosis or of mixing up her lab samples with some other patient's.' "

She flipped a page. "Here's the part you'll like. 'Patient tearfully stated that she could not possibly have gonorrhea or any other sexually transmitted disease because she had been married for seven years and had never had sex with anyone except her husband.' "

"Ew," said Watson.

She peered over her glasses and smiled. "Think about that one," she said. "And then get busy finding me another French red for our next celebration."

"Give me that!" said Watson, taking the HMO records and reading the notes for himself.

"From the looks of it," continued Rachel, "they had to carefully connect dots and spell it out for her without mentioning her husband's visit earlier in the week, which, of course, would be a breach of patient confidentiality."

Watson read aloud from the notes, " 'Patient was informed that she could contract the disease from *any* infected sexual partner, including her husband. When she refused to believe the results, the physician on duty showed her the gram-stained slides so she could see for herself.'

"So Lucy Martinez was right—he *was* cheating on her."

Rachel curled her lip and served him a look. "Yes, and men have also been known to wear pants. More important for you, a week before the murder, we have her on record swearing up and down that she never slept with anyone but her husband. Seven days later, she tells the cops she was having an affair with Elvin."

"Lethal," said Watson. "Myrna will force-feed her on the witness stand."

"Another loving couple bound for life by matrimonial vows," said Rachel. "You got lucky, thanks to Heather, and I've got more good stuff to show you in his neurofunctional profile. The stuff came in the night before last from the federal medical center in Rochester. Took an hour and a half even on the T3 trunk line."

She pulled out a keyboard tray and began summoning scanning images onto the monitors.

"First, the big find—we have a subarachnoid cyst. And the neurologists are recommending removal."

A set of sixteen ghostly images of transverse brain sections appeared. She clicked on one of them and enlarged it to occupy the screen. "Right there," she said, using her mouse pointer to indicate a pale, gray golfball shape nestled somewhere between the skull and the images of brain convolutions.

"It showed up first on the MRI, and then they did a PET to confirm that it was compromising blood flow to the frontal lobes."

"A hard mental defect or disease?" asked Watson.

"Nice and hard," she said, sounding faintly disappointed. "We won't be breaking new ground with this one. We may not even get to it if Mary's clinic visits come into evidence. Nothing less effective than a thoroughly discredited witness.

"The first image is MRI, very good for structural detail. You want to see the lesion? There it is. Now, here," she said, clicking two glowing multicolored brain slices onto screens. "If you want to see the *effect* the lesion has on blood flow and metabolism, you use PET or fMRI. On the left you have Mr. Whitlow's brain, on the right an image at the same level of a normal brain from another twenty-seven-year-old white male. The color blobs represent numerical values. We could assign any color to any number, but by convention the blues and purples represent low blood flow, ascending upward through the spectrum—blue, green, yellow, with orange, red, and pure white representing maximum blood flow."

Watson looked at the colored slice of Whitlow's brain, which was mostly blue or purple in the frontal lobes, as contrasted with the normal brain on the right, which was mainly red, yellow, and white.

"That's resting state," she said. "The difference is even more pronounced in the presence of external aggression. Here are PET scans from the same normal control while the subject is watching this computerized video clip of a spitting cobra blown up and displayed in 3-D multimedia. It's a standard image, so is the accompanying explanation. The researcher shows the subject a digitized, high-resolution color image of a black-necked spitting cobra, taking care to explain that it is capable of spraying venom over eight feet into the eyes of its victim, which sears the eyes into temporary and exquisitely painful blindness, while the snake moves in for a bite and injection of a neurotoxin that causes seizures, intermittent respiratory arrest, raging fever, and slow death.

"Certain circuits become more active according to the PET images, especially those older, lower parts of your brain where things like fear—primary emotions—originate. But the frontal cortex comes into play, too, because it regulates impulses and powerful emotions by way of feedback circuits wired to the amygdala and the limbics in general. That's just one visual stimulus. The standard protocol includes dozens more. Heartwarming images of mothers cuddling infants at their breasts. Sunrises, concentration camp survivors, crying children, blooming flowers, smiling faces, angry faces, and so on—all presented in controlled environments and accompanied by standard narratives designed to activate certain specific cognitive pathways in the human brain.

"We compile those images of brain activity and assemble an individual neurofunctional profile for each subject. We capture and record images of how the individual brain responds to stimuli, the very same stimuli and the very same test we administered to five thousand other people, including one or two thousand repeat felons, who heard exactly the same voice describe exactly the same snake, under exactly the same controlled circumstances.

"We assemble a database of such profiles. Then, we teach a computer to catalog the profiles, looking for similarities and differences. We teach it to sort and compare and compare again, using the same kind of compare-and-contrast cycles the brain itself uses—what we call recurrent networks—and we find out who has certain predispositions and who doesn't. Then we measure how well the subjects control those predispositions, by looking at the prefrontal cortex and the way it is wired to the limbics, specifically, you guessed it, the amygdala."

Watson stared at the PET image of Whitlow's brain. "Can those colored blots tell us just why he shot this deaf black guy?" he said with a chuckle.

"Not quite," she said, "but I can tell you plenty about him. As you've already seen, he exhibits hypometabolism in the forebrain, which means his frontal cortex doesn't get quite enough blood and oxygen to control those impulsive behaviors we talked about earlier.

"Male. Unformatted. Biological markers for sex and violence found in tissue biopsies and cerebral spinal fluid, including low serotonin metabolite levels in his CSF. He has genetic Type-2 alcoholism—the worst kind—check the low P-300 brain waves. Dysfunctional D2 dopamine receptors. Low MAO platelet levels. There is evidence of transient depression, no surprise for an accused murderer awaiting trial."

Watson stared blankly into the images of colored brain slices on the monitors.

"Got all that?" she asked, with a sly, sideways glance.

Monitors sprang to life with more vivid color images. She pointed at one screen after another. "PET, CAT, echoplanar fMRI, MEG, SPECT, and EEG. Visual depictions of glucose consumption, electrical fields, magnetic fields, and blood flow—all capable of individual display or superimposition. What do you want to know?"

"Is he crazy?" asked Watson. "I mean, in addition to having a hard mental defect."

"The lesion is confirmed by scores on the Halstead-Reitan and Luria-Nebraska Neuropsychological Batteries. Multiphasic personality inventories show elevated antisocial tendencies. Modern Racism Scale in the upper five percent. Solipsistic, narcissistic, atavistic, autistic, sadistic, in short some of the worst istics we've seen since the government started reimbursing us for finding them under the Federal Omnibus Scanning Technology and Forensic Applications Act of 1999."

She winked at him.

"Final diagnosis?"

"A classic Mitgang-Munchausen subanthropic homunculapathy. He's even worse off than you are."

Watson looked at her uncertainly.

She kicked him under the table. "I made up the last part, ya big dope. Just kidding."

She rolled a pencil between her lips and smiled at him. Her lips . . . "Stop me!" cried child Watson's inner adult, as he felt himself lean forward, quelling the urge to gorge on ripe, moist crescents smudged with burgundy lip color. She leaned over a printout of James Whitlow's EEG and read the interpretation to him. He wanted a peek at the pewter-colored lace nests where his twin obsessions were hiding out. A glimpse past the collar of her lab coat, down her throat, and into the neckline of her blouse revealed burgundy lace—a new color scheme—that matched her lips.

"Elsa," he said, "we need to go somewhere, for some grooming and maybe lice picking?"

"Can't," she said. "Too many other primate scientists still working, and I don't think you're ready for group sex." She raised an eyebrow. "Besides, last time you spent half the night complaining about how we needed to get to work and the other half asking your brain why it wanted to get laid in accordance with the Coolidge effect. So this time we are doing our work first. And if you fire up the guilt networks again, I'm putting you in the tube and taking some functional MRI films, so I can show them to my students."

"OK, what do the government's experts want to do?" asked Watson.

"The government's neuropsychologists are going to be saying that the lesion does not affect Mr. Whitlow's ability to appreciate the consequences of his actions. All these frontal lobe theories we've been throwing around are still new and arguable, but I'm pretty sure that we'll get our evidence in, and they will try to refute it with their experts."

She opened a folder and went in search of a report. Watson tried to catch her eye, but she was all business in a chilly way, and he wondered if it was only because it was daytime and business hours at the institute.

"They will also try to get some new-wave stuff in. You heard me mention the Modern Racism Scale? Pretty soft stuff. It's a tricky test designed to deceive the subjects into confessing their true racial attitudes. Still very subjective. So a new test has recently been devised."

"To measure racism?" asked Watson. "C'mon."

"It can be done," she said levelly. "No question about it. In fact, we can measure your attitude about almost anything, noninvasively."

"How?"

"Remember the first three hundred milliseconds? The gap between stimulus and response, between intention and deed? The preconscious?"

"Yes."

"I sit you in a chair in a controlled environment with a color monitor in front of you. I put what we call a good-bad response box in front of you, which is an input device to the computer. It has two buttons, one for your right index finger, one for your left. I start showing you words—good ones, like *beauty, peace, friend, flowers;* or bad ones, like *nausea, evil, cancer, death.* I measure exactly, in milliseconds, how long it takes you to judge the valence of the word, usually about five hundred milliseconds, half a second."

"OK," said Watson.

"Now, guess what happens if, a hundred milliseconds before I present a good word or image, I flash a bad word or image on the screen for two hundred milliseconds, just long enough for you to see it, but not long enough for you to think about it, and then I present the good word or image?"

"I throw up?"

"No." She laughed. "It takes you longer to decide that the good word or image is positive. It's called stimulus onset asynchrony. Let's keep it concrete. When we showed Whitlow a gorgeous high-res photo of a blooming orchid, it took him half a second to punch the good button. If we flashed a picture of a white face for two hundred milliseconds just before presenting the orchid, it still took him only about five hundred milliseconds to punch good for the orchid. If we flashed a black face for two hundred milliseconds before presenting the orchid, it took him almost one whole second to make his decision, because his brain must first override the initial negative associations of the first image."

"He's a racist because he can't push buttons fast enough?" asked Watson.

"It's good science," she said. "John Bargh at NYU. Russell Fazio at Indiana. If the subject has positive feelings about the first image, or 'priming image' as we call it, and has the same positive feelings about the second image, the 'target image,' then he responds quickly. If one is negative and the other positive, there is a measurable delay. Furthermore, the longer the delay, the more powerful the positive or negative associations adhering to the first, or prime, image."

"This is all going to mean something soon," said Watson. "I can feel it."

"Whitlow is a Pavlovian racist," she said, "with powerful, immediate negative reactions to black faces. That's no crime in itself, I guess. But I think the prosecutors will attempt to bundle these test results in with their psychological assessments, to show that any impulsive act undertaken by Whitlow against a black person would be accompanied by intense racial animus."

"But wait," said Watson. "Doesn't that mean he can't help it? His racism is involuntary?"

"Look at your statute," she said. "It makes it illegal to intentionally select a victim *because of* the victim's race, color, religion, national origin, ethnicity, gender, disability, sexual orientation, et cetera. It's a two-headed crime. There's the selection, which can be intentional, and there's the motivation, which, according to the government, may be voluntary, involuntary, conscious, unconscious. Doesn't matter."

"You're sure you aren't a lawyer?" Watson asked. "This stuff is science fiction," he said.

"The science is not fiction," she replied. "The only question is whether it is admissible evidence in a federal murder trial. If it comes in, I can't take the stand and say it's bad science, nor can I prove that Whitlow has automatic positive feelings about black people, because he doesn't. He has automatic, powerful negative feelings about them."

"More evidentiary theory," moaned Watson.

"You got it," she said. "And now that you understand automaticity testing, if you'd like to make an appointment, I'll rig you up and test your automatic, preconscious attitudes about your wife by slipping in a photo of her two hundred milliseconds before I show you a picture of that spitting cobra. You want?"

"Poor taste," he said.

She stood up and began stacking folders.

"Elsa," he said, "I . . ."

She smoothed his hair with her hand. "Cham, you have pretrial and motions in limine due. I have a shitload of Whitlow data to wade through."

"How about tonight?" he asked. "Late?"

"Male mice on nitric oxide," she said. "Can't. I'll call you, OK?"

CHAPTER 21

S he didn't call the next week, and neither did Sandra. Watson had to call the Memsahib to set up treaty negotiations on neutral ground. He had sent flowers, which hadn't helped. So far they could not agree on a location. Before long, they would be attending peace talks in Paris and fighting over the shape of the bargaining table. So far it was a case of trying to install Mistress 1.0 before uninstalling Wife 1.0. IRQ conflict.

He followed proper male protocol and threw himself into his work, efficiently cross-linking his career aspirations with his sexual drives in that harmonious state of being the Greeks called eudaemonia and Freud called sublimation. But he was having serious withdrawals from Sheila and Benjy—kid-flesh cravings. One of life's greatest pleasures was snagging a cooing nine-month-old from the crib at dawn, wrapping it around his head, and giving the little squirmer a serious belly raspberry while it giggled in his ear. Talk about fun! Then, off to work. But Benjy had been moved to the alpha male's house, being protected from convicts, criminal defense lawyers, and belly raspberries by R. J. Connally & Sons. Watson could imagine R.J.'s consternation over his son-in-law's dalliance with the criminal law. Real Money was nowhere in sight, unless Watson became a working fool of a criminal lawyer and hung out with the likes of Gerry Spence and Alan Dershowitz. Otherwise, Watson was off on what R.J. would call a preposterous departure from the true calling of Real Money.

Watson spent the week researching, drafting, and filing his pretrial motions. Then he received copies of Harper's handiwork: The government's filings were cookie-cutter motions and memos—a secretary had probably changed the names, the case numbers, the style and headings, from forms filed in other cases. Boilerplate legal jargon full of string-cited cases, little or no application of the law to the precise facts of the individual case. Watson's memos were handcrafted gems, written by the winner of the Ignatius University School of Law's Computerized Legal Research & Writing Award.

After he finished drafting and filing his responses to the government's motions, his thoughts turned to Palmquist, but every time he clicked on her in his Personal Information Manager, he willfully clicked NO when the software asked him: "DIAL WORK NUMBER FOR THIS ENTRY?" The last thing she'd said to him was "I'll call you."

Finally, one afternoon, his monitor beeped at him and he spotted E-mail with a Gage Institute return address. He clicked on it, feeling like a lovesick swain in days of yore breaking the wax seal of a perfumed envelope. Maybe his obsession had not touched these photons and screen blips with her fingers, but his bloodhound was in full cry at the mere sight of her name in electronic print. Craving purple prose poured from the portals of her soul, he found instead fat blocks of single-spaced print detailing the forensic implications of subarachnoid cysts. Not so much as a "How are you?" or "When can I see you again?" If he couldn't quite work up the moral nerve to mount the comely brain scientist, just what did he want from her, anyway? he asked himself. Declarations of love? Admiration? Professional respect? Reciprocal infatuation?

He thumbed through the folder of his-and-her medical records she had given him during his last visit. "Patient tearfully stated that she could not possibly have ... any ... sexually transmitted disease because she had ... never had sex with anyone except her husband"? He resisted the empathy required to imagine himself receiving such a diagnosis, the rush of attendant physical and mental symptoms induced by truth, betrayal, jealousy, hatred, desire for revenge, all converging at once. He moved on to her typed Whitlow notes instead: "The arachnoid cyst compresses the frontal lobes of James Whitlow's brain, restricting blood flow, lowering metabolism, making the so-called 'executive functions' in the frontal cortex less active and less capable of controlling violent or emotional impulses."

His phone rang twice. Outside call. "United States District Court, Eastern District of Missouri," said the caller ID software.

"Hello?"

It was Judge Stang's secretary.

"Ida?" he said, almost smelling lavender water.

Her voice was thready, kind, polite, and ultimately terrifying: Judge Stang wanted to meet with the lawyers again on the Whitlow case.

"Meet?" asked Watson with some trepidation. "You mean, for the pretrial conference? Already?"

"The judge has ordered the lawyers to appear in chambers," said Ida. "He didn't say anything about a pretrial conference. Those are usually scheduled and held in the courtroom."

A frisson of terror traveled up his spine. Judge Stang in chambers. Twice! On the same case?

"When?" asked Watson.

"Well," Ida sounded surprised. "Now. I assume he meant now." Watson heard her turn the receiver aside and speak to the judge.

"No," cried Watson in vain, "don't *ask* him."

"You wanted to meet with those lawyers on the Whitlow matter now, didn't you?" she asked.

"Where *are* the lawyers?" Watson heard the judge shout from his chambers. "What's keeping them? Didn't we order them to appear? And they have not appeared, right?"

Watson politely thanked Ida, hung up, and then hollered, "Myrna! Help!"

Watson left Harper a message, Harper left Watson a message, Harper left Myrna a message, and then they all ended up on a conference call— the three of them at a loss for why Judge Stang was summoning them to his chambers. Maybe it was a pretrial conference, and Ida just didn't realize it. Or maybe the judge wanted to hear the lawyers argue their motions in person. Unusual in federal court, but not unheard of. A settlement conference?

He grabbed copies of his motions and supporting memoranda, then looked at the stack of papers filed by Harper and decided he didn't need to bring copies of those.

On the way downtown, Myrna, who had been in stretch pants and an

Elvis Costello T-shirt, disrobed in the backseat of Watson's Honda and donned amazon courthouse armor. Gunmetal gray suit, white silk blouse, opaque brown nylons, gray flats. Just enough eyeliner, no eye color, amber hair drawn back into a tight bun, her face game and war-like. They toed off at the foot of the courthouse steps and assessed each other's appearance. She stood on her tiptoes and brushed off his shoulders, straightened his tie, stepped back to look him over.

"Middle button," she said, pointing at his suit. "Judge Stang does not tolerate open jackets. Am I OK?"

"Beyond corporate," said Watson.

Inside, they entered what Judge Stang had called "those talking time-and-temperature elevators" and rode to the twenty-eighth floor of the Courthouse of the Future, took deep breaths, and stepped out to meet destiny.

Myrna had told him that Harper was a big guy, but Watson had considered the source and forgotten about it until they walked off the elevator and were met by a tall, pacing man in a blue khaki suit, with shoulders too big to see around. Watson instantly recognized the familiar smoker's voice, but it was incongruously coming out of a lawyer with the physique of an NBA power forward. A blunt-cut and blown-dry shock of silver hair gave him a patrician distinction beyond his thirty-something years.

When they shook hands, Watson felt his own large hand get wrapped in fingers as thick as cigars and folded into a wide, dry palm. Harper's face was lean and tanned everywhere except where his golfing visor had been. At Stern, Pale & Covin, only rainmakers and shirkers had suntans. On a government lawyer, it probably meant only that Harper carefully took his leisure no matter what the demands of his sole client.

"Mike Harper," said the Assistant U.S. Attorney warmly. He seemed smooth, professional, collegial, radiating the easygoing self-confidence of a large, healthy specimen, with an apparent noblesse oblige for smaller people—until Watson noticed that he was pointedly ignoring Myrna Schweich. She was scurrying underfoot, looking for somewhere to throw her gum wrappers, because she could not smoke in a federal building and was reduced to chain-chewing sticks of Juicy Fruit.

Finally she stepped out from under Watson's elbow and put her little white hand up for a high five—a low five in Harper's case—"Hey, Mookie. How are ya?" she said.

Harper refused to look down at her and looked at Watson instead. "She'll do nothing but hurt your case. Have you met her clients? Does Judge Stang know about her?"

"Hey, asshole in the sky," she said, "I'm down here at just the right height to do some serious damage to the government's posture in this case."

"I have nothing to say to you," said Harper, glancing down from glacial heights of disdain.

"Aw," said Myrna, "Mookie's mad, Joey. We hurt his feelings. And they say it's the women lawyers who get emotionally involved."

"Let's go see the judge," said Harper irritably. "Sooner the better."

"You guys go on ahead," said Myrna, "I have to take a piss."

Harper and Watson found Judge Stang's outer office empty, with no sign of Ida except her four-footed cane, looking forlorn and abandoned in the center of the room.

Then they heard Judge Stang muttering again from within the penetralias of federal justice.

"They are saying I intentionally inflicted emotional distress on a lawyer?" said Judge Stang, apparently on a phone call. "Well, Judge, I can't help that."

When the lawyers peeked through the door into chambers, Ida caught sight of them, bowed, and whispered to the judge.

"They can wait until I rise from the dead, Ida! They kept the court waiting, didn't they?"

She flapped a palsied hand at them and motioned for the lawyers to sit on the cracked leather sofa in the outer chamber, while Judge Stang continued his phone conversation. Myrna showed up, fluttered her fingers in a familiar wave to Ida, and mouthed: "Hi, Ida."

"Yes, Judge Hunsicker, I know you are the chief judge of this district. But I have seniority. In my day, that counted for something. It's my word against some neurasthenic lawyer's."

There was a pause.

"I can't help it if one skittish member of the bar has a nervous breakdown. They didn't have to call an ambulance. That was for show! You've heard of the thin-skull rule with regard to unnaturally susceptible plaintiffs? Well, there's probably a thick-skull rule for fat-headed lawyers, isn't there? I've got three of them waiting to see me right now, and I suppose you'll hold me responsible if one of them breaks out in attacks of fantods and whim-whams?"

Another pause. The lawyers exchanged glances.

"Ida," said the judge, "Judge Hunsicker did it again."

"She hung up on you?" she asked. "The woman has no manners. She was brought up by a different class of people."

The judge sighed and then cussed under his breath. "All right, send in the clowns. Let's get this over with."

Myrna, Harper, and Watson all greeted Judge Stang, who swiveled away from them and looked out his window.

Watson immediately noticed that there was a single hard-back chair available this go-around. He saw Harper looking at it and was too late in making a move for it. Harper got there first.

"Mr. Watson," said Judge Stang, still not turning to look at his visitors, "would you please carry that chair back to the outer chamber. My last visitor was not a lawyer."

Watson gingerly picked up the chair and carried it out of the judge's office. Ida showed him its place against the wall. He heard Judge Stang speaking and rushed back inside.

"The court is not sleeping at night, and I'll tell you why. The court wakes up with chest pains thinking about how it is on the brink of hosting an unnecessary murder trial. A trial that competent, professional officers of the court should be able to settle. But, it is not being settled, which means that one or more of the lawyers involved is incompetent, unprofessional, or both. I intend to find out if it is one, two, or three of you who are incompetent and unprofessional."

"Judge, excuse me," said Harper, "just a clarification. Is this a settlement conference, a pretrial conference? Or perhaps a hearing on the motions now pending before the court? And if it's any of those, may the government request that a record be made of these proceedings?"

"Your boss, our aspiring senator, told you to say that, Mr. Harper," Judge Stang said.

Harper flushed. "That's not true, Judge, I was merely trying . . ."

"To set me up," said the judge flatly. "This is a conversation, Mr. Harper. Human beings have conversations in which they speak plainly to one another, instead of constantly holding forth in the fashion of assistant United States attorneys while records are made of their timeless oratory."

"Judge, I—" began Harper.

"Mr. Harper, we are neighbors. My house is on the corner of the busy intersection of Nowhere Street and Elsewhere Street. You are my next-door neighbor, you live on Nowhere Street, second house from the corner."

Judge Stang remained slumped in his recliner as he slowly swiveled around to face his desk. He seemed to be aging before their eyes, his chest caving in, his wispy, Wildroot-slicked silver hair falling out onto the lapels of his funeral suit. Still not looking at the lawyers, he reached out with a nearly fleshless hand and opened a handcrafted walnut and polished-brass humidor. He selected a cigar from the cedar and velvet-lined interiors (another ten-dollar Davidoff; Watson couldn't help noticing the trademark white-and-gold band).

"If you were gentlemen," Judge Stang said without looking at them, "I'd offer you cigars. But you're not, so I won't."

"Judge—" began Harper.

"Don't interrupt me, Mr. Harper. I'd like to taste this fine cigar for just a moment without having the portals of my ears soiled by the slubbery speech of lawyers."

Judge Stang selected a cedar match from an etched shot glass and lit it by scratching it on the leg of his desk. He puffed comfortably, turned the cigar sideways to check the burn, then settled back into his recliner.

"Every morning I sit at my window overlooking the four-way stop signs at the intersection of Nowhere Street and Elsewhere Street. I often see you leave for work of a morning, drive south on Nowhere, and stop at the four-way stop. And I notice that you, being a conscientious government official, always come to a full stop before crossing Elsewhere Street."

Judge Stang stopped and, for the first time, looked at Harper, whose mouth had come unhinged.

"Are you taking notes, Mr. Harper?"

"Notes, Judge?"

"Never mind," said the judge, swiveling slowly away from his audience and back around to his view of the river. "Each morning, at precisely seven-fifteen A.M., I watch Freddy Fuckhead, who lives on the other side of me on Elsewhere Street, come out to his car. Each morning at exactly seven-fifteen, I see him start his car, race the engine in a most obnoxious way, then proceed west on Elsewhere at fifty miles an hour, right through the stop sign without so much as touching his vehicle's brake pedal. I have watched Freddy do this every morning, of every business day, for the past four years."

The judge stopped talking, puffed, and stared out the window, watching the morning sunlight dapple on the surface of the widest river in North America.

"That's Mark Twain's river," he said. "Huck and Jim are probably still out there somewhere enjoying each other's conversation, while I'm stuck on land with sham kings and bogus dukes."

The judge silently puffed and continued staring. Harper and Watson looked at each other. Then Harper leaned a little off keel, sneaking a peek to see if Judge Stang had perhaps slipped away from them. When the judge began talking again, Harper snapped to attention.

"But this morning," the judge continued, "this morning, this crappy case was weighing on my mind, and I was suddenly overcome by a sudden urge to take a crap. So I got up from my place at the window and went to take a crap, at precisely seven-fourteen A.M.—sixty seconds before Freddy Fuckhead usually emerges to start his car.

"When I finally returned to my perch overlooking the intersection of Elsewhere and Nowhere, it was seven-nineteen A.M. I looked out my window and saw that a terrible accident had occurred during my bowel movement. Freddy Fuckhead had apparently broadsided your car, and both cars had burst into flames. You were stumbling around carrying your own head by the hair, and Freddy was smoothing the wrinkles out of his suit, which had apparently been rumpled by his vehicle's air bag.

"Now," said the judge, "in a civil action for negligence or in a criminal action for criminal negligence or motor vehicle homicide, your estate or the prosecutors, as the case may be, want to call me as a witness to testify that I saw Freddy Fuckhead run that stop sign every single weekday morning for four years, and that, even though I did not see him run the stop sign on the day of the accident, I am all but certain that he did it that day, too, and in all probability caused the accident."

Clouds of smoke billowed softly against the judge's window.

"Freddy is being represented by Ms. Schweich and Mr. Watson. When the prosecution calls me as a witness, she stands up and objects. On what grounds, Ms. Schweich?"

"Uh, Judge," said Myrna, "begging the court's indulgence and with all due respect, if I answer correctly, instead of a cookie, may I please have a cigarette?"

"State the grounds for your objection, Ms. Schweich," the judge commanded.

"Federal Rule of Evidence 404," said Myrna. "Evidence of crimes or acts other than those charged should not be admissible merely to show that the defendant, having committed other bad acts, has a propensity toward crime or bad character."

"Exceptions?" asked the judge.

"Such evidence may be admissible to prove some other fact at issue, such as motive, opportunity, intent, or other elements outlined by other rules. But on your facts, motive and intent are not elements of the charged crime, and so far I've heard no other fact at issue which the evidence would be admissible to prove. The other side wants you to testify that Mr. Fuckhead was routinely negligent and therefore was probably negligent on the day of the accident—exactly the kind of evidence Rule 404 was designed to keep out."

"You may have a cigarette, Ms. Schweich."

"I am deeply grateful to the court for its forbearance," said Myrna, instantly opening her purse and shaking a Gitane out of its blue package. She lit it and took a gasp of smoke into her lungs, as if she had just broken the water's surface after nearly drowning.

"Mr. Harper," said the judge, "according to the government's pretrial papers and in various motions pending before the court, you want to put in a lot of evidence about how this fellow told nigger jokes, said the word *nigger*, painted swastikas on water towers, got into a fight with a black football player ten years ago in high school, associates with groups who use the word *nigger*, uses his computer to talk with them, reads books about people who hate niggers, and has been examined by some psychologists who want to testify that they have tested this fellow and determined that he is a certifiable racist, is that right?"

"We do, Judge, because all such evidence goes to prove motive," said Harper. "And such evidence will help us prove that Mr. Whitlow intentionally selected his victim because of the victim's race."

"Is it a federal crime to be a racist?" asked the judge.

"No, Judge," said Harper.

"Not yet, anyway," said Judge Stang.

"But there are other federal offenses—murder for instance, or conspiracy to commit murder—and the statute requires a penalty enhancement if the trier of fact determines those crimes were motivated by racism."

"Motivated?" asked the judge. "Mr. Harper, state the difference between motive and intent."

"Intent is . . . what you intend to do," said Harper, "whether you committed a crime on purpose, as opposed to making a mistake, or doing something while sleepwalking . . .

"And motive?"

"It's what motivated you. Your reasons for doing what you intentionally did."

"Not usually a separate crime, is it?" asked the judge. "It's usually not even a separate element of a charged crime, is it? I mean, usually we want to know if the criminal act was intentionally done. We talk about motives to fill out narratives for the jury, or even to impose additional penalties at sentencing, but motive is not usually a separate crime, or an element of the crime itself, correct?"

"Correct," said Harper, "but society may identify and punish particularly deleterious motives if the legislature determines . . ."

"And there are good reasons for not making motive an element or a separate offense, are there not?" continued the judge. "How do you prove what someone is thinking about while committing a crime, and then prove that their thoughts caused the crime?"

"I think—" began Harper.

"I suspect you have woken up of a morning at least once or twice and been puzzled as to the bizarre mélange of motives which caused you to behave so abominably the night before, but we won't get into that. Do you ever wonder about your motives, Mr. Watson?"

"I confess, I do, Judge," said Watson, staring at the back of Judge Stang's head. "Sometimes I do things, and I don't understand why. Often I have mixed motives, but I can't sort them out, and then at other times I think I have certain motives, but I actually have other motives. And if I am confused and mistaken about my *own* motives, I shudder to think of a criminal trial, with a jury trying to puzzle them out for me, while I sit silently by enjoying my Fifth Amendment rights."

Myrna winked at Watson, puffed her Gitane, then extended the small, freckled middle finger of her right hand, and waved it in Harper's line of sight.

"Judge," said Harper angrily, "this has gone on long enough. I must insist . . ."

"IDA!" yelled the judge, without turning from his view of the window. "Would you please call down to Mr. Frank Donahue's offices and order him to appear before the court, in chambers. Now."

"Judge, I have authority from the United States Attorney to ask for a transcript of these proceedings. Furthermore, opposing counsel—one of them at least—is the most unprofessional lawyer I have ever met, and the court is also not advising us of its purpose in conducting this hearing . . ."

"This is not a hearing," said Judge Stang. "The court was very clear about that at the outset. It's a conversation, Mr. Harper. And the court has concluded that your end of the conversation is finished. You are advised to say nothing else until Mr. Donahue arrives."

Myrna smiled and lit another cigarette. Watson stared at the back of Judge Stang's head. Harper looked down at his folded hands and quietly fumed.

After several minutes of intense and uneasy silence, Watson heard a male voice in the outer office and recognized the squat, burly figure of Frank Donahue from news photos he had seen of him, with his shock of wiry red hair tinged with gray. He was short but carried himself with authority, green eyes darting, assessing the players in the drama he was about to enter.

"Ida, please show the United States Attorney into chambers," said Judge Stang.

"Good afternoon, Judge," said Donahue.

Judge Stang, still looking motionlessly out the window, spoke. "Mr. Harper, here, was unable to edify the court with a coherent opinion about the difference between motive and intent, and so I asked my secretary to ring your office, Mr. Donahue."

Frank Donahue checked Harper for a read on how far the proceedings had degenerated. Harper drew a breath and looked sideways.

"Maybe a concrete example will help," said Judge Stang. "You obviously *intended* to file this Whitlow case, because it's been filed, it has your name on the pleadings, and I trust you were not drunk, or sleepwalking in the throes of murderous somnolence, or in a fugue state, or suffering from more than the usual governmental mental incapacity when you filed it. But kindly advise us, Mr. Donahue, of your motive for filing it."

"Was I summoned here to participate in a metaphysical inquiry into culpable mental states?" asked Donahue incredulously.

"Pah"—a single plosive sent smoke aloft, where it hovered in the sunlight like a cirrus cloud around the gray crag of Judge Stang's profile.

"The court would never inflict such confusion upon itself, Mr. Donahue. The metaphysical and legalistical spectacles we've seen from you in the past are so profound they bewilder, astonish, and confound everyone, including yourself."

Donahue looked for a chair and then seemed irritably to recall where he was. "I am here as a representative of the United States government and in my capacity as an officer of this court," said Donahue, his gorge rising with his voice, "I will not . . ."

"The baldest, most self-evident fact does not go unchallenged in any proceeding distinguished by your esteemed powers of mental self-mutilation," continued Judge Stang. "The court can't think of another practitioner who takes such perverse and voluminous pride in self-inflicted perplexity. In short, Mr. Donahue, if you'd like, the court will take judicial notice that you are one sharp lawyer."

"If it please the court," said Donahue, "I'd like to request that a transcript be made of these proceedings . . ."

"So you can take me upstairs on a writ? File a complaint with the Investigative Judicial Council? An ice chip's chance in Hell. It does not please the court."

"All right," said Donahue, "then I am forced to *insist* on a transcript of these proceedings. The court's remarks are not proper . . ."

"PROPER!" shouted Judge Stang.

Watson felt sound waves from the judge's vocal cords blow back his hair and marveled at how a small, old man managed such vocal magnificence.

"Proper foolery!" he yelled. "You ask me one more time for a record or a transcript for your golfing buddies upstairs in the Eighth Circuit secular chapel of appeals, and I will hold you in contempt, sir. I will hang the sword of Damocles from the rafters by a human hair. Then, I will order you to stand under it and sing 'Chattanooga Choo-Choo' while my court reporter makes a transcript of it for you. Do you understand me?"

Frank Donahue puffed up his chest, his blue suit filling like a sail with windy indignity. "If this is to be another one of the court's sessions of hectoring and humiliation and, frankly, what is widely considered to be an abuse of this court's powers, then I—"

"IDA!" yelled Judge Stang, scowling down the length of his smoldering Davidoff. "Ida! Send one of the girls in."

Frank Donahue huffed with impatience, while Judge Stang watched the river flowing in the morning sun.

"Good morning, Judge." It was the brunette. She'd been a year ahead of Watson at Ignatius. Renee something. An untouchable beauty with a class rank in the single digits. She politely nodded at the lawyers, walked by them, and took her place attentively at Judge Stang's elbow.

The judge did not look up from his view of the river. "Is it a felony, a high crime, or a misdemeanor if I issue a contempt citation, suspend the sword of Damocles by a human hair, and order the United States Attorney for the Eastern District of Missouri to stand under it and sing 'Chattanooga Choo-Choo' while my court reporter makes a transcript of the proceedings?"

The U.S. Attorney sighed audibly.

Renee tucked an arc of dark, lustrous hair behind her right ear and smiled. "To be honest, Judge, we haven't looked at that precise issue, but the court will recall that we have on occasion looked at similar matters, some of which were not high crimes, misdemeanors, or felonies, and some of which could be so considered. For instance, it was not a high crime or misdemeanor for the court to order a bankruptcy attorney to masticate his own fee application. Our only caveat was that the lawyer should not be ordered to swallow after chewing, because an untoward airway obstruction might result in injury or death from suffocation, which in at least some jurisdictions might be considered misdemeanor assault."

"Go on," said the judge.

"It was not a high crime or misdemeanor for the court to order counsel at both tables to wear dunce caps for the duration of an evidentiary hearing in that class-action health-insurance case we heard last year. Perhaps the court recalls the attorney from California who appeared at informal matters with no tie and an open collar?"

"That surf bum?" growled the judge.

"None other," she said archly. "The court was not charged with any impeachable offense when it ordered the lawyer to put on *two* four-in-hand ties in Windsor knots before the court would entertain his motion to appear pro hac vice. But if I may . . ."

"You may," said the judge.

"Has the court considered the possibility that the strand of hair might break, allowing the sword to fall on Mr. Donahue's head, resulting in a head injury, which—"

"You mean, they would blame me for that?" asked the judge.

"They might, Judge," Renee gently advised.

"You mean, they might say the sword fell *because of* my alleged hatred of Mr. Donahue? Would they be saying I had mixed motives in exercising my inherent powers pursuant to Article III? My expansive, discretionary powers, delegated to the court by Congress and by the United States Supreme Court and by the Federal Rules of Procedure? You mean, all those powers of mine could be impermissibly tainted by some dark, unspoken motive? I could be impeached *because of* that?"

The woman pursed her lips and nodded. "Perhaps, Judge, but without more facts I—"

"But what if I ordered Mr. Donahue to stand under the sword *because of* the way he was acting? And *because of* his bullshit case which is defiling my docket? And *because of* certain mental afflictions of mine which make it difficult for me to control my intense hatred of lawyers? And *because of* . . ."

The judge stopped, picked up his teacup and touched it to his lips, then held it out and peered at it through his reading glasses. "Ida! Tea!" He selected another cedar match and struck it on the underside of his chair. "I confess I've forgotten your question, Mr. Donahue," he said. "Would it be easier for us to simply move on?"

"Move on?" asked Donahue.

"Yes, with the court's business. With our conversation."

"Judge, without in any way suggesting that I want a transcript or a record of these proceedings, the government requests that the court state the nature of these proceedings. Is this a hearing on dispositive motions?"

"Mr. Donahue," Judge Stang drawled, "your name is Polonius, and you have concealed yourself behind a tapestry in Queen Gertrude's bedchamber. I am Hamlet. I come on the scene. I hear something or someone behind the tapestry, and I say, 'How now? A rat?' and I stab my sword through the tapestry and mortally wound you. Queen Gertrude says, 'O me, what hast thou done?' I say, 'Nay, I know not. Is it the king?' "

Donahue took a single deep breath and hung his head in resignation.

"Did I intentionally kill you?" asked Judge Stang. "Did I think it was a rat, or a person back there?"

"These are fictional characters, Judge, I don't see—"

"Immortal fictional characters," said Judge Stang. "And even though we are safely within the parameters of standard criminal law, you have a thorny time of it unraveling my intent. Because a second later, I see that it is a rash, intruding fool—you, I mean, of course, Polonius—behind the tapestry, and I say, 'I took thee for thy better,' meaning I took you for the king, of course. But now we don't know if he thought it was the king before or after the stabbing occurred. Which was it?"

"I confess, I have no idea," said Donahue, "nor do I care."

"Now let's pretend there is an unconstitutional sentence-enhancing statute for any improper motive I may have had in stabbing you. Now we are off to the races, aren't we, Mr. Donahue? Let me proffer a few motives. You'll recall I was pretending to be mad in my play, and this deed was another in a series of ruses designed to make people think I was crazy. I was motivated by an intense hatred of rats and ratlike people. I was seeking revenge on my father's death. I was unconsciously lashing out at any and all authority figures because of my rebellious and melancholy nature. I killed you because I knew you would never consent to a marriage between me and your daughter, Ophelia. And so on."

"Well, Judge," said Frank Donahue, "if nothing else, we have the case of United States versus Hamlet well in hand."

" 'How now? A rat?' " chuckled Judge Stang, and turned around just far enough to trim the ash on his cigar in the stone ashtray on his desk, then swiveled back to his view. "I take one look at this statute, gentlemen, and I see trials. Lots of trials, each one lasting forever, while we try to find out just what kind of hatred our defendant specialized in. It's hard enough trying to find out what the accused *did*. Now you want to add to that another four days of trial to find out what he was thinking about when he did it?"

"Judge," said Donahue impatiently, "we move to—"

"After careful consideration," interrupted Judge Stang, "this court has determined that a hearing on these matters is not necessary. The court has before it written motions and supporting memoranda from both the government and the defendant, James Whitlow."

The judge swiveled and faced the attorneys.

"The court rules that all of the motions in limine filed by the defendant are hereby granted. The court further rules that all of the motions in limine filed by the government seeking to suppress evidence of the defendant's mental disease or defect are hereby denied."

"The government will seek an immediate, expedited interlocutory appeal of this proceeding and the court's orders," said Donahue firmly.

"I'm not finished, Mr. Donahue," said the judge. "In addition, for the reasons set forth in the defendant's proposed order and memorandum in support, drafted by Mr. Watson, here, the court hereby grants the defendant's motion to dismiss the government's charges under the hate crime motivation sentencing provisions."

"The court will be reversed on appeal," said Donahue confidently.

"Pah," said the judge, more smoke billowing aloft. "Why, I hadn't thought of that, Mr. Donahue. Now you've got me thinking. If that happens and this case comes back to my courtroom, I might have to sit on it until after the election."

Donahue turned to Harper and said, "C'mon."

The judge drawled on. "Of course, the election has nothing to do with this case, because you heard me ask the United States Attorney about his motives in filing it, and he said nothing about any election."

Harper and Donahue left. Myrna and Watson stood in front of Judge Stang's desk, breathing faster, flush with the spoils of victory.

"Fine work on the motions," said Judge Stang. "In your coming colloquy with the Platonic Guardians upstairs in the Eighth Circuit, you will probably win on most of your motions in limine because the government is overreaching in its efforts to put speech, beliefs, and associations before the jury. Besides, most evidentiary rulings are within the sound discretion of the trial court," he said, exhaling smoke in a sigh. "That's me."

"Yes, Judge," said Watson.

"But the court may have overreached itself in dismissing the hate crime business. That's going to be your real battle. You will be closely questioned on Wisconsin versus Mitchell."

"I know, Judge."

"The statute in Wisconsin versus Mitchell is different from this federal statute for the reasons set forth in your papers. Make sure you are ready to tell them why."

"I will, Judge."

"Ms. Schweich, if we come back for trial on this, you will behave yourself in my courtroom. No antics."

"I will do my utmost," said Myrna.

The judge snorted. "And if your utmost isn't good enough, and you act like an asshole, then I will call you an asshole in front of your client, the jury, the press, your mother, and so on."

"I understand, Judge."

The judge swung slowly back around to his window and sighed. "That's Mark Twain's river," he said.

"It's very beautiful today," said Myrna.

"I'm old and tired," said Judge Stang. "Human vices and the voices of lawyers trouble my sleep. I am not at peace. Soon, I will be dead. Frank Donahue will be senator. And you will all still be back here talking. I'll be slumbering in eternal bliss and you'll be giving tongue to base human urges. Fools! I cry, Make me merry. But they do not oblige."

"We'll make plenty merry after a ruling like that, Judge," said Myrna. "May we be dismissed if the court has no further business with us?"

"*Ida!* Show the lawyers out and bring my tea."

CHAPTER 22

Myrna climbed into the backseat of Watson's Honda and briskly disrobed, making like Joan of Arc after battle, using the clothes hooks as racks for her litigator's panoply of armor: worsted wool breastplate, burgundy scarf gorget, chain mail of silk blouse, gray skirt of tasses.

Watson tried to drive, but the adrenaline of conquest was singing in his veins and giving him the shakes. He had expected to go down in flames nobly defending Whitlow's constitutional rights, and this expectation had become an antidote to his fear of failure. No shame in losing a loser of a case for a loser of a client. Nothing wrong with a novice practitioner training on the legal equivalent of a cadaver. A young lawyer could have done himself proud by winning just one of his sixteen pretrial motions. Even a symbolic win on a "mere technicality," as the newspapers love to say, would have been ample reward. But to win all sixteen motions? Including a motion to dismiss the hate crime charges? Speechless delirium. He had at least temporarily altered the destiny of a murderer, upset the plans of the federal government, frustrated a U.S. Attorney and candidate for the U.S. Senate, and probably enraged half of the community—all by arranging letters and words on the aquamarine screen of his monitor, then printing them out and filing them in court.

"Looks like you and Frank Donahue will go at it," she said.

"Frank Donahue? I figured Harper would argue it."

"No way, Harper is Mr. Hollywood. Helpless without a script. Donahue will handle this one himself. He'll want to make sure the Eighth Circuit understands how important this case is to the office of the U.S. Attorney and to the office of the Senate."

Watson held off imagining what it would be like to square off against Frank Donahue in the U.S. Court of Appeals and savored the victory in hand. In law school, drafting legal memoranda had won him good grades and prizes. In federal district court, prize memos conferred tactical advantages on guys like James Whitlow, a bigot on taxpayer-funded life support. For the time being, Watson's memos had thwarted the will of the People of the United States of America, who wanted Whitlow injected with something that would do the job quickly and not altogether painlessly.

From the backseat, Myrna gave a short seminar on client relations and the criminal law, while changing back into black grunge mufti and her Elvis Costello T-shirt.

At pivotal junctures in any case, she advised, the client needs to be informed. When the news is bad, the lawyer should never mention the subject of fees outstanding. But when bearing glad tidings of great joy, such as the pretrial motions massacre they'd just wrought on the government lawyers, the communication to the client should always include a reminder of the fees required to render such excellent services. In Myrna's considered opinion, it was time to advise their client that Dr. Green's fees were soaring. They had just won an important tactical battle in what could be a long war—a campaign that could very possibly include two appeals: one before trial, one after. He should seize the day and secure another bundle of fragrant, green bills.

"Again?" asked Watson. "Ask them for more money? Already?"

"Better now than after we win or lose an appeal or a trial, dude," she said. "After that we may not hear from them again. Then what? Do we send them a statement of fees for services rendered? Attention: Order of the Eagles, care of Santa's Workshop, North Pole. We don't even have their address. Just between you and me I don't want to know their address. We kicked the government's well-funded ass with nothing but our canvas-topped tennis shoes, and now we need more money for steel-toed boots."

In describing the current posture of the case to their client, she advised, Watson should be guardedly optimistic, carefully exuberant, if such a thing was possible. Celebrate triumph without raising false hopes. They still had the court of appeals to contend with, but the deference that the court of appeals was required to give to Judge Stang's evidentiary rulings—what lawyers called the "standard of review" on appeal—was so much in their favor that some, if not most, of the evidence of racial animus would not be admissible at trial. More important, they had thrown a procedural hurdle in the path of Donahue and Harper, who now had to write a brief and argue an appeal in the Eighth Circuit before they could even think about going to trial.

"See what happens when you do your job?" said Myrna. "I'm the first to work with opposing counsel, until they try to do me in the eye. When that happens, I smack the other lawyer upside the head with a riot stick and break his teeth. Then I tell him if he ever, ever disses me again, I will go banshee. I will go Harpy, succubus, fuckubus, you name it. I will show up in his worst nightmare, sink my talons into his back, strangle him with piano wire, gnaw off his scalp with my fangs." She stopped for a breath. "Am I too wrapped up in my work?"

The snap and hiss of a match igniting led him to believe she was administering another maintenance dose of nicotine. Then he smelled burning herbs.

"Myrna! Are you brain damaged? We are in the car, for the love of . . ."

"Celebrate," she croaked in the breathless whisper of a pothead who has learned to talk without exhaling. "We owe it to ourselves. We've made a real difference in the life of a poor, helpless, downtrodden, defenseless bigot." She swallowed a cough without losing her hit.

"Where did you get that?"

"My purse," she said.

Watson flashed on the session in chambers, where Myrna had pulled a cigarette instead of a cookie out of her purse as a reward for her command of the federal rules of evidence. So, not only was she reckless enough to fire up a joint in a moving automobile on a major thoroughfare in broad daylight, but she also had waltzed through metal detectors operated by court security officers; into a federal courthouse; past regional offices of the FBI, the DEA, the U.S. Attorney; and into federal district court, where she appeared before Judge Whittaker J. "Black Jack" Stang—Ivan the Terrible, the Prince of Darkness—all the while serenely in possession of a Class I narcotic.

He needed to finish this case and promptly reassess his post–Stern, Pale office arrangements.

She passed a thin, pink joint wrapped in strawberry rolling papers up to the front seat.

"In the car?" cried Watson, waving it away. "Do you want to get arrested and tossed into the cell next to Whitlow's?"

The notion so amused her she lost her hit in a series of spasmodic chuckles. "We have our lawyers with us, don't we?"

Watson kept glancing into the rearview mirror, scanning for cherry-topped avengers, managing to get his pulse back under control when he didn't see any. He berated Myrna again; he didn't care if she endangered her own career, but he did not appreciate her putting *his* ass in legal peril. The next time he looked up at the mirror, he noticed a gray sedan. Noticed it, because it had been there before, or so it seemed. A few minutes ago? A gray Ford? A Taurus? A Probe? Two serious-looking galoots—almost twins, dark hair, dark suits, dark sunglasses . . . make that mirrored sunglasses. They didn't seem to be talking, just staring straight ahead at . . . Had they been there before? He'd checked the mirror before turning up the ramp onto Highway 40. Was this the same gray car he'd seen then? Nah.

He changed lanes. The gray car followed.

"Uh, Myrna," he said, glancing again into the rearview mirror, "I'm not buzzing a cop, I'm not copping a buzz—I mean, maybe I'm having some contact paranoia. There's a car behind us, possibly following us. Two guys in suits and sunglasses."

Myrna calmly exhaled her last hit, put the roach out on her tongue, and swallowed it. "If they want me for possession, they'll need a warrant and a stomach pump. Don't gape in the mirror," she said. "The worst that can happen is you'll get a clinic on probable cause and auto searches from a leading expert."

She fished a compact out of her purse, opened it, and dabbed at the corner of her lips with a tissue.

"Couple a serious fucks in suits," she said, tilting the compact mirror. "You got automatic windows?"

"Yeah," said Watson, struggling to keep his eyes off the rearview. "I do. And power windows will help get rid of the smoke. But what about the big wad of cash from Buck's lawyer I have in the trunk?"

Myrna emitted a vocal call that seemed to originate from somewhere in their evolutionary past. "YOU KEEP THE MONEY IN THE TRUNK OF YOUR CAR?" she yelled. "And you're beating me over the head about having a hit of pot on me? Please advise that we have a container search on our hands here and not plain view!"

"It's still in the envelope it came in," he said. "You told me bank deposits look like *income* to the IRS," he protested, thinking—more like internally screaming—*Not only do I lose my job! Now I lose my law license!* Maybe Sheila will bring a bumper sticker home from school that says: DARE TO KEEP YOUR DAD OFF DRUGS. Or maybe he could show up on Parent Career Day for a short presentation on money laundering.

"I have about ten safety deposit boxes in different names," she said. "Remind me to show you how they work. In the meantime, make some big cracks in these windows back here, while I get this license number down. Missouri 5YW-77F."

Watson heard a click and beep as she powered up her cellular phone.

"I know a friendly Department of Motor Vehicles dispatcher with main database access," she said. "Got her kid off with a suspended sentence for a weapons charge."

"Where do I go?" asked Watson, steadfastly staring straight over the wheel and concentrating on the logo of a Bunny Bread delivery truck in front of them.

"That depends if behind us we have government goombahs or some other variety of big tuna. Don't look in the rearview. Turn on your blinker, make a lane switch, and check them in the sideview."

Watson signaled and hopped a lane. "Still there," he said.

"Real stealth bombers, these guys," she said. "They need a siren and a couple wide-load warning signs."

"They're closer," said Watson.

"Libby? Hey there. Myrna Schweich. Can't chat 'cause I got a small emergency here. Can ya run one for me? Yep. Missouri 5YW-77F. Metallic gray 1992 Taurus. Right. Johnny Laws? No? Registered to who?"

Watson crossed to the far right lane, dropped to fifty-five, and glanced in the sideview. The Taurus followed him to the right-hand lane and didn't pass.

"WHAT!" yelled Myrna. "Wake me up and say it again. No way. That's positive? Thanks, Libby. Gotta go."

Another beep and click when she turned off the phone.

"Cops?" asked Watson, doing an admirable job of keeping his voice from shaking.

"Beat me naked with a bat," said Myrna. "Those plates . . . That car is registered to James and Mary Whitlow, 4279 Fairmont, Dogtown, South St. Louis. New registration. Not more than three days old."

"Not possible," said Watson, a glimpse in the mirror. Eerie visual disturbances, his brain metabolism suddenly accelerating, burning some new fuel mix of fight-or-flight secretions. The windshield was becoming a huge, wraparound, high-resolution video monitor, the rearview mirror a mini-live-action video inset. Level 5 in a 3-D multimedia experience called Lawyer Warriors. The clues coming onto the screen and over the audio interrupts were impossibly contrived and gamelike. And behind him, his virtual guide, a dwarf with red hair, some yappy know-it-all on the order of Microsoft's Bob, was telling him how to destroy their Level 5 enemies, so they could advance to Level 6.

"Can't be Whitlow's car," he said, hoping sheer force of will might warp reality back into a narrative that made some sense. Then he recalled his interview with Whitlow and Myrna's recitation of Dirt's report: Lucy, the neighborhood watcher and mistress of towing—hadn't she confirmed that Whitlow's car was a Ford Taurus? And the tow lot lady? *Title and a photo ID . . . and you will have to register it, pay any back taxes and licensing fees. Then, it's yours.*

"Does your dispatcher ever make mistakes?" asked Watson.

"Not so far," said Myrna. "You heard me ask her twice. And it ain't reported stolen either."

"Whitlow's car is following us," said Watson. He dropped all pretense and stared into the rearview mirror at two men in suits and shades, following him in his client's car. Maybe they had stolen it. His delight at escaping arrest was so intoxicating, he almost assumed his Lawyer Warrior avatar stance, ready to defend his client's property. What if he turned the car around, went back downtown, and filed an action for recaption and repossession? That would show them!

"Looks like somebody got the car out of the impound lot," said Myrna, whipping out her compact for another look. "Musta been Mary Whitlow. But neither of them look like they'd take being called Mary too well."

Her comment inspired two or three seconds of tense, prestorm silence followed by a burst of heat lightning in both their brains.

"Order of the Eagles!" they both cried.

"Shit," she said. "Militia goons. Gotta be, right? The cops wouldn't drive a suspect's car around and fuck up evidence."

"Gee," said Watson. "Do you suppose whoever it is has opened the trunk?"

Another beep and click from her cellular phone.

"Where do I go?" asked Watson. "We drove past Big Bend and we're coming up on Hanley."

"Get off anywhere you want. I'm calling the office. I'll tell you where to go in a . . . Tilly? What's happening? No, hold the messages. Anybody been there to see me? Two guys in suits and sunglasses? You told them I was in court? No, Tilly. I wish it was the FBI. Be there in a sec."

"Where to?" he asked, taking the Hanley exit, and checking the side-view as the Taurus followed them.

"They know where we live," she said. "They've already been there."

"And?" he asked.

"And what?" she said crossly, eyeballing her compact mirror again while pretending to tease an eyelash. "Go back to the office and we'll talk to them. That's what."

Watson cruised down Hanley trying to think of a polite way to ask if he could just drop her off. Instead he drove to the parking lot behind the building, trying to convince himself that gallantry and chivalry were useless vestiges, especially out of place here, where Myrna represented the gender in charge. He parked his Honda in the usual spot. The Taurus slid into a metered space on the street and waited.

"Don't give them the hairy eyeball search," said Myrna, gathering up her clothes and purse and walking toward the back door of their building. "Just get inside."

Watson locked the Honda with his remote and lingered momentarily, thinking that if his car were a computer file or a desktop object, he could set an extended attribute or an archive bit, and then he would be able to tell if anyone tampered with it in his absence. Or if the parking lot were the desktop of an operating system, he could just lock up the whole thing with a screensaver, so that no one could get into it without typing in the password. He was suddenly alarmed at the uselessness of his own thoughts, staring blankly at a car, wishing it was not a real car but an object on the colorful, orderly, well-maintained desktop of his operating system. . . . Clutch thinking. A real-world crisis manager.

"*Joe,*" said Myrna sharply, the look on her face expressing concern for his mental health.

"You don't think they'll, uh, do anything to the car, do you?"

"Not unless I hire them to do the job," she muttered. "Get inside."

The door into the building faced west. As they approached it, he kept waiting for a bullet to enter the back of his skull. Probably, he would not even feel it—a flash of light inside his brain—and plush curtains of blood would fall slowly over his eyesight, his matinee video screens would go blank for good.

When he opened the glass door and walked inside, the afternoon sun cast a shadow of his outstretched arm holding the door for Myrna, of his suited torso; the clean lines of his silhouette fell spread-eagle on the floor of the entryway like the outline of a fallen victim at a crime scene.

"*Some serious motherfucking professionals did this,*" the homicide detective would say. "*Probably Order of the Eagles, like their client. Birds of a feather. These two lawyer fucks probably never knew what happened. When those hollowpoint bullets hit the brain stem, they open your head like a fucking cantaloupe.*"

A split-second ejection to the afterlife. No time to make a confession or think about the meaning of life. It just stops, and then coarse people stand around talking about your remains, how you got what you deserved because you took too many risks, served the wrong clients, picked the wrong side, ate the wrong foods, smoked, and drank too much. Death—the ultimate defeat in the evolutionary fitness contest.

Myrna jangled her keys and popped the locks on her office door, tossed her clothes and purse on a chair, then walked around her desk and pulled open the big lower drawer. She plucked out a black shoulder holster, so delicate it looked like a one-cup leather bra. She slipped into it and yanked open the top drawer, pulled out a Smith & Wesson .357, snapped a clip into it, and popped off the safety.

Watson watched, unsure whether the resolute calm she displayed in arming herself inspired confidence or terror. It appeared that there was at least some chance that real bullets could soon be discharged with the attendant ambient audio of actual explosions.

"Jacket," she said, pointing at the wall behind the door, where a black blazer hung on her coatrack. He threw it to her. It matched her baggy black pants and covered the weapon. She faced him and patted under her arm.

"Ready?" she asked him. He nodded. She put her arms down, comically splayed and wiggled her itchy fingers, then drew the weapon, her right hand instantly retrieving it from under her jacket. She crouched into a standard two-handed shooting stance, the gun pointed at the peephole of the door.

"The clip holds eighteen Equal Rights Amendments," she said, tucking the weapon back into her holster.

Her phone emitted a single trill.

"Hi, Tilly. Two gentlemen? To see Joe? Do they have an appointment?" She held the phone away and smoothed her jacket over the bump of the holstered weapon. "Tell them we are preparing for a trial. They should make an appointment and leave their names."

Myrna paused, fished out a cigarette, and lit it with the skull lighter. She exhaled. "An emergency? Tell them my whole life is one big emergency, and five minutes is all they get. Send them to my place."

She hung up, tugged down her sleeves, and patted the jacket again. She stood behind her desk, lifted a piece of paper, and pretended to be reading it.

Two knocks.

"Yeah," she said. "Come hither."

The door opened. Watson recognized the top halves of them from his rearview mirror. Two large men, still in shades, leaned in.

"Joseph Watson?" said the first one, aiming black lenses in his direction.

"Yeah," said Joe. "Why?" He tried to sound tough and annoyed, a hard-bitten criminal lawyer who would never have worked at Stern, Pale, where visitors in suits and ties were greeted with "How can we help you?"

Would they reach for their weapons now? His only real-world referents for the physical specimens standing in the doorway came from Scorsese movies and video games—Greek SlaughterHouse and CarnageMaster. Multimedia violence and movie bloodshed were the closest he had ever come to physical danger. Every other threat he'd encountered in real, adult life had to do with purely psychological or intellectual threats, marital turbulence, academic performance, career-path obstructions.

The man's nostrils flared slightly. Watson instinctively moved his hand in search of a trackball or a joystick, something to click on so he could fire his turbocharged lasers and blow big, jagged holes in their virtual flesh. *Eat flaming death, Droids! I am CarnageMaster!*

Galoot number one walked in, folded his hands in front of him, and waited for his partner to shut the door and come alongside with a black leather briefcase in tow. Even close up, they looked alike—not quite twins, but probably brothers in more than crime. It was hard to tell with no eyes to look at. Stocky two-hundred-pounders, both straining at the seams to move up a size into new dark-blue and black suits. Above the shades, their hair was slicked straight back with scented styling gel, and below them, mugs with double chins. Tastefully subdued ties were done up just so on cotton oxfords with clean and neatly buttoned cuffs and collars. They had the look of former college athletes who, after fifteen years of selling insurance and buying a thousand or so twelve-packs, had gone into law enforcement or found a suitable militia and were now ready to remind the world about patriotism and decency and fighting for what is right.

Their sunglasses were busy with reflections of the office, including occasional tiny postage-stamp images of Watson and Myrna, swelling and shrinking in the convexity of the black lenses, swirling like those thumbnail animated Java applets you see in Web sites.

"We need to talk about James Whitlow's case," said the same bruiser, the one on Watson's right, who so far was the talking half and seemed to be carrying less fat and more muscle than the retiring mesomorph on the left, who, upon closer inspection, was also distinguished by a complexion that looked like a flesh-tone satellite photo of a lunar landscape. Introductions seemed unlikely, so Watson provisionally named the lead, talking male Alpha and the clone beast in tow Beta.

"If you gentlemen made an appointment, it's not on our calendar," said Myrna. "You are . . . ?"

"Ma'am, we work for some friends of Jimmy Whitlow," said Alpha, sounding almost polite, turning his head in Joe's direction. "The friends he told you might be in a position to help pay his lawyer fees."

His accent was somewhere between Midwestern and Southern, maybe Cape Girardeau, Rush Limbaugh's hometown, or at most, the boot heel, damn near Arkansas.

Joe opened his mouth even though he had no intention of saying anything. Myrna's face morphed into a great big "Say what?"

"Don't talk to these guys, Joe," said Myrna. "Friends of Jimmy Whitlow? Lawyer fees? You guys come in here asking about alleged clients? To me that means you are either from outer space or else you are cops."

Beta flinched and spoke for the first time. "We ain't cops," he said suddenly, as if this were too much slander for any man to bear. He twitched again, seeming to show conscientious restraint in not reaching for his weapon; then his vocal cords rumbled somewhere deep in his thick neck. Alpha turned his head slowly around, an apparent reminder to his associate about who was going to do the talking.

Myrna's back talk made Watson nervous. He was wondering if she shouldn't be polite and let old Beta vent a little, if it was a choice between that and him discharging bullets. The man's acne may have occasioned an unhappy adolescence and chronic low self-esteem. Watson wanted to help Beta feel better about himself, manage his anger, talk about his feelings.

"You guys got wires on?" asked Myrna. "Christ, you might as well pull out those gold badges and use 'em for tiepins. Undercover from Hell to breakfast, Joe."

"Lady," said Alpha, "we ain't cops. We work for some friends of Jimmy Whitlow. We can't get to him anymore, because the feds took him to Minnesota."

"Cops, robbers, meter readers, Jehovah's Witnesses, good fathers, war veterans," said Myrna. "I got no idea. I take it you ain't showing IDs. You want to tell us something? We'll listen and see does it make sense, but we don't know anything about any friends of Jimmy Whitlow. And we don't know sheep shit from Tootsie Rolls about anybody paying anybody's lawyer fees."

Alpha's shoes creaked when he shifted his weight and rolled his shoulders like a gorilla, except that he was too swollen around the middle to be a primate; he and his brother were more like dark polar bears, but their thickness and ursine stolidity seemed to be animated by intelligences a rung above gorilloid.

"I'll be brief," Alpha said, as politely as a salesperson making a cold call. "Tell Jimmy Whitlow we are missing the delivery. And we need to know who took it. Him? Or her? Or somebody else? Because until we find that out, we ain't paying one dollar for nobody's lawyer fees."

Myrna put one hand to her forehead and the other out in mock protest. "Whoa. Too much, too fast for me. Joe, get a pen and write this stuff down. A delivery of something, you say? And somebody paying lawyer fees?"

"I didn't say that," said Alpha. "I said nobody is going to pay a dollar until we get back what's missing and find out who took it."

Myrna froze and mulled that one over for all of second. "Oh," she said, fetching her cigarette from the ashtray for a puff. "I thought you were trying to say somebody had paid up Jimmy Whitlow's lawyer fees. We still owe Dr. Green a lot of money, and we just bought ourselves a pretrial appeal." Her voice dropped as she artfully slipped the name into her sentence. Her manner was casual, but she glanced through smoke and watched Alpha's response.

"I said," Alpha repeated, flushing slightly, "we don't pay one dollar of lawyer fees until we get a straight story and both briefcases." Then he bowed slightly and asked, "Who's Dr. Green?" His manner was deferential, as if he would be the first to admit that he might not have the right to know.

Watson was beginning to understand that these were bad guys who had been to charm school, where they had been trained to present the best possible front at all times, the better to conceal malignant hatreds and ugly social agendas. If they could all go out for drinks and dinner, Watson would probably go home convinced that some synergistic mix of hatred and patriotism was the answer to our nation's problems.

Myrna took a long look at what she could see of Alpha's face, then she smacked herself in the head with her palm. "I am up-fucking big time," she said. "Dr. Green is our expert in another case. Right, Joe? What is it, that prisoners' rights case, ain't it?

Joe nodded.

"Ai, yi, yi," said Myrna. "So many cases. Sorry, boys, I get them mixed up."

"You are one of them free appointment lawyers, right?" Alpha asked, turning suddenly in Joe's direction. "Jimmy ain't paying you, is he? Buck ain't giving you money, is he?"

Watson glanced at Myrna. "The court appointed me to represent James Whitlow," said Joe.

"What about you?" said Alpha, wheeling his mirror shades in Myrna's direction. "I guess we pretty well know you don't work for nothing."

Myrna blew a ribbon of smoke in Alpha's direction. "Joe's a buddy. He used to work for me. I'm helping him out. Giving him some advice. That OK with you?"

Alpha set his jaw and said, "We got word that Jimmy needed money for investigators and experts and such. We can't help Jimmy Whitlow with lawyer fees until we find out what happened to the delivery."

"Happened?" asked Myrna.

The two visored heads turned together again.

"When Jimmy was in Des Peres County," said Alpha, "we asked him what happened to the briefcases, and he told us his wife put them in the trunk of his car after the . . . person died, and before the cops came."

"No shit?" said Myrna.

"Jimmy said she *said* she put them in the trunk of the car," inserted Beta, who was apparently eager to display his alertness to the nuances of hearsay. "He didn't actually *see* her put them in the car. He was in the house. He didn't see what she done with them."

Alpha's shoes creaked again when he turned to look at Beta, using body language meant to convince his junior partner that his next interruption would be his last.

"Jimmy claims he told her to put the briefcases in the trunk," said Alpha by way of clarification. "So then we went to Miss Mary. And we said, 'Where's the briefcases?' And she said, 'Jimmy put them in the trunk of the car.' "

"Pretty easy so far," said Myrna. "Sounds like the briefcases are in the trunk of the car."

"*Were* in the trunk, maybe," said Alpha. "The car got towed and Miss Mary had to go get it out. So we offered to follow her when she went to fetch it. She ran into some trouble there because it weren't registered and she had to dig around back at the house to find the title. Next day, we followed her back out to get the car and sort of helped her look in the trunk, where we found *one* empty briefcase."

Beta flourished the black leather briefcase, popped the locks on it, and splayed it open on Myrna's desk.

"Empty," he said. "Nothing in it but a fucking calculator."

Watson saw a device with a liquid crystal display and a keypad protruding from the flap in the divider. It was no calculator, but it looked familiar. He'd seen it before, or maybe a picture of it. A news photo?

"So we got how many missing briefcases?" asked Myrna. "Two? Three? Joe, are you getting this down? We gonna have to send a message from these gentlemen to Jimmy Whitlow."

Joe grabbed a legal pad and mumbled, "He says she says she put them in the trunk of the car. Three briefcases."

"I never said it was three briefcases," said Alpha. "It's *two* briefcases." He turned and looked at his companion. "Well, really I guess we are talking about one briefcase. That there is the other one, which we found in the trunk of the car, but there ain't nothing in it. Which means somebody put everything into one briefcase and took it out of the car, or maybe never even put it in the car."

"Stop right there," said Myrna. "What car?"

The heads turned together.

"We got Jimmy's car," said Alpha. "We got one briefcase. But there ain't nothing in it. All of it is missing, and we want it back."

"Got that, Joe?" asked Myrna. "They want *all of it* back."

Alpha bristled, apparently reviewing the conversation so far and concluding he'd said too much.

"Tell Jimmy Whitlow, no lawyer money until we get it back with a straight story about what happened. If not, he better be damn sure he don't know where it is."

"You bet," said Myrna. "And we will tell Jimmy Whitlow everything you told us to tell him. Is there a number he can call?"

Alpha stared, too dumb to tell whether Myrna was being smart with him. "He knows how to reach us," he said.

Watson cleared his throat and carefully acknowledged Beta with a deferential glance before addressing Alpha. "If the cops had the car towed, maybe they took whatever was in the briefcases. Is that possible?"

Both men stiffened, and their faces blanked in the throes of radical new ideas.

"Uh," said Alpha, "we don't know for sure, but we don't think it was the cops who had the car towed."

"Why?" jeered Myrna. "Because they didn't send you a fucking letter? If the cops took it, they are probably looking for the guys who are looking for whatever is missing. Or maybe they are asking Mary Whitlow about what they found in the trunk of her car. And maybe she is telling them that you are looking for what they got out of the trunk of the car. Anything is possible."

"What about Buck?" asked Alpha. "Have you talked to Buck?"

"Buck?" said Myrna. "Who's Buck?"

Alpha looked at Beta, then bore down on Myrna. "Lady, I said we ain't cops. So cut the crap. Mary Whitlow claims that Buck talked to Jimmy about all of this. And that means we want to talk to Buck. But it seems that Buck is suddenly out of town. So, if Buck calls you, you tell him to call us."

"Buck," said Myrna flatly.

Alpha fixed his gaze on Myrna. "Buck ain't paying you, is he?"

"Nobody pays me," said Myrna. "As soon as they do, I'm gonna get myself a real office instead of this shithole."

"We figure he might call you because you got him out of trouble last time," said Alpha.

Myrna shrugged and glanced at Joe. "Whatever you say, gentlemen. If anybody named Buck calls we will tell him two big guys are looking for him."

Alpha motioned toward the door and let Beta go first. Then he grabbed the doorknob, turned, and said, "And if we don't hear from Jimmy and Buck real soon, we will come back here."

The door shut. Myrna heaved a big sigh through pursed lips and puffed cheeks. They both tiptoed to the door and listened to the men grunting to each other and leaving through the back door.

"Fuck me a new asshole," she whispered.

Watson was shaking all over and wondering where he could find some alcohol, like right away. Then, he would need a phone to call Sandra and tell her she had been right. Yes, honey! Darling! *You were right!* I have endangered myself, my career, my home, my children. I am going back to Stern, Pale on my hands and knees. I temporarily lost my mind. Synaptic brownout. I was not myself. I was beside myself, watching myself. Somebody else was moving my entire body.

"Militia, right?" hissed Watson.

"Maybe *patriots* would be a better word," she said, "since, according to Harper, your client is one of them."

"Who's paying us if they aren't?" asked Watson. "And *you*," he said, anger getting the better of fear. "You're Buck's lawyer. You sent me that letter."

Myrna looked away and mumbled something, then marched over and grabbed the Gitanes from her desktop.

She looked at him hard, wrinkled her nose, and took a deep breath.

"Joey, sit down," she said, as she walked around to the other side of her desk. "We need to talk a little."

Her tone suggested they had more than a little to talk about, and he didn't like the partneresque maneuver of retreating to the control side of a desk.

"I told you how the criminal bar sticks together when the prosecutors and the press and the IRS come around wanting to examine our billing records and seeking privileged information about who is paying who. Well . . ."

"Well what?" asked Watson. "I'm not a prosecutor or the IRS."

"Buck sorta called me after Jimmy Whitlow got arrested. You were still down at Stern, Pale."

"Buck called you?"

"Yeah," said Myrna, "because this friend of his had been arrested for killing a black. Money might be available, but it would be the kind of money the government couldn't know about. I couldn't take the case, because then the government might try to hook Jimmy up with Buck and the paintball warriors, because awhile ago I represented Buck on a little weapons charge, which only happened because Buck ended up in a building that had some rocket-propelled grenades and a shoulder-launched surface-to-air missile in it. God as my witness, they weren't his. He didn't even know they were there! Anyway the government floated some conspiracy shit, trying to say Buck was one of these Eagle Warriors or whatever. And me and the other lawyers got them off. Case closed."

"Why didn't you tell me about this?" asked Watson.

"I didn't know!" she said. "Buck said it was just a regular fuckup. Crime of passion. No militia business. Cash money. But we needed to be careful because . . ."

"Because Jimmy Whitlow *belongs* to the fucking militia, right?" yelled Watson, almost hitting a woman.

"I don't remember," she said. "I don't think he said it that way. Anyway, then we found out you got appointed, and I thought, Small world! And we started thinking could you maybe help," she faltered, "or better, could we maybe help *you* with the case. And then we started thinking, what if those Stern, Pale white-shoe bastards started pressuring you and what if you couldn't devote enough time to the case? And then Buck sorta let it be known that this money could be made available. 'Course, I never ask where money is coming from, but I sorta let Buck know that you probably needed money. Especially if it came to pass that you would have to quit the big firm."

Watson felt his internal temperature drop with the chilly realization that yet another professional was using him—for his own good, of course. And now, here was the professional equivalent of his big sister telling him he was sorta, kinda, something like a marionette on a stage run by militia defense lawyers.

"What else did you sorta tell them?"

"Well, really it was Buck doing the telling," she said. "He knew you had been appointed. I said I knew you, and he said there were certain interested parties."

"Parties interested in?"

"Jimmy Whitlow," she said, reaching for the Gitanes. "And Buck sorta wanted to know what kind of a job you would do. And I said, of course, I thought you would do a great job on the research and writing angles, because you had done research and writing for me."

She lit up and inhaled.

"And?" asked Watson.

"And he sorta said, 'Yeah, but what if Jimmy Whitlow had really done it? Would Joe still be all fired up on the con law issues? Would he still go the extra mile on the research if there was some evidence about how maybe Jimmy Whitlow had . . .' "

"Killed a black guy because he hates black people," said Watson, feeling his face get hot.

"Joey," she pleaded. "He was probably just talking about the killing part or the militia business. I got no idea! I'm every bit as much in the dark on this as you. I thought the Eagle Scouts were paying us! Like I said, I don't ask money questions. Buck's pulling some shit. Or your client is pulling some shit. Or the Eagle boys are pulling some shit. All I told Buck was that maybe you wouldn't be working in a place like that if you had more money, which would give you a choice in the matter."

"You told them I could be bought?"

"I told them you'd probably rather be doing something else. Criminal law. Isn't that what you told me? Didn't we used to talk about that? Before the wife took charge of your career?"

He felt a shadow fall somewhere behind his eyes.

"Whoops," she said. "That was not what I meant to say."

"Who's *them* and why didn't you tell me about *them* before?"

"Them who?" she said. "You think I know? It ain't them, apparently. It's fucking Buck. Buck is fucking me. He's fucking you. The only person he ain't fucking as near as I can tell is Jimmy Whitlow. I didn't know anything about any missing briefcase. Maybe Mary Whitlow has the briefcase. Maybe the cops have the briefcase!" she exulted. "By the way, put your feelings aside and let me say, that was pure genius, Joey. I don't know for sure, but you may have saved your client's life and damn near resolved the case with one crucial remark. Brilliant!"

"You told them I could be bought," he said bitterly.

"Joey, you ain't a hard guy to get to know. You sorta play the ingenue, but I told them I didn't know how hard you'd be working for old Whitlow if there was any indication that, let's say, if there was evidence that he . . ."

"And now you're going to tell me there *is* some evidence of that?"

"Mother of Christ, no!" she said. "I told you every idea I got about what happened." She patted another manila folder and teased him with a look. "And I got some new ideas now, and some more good dirt from the Dirt-Meister. I guarantee you, between Dirt and me and you, we'll figure out what the fuck happened." Her eyes brightened. "Or you'll kick so much butt in the court of appeals it won't matter what really happened."

"I don't work for you," said Watson. He pointed a rigid finger at her. "I quit."

"Quit what?" she asked. "You can't quit the case. You entered your appearance as retained counsel."

"Because you told me to!" Watson shouted. "No, I quit you. I need to find another place to work."

"Don't do that," she cried. "Aren't ya even curious? I mean, what about Dirt? You gonna fire him, too? Your investigator? Without whom we would know next to nothing? You'd be cutting off your dick to spite your balls, or however it goes. You'd be cutting off the pros to spite your case." She patted the manila again.

His eyes went from the manila to the briefcase Beta had left on Myrna's desk. Hers followed. Watson walked over to it and reached out to pick it up.

"Uh-uh," she said, reaching into her desk drawer and pulling out a box of latex gloves. She peeled off a left and a right and handed them to him.

"See, you need me. Even if I am—"

"You are a bitch," said Watson.

She put one hand on her breast and sketched a theatrical flourish with the other, as if she were a heroine in a blood-and-thunder melodrama. She dabbed at the corner of her eye with the back of her wrist. "You deserve better." Then she made Groucho eyebrows and added, "But you won't find better, because I'm the best in town."

"Best liar, maybe." He put on the gloves and gently removed the keypad device from the briefcase. He recognized it from the *Post-Dispatch* photo of Elvin holding it up. The same letters VTD at upper left. "Voice Transcription Device."

"A Tireless Advocate of Using Technology to Overcome Disabilities," he recalled from the caption below the photo.

"That's how they talked to each other," said Watson.

Myrna blew a thin stream of smoke from the corner of her mouth and looked at the VTD. "Talk? You mean that TDD thing that goes over the phone lines?"

"No, not the TDD—the VTD," said Watson. "Mary didn't know sign language. Elvin was deaf. That is a Voice Transcription Device. It prints spoken words on a screen. If it was on during his last visit, then—"

They looked at each other.

"If it was on when he was . . . in the Whitlow house," said Watson. "If it was left on, the battery's dead. But it probably has an autosave feature that stores whatever is in memory before the battery dies. Just like a laptop."

Watson extended a gloved finger toward the button on the device that said POWER.

"Don't fuck with it," she said. "We need to have a VTD party with witnesses. We call the company that made the thing and have them send out a local service or tech person. Get a notary public or a nun in here to watch. We get it dusted to see who all has touched it besides Elvin. Then we have lots of witnesses about the state of the device when it was powered back up."

As usual, she was right, and he despised her for it.

"I gotta warn you," she said. "Before you go powering that thing on and printing it, you better know that whatever you get becomes evidence. For better or worse, for richer or poorer. There's every chance you'll end up having to turn it over to the other side. All of it, no matter what it says. Might be something you want to ask your client about. *Before* you turn it on, or print it out."

"I'll ask him," said Watson grimly.

She smiled at him. "Don't hate me for being a lawyer, Joey. I can't help it."

He gingerly tucked the VTD back into the briefcase, folded it shut but left the latches open, and left for his office, ignoring her as she crooned, "It's really, really good. I can't believe you don't want to know what it is."

He went into his office, resolving to call Sandra and surrender himself to her and the kids. He could go home and rejoice in the bosom of his family. No hate criminals or clients, no mendacious lawyers, no terrifying judges or combative government lawyers, no insidiously polite militia goons (unless they decided to come to his house and kidnap the children!).

Inside, he found a multipage fax spindled on the tray of his machine. An Ignatius Medical Center transmittal sheet and an attached printed form with blanks filled in by handwriting. "Consent to Emergency Medical Treatment." The message box on the fax cover sheet was from Rachel:

> Joe, tried to call twice today. As you can see from the attached, James Whitlow is going into surgery tomorrow morning at six A.M. to remove the subarachnoid cyst.
>
> Possible risks. He consented to any and all necessary treatment on the stipulation that postsurgical rehab and confinement be in a federal medical facility, with recommendations for leniency at sentencing in the event of a conviction. I think we can make a decent argument, based upon a reasonable degree of medical certainty, that this lesion was wholly or partly responsible for any impulsive or antisocial tendencies.
>
> After surgery, he'll be transported back here to our secure psychiatric rehab wing. I'll get regular updates by phone and file transfers, so call for information.
>
> What happened in court?
>
> RP

Chapter 23

Rachel Palmquist didn't have to wait long to find out what happened in court; neither did the rest of St. Louis. A headline in thirty-six-point type announced it first thing next morning: HATE CHARGES DISMISSED IN MURDER OF DEAF MINORITY. The *Post-Dispatch* recycled the original photo of Whitlow from the first day of his arrest, handcuffed and scowling with his best white-trash, vinegar puss, over the caption: "Technicalities May Free Accused Hate Killer."

Watson read the article, experiencing a peculiar mixture of pride and despair, wondering where he would turn for help now that his mentor, his would-be mistress, and his wife had all betrayed him. If nothing else, he was charming all the important women in his life.

He'd tried unsuccessfully to call Whitlow at the federal medical center in Minnesota twice last night. This morning, by the time he made it through the phone menus and voice-mail mazes to a human being, Whitlow was already under the knife. It would be several days at least before his client would be able to answer questions about missing briefcases.

The news story included a thumbnail bio on Joseph Watson, "appointed by Federal District Judge Whittaker J. Stang to defend James Whitlow, an indigent, who had been charged under federal hate crime laws in the slaying of Elvin Brawley, a deaf poet and leader of the black community." Even Watson's employment arrangements were front-page news: "Joseph Watson, a graduate of Ignatius Law School's class of 2001, was appointed to the high-profile hate crime case while still an associate at the corporate law firm of Stern, Pale & Covin. Sources say that when the case began to take up almost all of Mr. Watson's time, the young lawyer resigned to devote himself full-time to the defense of James Whitlow and to start his own practice."

Resigned? No use chasing that one down. Arthur Mahoney would blame it on the reporter's misunderstanding of Stern, Pale's plain-vanilla, bias-free, noncommittal Notification of Employment Status change—the same one used to describe the departure of any lawyer from the firm. A confirming letter would arrive soon after containing the exact wording of the statement as issued by the firm and its management. And no use arguing with the gymnastic journalist who reported the dismissal of some but not all charges as "freeing" a hate criminal. Most of St. Louis would come away from the story with the impression that some rookie tyro lawyer named Watson had used lawyer tricks to grab some publicity and spring a homicidal racist from prison. Concerned Citizens would be out in force with cellular phones on the lookout for a white patriot waving an AR-15 semi, screaming racial epithets, and looking for children of color.

A sidebar displayed a chronology of Whitlow's past, including a reprise of the water-tower swastika incident and a few tantalizing morsels from an "anonymous source in the U.S. Attorney's office" about how investigators were pursuing the defendant's "possible links to the white supremacist militia group known as the Order of the Eagles, a right-wing hate group, widely reputed to be responsible for the 1999 Washington, D.C., blast in which a car bomb killed two government officials and injured many pedestrians in front of the Department of Education."

Pages two and three had more articles on hate crimes and how they were destroying the social fabric of the entire nation. More congressional hearings loomed on the political horizons, because it was an election year, and the escalating frequency of hate crimes was a volatile topic on the talk show circuit, in the papers, and on the public's mind.

The biggest, most dramatic photo (shot from below) was of Frank Donahue, U.S. Attorney, his fist shaking, wrath contorting his face, as he railed against racism and hate crimes on the courthouse steps, over the caption "Hate Criminals Beware":

Shortly after the ruling, U.S. Attorney Frank Donahue, front-runner in the upcoming race for Missouri's open Senate seat, raised his orator's voice and mustered all of his renowned eloquence to decry the wave of hate crimes sweeping the nation. "I am here to put bigots, racists, gender criminals, abusers of children and despisers of the disabled on notice that my tour of duty as a United States Attorney is not over yet. I intend to devote myself and the powers of my office to punishing those who terrorize minority victims and express their hatred of differences by perpetrating violent crimes on those least able to protect themselves.

"Crimes committed out of hatred against a person or group of persons because of their protected characteristics are federal crimes," said Donahue. "Congress passed these laws, and the people want them enforced. In my opinion, James Whitlow killed a hearing-impaired African-American man first with his words and then with bullets. Two crimes, not one. Judge Stang's ruling says to the people of this community: Hate doesn't matter. I say hate *does* matter to the people who are victimized by it."

Members of Mr. Donahue's staff described Judge Stang's ruling as a temporary setback based upon the court's "erroneous and highly theoretical interpretations of the First Amendment and certain evidentiary rules."

To Watson's dismay, Frank Donahue's front-page tirade was a mere exchange of pleasantries in the sunny vestibules of the community's collective consciousness compared to the toilets of psychic outrage waiting for him back on the op-ed page.

A local columnist lit into Watson under the heading: "How Does It Feel, Attorney Watson?" The article took the form of a series of rhetorical questions aimed at his missing sense of decency:

How does it feel knowing that you are defending bigotry, hatred, and violence?

How does it feel knowing that your constitutional shenanigans have allowed a racist hate-monger to murder a man because of his skin color and go free?

How does it feel knowing that your labors have aided and abetted a bigot, a man who deprived his own deaf child of American Sign Language?

How does it feel knowing that you will be holding this bully's coat for him, so he can go off and kill again in the name of hatred?

How does it feel when you try to sleep at night, Mr. Watson?

If it's any consolation, St. Louis sleeps no better than you do, because we know that, with your help, a bigot seething with hatred will soon walk the streets again.

He skimmed over two letters to the editor on the opposite page, one from a proponent of the Violence Against Women Act, the other written by a spokesperson from Americans for a Hate-Free America. He stopped answering his phone after a journalist called to ask if he would have any compunctions about representing the Ku Klux Klan, assuming the fee was in line.

Sandra would read this newspaper, he thought. And, what? Weep? Curse his bones? *"Look, kids, Daddy's picture is in the paper again. He's really doing well representing racist murderers. And look where it says that he may get a chance to work for Lorenzo 'Bloody Turk' Garroti and the Mob. Wouldn't that be something? Aren't you proud?"* He felt another sudden, visceral urge to return to his days of being a nice, uncomplicated computerized legal research expert. Papa Joe Provider, Esq., Mr. Needle in the Haystack for the partners needing supporting case law. A lotus-eater staring blissfully into a screenful of sumptuous icons, lounging around, wired into his workstation, manipulating files, searching databases, cutting, pasting, storing, retrieving. Instead of being hanged in effigy on the front page of the *Post-Dispatch,* he could go back to creating motions and briefs, papers that disappeared into the great maw of nameless civil litigation and transported their author to wealth and oblivion.

And at the end of very long days, he could go home, where he would once again be revered for being sensible, even-tempered, steady. He and Sandra would grow old, beaming wise smiles at each other from opposite sides of the fireplace, quietly watching their Real Money double every seven years according to the Rule of Sevens. Instead of being *in* the *Post-Dispatch,* he could be peacefully reading it in a hot tub out in Ladue. *"Honey? Did you see where the long bond is up six ticks, today? We're still fifteen per in the bond fund? Or did we shift into gold futures?"*

He had secured a major strategic victory using nothing but the mighty keyboard. A definite high, but if he tried to call Sandra on the outside chance that she might share some small part of his giddy triumph, R.J. or his mother-in-law might answer instead. So he grabbed a piece of his new stationery and tried to write a version of the sentiments that had swept through his brain after the departure of Alpha and Beta: "Honey! Darling! YOU WERE RIGHT! I have endangered myself, my career, my home, my children. I am going back to Stern, Pale on my hands and knees. I temporarily lost my mind . . ."

He read that one over and threw it away. Then he took a new piece of stationery and wrote: "I love you. I miss you. Joe."

Better, he thought. A genuine, noble sentiment, sufficiently ill-defined to satisfy the lawyer in him, containing nothing that would get him into trouble during a subsequent argument.

When he tried to reach Rachel for some celebratory cheer, he had to make do with a voice-mail greeting. He pressed 0 for operator and paged her. No luck. She was probably deep inside a rat brain and unable to make it to the phone. Brain surgery on his client? Nice of her to call and seek permission. From the sounds of it, Whitlow had consented to anything and everything on the promise of being kept out of Des Peres County jail.

He left her a voice-mail message demanding an explanation for the rush to surgery. What he got for an answer was another impersonal E-mail:

Joe:

Stacked up here. Can't call.

Arachnoid cyst in the left Sylvian fissure effacing ventral frontal, anterior temporal, and insular cortical gyri and displacing the associated cerebral vasculature, restricting blood flow, lowering metabolism, resulting in impairment of the frontal 'executive functions' that control violent or emotional impulses.

Lesion potentially serious. Removal or shunting indicated. Won't know until they get in there and look at it. Not worth risk of waiting.

Whitlow due back here in our facility in ten to fourteen days.

RP

The Eighth Circuit had put the case on a fast track. Briefs due in ten days; oral arguments five days later. An expedited, interlocutory appeal. The schedule suited Watson, because he'd already researched the law to the ends of the on-line services and had written the brief four or five times in his head, not to mention his pretrial motions on essentially the same subjects.

Briefs would not be a problem. But what about oral arguments in the federal court of appeals? One rung below the United States Supreme Court? "This ain't moot court, Maynard," as Myrna had so aptly put it. He would be representing appellee Whitlow in a fight to the theoretical death on the battlefields of constitutional law against the appellant, the People of the United States of America. Sword, word, and foul play. May the best casuist and subtle slipper win. "Never mind the truth, Counselor, please square it with precedent. We want to hear how your proposed ruling is safe, does not disturb precedent, and jibes with everything else we've let pass in the carnival of human depravity we preside over every day."

Harper and Frank Donahue would be assailing Judge Stang and his rulings, and Watson would be defending him. Whitlow would fade into the background, so that Watson could proudly display his new client, the District Court, and its well-reasoned opinions, which the other side would be assailing for purely personal gain and base motives. According to his appellate advocacy instructors, you couldn't say it, but if you could, it would sound like this: "May it please the Court. I am here on behalf of my client, it's true, but more important, I am here on behalf of the United States District Court and its well-crafted order and judgment rendered below." Being Whitlow's lawyer would daunt and test the mettle of any lawyer, but then throw Judge Stang in to boot—the silverback male in the primate hierarchy of the St. Louis bar. Would Judge Stang be forced to suffer the insult and judicial ignominy of having Donahue bring his publicity stunts back to his courtroom? Or would the mighty judge's handpicked young lawyer serve him well, defend his reputation, preserve his authority to run his own courtroom?

Before he could finish the job of exaggerating his own importance in the world, his phone rang once, meaning it was Myrna calling from next door. If he didn't answer, she would come over and knock on his door.

"What?" he said.

"Joe," she said in the polite tone she used only when clients were present, "if you have a minute, Mrs. Whitlow is here to see us."

"Mary Whitlow!" said Watson. "She's here? In your office? We can talk to her?" he asked, still stuck in his civil litigation mentality. "I mean, she can talk to us?"

"I'm talking to her right now," said Myrna. "If you come on over, we can all talk. It's called the freedom of association. You may have read about it in law school."

Myrna was blatantly untrustworthy, but what could be done about that? The case, his client's fate, and Watson's present circumstances seemed inextricably bound up with a crass, shifty, five-foot-tall orange-headed criminal lawyer. Sure, he could manage the appeal. He'd written lots of briefs and done practice arguments in moot court. But even if he won in the Eighth Circuit, the case would be remanded for trial. And then what? Maybe Myrna was no good for Joe, but she would certainly do a better job at trial for his client. Hadn't he worked with duplicitous assholes before? Sure, in a firm with four hundred lawyers, one must learn to get along with duplicitous assholes. Wasn't that what lawyering was all about? She was an improvement over Arthur. If she'd used him, was it because she was acting like a lawyer, and he was acting like a gullible dupe?

Maybe Myrna was in cahoots with Buck, Mary Whitlow, Harper, Palmquist, Arthur? And his job in this hierarchy of professional, unprofessional, and nonprofessional villains and competing egos was to go off and be Bartleby the Scrivener for the powers that be. Do some research and writing to keep Judge Stang happy, while the real lawyers decided the defendant's fate.

Watson put on his sport coat and found a lawyerly-looking folder to accompany him. During the short walk into the next room, he braced himself for a confrontation with his client's mortal adversary by conjuring memories of the various villainesses he'd met in print over the years—Madame Defarge, Lady Macbeth, Blanche DuBois, Morgan le Fay. But instead of finding a calculating virago and literary prototype with key-cold eyes, he opened Myrna's door and found a frightened, overweight woman in nappy black polyester slacks and a blue smock with ACROBAT PRINTING & GRAPHICS stitched into the lapel. Her hair was brown, limp, straight, clinging like a greasy silk scarf to her fat head. Her eyes looked like black marbles pushed into the swollen features of her face.

Suddenly Watson could think only about how his client had given this woman—his wife!—a venereal disease, or so it appeared from the medical reports. She was a definite two-bagger. Had she let herself go? Or had Whitlow married her because she'd had something else he needed? A car? A place to stay? The thought of Whitlow ... infecting this unsightly woman while he whispered lies into her unwashed ears made the procreation of the entire race seem a sordid, bestial business, indeed.

And what moral promontory afforded him this disdainful view of the family Whitlow's dirty deeds? He'd come pretty close to breaching the domestic antiviral firewalls himself. Maybe Sandra was meeting with a different sort of lawyer right now, taking a look at family law options? Maybe she was down talking to Drath Bludsole at Stern, Pale. *"Conflict, Mrs. Watson? What conflict? He doesn't work here anymore, remember?"* Maybe she was getting the sort of domestic relations advice he imagined himself giving in answer to Whitlow's incessant "What would you do?" *"Number one: Do nothing to betray your knowledge of the affair. Number two: Hire a private investigator with a telephoto and get some pics of him and Dr. Stone Fox desecrating your conjugal bliss . . ."*

Instead of shaking Watson's hand, Mary extended damp, pudgy fingers and let him grasp them. She didn't look at him when he said, "A pleasure to meet you, Mrs. Whitlow"—a mannered contrivance he regretted the instant it left his lips. Her fingers felt like raw breadstick dough when he squeezed them.

"I can't be talking to you-all," she said, fetching a pack of Kents from the side pocket of her smock. She apprehended Joe in a single suspicious glance, then turned back to Myrna and showed her the unlit cigarette, which quivered slightly in her trembling fingers. "I got one thing to say."

Myrna put her hand on the skull lighter, then thought better of it, opened her desk, retrieved a book of matches, and handed them to Mary Whitlow.

"The government is after me," she said, "and they ain't the onliest ones after me. I don't know what all Jimmy told you." She looked at both of them for a reading and received only blank looks.

"What a client tells his lawyer is privileged," said Myrna politely, "but—"

"You mean secret," interrupted Mary. "OK, I got my own secrets, and I ain't telling them." Her voice shook. She lifted her head and mustered a look of defiance, which was quickly deranged by twitching facial muscles. "Maybe he don't care if he dies," she said, tears beading at the corners of her eyes. "But I got a deaf boy to look after."

"So does he," interjected Watson.

"Maybe if you told us what it is you need to get back," said Myrna soothingly. She rose out of her chair and walked slowly around the desk. "And who is threatening you. Maybe that would help us explain things to your husband. We can't talk to him just now because the government is doing some remedial brain surgery on him."

"I ain't telling shit," Mary said in a quavering voice. She looked away from Myrna and glanced at Joe, as if daring him to ask her something. "Every time I talk, things gets worse. And what I say gets twisted around to help whoever get whatever."

"Because you've been talking to the government," said Myrna. Her voice sounded compassionate, respectful, tender—in short, utterly foreign. "Maybe the government lawyers have been putting words in your mouth, doctoring your testimony, cajoling you into seeing things their way. I know how they do that. And when that happens sometimes people don't know where to turn, who or what to believe. They live their whole lives trusting the government. And then? They get arrested or questioned and find out what the government is all about."

"That ain't me," Mary snapped. "I know what the government's about. I still ain't tellin' shit. Because I know what you're about, too. And him," with a jerk of her head in Watson's direction. "And them."

She breathed faster and resettled herself in the chair.

"But eventually," purred Myrna, "you'll tell everybody, won't you? The judge, the jury, the press, because you are going to testify in federal court. Twelve jurors are gonna stare at you and ask themselves, 'Is she lying? Is she telling the truth?' The government may act like your friend now, but eventually they'll come after you, too. Then you will get a promotion, from witness to defendant."

"For what?" she snapped and braced herself. "I didn't kill Elvin Brawley. James Whitlow done that." Her lips trembled, and she covered her face with hands that had been stained by toner cartridges and print ribbons.

"Pretend he did kill Elvin," said Myrna. "Then things look bad for him, right? Which I guess could be good or bad for you."

"Oh," said Mary sarcastically, "another lawyer gonna explain good and bad to me? I had the devil's own time telling them apart, so I give it up. Now I do for everybody what they done for me—nothin'." She leaned forward and spit the word from her mouth. "How 'bout what that bastard dickhead done to me?" she asked. "But that ain't your business, is it?"

"My business is to keep the government honest," said Myrna. "I make sure they don't abuse power and take advantage of regular people like you and me."

Myrna watched Mary exhale and then reached for her Gitanes.

"So what is it you want us to tell your husband?"

"I get my half back and maybe things change for him," she blurted. She stuck the cigarette in her lips with shaky fingers and looked as if she'd regretted even this sudden communication. "Maybe I go away."

"Joe," said Myrna, "let's write this down and make sure we get it right."

"Don't write nothing down!" she shouted. "I didn't say nothing anyways. You tell him what you maybe heard me say." She rose abruptly. "I'm gone."

"Least now we got a pretty good idea she ain't wearin' a wire," said Myrna.

"I ain't here for the government," Mary yelled.

"Good, then sit down," said Myrna. "Unless you want us to tell Jimmy your message is 'Nothin'.' "

Mary warily sat back in the chair and regarded Myrna with hatred in one eye and fear in the other.

"A trial is nothing but stories," said Myrna. "Lots of different stories told to an audience in a big room that feels a lot like a church. Your problem is you got a bad story, ma'am. You can explain the parts that don't make sense to me, or I can just call the Assistant U.S. Attorney. He runs a little thing called a grand jury, where he can maybe ask you what was in them briefcases everybody is looking for."

Mary glanced at the drooping ash on her cigarette and tried to steady her hand. Myrna looked in her eyes, then stared at her shaking fingers.

"How 'bout an ashtray?" Myrna asked, taking a puff on her own cigarette, "before you shake that loose?"

"I got nothin' to say about briefcases," said Mary.

" 'Nothing' would be great," said Myrna, "if you could get away with it. But when you take the witness stand, saying 'nothing' ain't gonna wash."

"I'll tell it the way it happened," said Mary bravely.

"No shit?" asked Myrna. "The whole story? You gonna tell the court about the Order of the Eagles? And how you are Militia Momma? What are you this year? The secretary? The treasurer?—I forget. You gonna tell them how you handle all the printing of the newspapers, newsletters, mailers? All the shit that gets sent out to the four corners of the world? You gonna tell them all that?"

Mary's face locked up in a ghastly mask. Myrna came around her desk, turned hard at the corner, and stabbed her cigarette out in the ashtray. She swept into the woman's personal space so abruptly that Mary raised her hands. "You may *think* you been fucked in this life," said Myrna, "until I get you on that witness stand, girl. Then you gonna get fucked so hard blood's gonna come out your ears."

"Myrna," said Joe, stepping forward, as Mary covered her face again and sobbed.

Myrna walked back around her desk and started going through the same pile of papers she had been patting and trying to bait Joe with the day before. Myrna glanced once at him and winked. "Or maybe you've already told the cops all about the briefcases and militia business, in which case I'd be thinking about when the Order of the Eagles will find out about that. Either way, you are in no position to be feeling us up for an offer to tamper."

Myrna's eyes gunned through a blue haze of smoke. She waved a newspaper aloft, then stopped and grabbed another before she came back around the desk. She handed one to Joe and showed the other to Mary Whitlow, who made no effort to take it from her.

The masthead was writ large in a fancy headline font, like garnish for the Magna Carta: EAGLE EYE PATRIOT NEWS. If the headlines were any indication, it was a newspaper for racially minded folks. STUDY PROVES BLACK IQS 30% LOWER THAN WHITES. A boxed column lower right: BLACKS CAUSE 90% OF VIOLENT CRIMES.

Inside, things got worse. RUNNING NIGGER TARGET POSTER SALE, said the ad on page three. GENETICISTS URGE RACIAL PURITY, read one headline, with a boxed quote: "Mixed race marriages are destroying the social fabric of America. . . ." WHITE FETUSES ABORTED AT SEVEN TIMES THE RATE OF BLACKS, said another heading, followed by a caption, "Welfare State Breeding Criminals and Then Writing Them Government Checks." On page four, BABY KILLERS BOMBED! followed by a piece on how to make sure you aim for the head of the clinic doctors, or use armor piercing bullets at a range of under five hundred feet.

"Top of page five," said Myrna.

Watson's brow bled sweat as he saw an editorial: "Tax Revolt, Not Another Dime of My Money for Raising Nigger Criminals," complete with a byline and handle: Thor61, Whitlow's virtual ID, if Harper was telling the truth.

"Now," said Myrna, "if the government gets ahold of these, we will be fucked naked in Timbuktu. Back page," she said to Joe.

He turned it over, where a box on the back contained publishing information:

> This newspaper is published by armed patriots who are ready to protect the great future of this country and are dedicated to recapturing the media and the federal government from the Jews and the niggers.

> This publication contains opinions protected by the First Amendment of the United States Constitution. It contains opinions and ideas only and should not be read as fighting words, specific instructions, or incitement to lawless behavior.

> Thanks again to Zara42 and Thor61 for their hard work. Special thanks to Thor's wife, MW49, our treasurer and newsletter editor.

> Willing To Die Free & Proud. Order of the Eagles.

"Our treasurer MW49? Thor's wife? MW? We've both led such bad lives, Joey," said Myrna, "we couldn't be that lucky, could we? Couldn't be her, could it?"

Mary's nostrils flared with her breathing, but she stared at Myrna, with tears leaking at the corners of her eyes, and said nothing.

Watson suddenly realized he had not yet had the chance to tell Myrna about the his-and-her medical reports, and was glad he hadn't. She'd be rubbing Mary's face in gonorrhea by now if he had.

"He's a lying racist shithead. She's a lying racist shithead. Let's pretend they both belong to the Order of the Eagles and neither is taking sign language lessons. Why is a black deaf guy coming to their house every now and again with a briefcase and staying for three minutes? Drugs? Who's buying and who's selling? And why would racists do business with African-Americans?"

"Elvin wouldn't do business with nobody 'cept me," said Mary. "Alone. The nursery monitor was Jimmy's idea. Jimmy Whitlow's wife alone with a nigger? Not on planet Earth, unless he could hear what was happening from twenty yards away."

"And what was going on?" asked Myrna.

Mary lifted her chin. "Personal shit."

"I don't know what this is all about," said Myrna, "but it ain't race, not mainly anyway. Lots of hate flying around, but hatred because of race? Because of disability? We don't see the n-word or anything about deafness until Mary starts talking to the FBI. My guess is that they have information about Whitlow and his buddies, maybe information about her, too. But they don't have enough to bring a conspiracy charge and link it to a real militia crime. So, let's say in the course of telling the FBI what really happened old MW slips and uses the n-word or says something about Elvin being deaf. Then what?"

"Then I get arrested for hating niggers," said Mary, challenging her with *another* look.

"Nah," Myrna said. "If they get on your bad side, they lose the only witness who can put an Order of the Eagler away for life? No. I think it goes this way, 'Nigger?' asks the field officer. 'Who used that word? Surely you didn't use that word, did you, Mrs. Whitlow?' " Myrna said, glaring at Mary Whitlow. " 'Why, that kind of word makes us wonder if this was a hate crime. Yes, that's right. Extra penalties, big ones for a hate crime, but only for criminals who have committed some other separate crime, like shooting a black man or a disabled person. So you were saying? Who said nigger? Was it the bastard dickhead who said it? Think back. Did he say it at any other time just before the crime was committed, or maybe while the crime was being committed? Because if he did, that would be serious, indeed. Did he say anything about Mr. Brawley's disability?' "

"Fuck you, lady," said Mary.

"I'm getting warm," said Myrna, "don't you think, Joey? I gotta talk to my receptionist about an appointment I got waiting. Can you two hold on a sec? Unless Mary Whitlow has somewhere to go?"

Myrna nodded hard at Joe, motioning him into the hallway. Once outside her door, she said, "In case you've never done this before, it's called Mutt and Jeff, OK? You go back in there and tell her I'm a ruthless, crazy bitch from Hell and there is no telling what I will do. I might call Harper on her. I might hand over the Eagle Eye newspapers to the government. I might get her charged with tampering or blackmail. Nice touch trying to stop me going after her. Brilliant. You got real instincts.

Try and get her to confide in you. Tell her you can help her figure out what to do. She's sweating. She's got the Eagles after her and the government. She is trapped and terrified. Use her fear."

She pushed him back through the door into her office and closed it.

Mary Whitlow craned her fat neck around.

"Ms. Schweich has a client she needs to speak with momentarily," said Watson, taking the chair opposite Mary and putting his hands on his knees.

"Yeah," said Mary, "maybe she'll fall and break her neck on the way."

Joe watched her fingers shake as she lit another cigarette.

"I . . . guess . . . you don't know what to do now," said Joe. "If I can help . . . ?"

"Fuck you," said Mary.

"I was appointed to be your husband's lawyer," said Joe. "I'm just trying to help him. If you have a message for him that you think will help him. Or maybe help you—"

"You fuck around?" she asked suddenly.

His mouth opened and he looked at her white face, now rigid with hatred. He wasn't sure if he'd heard her right, or if his own obsessions were leaking out again and infecting the world. She puffed and regarded him with a fixed, squinted gaze, pointing with her cigarette at the wedding band on his left hand. "I said, do you fuck around?"

"What?" he asked, feeling blood rushing under the skin of his face.

"I thought so," she said. "They all do. And after they fuck around on you. They lie about it."

"Ms. Schweich wanted me to ask you about—"

"You Catholic?" She glanced at him again. "You went to that Jesuit high school with Jimmy—ain't that what the paper said? Jimmy made me turn Catholic, too. Said I had to or he weren't gonna marry me. Then he went on and on about how adultery is a mortal sin, right up there with murder," she said, tamping her ashes in midair and watching them fall to the floor. "Fucker."

The medical reports Palmquist had given him scrolled by in his imagination as if on a ticker at the bottom of the screen called consciousness: *"Patient stated she could not possibly have . . . a sexually transmitted disease, because she had never had sex with anyone except her husband."*

"Jimmy told me that if I ever fucked around on him, he would shoot me in the head and blame it on a nigger."

"And according to your statements, you did fuck around, didn't you?" asked Watson, deciding the best policy was to try and meet her at her level. But having mustered the courage to look her in the eye and confront her with her own story, he knew instantly that he could never go where she was. She gave him a killing look—a hockey mask from a horror movie. He could hear air being sucked into her nostrils. Her black eyes shone with fevered loathing. Maybe Othello looked like this the night he strangled Desdemona. Black vengeance come from hollow Hell, her bosom full of aspics' tongues, a big toad-woman living upon the vapors of dungeons. But *Othello* wasn't real, he reminded himself. No, it was like a verbal video game for hip literary types. A cartoon of emotions fossilized in print. And Othello had only a purloined hankie for hard evidence—imagine if Desdemona had given him a dose? Mary Whitlow was sporting the real item.

She drew a deep puff from her Kent and blew it at Watson, then clenched her teeth and said, "Jimmy never did say what would happen if he fucked around on me." Her eyes glinted. She took another puff and rolled the cigarette in her fingers, dyed black and orange from print and tobacco. "I guess he knows now."

Chapter 24

Watson quietly neglected to invite Myrna to the Voice Transcription Device party. Instead he had the machine dusted for prints at a private lab the next day. Then he called VTech Industries, the local distributor, and arranged an appointment with John Crowell, the senior VTech service representative. By phone, Crowell explained that the VTD operated at maximum accuracy only if it contained the speaker's vocal profile—a list of approximately one hundred sounds spoken aloud and stored in the machine's memory—which in the best of cases enabled the program to recognize and transcribe an individual's voice into printed words. With the profile in place, transcription accuracy ranged between 80 and 90 percent, with frequent errors, especially for homonyms *(to, two, too; some, sum)*. Without the profile—for example, when the speaker was a casual acquaintance or infrequent visitor— transcription was a hit-and-miss affair, averaging 40 to 60 percent accuracy.

Crowell explained that voice recognition technology still suffered from the same inexactness and inaccuracies that had bedeviled the computer industry's quest for handwriting transcription and pen-based computers. VoiceType technology had been developed by IBM back in the mid-1990s, and by 1996 had begun showing up in operating systems such as OS/2 Warp 4. VoiceType dictation was the first office application, followed a few years later by handheld VTDs—assistive devices for the deaf—intended to display reasonably accurate transcriptions of spoken communications on the liquid crystal screen of the VTD. Most of the devices also contained a keypad, so the deaf person could then quickly type a response on the screen and show it to a hearing person. Or even play it for them, using the device's voice synthesis features. But so far, according to Crowell, practice lagged behind promise: Errors were still frequent and egregious.

When Watson told his would-be expert that he needed someone who could testify about the device and whatever was stored in its memory, Crowell was cautionary. Using a VTD to prove what someone said or didn't say in any given session was probably not possible. But, he added, if Elvin Brawley was using the device to type messages to whomever he had been talking to in any given session, the machine's memory should contain an accurate record of what he had typed. Trying to prove what Mary Whitlow said or didn't say would be a different matter.

Watson drove out Highway 40 to an office park in Chesterfield, where he met Crowell, a tall, stoop-shouldered, fifty-ish technician with a jeweler's loupe mounted on the frames of his bifocals. Crowell showed Watson into a workshop lined with folding tables and stacked with gutted electronic equipment, disemboweled chassis sprouting spangled, multicolored wires, unmoored circuit boards leaning in cross-hatched heaps.

"Have you used one of these before?" Crowell asked, sitting at a circular table under a hooded row of fluorescent worklights and showing Watson a chair next to him.

"No," said Watson.

"Let's play with another one before we boot yours up," he said. He rose from the table and fetched another VTD, setting it between them. "It's an 880," he said, "same model as your victim's machine." He pivoted the device and pointed the LCD panel at Watson. "Microphone," he said, pointing at two tiny slits in the corner of the cover.

Crowell pushed a button and powered on the device. "READY" flashed on the LCD. Then Crowell pushed another button, and the message "BEGIN TRANSCRIPTION. LISTENING . . ." appeared on the screen. Crowell began speaking in a clear, distinct voice, with a slight pause between each word.

"When I put it in transcription mode, it attempts to translate every vocalization it receives into printed words. Period. Punctuation is absent unless the speaker provides it by saying period, comma, and so on."

Watson watched as Crowell's words, or rather, something like Crowell's words appeared on the LCD screen: *"When I pudding transcription mode it contempt too translate aviary vocalization it release into print words. Punch your station is absent unless the speaking provides it by saying., and so on"*

"You see?" said Crowell. "Pretty rough."

"You see pretty Ralph" appeared on the screen.

Then Crowell spoke even slower with more emphatic pauses. "It does better if you speak carefully and use simple words. Period."

Watson watched the machine display: *"It dozen better if you speak careful and used simple words."*

When Crowell began speaking normally again, the screen filled with near gibberish. He turned off the device. "It also only recognizes words in its database of common speech. It does not transcribe profanity, slang, esoteric words, and the like. Watch." He powered the unit back on. "Fuck you, asshole."

"Frog you gas hole" appeared on the screen.

"Our customers who lease these provide them for their deaf employees to help satisfy the reasonable accommodation requirements of the handicap laws. And the technology does *help* deaf people communicate with hearing people who don't know sign language. When attempting communication with someone who knows no sign language, deaf people get most of their information from lip-reading and from the speaker's facial expressions. This device really provides them with just another uncertain set of clues to help them guess what is being said by a hearing person. Watch my lips," he commanded. "What's that big loud noise. What's that big loud noise.

"Now, watch my lips again," he said. "What's that pig outdoors. What's that pig outdoors. See? To a deaf person, they look exactly the same on the lips. Now . . ." He powered on the VTD.

"BEGIN TRANSCRIPTION. LISTENING . . ." said the screen.

"What's that big loud noise," said Crowell. "What's that pig outdoors."

Watson watched the screen as *"What sat big loud noise what sat pig outdoors"* appeared.

"See," said Crowell. "It helps, but it's far from accurate." He powered off the machine and returned it to the shelf.

"The technology depends on very sophisticated hardware and software. Skeptics would say it has been just around the corner for three decades, and still not here. Every time a CEO or a lawyer or anybody else who dictates for a living hears about it, they want it, because they think it will replace their secretary and save them from learning to type. Unfortunately, the proof isn't in the pudding. Yet," continued Crowell, with a wry smile, "because it's still just around the corner. Until then, if the thing is being used for dictation, somebody must go back and edit the transcription. You can appreciate the hurdles in speech transcription if you imagine a device capable of accurately transcribing a Boston accent, a North Carolina drawl, and Jamaican Creole. It's all English, but tough to teach a computer."

Crowell snapped on a pair of rubber gloves and removed the back of Elvin Brawley's machine. He installed a fresh battery pack, then pushed the power button. Watson held his breath and watched the LCD come to life.

"AUTOSAVE ON SHUTDOWN," said the screen. "THE SESSION DATED 14 JUNE 2002 WAS SAVED AT 17:45 ON SHUTDOWN."

"That's it," said Watson. "The day of the . . . The day it happened."

"Somebody turned the machine off before the battery died," said Crowell.

"PRESS 'Y' NOW IF YOU WANT TO RETRIEVE THE TRANSCRIPTION SESSION TIME AND DATE STAMPED FRIDAY 14 JUNE 2002 AT 17:45."

Crowell touched Y.

"Looks like the only saved session," he said, "which isn't unusual. The system resources required to store and run the program itself don't leave much room for storing multiple long sessions. Users are encouraged to offload to their PCs if they want to save multiple sessions."

"But we do have at least one session?" asked Watson.

"Looks that way," said the technician, as they watched the screen fill with characters:

```
14 JUNE 2002 17:41
BEGIN TRANSCRIPTION. LISTENING...
Got it set up
Got my voice
OK
```

```
When I told you the lessons are too expense if
YOU FIND BETTER LESSONS FOR CHEAPER THAN BUY BETTER LESSONS
```

"His should be the caps," said Crowell. "The caps should be what he is typing back to her in response to her comments."

The session continued scrolling by on the screen:

```
Maybe we will buy lessons from somebody else
Then is last lesson one less they tell me different
I DON'T MAKE MORE LESSON BUT THIS LESSON YOU STILL WANT? FOUR
FOR ONE? THE SAME AS ALWAYS?
14 JUNE 2002 17:42
Yes for for one I have the money
YOU SAID YOUR HUSBAND GO?
Gone yes
YOU SAID YOU WANT ME TOUCH YOU?
Yes
YOU WANT ME TOUCH YOU?
Yes and I will too
14 JUNE 2002 17:45
James help me vinegar is common anthony
   Help me he's gone crazy
   Vinegar is common anthony help me
AUTOSAVE, CLOSING SESSION.
```

Watson and Crowell replayed the session.

"That's it?" asked Watson. "Can we print it?"

"Sure," said Crowell, turning in his chair and grabbing a bubble jet printer from a nearby table, then cabling it to the VTD.

While Watson waited for the printout, he imagined Mary and Elvin in her living room. Her saying something like the lowercase words. Elvin typing the uppercase ones. And Whitlow, who was outside with a nursery monitor would hear—what? Only whatever Mary was saying, and not what Brawley was typing. In other words, when Elvin had typed: "YOU SAID YOUR HUSBAND GO?" Whitlow would have heard only "Gone yes." When Elvin had typed: "YOU SAID YOU WANT ME TOUCH YOU?" Whitlow would have heard "Yes."

Watson looked at the time entries printed in the margin of the sheet. "Would the times be accurate?"

"Should be," said Crowell. "Probably the most reliable information on the screen."

Watson studied the three time entries. The first, lengthy series of comments about expensive lessons apparently took about one minute, separated by 17:41 and 17:42, which seemed about right if one factored in lags for doing the keypad work and reading the screen.

"Would they be sitting together turning the thing back and forth? The way we are now?" asked Watson.

"Probably," said Crowell, "especially since he's typing back to her."

The second batch of comments was about one third the length of the first, but it began at 17:42 and ended at 17:45, when, according to the machine, Mary Whitlow said repeatedly: "James help me vinegar is common anthony."

"Why does the long series of comments take one minute and the second short one take three minutes?" asked Watson.

Crowell looked at the printout. "Well, during the second session, they were either communicating really slowly," he said, noting the time discrepancies with a pencil, "or, judging from the first patch, they communicated for half a minute with two and a half minutes worth of silence in there somewhere."

Watson imagined Elvin and Mary sitting at the table looking at his VTD screen: YOUR HUSBAND GO? And Mary says, "Yes." And Whitlow, sitting out in his Ford Taurus with the nursery monitor hears his wife say, "Yes," and thinks, *Maybe he asked her for a light?* He does not hear: YOU WANT ME TOUCH YOU? Only "Yes" and "Yes and I will too."

For the first time, Watson considered Elvin. *What about Elvin? What would Elvin hear?*

"I can send you lists of the most likely near hits on these words that don't seem to fit. *Vinegar, common, anthony.* She probably said something else. Sometimes it helps to look at others in the same phonic spectrum. For instance, *common* gets mixed up with *come on, coming, calm down,* and so on. Maybe that would help."

Watson looked down at *vinegar* and felt sick to his stomach. Two minutes of silence after Mary said she wanted him to touch her? *And what would Elvin hear?* What if he couldn't even see her face? What if he was busy touching her, or she was busy touching him, and not looking at the VTD? Elvin would hear nothing. And unless he could see her face or the VTD, he wouldn't even know she was talking.

Vinegar is common anthony.

For no apparent reason, he suddenly recalled one of the articles retrieved by his Internet spider named Rachel: "Are Animals Capable of Deception?" The answer: an emphatic yes, as evidenced by Frans de Waal, who observed subordinate male chimpanzees after they had furtively sought and obtained sexual favors from adult females who "belonged" to dominant males. If the alpha males discovered their subordinates in flagrante delicto, the young bucks covered their erect penises and made nice. *Just talking, Boss. Watercooler stuff. No big.* Watson could vividly imagine himself covering his penis with his hands if Arthur, R. J. Connally, Judge Stang, or his faithful father caught him at the portals of Palmquist's pearly pink gates. *"No, really, I was just looking out for the interests of my client."*

"That would help a lot, if you would fax the other possible matches to me," said Watson. "I'll just go back and work on them in my office. But"—he looked at his watch, feeling his stomach cramp, pretending he had just noticed the time—"uh, I have to file something in court," he lied.

"Most of it looks fairly reliable," Crowell said, staring at the screen, "especially the simple words. But, even if you figure out what she said when the machine typed *vinegar common anthony*, it would be tough to prove it in court."

"Yeah," said Watson. "I see what you mean." He thought of Mary Whitlow squirming in Myrna's office. Vengeance pinching her dough-face into lobes and blisters of rage. *"Jimmy never did say what would happen if he fucked around on me. I guess he knows now."*

A chill gripped the insides of his ribs, along with a sudden irresistible urge to think of his client and his avenging wife the way Dr. Palmquist thought of them: big mice. Or maybe white-trash vervet monkeys.

He thanked Crowell and walked out to his Honda, looking around at the minimalls and movie theaters teeming with other primates going about their monkey business. Material brains in material girls and boys, programmed and being programmed to survive. The human race seemed to regress before his eyes, and he was slouching backward with them. The Whitlows were troglodytes fresh from the caves. And he was—what? Before long he would be a small-brained, small-minded (is there a difference?) moral dinosaur gasping in the poisonous atmosphere of modern ideas. Nature has a brain, and Watson and the Whitlows and Myrna and Judge Stang were all just a small bundle of neurons in an organism that lived forever and was populated by humans, and other animals—diseases, growths infesting the earth's skin.

As he took the ramp back onto Highway 40, he thought about Mary Whitlow. Her statements—from field reports and TDD printouts, in person, on the VTD—bobbed like corpses in the swamp of his thoughts, and sank again, taking with them his opinion of the human race.

The day after she found out her husband had cavalierly administered VD to her during a session of love-making, she typed a message to Elvin Brawley: "I just want us to be alone together. And next week, James will be gone to Nevada. I want to see you and have you touch me with your signs."

To the MP in the emergency room: "I was with my boyfriend. I was getting ready to go down on him. His pants were unzipped. My husband came home and shot him. He made me call the police and tell them it was a rape."

"James help me vinegar is common anthony."

His car took the exit to the Gage Institute at Ignatius Medical Center. He hadn't thought about going there, really, it just sort of happened. If the nuns were to put him on trial for driving his car to this location, perhaps he could formulate a defense based upon a mental defect or disease. He clearly knew and appreciated the difference between right and wrong, but he was unable to conform his behavior to his own moral code. Episodic dyscontrol? Mental defect? Irresistible impulse?

Call her what you will, he found the target of his irresistible impulse sitting in the L of her worktables, hunched over her keyboard and a tray containing a pink organ, about the size of a big garlic bulb, suspended in solution. She glanced up at him and said, "Oh. Hold a sec." She addressed her monitor and continued clicking and adjusting entries in the dialogue box of a database matrix.

A part of his brain asked the other parts, *Why am I here?* He was sleepwalking, a melody stuck in a repetitive, self-destructive fugue. His optic nerves translated images of her near-perfect, biology-of-beauty face back somewhere in his visual cortex. Fears from too many different parts of his life were swarming like bugs on the surface of the pond called consciousness, the same swamp containing Mary's vinegar and lies. The fold of her lab coat opened on another tight Lycra sweater (navy blue, this time), revealing the rondure of her right breast—plump, gibbous, swelling in the shadows. He spotted another floral motif straining under the sweater. Probably from a new line of lingerie called the Near Occasion of Sin. His spinal cord sprouted what felt like an extra column of lumbar disks in his pants. *I'm ready now.*

His nose quivered at the faint odor of pickling solution. Formaldehyde? Formalin? He studied the fleshy-looking specimen, which was shaped like a very small trussed raw turkey—covered by the same pinkish-white wrinkled skin with permanent goose bumps—suspended by wires in the solution, with a couple of clear tubes running into it.

"What is . . . ?" began Watson, his queasiness approaching nausea again, hoping whatever it was had not come from a human being.

"Isolated and perfused whole brain, in vitro," she said.

"Isolated?"

"Whole brain," she said.

"Of?"

"A reptile," she said. "A small lawyer," she added without laughing. Then she laughed. "Guinea pig, really. Why?"

"How long has it been dead?"

"Hah," she cried. "Dead? This isn't dead, Counselor. Undergrads work on dead guinea pigs. When I first met you in Arthur's office, we talked about beheadings, remember?"

"I do," said Watson.

"This is the opposite of a beheading. This is a *live* guinea pig, minus its supporting vessel. Unencumbered, as it were. Free to dream without the constraints of senses and the thousand natural shocks that flesh is heir to," she said, her eyes lustering with a visionary gleam. "Unburdened of bodily cares, free to think thoughts beyond the reaches of body and soul."

She clicked and slid her pointer around the screen, opening and closing windows. Entering data.

"You're serious—it's alive?"

"Better question," she said, still without looking at him, "how would you prove it is alive? How to prove it is still thinking?"

Watson stared at the pink lump. "Give it beer and see if it gets drunk?"

"What if we can teach it a conditioned response?" she asked him. "If it can learn, it must be conscious, right? Remember the septal pleasure centers I told you about? Well, we get a microelectrode in there and make the pig brain feel better than sex on cocaine in clover by juicing the septals with a few millivolts. Most people have heard of the Olds and Milner experiments where they got a wire into the septal nuclei or the medial forebrain bundle of rats and rigged it so the rats could stimulate themselves by pressing a bar."

"Yeah," said Watson, "and the rats stopped eating and drinking. They just kept pressing the bar until they died."

"Right," she said. "It gave new meaning to the conditioned response phase known as extinction. Seven thousand self-stimulations an hour! Raw pleasure the only explanation. Pleasure to die for. Anyway, so we take our little bodiless guinea pig brain and we get our microfine wire in the septal nuclei, and then we pick any efferent nerve whose pathways would normally conduct impulses that would trigger a voluntary or semivoluntary motor response, say, the nerve that controls the blinking of the animal's eyelid. We hook a little sensor up to that nerve so we can measure impulses along the nerve and detect the sort of impulses that would normally trigger an eyeblink. And then we teach the animal, or rather, the animal's brain, to send those impulses. We reward every eyeblink impulse with septal stimulation. Faster and faster, so that if it had an eyelid, it would be blinking hundreds of times per minute. Pretty soon our conscious guinea pig brain is blinking its phantom eyelid seven thousand times an hour."

Watson blinked.

"Imagine you could have an orgasm just by blinking," she said.

In place of the little pink trussed turkey of a brain in solution, Watson imagined his client's mole-gray and shell-pink blobulous engine of reason, bobbing in solution, wired and tubed for sustenance, while she went to work on it, rerouting synapses, touching up the contact points on various wet, tubular, coiling circuit boards. Then she could just reinsert it, back into its low-end chassis?

He tried to imagine free will, altruism, any soulful notion inhabiting Whitlow's stew of stringy neurons, and he failed. Palmquist would call it eliminative materialism. The brain is only matter. Whitlow's reasoning, intention, remorse, aspiration, his rancor and fear—artifacts and nothing more. Cellular static. Perhaps these mental events *felt* important and meaningful to his brain, but in a world constituted of matter only, thoughts, dreams, and soulful longings were as meaningless as the bioluminescence of comb jellies and mollusks.

"I am assuming that you did not come here to watch me work on the isolated whole brain of a guinea pig," she said.

"I came here because you are not returning my calls," said Watson. "I've been in hourglass mode for a week."

"When I'm swamped, I revert almost exclusively to E-mail," she said. "Don't you?"

"Yeah," said Watson. "And I would never squander the time it takes for a phone call over something as trivial as brain surgery."

"It was voluntary," she said. "He signed all the papers. We've got him on videotape with two doctors who explained all of the procedures and risks. We even asked him if he wanted to talk to his lawyer before consenting, and he said no. I think his words were, 'Just get the fucking thing out of there. And keep me out of Des Peres.'

"As for our case," she continued, "we've done too good of a job. It probably won't even go to trial. The anomaly is way hard. Too hard. Too easy. We won't be breaking new ground there. It's a big cyst. Probably been there his whole life, though it may have been different sizes. It didn't show up on the scans they did of him when he had his first bout of seizures, but that was seven years ago, and they were using beta-maxed scanners with shitty resolution. Toy cameras compared to the Cray-driven machines they used on him up in Minnesota."

"So now," said Watson, "you've lost interest in the case?"

"I am your neuroscience expert," she said. "If it goes to trial, I'll testify, and the worst he'll get is manslaughter. We are back in occupied territory. PET scans and fMRI to demonstrate a hard defect and consequent loss of impulse control? Very well settled, as you know from your research. Relax," she said with a smile. "We can go on autopilot. And you have Mrs. Whitlow's medical records, proving she was lying about the affair. You should be celebrating."

"*We* should be celebrating," said Watson.

"Another case came in from Reno, Nevada," she said. "A hot one. The guy strangled his wife after he caught her having an E-mail relationship with a technical support guy at Oracle 2000. The scans are showing frontal lobe hypometabolism, without any neoplasms or lesions to blame. Very cutting edge. Any defense will be based entirely on scan interpretations and neurofunctional profiles. The prosecution's neuroscientist is the number two PET man in the country. I have a major war shaping up."

"I understand," said Watson.

"I knew you would," she said. "That's why I sent E-mails instead of calling. I don't get to my voice mail until almost midnight, and I didn't know if it would be safe to call then."

"And I think I also just wanted to see you," he said, feeling his backbone feeding impulses into his—what would you call it, a soft bone? A temporary bone?

"Yeah," she said. "I've been thinking about that, too. You're Catholic, I'm agnostic. You use Windows 2000. I'm an Ultra UNIX person. Not only do we have religious differences, we have incompatible operating systems. In terms of networking options—you're married, I'm divorced."

"I wasn't thinking of proposing marriage," he said, adopting a seize-the-day posture he thought would appeal to her.

"Let's think of ourselves as noninvasive electrodes," she said. "We either give each other pleasure, or we do not. Didn't you tell me you used to be into primatology?"

"I was," he said, "in college."

"Sex is the highest form of primate play. But not for you, right? For you, it touches off complicated moral reasoning, a sort of infinite loop between the anterior cingulate and orbital frontal cortex—circuits you'll probably never be able to escape. You've heard of neural Darwinism? The environment—nurture, if you prefer—can actually alter the hard wiring of the brain. That's what happened to you. Catholicism has implanted a complicated set of conditioned responses. It's rewired certain parts of your brain. I like to play. Your play is encumbered by moral cobwebs. Doesn't sound like fun for either of us."

"But—" he began, and then stopped. How could he argue this one? The diagnosis was too personal and accurate.

"Besides, you're married, remember? That means you are constantly multitasking, which requires a ton of RAM, and gets exceedingly complex, especially when you are trying to run older, primitive religious programs in the same sessions with the newer ones, like advanced cognitive neuroscience."

He looked at the guinea pig brain, smelled the formaldehyde, listened to her withering deracination of every one of his cherished concepts about the soul, free will, beauty, truth, guilt, religion.

"Besides," she said, "after I finish the Reno case I'm leaving for a fellowship down in South America."

"For vacation?"

"The project is running into too many obstacles in this country. We are opening satellite programs in other countries, where the governments are more receptive to genetic and medical solutions to these problems. Here, if you want to study a male on death row, or, God forbid, if you propose that violent crime may have a genetic or a biological component, your funding gets cut off because people don't want to *know* if violence is predictable, diagnosable, or treatable. When we submit a proposal suggesting that violent crime may have at least some biological or genetic components, we get vilified in the press for being genocidal. They think we are planning to scan criminals and then execute them before they commit any crimes."

"Yeah," said Watson. "Maybe you should tell them you just want to do brain surgery on criminals and repair them."

"I am confident your client will get some relief from the surgery. What will he be like without the lesion? I don't know. What was he like before it grew? We don't know, because we don't know when it grew. Some grow very slowly over decades, some grow to affect cerebral capacity within six weeks. Was the lesion there when Whitlow had his first episode of violence? Maybe. Does it matter? The point now is that we can use it for a defense, and medical intervention is at least possible, with a reasonable chance of success. But I can't speak for the psychological, the personal, the moral repercussions. That's for your client and you to decide. I don't think he'll be talking it over with his wife."

"If he can still talk," said Watson.

She shook her head. "Start by asking him if he is happier. A subjective before and after? And go from there. We can't say for sure what he will be like after the operation. He may be 'better' in terms of controlling his temper or modulating his intense hatred of black people, but if they take too much tissue or the wrong kind, it may make it impossible for him to hate *anybody*. Unable to respond quickly and violently to sudden attacks from the environment. Not good for long-term survival, because it would impair normal suspicion and aggression."

"But nobody's worried about his long-term survival," said Watson.

"Not you, certainly." He scowled at her, and she smiled back.

"Now what? Am I turning you into stone? I'm a monster, right? Look, the technology for this is on its way. If your client were a peaceful taxpayer, I would be the first to recommend that we not monkey around with parts of his brain that control his personality. The techniques are still so primitive—it's like playing a piano with our elbows. The neural

networks and clusters are all stacked on top of each other and intercon-
nected. It's like trying to remove only the pornography links from the
World Wide Web. It can't be done, because ultimately everything is connected to everything else.

"It's research. Our sister projects in other countries have had demon-
strable success modifying pathological neural networks and alleviating
the behavior disorders. Maybe you should think of the alternatives.
Most of our subjects are repeat offenders, violent criminals. I think it's a
bit more humane than execution."

"A bit," said Watson. "When is he due back?"

She turned and clicked into her calendar. "He's due back here in the
Forensic Psychiatric Wing of Ignatius Medical Center next Wednesday.
Four, five days."

"The day after oral arguments," said Watson.

"That's right," she said. "The Eighth Circuit. Good luck. I'm sure
you'll do a great job."

"Thanks," he said.

"And patient Whitlow's in fairly good spirits, according to the post-
surgical scans, that is. Resting-state blood flow to the frontal lobes has
increased by about twenty percent. No sign of chronic or acute depression on his PET. Maybe he's happy because his lawyer is doing such a
good job for him."

"Or maybe they removed the depression circuitry when they were in
there," he said acidly.

"You're an incorrigible moralist," she said with a friendly smile. "It's
endearing in a way. You keep looking at my pig's brain. I know what
you're thinking. The answer is yes. It's black art, but it's doable. We
could do the same thing with a human brain. Easy. Not only that, I
predict that within our lifetime, they'll manage two-way patches to
artificial intelligence. They've already hooked up silicon chips to leach
neurons with bidirectional signal processing. Deep voodoo. Past cool
and headed for absolute zero. You want me to zap you the extracts
on it?"

"Maybe after the case is over," he said.

"And hey," she said, "my colleagues down in Neuropsych are working on adding a Religion Scale to the standard neurofunctional profile.
They're building a database, scanning volunteers, and so on. If you're
interested, it would give you a chance to see the hottest machines in action. Completely noninvasive. Just let me know if you want in on it."

Watson listened to her techno-chatter and said nothing. He wanted to leave but couldn't. He needed something from her. What? Maybe she could scan him and see an image of it. Maybe she was like Circe, who had no use for men, once she had turned them into pigs and asses. And Watson was no Odysseus, because he'd lost his head and turned himself into a pig. Now she was bored.

"I really did enjoy working with you," she said. "Maybe I'll see you over in the forensic wing when your client gets back, if I'm not out in Reno."

"Maybe," said Watson.

"Someday you'll thank me for this," she said. "After our night in the storage room, I started thinking: What if I were a nice woman with two kids married to a nice guy like you? And someone like me came along?"

"This sounds like a conscience in bloom to me," said Watson. "I thought you said you didn't believe in it."

She smiled. "On the other hand, as you know, even chimpanzees display altruistic behaviors. Right?"

"There is almost always *some* explanation, isn't there?" said Watson, mocking her with lines from the speech she had given him on the mats in the storage room. "The brain almost never says, 'I don't know,' when asked about its own perceptions."

"You got me," she said. "But you still need to take your cue from the rest of your body and obey your cortex, instead of your limbics. Go back to the family where your brain keeps sending you."

"And where does your brain send you?" asked Watson.

"Where I need to go right now," she said, with a tight smile. "To the lab."

CHAPTER 25

He could remember a time when he was flush with family and fatherhood. He could make love to his wife. And after George, the father of his country, had slaked his standing lust, maybe Benjy would wake up during the night, and Watson could shift into Dad Mode. He could swing Benjy aloft, feel him drool in his ear, and hear his one-year-old son say, "Bwah, gabah, dah." Poetry, biological music, vocal cords from his descendant, pure preverbal human affection, untainted by lies, guile, artifice, and self-aggrandizement.

"May it please the court," Watson could say to the learned judges of the Eighth Circuit Court of Appeals, "this case hinges upon a complex interaction of state and federal law, of statutory construction and constitutional hermeneutics, of federal jurisdiction and esemplastic common-law theory, but I can sum it all up, your honors, in one simple locution: Bwah, gabah, dah. See, op. cit., id., passim, ibid., *In re Bwah, Gabah, Dah*, 708 F.3d 115 (8th Cir. 2002)."

Now, abandoned on the eve of oral arguments, the only stable operating system left was Warrior Mode. He booted into it with a vengeance, shunning all contact with females. Abstinence. Fasting in preparation for oral combat with the U.S. Attorney for the Eastern District of Missouri.

He stayed at his office until 10:00 P.M., then drove home to his big, empty house. He parked the Honda in his gravel driveway (the one that should have been paved by now with his Stern, Pale bonus). He fetched snail mail from the box and walked up the sidewalk to his front door, picking up newspapers along the way. He was trying to read the urgent warning on the envelope of another payment-due notice, but it was too dark. He looked up to take the first of two steps onto his front patio. Someone had scattered rocks, chunks of gravel on the cement. Kids? Not *scattered*, he realized with a shudder, as a pattern of letters emerged in the penumbra from the yard light. Letters, written in gravel: D-E-L-I-V-E-R-Y-? He spun around and scanned the dark suburban landscape for snipers and car bombers; maybe Alpha or Beta were sitting in a gray Ford Taurus? He peered again at the message: DELIVERY?

"Shit!" He spilled mail and dropped his key ring trying to jam the house key into the lock.

He called Myrna at home. One of her little girls answered the phone. He swallowed panic and rage, and became a well-behaved, solicitous adult. "You're watching TV with Mom? That's nice. That sounds like fun."

"Yes," said the little girl. "It's a show about some mean policemen who are trying to put people in jail. They just want to be mean and arrest people and get them to confess before they can talk to their lawyer."

"Oh," said Watson. "You *are* watching TV with Mom. Listen, this is Mr. Watson. I need to talk to your mom. It's very important." *Before we are all dead or in jail*, he thought.

"Joey," said Myrna, "I knew you couldn't stay mad at me."

"Myrna, there's a message on my front patio written in gravel. They are still looking for the delivery. Big capital letters. It says 'Delivery question mark.' "

"Hold on," she said. "I gotta tell you something very important. This is big. Huge! It could get everybody put away for natural life. Are you ready?"

"What?" he asked. He heard a high-pitched trill, like a computer logging on. It cycled through a series of high- and low-pitched codes, then stopped.

"OK," she said. "We have a clean line. No taps. Go ahead. Wait, you ain't using a remote are you? Are you hardwired into the wall?"

"Yes," he said. "What? What's so important?"

"Important?" she asked. "Oh, me? You mean the very important la, di, da? I only said that in case they were listening, in which case they would stay on the line while I checked it with the sniffer, because you were starting to talk about stuff that could get us all in trouble."

"*Delivery*," he said, gritting his teeth. "Written in gravel."

"In gravel?" she said. "Those clever motherfuckers. That's how they got around the vandalism statutes at the abortion clinics. You're the hate crime expert. If there's no underlying crime, there can't be any enhancement for the hate, right? So instead of spray painting the clinic sidewalks and committing vandalism, they snuck in at night and rearranged the mulch and pea gravel or whatever they could find and spelled "Baby Killers!" Like I said, clever motherfuckers."

"I don't care if they are clever or fuck their mothers," shouted Watson. "They were at my house! Got it? They want to know what happened to the delivery. Whatever was in the briefcases. Did you talk to Buck?"

"Calm down, Joey," she said. "They won't fuck with your house. The wife and kids ain't back yet, are they?"

"No," he yelled, "but I want to live to see them come back home if possible."

"Don't freak, dude," she said. "If they knock on your door, tell them to meet me at my office in the morning. I talked to fucking Buck, for Christ's sake. According to him, the briefcases were full of hate literature and militant pro-life shit. How to make bombs out of fertilizer. How to drop ATF agents with deer rifles. Mary and the black dude were doing all the print work for the national organization and several of the regional offices, to boot. Acrobat Printing and Graphics, remember? Major print jobs for the Order of the Eagles. Buck says the black dude didn't care about working for racists because the money was so good, but after he made his nut, he started wanting out."

"So they killed him?" asked Watson shrilly.

"Did I say that?" she asked. "I'm telling you what Buck said, OK? We don't know what was going on with the deaf black dude. Maybe we will never know. We still don't know what his priors were, because Dirt's source in the Bureau is on vacation. He has at least one alias, but the priors are federal and hard to get. We should have it well before trial, but in the meantime, we don't know shit about him except he was deaf and into engraving and printing and computer graphics. According to Buck, this was just a regular drop-off, until Mary Whitlow set up your client for a murder. Did you get the machine looked at? That VTD dealybob?"

She slipped the inquiry smoothly into the conversation, trying to seduce him back into Teamwork Mode.

"I did. I'll tell you about it tomorrow. If I live till then. I have oral arguments at nine-thirty."

"I know that," she said. "Frank Donahue's probably deep into scotch down at McGurk's Pub, waiting to get his beard plucked and his ass kicked. You'll show him, Joey."

"So these lessons Mary is talking about," he said, thinking out loud. " 'I'm ready for another lesson. I have the money for the lessons. The lessons are too expensive.' That's—"

"Probably code," said Myrna. "They were smart enough not to talk about their business over the phone lines, especially when TDD printouts come out the other end."

"So then why *two* briefcases? Did he bring two briefcases full of literature?"

Myrna paused. "What if he brought the pamphlets and newsletters and shit in one. Then, she's got the money in the other. They switch."

"And where's the money?" he asked.

"Good question," she said. "Beat's the Buck out of me. He claims he don't know either. Buck's story is that the Order of the Eagles is breaking up. Too much heat and notoriety. Factions are forming. And he and Jimmy Whitlow are blood brothers or some shit. Maybe they are going off to start another Cub Scout Den, or something."

"Something's not right," he said. "Why do those guys want the delivery so bad if it's just a bunch of newspapers? Can't they print some more? I mean, who cares?"

He could hear her exhale cigarette smoke. "Well," she said, "maybe there was membership stuff and minutes of meetings and all kind of militia business printed up in there. Enough to get them all walloped on conspiracy charges and socked away on hate crimes. I don't know. But they do seem to want it bad, don't they?"

"And where is it?" asked Watson.

"Buck claims he don't know," said Myrna. "His story is either Mary Whitlow has it, or the cops have it."

"He's lying," said Watson, "and maybe you are, too."

"Joey," she protested. "Stop that."

"Remember the impound lot inventory sheet? *Two* briefcases. Not one. Two in the trunk when Dirt visited the lot. Mary goes to get the car out of the lot with the two lugs who visited us in the office. When they open the trunk, they find one almost empty briefcase. Because Buck hopped the fence and got the other one. Which is what Whitlow was talking about when he told me, 'Never mind about the impound lot. We took care of the impound lot.' "

"Possible," said Myrna. "Without getting into it, I think it makes more sense that the cops took it. And they don't want us to *know* they have it, because they are downtown huddled around a pile of militia publications figuring out how many Eaglers they can nail on conspiracy charges."

"But why would they wait?" he protested.

"What's the rush?" she said. "It's like staking a dealer's house and putting tracers on his lines. Pretty soon you've got more criminals than you know what to do with. Let me tell you something else, if we wind up in a small room with some Eagle Scouts, don't be making cogent arguments about how Buck has the other briefcase."

"Because he's your client," Watson said acidly.

"That's right," she said, "and Jimmy Whitlow is *your* client."

"And they're paying us with the money Mary Whitlow was using to pay for the delivery, right?" asked Watson.

Silence. "That's what I'm talking about," she said finally. "That kind of talk will either get us killed or thrown in jail. The scenario that makes the most sense based on the evidence we've seen so far is that the cops have the other briefcase and whatever was in the briefcases."

Watson heard Whitlow's voice playing in his mind's ear: *"We took care of the impound lot. Which reminds me of the most important thing. Buck found some money. Some good money, actually."* Then he flashed to Mary Whitlow, sitting in Myrna's office: *"Tell him I get my half back and maybe . . ."*

"I'll see you at the office," said Joe.

He felt mortal terror for the third time in as many days and again wanted only to go home—home being wherever his wife and kids were. How did the Bible put it? "That is why a man leaves his father and mother and clings to his wife, and the two of them become one body." If only, and one brain, too? How consoling it would be to leave mother militia and father Stang and just go cling to his wife. Maybe Sandra had opened his letter today?

He peeked out the blinds while drinking a Budweiser nightcap, took a warm bath, and reread his fifty-page brief. If he closed his eyes he could almost recite it word for word. Every sentence had been honed and polished before he'd filed it in the Eighth Circuit. It was an essay and a legal brief, stuffed with case law and quotes from First Amendment scholars, George Orwell, Clarence Darrow, Floyd Abrams, Demosthenes, Oliver Wendell Holmes, and Nietzsche. Afterward, he drank milk, counted sheep, and then stared up at the ceiling, as quotes echoed in the chambers of consciousness.

He put the covers over his head and listened for lurking militiamen. Alone again in his big, empty house, he manfully tried to convince himself that he did not need sleep. *I do not need to sleep*, he told himself, over and over, until the glowing tumblers on his digital alarm whirred and rotated from 12:59 A.M. to 1:00 A.M. *The loss of a single night's REM is irrelevant the night before a stressful event. Adrenaline will take over during battle, and sleep won't matter*, he thought, calling to mind the various articles he had read on sleep.

As the wee hours crawled by, he issued several more imperatives, commanding himself to believe that he did not need sleep. Why? So he could go to sleep, that's why. Some part of his brain still believed it needed sleep for optimum performance, even though it didn't. He did not need to rehearse his presentation or review the briefs. That was all done. It was already in place in his neural networks. No need to disturb it. Preparation was finished and only the battle itself left to endure.

If he were Henry V on the eve of the Battle of Agincourt, he could sneak among the encampments of his neurons and neural networks, his neuroses and phobias; creep among the various grumbling factions of his unconscious, his preconscious, and his subconscious; visit fortifications in the neocortex and talk to the brutes manning his limbics; drop down to the brain stem and inspect the autonomic nervous system; eavesdrop on an argument between his Id and Superego:

Superego: "We must acquit ourselves with valor in the Eighth Circuit Court of Appeals on the morrow."

Id: "And then celebrate afterward in the primate labs by feeding the dumb glutton a plaster of warm slickness from the Venus de Neuro."

At first light, he could give a St. Crispin's Day speech to rouse the rest of himself to battle.

But alas he was not an army of neural networks or a commonwealth, or a parliament, or a symphony of brain cells, he was himself. And after oral arguments, he would be either victorious or vanquished. Sleep? He did not need to sleep.

He covered his face with the pillow and tried not to think about how, in eight and one half hours, he would be standing at the lectern on the top floor of the Courthouse of the Future addressing the United States Court of Appeals for the Eighth Circuit. Three federal appellate judges with approximately 130 years of combined legal and jurisprudential experience behind them would be asking him questions about the law of the Whitlow case and Judge Stang's orders and rulings below. If he answered wrong, Whitlow could die, and Judge Stang could be forced to endure what for him was a fate worse than death: reversal and remand for trial.

Tomorrow he would be an appellate lawyer. Not the trial lawyers he'd seen in movies. Trial lawyers make their living as players in a semi-scripted production called a trial, which often appears to the audience as some weird blend of theater, combat, and tedium. A good trial lawyer already knows the answer to almost every question before the witness answers. Success is often a matter of keeping unfavorable evidence away from the jury, getting permission to introduce favorable evidence, and then arranging predetermined segments of testimony into scenes, acts, and the final drama of closing arguments. The jury is the audience; the lawyers, the playwrights; the courtroom, a black box or stage, where only certain players and speeches are permitted with competing visions of the truth, irreconcilable versions of "what really happened." The show can go on for days, weeks, months. After it's over, the audience votes.

Appellate lawyers get twenty minutes apiece to make their case to gowned and graying appellate judges. Twenty minutes, whether it's a breach of contract suit between two corporate titans for $1.2 billion, or a wrongful discharge claim of a single union employee. No witnesses. No juries. No new evidence or objections (if they weren't introduced or preserved in the trial court or in the pretrial motions and memos, they are lost forever). Appellate judges are free simply to listen or to interrupt the lawyers with obscure questions on two dozen different points of law. The appellate lawyer must be prepared for those questions, or confess ignorance—something lawyers seem congenitally unable to do. So, Watson had to be prepared to give anything from a twenty-minute, uninterrupted speech to a one-minute summary of essential points squeezed in after nineteen minutes of close questioning from the bench.

At one-thirty A.M. he broke his promise to himself not to engage in more overpreparation. He switched on the bedside lamp and fetched out the paper profiles he'd done on each of the judges assigned to the panel. The new search engines made it possible to find every published opinion rendered by any judge and sort it according to issue, West key number, criminal or civil, the court where the case had originated. His best bet was Judge Roger Horn, a sixty-six-year-old country lawyer from Poplar Bluff, Missouri. Horn was a former defense attorney and state legislator who had reversed Judge Stang only twice in twenty years in the Eighth Circuit. Horn was also a First Amendment absolutist and had written opinions reversing convictions for draft-card and flag burning. Nationwide, the odds of winning a reversal of a criminal conviction in the federal court system runs at a puny 4 percent. Judge Horn had, by way of majority and dissenting opinions, shown a willingness to reverse criminal convictions almost 8 percent of the time.

His worst bet was Judge Jordana Mallory. She had been a big-firm partner at Fishbeck & Klein, the number two firm behind Stern, Pale, then she had become in-house counsel at a local chemical company. She had been a controversial district court judge because her background was almost entirely corporate, and it showed in her con-law and criminal-law opinions: fuzzy logic and short, conclusory opinions. She had dissented in two school prayer cases and closed one of those opinions with the statement: "Surely there is room for both the First Amendment and Our Creator in the classroom." She was an avenger when it came to pornography and had been an early and vocal supporter of the penalties for "indecency" set forth in the Communications Decency Act. Watson had pretty much given up on trying to convince her that the hate crime statute violated the First Amendment. He planned instead to keep her focused on the evidentiary issues, where he could appeal to her memories of being a controversial district court judge who was constantly being second-guessed on appeal.

The wild card was Judge Geoffrey Willard, an Arkansas district court judge sitting by designation—which meant he had been recruited to help appellate judges handle the burgeoning caseload of matters federal. He was a relatively unknown quantity because district court opinions, especially criminal dispositions, often go unpublished. He had presided over school deseg cases and some class action Title VII cases where his rulings had been conservative and well reasoned. But as near as Watson could tell, the judge's conservative bent also included the usual tough-on-crime strain. He had been prepared to write off Judge Willard, too, until a spider and an off-label browser had brought back an obscure hit from a Little Rock Web site. It was a local bar journal article called "Hate Crime Hysteria," by Judge Geoffrey Willard, written back in the late nineties, just after they passed the federal law providing augmented penalties for church burnings. It was a glimpse into the mind of a judge who was skeptical, one, that church burnings were racially motivated, and, two, that a federal statute outlawing hatred would discourage anyone from burning a church, when the penalties for plain arson already dealt in decades of hard time.

Then Watson decided to reread Wisconsin v. Mitchell for the—what? Twentieth time? He flipped open the cover page and thought he heard the lock turn in the front door. Or had he imagined it? He froze and listened.

Alpha? Beta? An Order of the Eagler with an explosive device? Somebody looking for Jimmy Whitlow's lawyer? Buck? Here he'd squandered all of his energies preparing for intellectual battle in the Eighth Court of Appeals. Federal appellate law—the legal equivalent of brain surgery. How ironic if, instead, the pivotal clash took place in the swine ring, a muscle game, where ruthless violence reigned supreme. He'd spent most of his life reading and writing, speaking, talking, deploying words—a cluster of linguistic skills that would be of precious little use in a contest with Alpha and Beta.

He heard the door open in the foyer. Somebody was trying to be quiet, because he heard only a single whoosh of the door brushing free of the weather stripping. He threw off the covers—to do what? Get a toothbrush and sharpen it up real quick? Brandish a fingernail clipper?

He heard soft footsteps on the stairwell. Fuck! How many times had he resolved to get himself a nice semiautomatic weapon and keep it in a lockbox next to the bed for just this occasion? But whoever it was must have had a key, unless they'd picked the lock?

"Joe?" asked a woman's whispering voice.

"Sandra!"

He fell on the bed and gave himself cardiac massage.

She looked down at the stacks of paper scattered around the bed and her mouth twisted into a just-as-I-thought smile.

"What are you doing here?" he said. "I mean, I'm so glad you're here. I'm glad to see you. I . . . have oral arguments tomorrow, in that prisoner case."

"I know *that*," she said. "That's why I'm here. Who put rocks all over the front porch? Was the UPS guy here? It says 'Delivery?' "

"It's a prank from . . . from some weird people I met," he said.

"I'll bet you're meeting weird people every day," she said and sat on the edge of the bed.

She wore an overcoat. Her hair was in French braids—his favorite arrangement. He smelled perfume and other fresh scents. Conditioner? But she didn't seem warm or particularly forgiving. Just matter-of-fact.

"You can't sleep," she said bluntly. "I knew you wouldn't be able to sleep. Remember the bar exam?"

Dark night of the soul. A seedy hotel room in Jefferson City, Missouri, the state capital, where all aspiring Missouri lawyers converge for the festival of anxiety, angst, and terror known as the bar exam. For two days, they cram and contemplate suicide. No one sleeps. Instead they lie abed and wring their withers about how their entire future and the welfare of their families will depend upon which circles they darken the next morning with a Number 2 pencil. The night of the bar exam, Sandra had hired a sitter for Sheila back in St. Louis, then had driven two hours to Jeff City so she could show up in his room at 10:00 P.M.

"Remember the night before the con law exam? Before First Amendment law? You can't sleep," she said again, in a level tone.

"And you won't be able to sleep," she said.

He looked at her eagerly, as if to say, *This is a peace offering, right? Are we making up? Am I forgiven?*

"I don't *want* to sleep with you," she said. "I'm still furious. Hurt. My family . . . And I don't understand what you are doing with yourself. This criminal case is a big mistake. Major career error. Everybody I've asked about it agrees with me."

Her voice broke, and his backbone cracked on the wheel of conscience. *I should have pleaded him out! Avoided the brain scientist the instant I saw her. I knew what to do. I just didn't do it! And then, after that, I knew what not to do, and I went ahead and did it anyway!*

"You have placed this passing infatuation with criminal law above your family's welfare. I can't do anything about that. But, now that you've chosen this . . . course, I don't know what to do. We're married," she said. "Are we getting divorced?"

"No way," he said without hesitation. "Why? Is that what you're thinking?"

"Never," she said, her eyes watching his, waiting for him to blink first. "Never."

Whew!

She glanced down at her hands and shrugged. "Unless I found out you were sleeping with somebody else. But I *know* you would *never* do that." She tossed her head, shaking off the notion of anything so preposterous. "Never mind adultery. Just the implications of willfully exposing your entire family to disease. Your unborn children." She shuddered. "That would certainly do it. In that case, divorce would be mandatory," she said. "But I wouldn't marry a creature like that."

"Nor would I," said Watson. *Premeditated, willful disregard of my own family? Adultery? Second only to murder when prizes for original sins were being given out. Because of what? Biological programming? Neural Darwinism? Genetics, serotonin levels, ape-hierarchy politics, evolutionary psychology? I wish! God, I would give body and soul if it were true. Life would be so much easier! I am protoplasm, I could say each morning upon awakening, I will do whatever is necessary to further my own agenda and the welfare of my immediate biological family and a few close friends, like-minded alpha males and females.*

"So," she said. "My husband has decided he wants to be a criminal lawyer. Not something I planned on. Not something I understand."

"San, I . . . I think it must be a law school thing. They brainwash you to think of your client first."

"Whatever," she said. She looked up at him suddenly. "And you can't go back to Stern, Pale after it's over?" Her tone was plaintive; she was pleading for one ray of hope. "Any way at all that could happen?"

Watson shook his head. "They put a bag over my head and marched me out at dawn to be shot," he said. "I'll join Jimmy Whitlow in prison before I go back there."

"I understand," she said with a sigh, undoing the buttons on her coat, and he caught a glimpse of rose-colored satin. Another teddy.

He felt nerves sprouting, blood rushing to his pelvis. Everything was going to be all right again. He was forgiven. He could start his whole life over! He searched her face for the same glad eyes that had sent him to the carpet so many times during the mad rush of infatuation that had swept over them like mental illness before they were married.

Instead, she was solemn. Glum.

"I guess I'm willing to try this criminal law business, if it means you will be home more."

"I promise!" he said, bowing down before the queen. "You won't be sorry. I'll be my own boss."

"That's what worries me," she said.

"No, really," he said. "I'll have so much more free time. You'll see!"

"Will I?" she said, slipping out of her coat.

"As soon as this Whitlow case is over," he said. "I promise."

"Stop talking," she said. "Do it, and go to sleep."

CHAPTER 26

Judgment day. He left two hours early as a precaution against systems failures—car breakdown, traffic, metropolitan dysfunction, poor health, nuclear accident, earthquake, flood, fire, war, windstorm, act of God. He arrived downtown at 7:00 A.M. Oral arguments were scheduled for 9:30.

At the Market Street exit, he saw the Old Cathedral, pink and forlorn in the morning light. Instead of just driving by it, the way he had done for over a year on his way to Stern, Pale, he pulled into the parking lot and looked up at the stone façade. He considered his motives for wanting to go inside. For what? Good luck? Maybe his brain was wistfully yearning for otherwordly consolation, some balm for his overloaded mental circuits, spiritual salve for his sore somatic markers. Maybe prayer was a vestigial ritual originally developed to ward off startle patterns and panic disorders, to enable the organism to perform under stress, thereby maximizing fitness? Prayer was probably just an instinct in extinction, like altruism, which had served its purpose in advancing the social organism called the human race, and was now being phased out to make way for—What? Neuroscience? Cyberspace? A new brand of fitness?

Inside the Old Cathedral, he crept down the nave midway to a pew,

a middling location appropriate for a lukewarm Christian, neither hot
nor cold, the sort that, according to Revelation, makes the Divinity want
to spew them from His mouth. ("How I wish you were one or the
other—hot or cold!" He could use that line on Palmquist.) His footsteps
echoed in whispers from the vaults and ambulatories, arches and log-
gias. He felt the carved eyes of saints and fathers of the Church watching him from their alcoves, as he knelt in a wooden pew and bowed his
head. Streaks of painted light slanted in from the stained glass windows. Sacred odors rose up from his childhood: cedar and rosewood;
incense from smoking thuribles, beeswax, smoldering wicks, and ashes;
starched soutanes, chasubles, and albs; unleavened bread; the scent of
lilies and perfumed graveclothes.

Watson shrank and felt himself become a homunculus once again, a
ghost in the machine. He was seven years old, renewing his baptismal
vows in St. Dymphna's Cathedral. *"Father, forgive me, for I have sinned."*

A severe, bull-voiced Roman senator in vestments, his white hair
parted and looking as if the Holy Spirit had perched on his head and
spread its wings. *"Do you renounce Satan and all his works?"*

Watson's scalp grew tight with Dante's fear. Satan was there somewhere, but he always moved one millimeter outside the peripheries of
human vision (except on special occasions, when he came out for a good
laugh at, say, a lawyer trying to pray).

"Do you renounce Satan and all his works?"

A cold wind had blown through his seven-year-old skin, bringing
with it the age of reason, thrilling his bones, horripilating its way up his
spine. Somewhere in his monkey brain he had neural networks that still
tingled with reverence and awe at the epiphenomenon called conscience.

Church. Just a nice building? God's mausoleum? An access node
where one could log on to SoulNet using dial-up networking, go to
www.divinity.com looking for WebMaster God?

He had trouble remembering the procedural rules. Probably he
should first be contritely sorry for the near occasion of adultery, which
he would probably be able to avoid, now that Palmquist had lost interest in him and his client. But was this theologically correct? What if, instead of preparing for an inquisition on First Amendment law in the
Eighth Circuit Court of Appeals, he had smashed the car into a bridge
piling on the way downtown and was trembling in the vestibules of the

afterlife, waiting to be asked ultimate questions from his Catholic youth? *Why did God make me? To know, love, and serve Him.*

"Mr. Watson, tell us please, what is *perfect contrition* and how does it differ from *imperfect contrition*?"

"Yes, Your Honor. Perfect contrition is sorrow for and detestation of sin with a true purpose of amendment, arising from a love of God for His own perfections. Imperfect contrition is sorrow for sin motivated by some inferior impulse, as fear of divine punishment—theophobia (fear of God), stygiophobia (fear of Hell), kenophobia (fear of voids)."

"And do you now have perfect contrition?"

"Who, me, Your Honor? Perfect contrition for what?"

"How about adultery?"

"Adul—? You mean, that hand job? Since when is heavy petting adultery? Recall, please, that I was bound, restrained, helpless at the time. If that's adultery, then the controlling statute is fatally overbroad, and it's a harsh universe you're running here, don't you think? At the very worst, I would call it quasi-adultery, for which I am now formulating quasi-contrition. I am doing the very best I can, here."

"But you saw the woman again after that. And you wanted to commit adultery with her, didn't you? You set out with the intent to do just that, didn't you?"

"But I didn't, did I? Because my brain wouldn't let me. My well-fortified conscience disabled my manhood. Doesn't that count for something?"

Psychomachia—the warfare of the soul. Who said: "I fear we cannot get rid of God because we still believe in grammar"? Does God play at billiards? Dice? The thunderclap of ivory planets splitting the air. The big bang followed by the whisper of white molecules colliding. Crisis theology. Pascal's wager: If there is a God, you win; if not, you won't know the difference. There, now he could cite specific instances when he had felt remorse, attempted prayer, and failed. If he could go to his knees, or lower, then he could ask for help in oral arguments.

He looked up at the tabernacle, a forbidden zone he'd seen during a tour of St. Dymphna's, just before his first communion. It had small, heavy gold doors, which swung out to reveal a lustrous panne satin interior, looking a lot like the inside of a coffin, but smaller.

"During mass," Sister Mary Vendetta had explained, "the Eucharist is offered up for us on the altar, but whenever mass is not being said, the Body of Christ is kept in the tabernacle."

Perhaps, giddied by the gravity of the situation, young Watson had mistaken the mighty, white high altar itself for the tabernacle—the overall concept being that of a capacious mausoleum, complete with ornamental sarcophagi, and a gold coal chute (the tabernacle), where bread and wine, manna and ambrosia were passed in to sustain and nourish the Living Body of Christ, who was reclining on a divan inside the altar, being fanned by eunuchs with palms and punkahs, and nibbling on grapes dropped into His mouth by fawning slave girls. Thus his nimble seven-year-old imagination had resolved the paradox that Christ had died for his sins, His Body was in the tabernacle, but He was also alive, and would live forever and ever.

Watson could walk up there now, perhaps. Turn the small, heavy gold key in the tumblers. The doors would swing open, a small coffin would slide out on casters, like a drawer in a morgue. The chthonic glow of candles flickering off the slick black casket. He could open the hinged top half, stand on tiptoe, peer into swirling satin, and see the embalmed body of James Whitlow. Rigor mortis rictus and risus sardonicus, hands crossed on his bosom, his tattoo plainly visible in the candlelight: JESUS HATES NIGGERS.

The courtroom had the same sacred, eschatological feel. Burnished wood and timeless marble; robed, somber dignitaries gravely contemplating Justice. But the sanctity of the court of appeals was technologically enhanced. Each of the appellate judges had a monitor, a pointing device, and a recessed keyboard at his disposal. The lectern had a small readout displaying the time remaining in the practitioner's oral argument.

It was a courtroom, all right. But the jury—the collective representative of common humanity—was nowhere in sight. One look at the panel of stern judges and Watson instantly wished he could argue to a jury instead. In the stifling formality of this star chamber, a jury trial would be a mud-wrestling melee by comparison. Instead of talking to what Myrna referred to as twelve Kmart checkout clerks, Watson would be trying to persuade three gray eminences who'd heard it all before. He managed an out-of-body experience for a split second, during which time he saw the parade of advocates who had appeared before these judges for years. Every working day, for decades, these aging men and women had sat and heard lawyers argue their cases. Heard Mr. Stammer clash with Ms. Hedge. Counselor Canny take issue with Solicitor Spleen. Heard the neophytes' whine and saw the sleight of the old hands. Heard them circumlocute and stall, with their "I would argue that," or "I would respond by saying that," instead of just arguing or saying it.

The format was more oppressively restrictive than a Spenserian stanza, but tight shoes only made the lawyers learn new dances. Alone, facing three judges with no evidence or witnesses, the veterans become masters of paralipsis and insinuation, rodomontade and heartfelt hyperbole, vainglorious oratory and rigorous rhetoric. But alas, none of it seems to matter in the end, because—that's right—the judges have heard it all before. If the statistics gathered by the judiciary committees are accurate, appellate judges usually decide cases after reading the briefs and before oral arguments. Knowing that, a guy should be able to sleep the night before oral arguments.

He took a seat on a bench that was very like a pew without kneelers. He watched lawyers filing in. Here and there, journalists with notepads. Not a crowd, but certainly more than the usual assembly of lawyers with cases to argue. Frank Donahue swept in with Harper and a clerk in tow.

"Well, young man," Donahue said warmly, "here we are." He smiled and shook Watson's hand. "Mr. Harper and I are still willing to play dead and let your client off with natural life."

"When my client recovers from brain surgery at the hands of government doctors, I'll ask him if he'll go for it," said Watson.

"Yes," said Donahue, "I heard they were going to try to fix the fellow's brain. Take out the hate glands, maybe?" He winked at Harper.

"Too bad about Judge Willard," said Harper.

"Too bad?" asked Watson.

Donahue nodded jovially. "Too bad for your client. He's the toughest district court judge in Arkansas. Positively loathes criminals."

"You mean he *hates* criminals?" asked Watson. "If he hates anybody he better watch himself around you guys, huh? Besides, he may hate criminals," said Watson, "but he wrote an *Arkansas Bar Journal* article called "Hate Crime Hysteria" back in the nineties, just after they passed the federal law against church burnings. I'll send you a copy if you'd like."

Donahue glared in Harper's direction. "I'm sure we found that one. It's his sentencing background that would give me the chills if I were you."

"I suppose it would if we were going to a sentencing hearing," said Watson.

Donahue squinted at him and elbowed Harper. "Very tart, this one. A little too flip. We'll see if Judge Willard takes some of the tang out of your sass, boy." He extended his hand. "Good luck, young man."

Watson shook Donahue's hand and then Harper's. And thought about going to the rest room with dry heaves.

He felt a light touch on his right elbow just as the clerk said, "All rise." He strained to see who it was in the corner of his eye, but no one was there. Another touch, from below? A child? He looked down and saw Myrna Schweich standing behind him in full corporate dress. She tugged his sleeve until his ear was at her level.

"Your dick is so big it is a fucking war club," she whispered. "Donahue is a lazy blowhard. He's a short guy with little hands. You know what that means. You? Look at you. Six two. Big hands. Manly man. You know ten times more than he does about the law of this case. The man does not read. Pull out that big cock of yours and beat him to death with it," she hissed.

Her exhortations had the intended effect. Maybe she was right. Where would a guy like Donahue find the time to read a brief, let alone cases cited *in* a brief?

"United States Court of Appeals for the Eighth Circuit is in session. The first case on this morning's docket is United States versus Whitlow. The appellant has reserved five minutes for rebuttal."

They would be arguing legal theory in a vacuum, hermetically sealed against any factual considerations. When Judge Horner asked him about the First Amendment and the federal penalty enhancement statute, Watson could not say, "Guess what, Judge? Did you know that Mary Whitlow is in this militia business up to her eyeballs?" He couldn't mention the missing briefcase, the VTD and its incriminating statements, the venereal disease, Alpha and Beta. Those were all trial court matters, messy factual discrepancies to be worked out below. Up here, in the chambers of pure legal reason, the only questions were legal ones: Did Judge Stang correctly rule that the federal hate crimes statute violates the First Amendment? Did Judge Stang correctly rule that evidence of tattoos, racial jokes, racist reading materials, arguably racist behaviors such as Whitlow's display of a Confederate flag, were inadmissible to prove racial animus because the prosecution had failed to link those activities to the murder?

"United States versus Whitlow," called the clerk. And Judge Willard looked up from his notes.

"Good morning, Mr. Donahue," said Judge Horner, who sat in the middle, flanked by Judge Mallory on his right and Judge Willard on his left.

"Good morning, Judge," said Donahue, swaggering to his place at the podium.

"And is it Mr. Watson?" said Horner, smiling indulgently at Watson. "For the appellee, James Whitlow, is that right?"

"Yes, Your Honor," said Watson. *Would it were otherwise! I'll go first if the court wishes!* As always, the complaining party went first, which meant that Watson would have to sit and watch a professional orator with twenty-five years of lawyering under his belt perform before taking his own turn at the podium.

"May it please the court," Donahue began, "I represent the people of the United States of America. We are seeking to enforce a penalty enhancement statute which Congress passed some time ago to provide additional penalties for crimes motivated by particular types of hatred. Despite the somewhat hysterical contentions set forth in the defendant's brief, this statute does not punish thought, or ideas, or beliefs. It punishes criminal conduct. The defendant, James Whitlow, is free to think any thoughts he pleases. He is free to be a bigot and think bigoted thoughts. But when he expresses his thoughts with conduct, namely, the murder of a disabled citizen of color, his conduct and his motivation for that conduct may be punished."

"Mr. Donahue," said Judge Horner, "I'm looking at the title of this statute as it is set forth in the United States Code, where it says, 'Hate Crime and Vulnerable Victims.' Are you telling this court that Congress was not targeting bigots and their proclivity for hatred when it passed this statute?"

"The statute is aimed at discriminatory *conduct*," said Donahue. "If there is no underlying criminal conduct, then no penalty applies. The statute punishes perpetrators who intentionally select victims because of certain protected characteristics. It does not target bigotry or racism or any other mind-set or idea."

"Because if it did it would run afoul of the First Amendment, wouldn't it?" asked Judge Willard.

"An argument could be made to that effect," said Donahue.

"And you're not taking off after bigots, are you, Mr. Donahue?" chuckled Judge Willard.

"Bigoted criminal conduct," said Donahue, "as set forth in this statute, which was very carefully crafted to accommodate the First Amendment."

"I see," said Judge Willard. "That must have been your evil twin in the *Post-Dispatch* railing against bigotry last week."

Soft laughter from the lawyers awaiting their turns, which Donahue quelled with a loud voice. "I hope I am entitled to publicly express my own antipathies for bigotry and still discuss the constitutionality of a statute aimed exclusively at discriminatory conduct. I find bigotry personally abhorrent," said Donahue, "but I am also aware that it is protected by the First Amendment. Our Supreme Court has told us time and again that the First Amendment does not protect violence or criminal conduct, even when the defendant claims to be expressing himself by using same. This statute does not target bigotry in the air, as it were, it targets bigoted conduct."

"And *only* bigoted conduct?" asked Judge Willard. "It's not overbroad?"

"I don't believe so, Judge."

"Have you seen this program— What's it called?" asked the judge. " 'The Fugitive'? And they made it into a movie, didn't they? This Fugitive fellow is constantly looking for a one-armed man who supposedly killed his wife. Do I have it right, Mr. Donahue?"

"I think so, Judge, but I fail to see—"

"I'm wondering what would happen if our Fugitive caught a one-armed man—the *wrong* one-armed man, as it turns out—and assaulted him. His victim has only one arm, so he's disabled under the terms of this statute, is he not?"

"Yes," said Donahue, "but—"

"And, of course, our Fugitive—what's the wording of the statute?" Judge Willard picked up a piece of paper and read from it. "Our Fugitive 'intentionally selected his victim *because of* the victim's disability,' isn't that right? But this *selection* has nothing to do with discriminatory conduct, does it? The Fugitive is simply trying to find the man who killed his wife, right? Yet under this statute he would receive extra penalties because of this intentional selection."

"In the confines of your hypothetical," said Donahue, "he would."

Judge Mallory interrupted and tried to ride to Donahue's rescue. "Well, it's not just a hypothetical, is it, Mr. Donahue? The case cited by the defense, Aishman versus California, in which the defendant and his friends went looking for Mexicans, because his wife told him a group of Mexicans had raped her? Were these men looking for rapists or Mexicans?"

"In that particular case," said Donahue, "I'm not . . . I believe they were . . . "

He hasn't read Aishman, Watson marveled. Incredible! Judge Mallory was pitching him one underhanded across the plate. The answer would be "both." He was looking for Mexican rapists. He can hate rapists all he wants, but if at least part of the reason he selected his victims was *because of* their nationality, he runs afoul of the statute. When the husband in Aishman came home from beating Mexicans with a baseball bat, he told his friends he had been "hitting home runs with Mexicans." Donahue wasn't going to make any hay with that line, because he hadn't read the case. Myrna was right!

"I concede that in some very narrow circumstances," said Donahue, "the statute may reach conduct not motivated by discrimination, but I would weigh those unusual circumstances against the grave problems the federal government faces in trying to stem the rising tide of bias-motivated violence and property destruction. These arguments were heard by the United States Supreme Court in Wisconsin versus Mitchell and the Court ruled that the Wisconsin statute was constitutional. Wisconsin was entitled to administer greater penalties for an assault in which the attacker intentionally selected a white victim."

"That seems to be the case in so many of these high-profile cases," inserted Judge Mallory. "Is there a danger these statutes will be used disproportionately against minorities who are accused of attacking what they perceive to be their social oppressors? Seems to me it's the prosecutors who decide what is and isn't a hate crime. In the Wisconsin case, which came up so often in the briefs, it's a black teenager who intentionally selected a white person."

"Proof positive that the statute is content neutral," said Donahue. "Every argument set forth in the defendant's brief was made in the

Mitchell case, and the United States Supreme Court rejected every one of them. This court is obliged to do the same under the doctrine of stare decisis."

"Don't overstate your case, Counselor," said Judge Willard. "That is not quite true. *Some* of the defendant's arguments were made in Mitchell, and *some* of the defendant's arguments are new arguments, because we have a new and different statute, isn't that right?"

"Not in any material respect, Judge," said Donahue quickly. "The sentencing commission looked at the Wisconsin statute and the Supreme Court's opinion in Mitchell very closely before drafting this statute, and this court—"

"And because we have a *different* statute," interrupted Willard acidly, "then we have a *different* case, and this bloviating reference of yours to stare decisis belongs in a theater, not in this courtroom. The Wisconsin statute was constitutional because it was discretionary, Mr. Donahue."

"I'm sorry, Your Honor? I've lost the court's train of . . ."

"The Wisconsin judge could administer the penalty enhancement or not, depending on the circumstances. Right? The statute simply expanded the range of available penalties from a four-year maximum sentence to seven, eight, or nine years, right? But here, this statute *requires* an enhancement of six levels under the sentencing guidelines if the perpetrator intentionally selected his or her victim because of a protected characteristic."

"Yes, but . . ."

"And our Fugitive is going to get a second, separate penalty for intentionally selecting a disabled person, even though he had no intention to discriminate against a disabled person per se—he simply wants to kill the man who murdered his wife, conduct which is already punishable under the homicide statutes. Nobody wants to set him free. But we don't want to give him extra punishments for something he didn't do. A federal sentencing judge bound by this statute is powerless to withhold the enhancement, even if it is clear that no discriminatory conduct has occurred."

"That's true, Your Honor," said Donahue, "but again . . ."

"And we have exceeded the bounds of the Mitchell case in other respects as well, have we not? You'll recall that in Mitchell, the defense made the same argument that's being made here, namely, that there is a very real possibility that a defendant will be punished for his beliefs or for expressive conduct which may have occurred years before the crime.

And the Supreme Court said"—the judge rustled papers and retrieved a document—" 'We are left then with the prospect of a citizen suppressing his bigoted beliefs for fear that evidence of such beliefs will be introduced against him at trial if he commits a more serious offense against person or property. This is too speculative a hypothesis to support Mitchell's overbreadth claim.' "

Judge Willard looked up over his reading glasses at Donahue. "But it's no longer speculative, is it, Mr. Donahue?" asked the judge. "Because in this case the government wants to introduce evidence that Mr. Whitlow displayed a Confederate flag once upon a time, or that he told racist jokes, or worried about his property values, or painted a swastika once as a college prank. Has the government attempted to tie any of these events to the crime being charged here?"

"We were prepared to do just that at trial," said Donahue.

"But you didn't get to trial, did you?" said Judge Willard, "because you couldn't satisfy Judge Stang's concerns about how you were going to tie all of this character evidence to the charged crime. It's a question of proximity, isn't it? How proximate is the conduct to the thought?"

"We had evidence that this defendant was spewing racial invective in a crowded bar just days before the crime was committed," said Donahue.

"Did this evidence contain any indication that the defendant was going to attack any member of a protected group? Did he threaten to go out and kill a black person, or did he tell somebody he would really like to shoot a deaf person?"

"Not in so many words, Your Honor, but when taken as a whole, his speech on any number of occasions is rife with violent antipathies against groups protected by this statute. All of this evidence taken together is probative and admissible on the question of his real motive in committing this heinous crime. And I would add, Your Honor, that under the terms of the statute as it has been interpreted by the courts, it is not necessary for the government to prove that the defendant, James Whitlow, selected his victim *solely,* or *exclusively,* or even *predominately* because of the victim's race or disability, only that his prohibited animus played *some part* in his motivation for the crime."

"Now I feel better," snapped Judge Willard. "If one percent of our defendant's motive for intentionally selecting his victim was *because of* the victim's race and disability and ninety-nine percent of his motive was *because of* his wife's infidelity, then we'll double or triple his sentence to make sure that no stone goes unturned in obliterating even minuscule amounts of bigotry, is that it?"

"With all due respect," said Donahue, "the court's hypotheticals are both erudite and creative, but my office is charged with applying statutes to real-world crimes."

Watson held his breath and watched Donahue taking on more water. Judge Willard was an archangel come down from heaven. Watson's ally. Stang's alter ego. He was waiting for Judge Willard to wink at him, or give him a nod. What a pal! The good judge was arguing Watson's brief for him. How was it these old men seemed so effortlessly insightful?

"Mr. Donahue," said Judge Mallory, obviously trying to give Donahue some relief from the onslaught of Judge Willard, "are there any limits to the government's powers under these statutes? I mean, we have extra penalties for intentional selection of victims based upon their perceived race, color, religion, national origin, ethnicity, gender, disability, sexual orientation, and views on the issue of reproductive rights. Suppose we add views on the issue of hazards presented by the ozone layer, or views on the draft in times of heightened national security, or views on whether the earth is flat? Would adding those categories render the statute constitutionally infirm?"

"The categories currently contained in the federal hate crimes statute all further legitimate state interests," said Donahue. "I think the Supreme Court's opinion in Dawson would prohibit extra punishment being given for abstract beliefs that are not related causally to the charged crime. For instance, if we tried to make a statute providing that all drunk drivers will have their sentences doubled if it can be shown that they are also racists, that would present constitutional problems, but that is not the case here."

"OK," said Judge Mallory, and went on to make his point for him, lest he drift back into the line of Willard's fire, "so it isn't the goodness or badness of the idea that we are talking about, it's whether attacks on the basis of that idea are a particular problem? As in the case of the views on reproductive rights, a category Congress added to the statute in 1999? We don't care if criminals are for or against abortion, but we do care and we give them extra penalties if they attack someone or destroy someone's property because of their views on this politically volatile subject, is that right?"

She was feeding him baby food with a rubber spoon.

"Absolutely correct, Judge Mallory," said Donahue. "The question is whether violence motivated by hatred of the particular categories presents a significant law enforcement problem in the traditional criminal context."

"Your time is almost up, Mr. Donahue," said Judge Willard. "One more time: How do you answer the arguments in the defendant's brief that this statute is not governed by the Supreme Court's analysis in Wisconsin versus Mitchell because it is not a discretionary sentencing statute but a call for separate, required, extra penalties, no matter what the circumstances of the case? The defendant's brief laid it out for you very well. But the government's reply brief reads like a law review article on the sentencing guidelines without ever engaging the ultimate issue. Is this statute discretionary? And if not, does that present us with a problem of overbreadth for our Fugitive and his quest for the one-armed man?"

"Judge Willard," said Donahue, "our brief dealt at length with the sentencing guidelines because they inherently tie the hands of judges and diminish their discretion in sentencing matters. That does not render them unconstitutional."

"But that's because they are simply assigning penalties for stated crimes. Give me an example of another crime for which the law provides a separate, required, nondiscretionary enhancement solely because of the defendant's motive?"

Murder for hire, treason, murder of a police officer, voyeurism. Watson clicked them off mentally, along with his memorized rebuttals for each one. Most of them were circumstances, not motives, easily proved with objective evidence, unlike the prohibited motive called hate. If the defendant was paid for the murder, it's murder for hire, but there is no such simple litmus test for the psychic state called hatred.

Donahue's mouth opened but nothing came out. "I seem to recall some examples set forth in our brief," said Donahue, "and we can make a separate submission calling the court's attention to those passages if . . ."

The red light on Donahue's lectern came on.

"I see my time is up already," said Donahue. "May I briefly conclude?"

"No," said Judge Willard. "The courtroom is full of lawyers waiting to argue their cases, Mr. Donahue. If we allow you to briefly conclude, the lawyers in the next case will ask for extra time to briefly conclude, and the lawyers in the next case will ask for extra time to voluminously conclude . . . and so on until it's dark outside. Please sit down."

"Mr. Watson," said Judge Horner.

Watson walked to the podium, trying to hide his deep breaths from the court. He placed his folder with his notes in front of him and saw print swim before his eyes.

"May it please . . . the court," he said. "I represent the defendant James Whitlow. Clarence Darrow once said, 'There is no such crime as a crime of thought; there are only crimes of action.' "

"Mr. Watson," said Judge Horner, "we appreciate the Clarence Darrow quote but we don't need to hear oral argument from the defendant in this case."

Watson trembled and looked up at the judges. He must have misunderstood Judge Horner. Judge Horner couldn't have said that the court was not going to hear his oral argument. That was not possible.

Judge Mallory wore a sour look on her face and wrote something on her legal pad, but Judge Willard and Judge Horner were smiling. Mocking him?

"That's all," said Judge Horner. "Thank you. We do not need to hear oral argument from the defendant in this case."

"But . . ." said Watson. He felt the floor heave under his feet. He was being dismissed before he could even argue! Why? Had he failed so abysmally that they didn't even want to hear him? Was his brief that bad? Was Whitlow's case so hopeless?

"We will issue our ruling in this expedited interlocutory appeal, probably sometime after lunch," said Judge Horner. "That's all. You may sit down."

Watson's mouth stuck open and he stared.

Judge Willard leaned forward and nodded, then whisked him away with the back of his hand.

"But—" began Watson.

"That will be *all*," said Judge Horner, his tone suggesting he was about to rise from his chair and carry Watson away from the podium.

Tomorrow's *Post-Dispatch* flashed before his eyes: HATE CRIME CHARGES REINSTATED: JUDGE STANG SUMMARILY REVERSED.

Watson picked up his folder and staggered back to his seat in front of Myrna. Half the lawyers were smiling at him, and the other half were leaning their heads together and whispering. Mocking him? Because the Eighth Circuit had not even allowed him to argue his case? Were they making fun of him? Was the case such a loser that the court had decided it didn't want to hear oral arguments?

Myrna was beaming. Donahue and Harper were leaving the courtroom.

"They didn't let me argue," whispered Watson. "My argument. They didn't let me . . ." His careful presentation, his magnum opus on the First Amendment—his brief!—from which he had distilled an outline that fit on a single page of boldface headings and case titles, each of which were the jumping-off points for five-minute compelling arguments on points of law posed by questions from the bench? Questions never asked? The presentation never made? Useless? Not worth hearing?

"They said I couldn't argue," Watson repeated, his empty stomach squirming as he stared into Myrna's bright, smiling face.

She pulled him down to her level and whispered in his ear. "That's because you already won, ya big fuckin' dummy."

CHAPTER 27

Watson found his client propped up in a hospital bed, cuffed in four-point leather restraints to stainless steel side rails. He had just enough slack in the lines so he could hold the *St. Louis Post-Dispatch* and read articles about himself. Without hair, his features seemed even more severe, the flesh of his face thrown into relief against the white of the pillowcase and bandages.

"You're his lawyer, right?" said a nurse, his finger on the bed's control pad opposite Watson.

A motor whirred and the head of the bed slowly elevated.

"I am his lawyer," said Watson, recalling the joy he had once felt in representing a real person, albeit a racist, falsely accused of killing because of racism. How to sort out the feelings he had about defending a racist who possibly had done everything he'd been charged with, and more?

The nurse touched the turban of bandages on Whitlow's head. "I need to change the dressings and put some more antibiotic ointment at the site." He began unwinding the bandages, while Whitlow folded up his newspaper and patiently waited.

"I get put to sleep like a dog in a kennel," said Whitlow cheerfully, "and when I come to, I find out my lawyer has kicked the government's ass to Hell and gone. And, hey," he added, opening his restrained hands and showing Watson his new digs, "I ain't in jail! I'm in a hospital."

"Don't jinx it by celebrating too soon, Jimmy," said Watson, hoping his client would notice the nickname and wonder how his lawyer had come by it. "We could still have a trial, or the U.S. Attorney could ask for a rehearing en banc, which means he would request a rehearing before a seven-judge panel. He could even appeal to the Supremes if he wanted to. He has to weigh the benefits of a win against the risks of having another failure splashed all over the papers during his Senate campaign."

The nurse lifted the last wrap from Whitlow's shaved head, revealing cross-hatched sutures holding a scimitar-shaped incision together. He squeezed ointment out of a tube and dabbed it along the angry seam, while Whitlow winced and held his head still. The nurse finished his work, rebandaged Whitlow's head, and left the room.

"And no matter what," added Watson, "you're still looking at manslaughter, at least."

"All I know is it don't look like they'll be able to kill me just yet," said Whitlow, returning to his newspaper. "If they offer manslaughter, you take it."

He glanced sideways at his lawyer. "So, that seizure stuff *did* turn out to be important for my case, huh?"

Watson sat down in a chair next to the bed. "Yes. It certainly qualifies as a mental defect or disease. It sounds like you had a cyst they needed to take out."

"And they was saying I might get a break at sentencing if the surgery fixed my temper and my bad attitude, right?"

"The consent forms look that way," said Watson. "I wish you had told them to call me before you signed them. If you read them closely, the prosecution has simply agreed to file the medical reports and the consent forms at the sentencing hearing, along with a rather ambiguous recommendation for leniency."

"But they'll do some more psycho tests on me again before that, right? And if it looks like the surgery worked, then I might get off easier, huh?"

"Maybe," said Watson.

"Well, you heard it here, first," said Whitlow. "I ain't the same person. The surgery fixed me up with a brand-new brain-box."

"It did?" asked Watson.

"You bet," said Whitlow. "It's a medical miracle." He gave Watson a wide-eyed, tender look. "For the first time in my life I know what it feels like not to hate. It feels so—"

"You feel better?" asked Watson.

"Feel better?" said Whitlow. " 'Feel better' is what you get with a hundred-dollar hooker. I ain't talking about *feeling* better, lawyer. I'm talking about how I don't hate niggers no more. Niggers are just as good as everybody else. In fact, there's plenty of white trash strewn all over the place that is much worse than your average Negro of colored. I know that now. I can see it as plain as high noon on a clear day."

Watson searched his client's face for traces of guile or sarcasm and found only buoyant optimism.

"You take this newspaper," said Whitlow. "Used to be like I couldn't read the fucking newspaper without blowing a blood vessel gasket. Looky, right here," he said, pointing at an article that had the word *Choice* in the header. "It's all about partial birth abortions. Now, back when I still had that cyst I'd read something like that and my brain would catch fire, because I'd think, 'Look at this piece of shit! We got the fucking Holocaust happening right under our fucking noses. Two million babies a year getting flushed down the toilet. And they call it Choice!' Then I'd call up my buddy Buck, and we'd talk about going out and bagging one of these bloodsucking, moneybag abortionists—maybe collect the head and hang it on the fence outside the clinic."

Whitlow shook his bandaged skull, as if ruefully remembering his old self. "Today, I picked up the paper, I read that article, and I said to myself, I says, 'Self, ain't this a great nation we live in where we can all have different opinions about important things and still set down to eat at the same table?' I said, 'Self, don't it take all kinds to make a world? What if we was all the same? Things would get pretty fucking boring, right?' "

He looked up from his newspaper. "I can think now," he said earnestly. "I can see things clear as day. Now, I know you ain't gonna believe this. So maybe you should just let me do the talking myself when it comes to telling the judge about it. But if I get outta here, I'm fixin' to get me a job at Planned Parenthood. I know, you think I must just be saying that. But don't it make sense? I mean, *choice* is the only thing that makes sense, right? Nobody is saying you *got* to kill your baby. Hell's fire, no! What we are saying is you got a *choice:* You can *kill* your baby, or you can *keep* your baby. Because it's America, right? What gets me is

I couldn't see it before, because I had that fucking cyst taking up half of my brain. It like was pressing on certain circuits so I kept getting stuck on the baby part. It ain't a baby. It's a choice. It's all about rights for women. And without I had the brain surgery I never coulda seen it."

Watson almost leaned over, he was staring so hard at Whitlow.

"And see," said Whitlow, his eyes shining, "it don't stop with just *seein'* what is plainly right there in front of me—stuff I couldn't see before. It's like the new me wants to go one better. The new me ain't happy till he thinks of a way to make things even better. So, what I say is we give the women *more* rights, *better* rights, and another running twelve months' worth of choices to boot. Suppose these poor women just *think* they want to have a baby, and then once it comes out they decide it ain't the right kind or is nothing but a butt-load of trouble? Then what? The new Jimmy Whitlow will tell you what, we just go ahead on and extend this choice business all the way up to the first birthday to make sure the woman knew what she was in for before we make her go on and raise the thing. See? More choice," he said. "Why? Because they got that fucking tumor out of my head, that's why." Whitlow turned back to his newspaper.

"They still saying I hate niggers?" he asked.

"I think so," said Watson.

He shook his head again, as if he were his own rebellious teenage son. "Why was I like that? Why couldn't I just be good? You know," he said, with a contemplative frown, "I think I always *knew* I was bad. I mean, what most people would say was bad. I figured that if I died, like right now, I would go straight to Hell. If I thought about it, I just *planned* on going there, because I couldn't act or think any different than just plain bad. But in the back of my mind I guess I always knew that couldn't be right. It couldn't be that I was just bad and nothing to be done about it except go to Hell. Something had to happen."

He looked up at Watson again. "One time I walked all over a cow pasture during a motherfucker of an electrical storm, because I wanted to get struck by lightning the way St. Paul done. Then I could just wake up different. But it never happened, and I never won the lottery either. But this surgery." He opened his hands and looked at the ceiling. "It's a miracle. I'm a different person."

He turned a page in the paper and snapped it open for another look. "And here's another one I read with my new brain. See this one here on how they want to increase our taxes so they can give out more

Medicare? Now if I was my old self, I'da been cussing lightning bolts about how I can't pay my own kid's medical bills, because the government takes my money and gives it to old people, who all got more money than I do. I ain't got health insurance, but I'm supposed to *buy* health insurance for these old stiffs, so they can get pacemaker number two put in and go play golf in Florida."

His head slowly wagged with the weight of memories from his past. "That was the *old* Jimmy Whitlow. Because today when I read about the government wanting to up the taxes for Medicare, I said to myself, I says, 'Self, ain't it great how the government is trying to help old fuckers like Harmon Mayhew, who lives down the street from us. Harmon's pushing eighty and don't do nothing but drink all day long, and that tends to make him sick because he don't eat—just drinks Jim Beam. He's got a four-car garage full of antique cars they say are worth over a million dollars. But he won't sell a one. And, praise God, he don't need to, even though he is always having to go to the doctor, which is free because of Medicare. And the ambulance has come around twice—wait, three times—because he keeps falling asleep in bed with a lit cigarette. Now, I know for sure that if it weren't for Medicare, Harmon woulda died twenty years ago. So this morning, when I read about more Medicare taxes in the paper, I says, 'Self, ain't it great how the government is taking my money to buy Harmon Mayhew a new liver?' You see?" said Whitlow, touching himself on the side of the head, "because they fixed whatever was pressing up there. Now I can see what's really happening.

"But again, just seein' ain't enough for me now. I gotta go one better. The old Jimmy Whitlow woulda thought, 'Let's go blow up a government building before they take *all* our money and give it to old winos on respirators.' But my new brain? My new brain gets this great idea because the blood is flowing into all the right places. It come to me in a flash, about how to make people see how taxes is nothing but helping people. What they should do is pass a law where instead of taking the money out of your paycheck automatic, they just go ahead and let you take it home. But then under the new law you got to take your money out of the bank once a month and walk down the street and *give* it to Harmon Mayhew, in person, face to face, and to every other old sick fuck on your block on Medicare. Then you could see goodness right there in living color. You could say, 'Self, you can't buy penicillin for your own kid, but your kid ain't dyin' yet like poor Harmon, and look what your money done for this helpless dead drunk old fart who can't tie his fucking shoes anymore. Your money went and bought him a new mechanical liver which costs more than New Jersey, and it comes with a shopping cart, so he can wheel it around on the golf course all day and putt.' You wouldn't hear no more complaining about taxes if you did a scheme like that. No, sir!"

"What was in the briefcases, Jimmy?" asked Watson.

"The what?" asked Whitlow.

"The briefcases from the back of your car. What was in them?"

"Whew!" said Whitlow with a shudder. "You're scaring me, lawyer. I don't have any idea what the fuck you are talking about. That scares me, you know why? Because up in Minnesota they was talking about that same amnesia stuff that we was talking about when I was over in Des Peres. Is briefcases a thing I should remember?"

"Was it the money? Was it money that you and Buck wanted to get out of the car?"

"Whoa," he said, putting his cuffed hands out. "Doctor told me to rest. This is too many for me. Was I supposed to get a briefcase for Buck? Help me."

"You said Buck could maybe get you some good money if he could get to your car, remember?"

Whitlow shook his head and hissed. "Shit. See there? Just like a lawyer. I'm looking at the death penalty. I'm trying to make my way after having my brain operated on. And you? You wanna talk about money?"

"Two guys chased me down in your car, Jimmy, and they want to know what happened to the delivery," said Watson, his voice shaking. "You remember when you were in Des Peres. Scared? Because people wanted to kill you? Well, now people want to kill me because they want whatever Elvin Brawley was bringing to your house."

"Wait," he said, lifting his restrained hand and touching his temple. "Bells are ringin' but it's ever so faint. That name . . ."

"The victim," said Watson. "The black, deaf guy you shot."

"That's it," he said. "They said this might happen." He shook his head. "I can see so much clearer, and I know what's right and wrong, and the hate is all gone, but I can't remember jack shit about facts and such. 'Specially I think they took out all the stuff that happened right around the time the Afro-American died. They burn it out of there with lasers is how they described it to me and suction out parts of your brain with glass tubes. It's gone."

"Forget the murder, then," said Watson. "But there's a few things I need to know."

Whitlow frowned. "The law says you can't hate niggers. If you hate niggers, it means you are a sick deviant psycho motherfucker. So I said, 'OK, I won't hate niggers, if I can help it.' And they said, 'Part of the reason why you hate niggers is because you have a brain tumor and it is pressing on certain parts of your brain that keep you from seeing that it is wrong to be violent and hate niggers.' So I said, 'Well, we got nothing to talk about. Go ahead on and take out the parts you don't like, and let's see.' And they said, 'Yeah, but you might get some side defects, like maybe you ain't gonna remember your fucking name when we're done.' And what did I say? Did I say no? I said, 'Get that bad part of my brain out of there. Be gone, Satan! I'm gonna be reborn with a new brain that don't hate niggers.' That's what I said. I done my part. But now I can't remember shit about this killing business. It's lost in a fog.

"And besides, that was the old Jimmy Whitlow. He ain't here no more. He's gone. And if I'm supposed to know something about briefcases, well, it musta gone with him."

CHAPTER 28

"Odor," said Judge Stang. His back, as usual, was to the lawyers, and Watson and Harper, standing, as usual, could just see his grizzled scalp sticking up like a weathered hillock on the red leather horizon of his recliner's headrest. The judge fingered the file and the newest submission of evidence and evidentiary motions in United States v. Whitlow. Watson had filed copies of Mary Whitlow's medical reports, including her statement that, during the last seven years, she had never had sex with anyone except her husband. He had also included highlighted copies of Mary Whitlow's TDD communications with the victim, showing that the day after receiving a diagnosis of venereal disease, she had invited him to her house for another sign language lesson, had told him that her husband would be out of town, and that she wanted him to "touch her with his signs."

His clerks had distilled the salient points of the submissions into a one-page memo and had clipped it to a tabbed folder containing the documents. The judge looked up from the paper and gazed out his window, taking in the view of the Mississippi, which looked like a slag run of cold lead drifting downstream under a sunless sky.

"This case stinks all the way to hate heaven, doesn't it, Mr. Harper?" said the judge. He fetched a cigar clip from the fob pocket of an ancient gray vest. He retracted the blade of the small guillotinelike assemblage and stared into the hole.

"But as near as I can tell these pungent varietals of hatred don't come under any of the categories covered in your statute. Can't the government recast this whole mess as a gender crime? I mean we have a man, and we have a woman, and they obviously hate each other. Can't we argue that they hate each other *because of* their gender?"

Harper cleared his throat and shifted slightly. "Our office has considered the possibility of a charge under the Violence Against Women Act, but so far no such charge has been filed."

"Because everybody had race fever and hate fever on the brain when they took the woman's original statements," said the judge, "and now it's too late to go back and interpolate some vile female derogations for a gender crime charge. I understand."

Harper bridled at the judge's insinuation. He opened his mouth and drew a breath. Then his shoulders sagged, and his mouth closed.

"This case does have a distinctly human stench about it," said the judge. The recliner's swivel mechanism groaned as he adjusted his view of the river by a few degrees.

"I dare say, Mr. Watson, you've made the government a trifle gunshy. Mr. Donahue isn't here, and the case has instead been returned to the capable hands of Mr. Harper."

"Mr. Donahue asked me to apologize on his behalf," said Harper. "He has engagements in Washington, D.C. He'll be unavailable for the next two weeks, at which time he will be able to devote himself almost exclusively to this case until it is resolved."

The judged chuckled softly. "That's so rich, Mr. Harper, it hurts my fillings. Mr. Donahue doesn't really think this psychotic fetish he's calling a case is going to be stinking up my docket for the next two weeks, does he?"

"Judge, I . . ."

"This will be *some* trial, Mr. Harper. Your hate crime business is gone, along with the Confederate flags and tattoos. Just what are we going for now, motor vehicle homicide? Improper mooring of a watercraft?"

"Mr. Donahue feels quite strongly that—"

"How many times does he want to lose this case in color on the front page of the paper, Mr. Harper?"

"Judge, I can't speak for Mr. Donahue's position with regard to . . ."

"YOU WHAT!?" shouted the judge in a voice so loud that Watson felt sound percuss the skin of his face. "YOU CAN'T WHAT?"

Harper looked once at Watson and struggled to speak, "I said—"

"You can't *speak* for Mr. Donahue? I fear for your soul and body, Mr. Harper, if you are telling me that you came to a settlement conference without authority to settle the case. If that's true, the ghost of your career will wander these halls until your foul, unnatural crimes are burned and purged away. You have authority, don't you? Full and complete authority?"

"Judge," said Harper. "I'm only an AUSA. A case with this kind of profile will require Mr. Donahue's approval, at least, maybe even approval from our Washington office. I can't—"

The judge spun around in his recliner and threw the folder of papers on his desk. He clutched his chest and snarled at Harper.

"It's Friday and it's two o'clock," he said, glowering up at Harper, who was terrified, probably because the judge had hardly glanced at him over the years, much less brought his lights full bore on Harper's own. "Out in the hallway, twenty feet from my door, is a pay phone. Go to that phone, Mr. Harper. Pick it up, and *find* Mr. Donahue. Tell him that he will give you full and complete, *final* authority to settle this case *today*, or I will issue a summons for him and for anybody else who needs to approve the resolution of United States versus Whitlow. Then I will have the marshals drag their FAT GOVERNMENT ASSES IN HERE IN CHAINS! *GO!*"

"Yes, Judge," said Harper, sidling toward the outer office, where Ida was knitting.

Ida reached up and touched the dial of her flesh-toned hearing aid, then glanced up at Mr. Harper. "Is the judge calling for tea?"

"MR. HARPER!" shouted the judge.

"Yes, Your Honor," said Harper, pausing at the door.

"If you have small children or any other family matters to contend with over the weekend, please arrange to have someone else assume those duties. We will be staying here, in this courthouse, until this case is off my docket. All weekend, if necessary, understand? And if I die, or if you die, or if, because of force majeure or some act of God, we are not able to settle this case by Monday morning, then tell Mr. Donahue that trial will begin at nine-thirty A.M., Monday morning. Is that clear?"

"Yes, Judge," said Harper.

"Tell him also we will be using the same jury pool we used in that drug courier case his office lost last week. Remember? The one where the defendant had two kilos in his golf bag, signed a confession, made bail, and then asked if he could have his drugs back before leaving jail? Ask Mr. Donahue if he remembers what the jury did to his office on that one. Not guilty! I will be using the *same* jury pool in this case. Monday morning. GO!"

"Yes, Judge," said Harper, and left, by way of Ida's office.

"The gentleman's room is two doors down on the right," she said as he passed.

"You probably don't know about that yet," the judge said to Watson, "because your feet are still tender. Federal jurors sit for six months in rotating pools. By the end of the six months, I know every single juror. At my age, I've seen them twice before. If I take a notion, I can fuck either side by seating the jury pool in such an order that the side I'm mad at must squander all their peremptory strikes and still wind up with people who are going to find against them. Remember that. Federal judges have damn near absolute power to fuck and scuttle your case if you piss them off. You heard it here first."

As Judge Stang spoke, a shaft of sunlight broke through the clouds outside and slanted in his window.

"Ah," he said, "that's what I've been waiting for." He leaned back until his shoulders caught a patch of warm light. "Keep coming, sun." He looked over his shoulder at the clearing sky. "If that sky opens all the way up, we'll get rid of this case in an hour."

Watson smiled and looked at the widening hole in the cloud ceiling, wondering if the judge meant he was going to call down some divine influence to settle itself on the proceedings, cast demons out of the lawyers' brains, and calm their disputatious natures.

"You can force a resolution using terror or tenderness. Meathooks or molasses. Terror is my personal preference, but today you'll see both. Mr. Harper is a golfing fool, perhaps you know that? It's Friday. Two-ten by my watch. He's probably trying to make a foursome out at Bellerive by, I'd say, five. And if the sun stays out, this case will be settled by four-fifteen. Until then, I will subject Mr. Harper to verbal Chinese water torture."

Watson kept nodding and smiling at what he hoped were appropriate junctures in the judge's speech, until the judge stopped and looked into his eyes.

"Your top and bottom are?" he asked. "Well, never mind that," he said, waving the thought away with a bony hand. "The government will come back in here and pretend like they are doing you a big favor by stepping down to second-degree murder, which will put you at number thirty-three under the sentencing guidelines. Eleven years minimum. Would your man go for that?"

"I would advise him not to take that, Judge," said Watson. "If we have to, Ms. Schweich and I will try this case on Monday morning. She could make the defendant's wife, the government's main witness, look very ugly on the stand."

"So could you," said the judge. "But then you've got the uncertainty of what the jury will do. What are you after?"

"Manslaughter, Judge. But manslaughter is where I want to end up. If I start there, they'll try to take me up a big notch to second-degree murder."

"Manslaughter will put you at level twenty-five under the sentencing guidelines. Five years is the lowest I can go there. He'll probably get out sooner."

"A single charge of voluntary manslaughter," said Watson. "And because of the surgery and the ensuing testing, my client should be allowed to spend as much time as possible in forensic psychiatric facilities."

"What if Mr. Harper says no?" asked the judge. "I'll be asking him to ride a bicycle without a seat."

"Then we will come away with manslaughter or better starting Monday morning," said Watson. "Maybe I'm wrong. I have one other stipulation. That the plea agreement dispose of all charges arising out of the incident in question, including charges based upon any evidence seized from the premises of the base quarters where the defendant lived with his wife, and any evidence seized from the trunk of his vehicle, which was towed the day of the shooting. If we could get a package like that, we would take manslaughter."

Mr. Harper appeared at the door of Judge Stang's chambers.

"Back with full authority, Mr. Harper?"

"I have full authority up to a point, to take certain—"

"FULL, UNQUALIFIED AUTHORITY!"

The judge's voice probed the upper registers of Watson's cochlear nerves, and he wondered again where Judge Stang kept his arsenal of decibels. He could scare God off the Mount and deafen Moses. The judge pressed his gnarled fingers to the bulging veins in his temples. Then he carefully spread his mottled gray hands on the desktop, as if to grasp a physical object and prevent the onset of a felony or a high crime. He stared at his own fingers—skeletal phalanges and vasculature wrapped in papery skin.

"Call Mr. Donahue back," he said slowly and carefully, "and tell him that I want to be absolutely certain that you have final authority for an offer of voluntary manslaughter. Level twenty-five on the guidelines. Tell him there is no way in Hell I will make you agree to it, but at this juncture in these negotiations, it is imperative that I am able to represent to the other side that you have final, complete, total authority to accept a plea-bargain agreement for a single count of voluntary manslaughter."

"But—?"

The judge held up his hand and waved Harper away with a single, back-handed flap.

As soon as Harper was gone, Judge Stang squinted and looked up again into the clearing sky.

"Ida. Bring me some settlement forms! The ones slanted in favor of the defendant, please. Oh, and the letter from Mr. Spence."

The judge chuckled to himself, and Watson politely smiled, pretending he was sharing the subject of his amusement.

"Fetch a chair out there for yourself," said the judge.

Watson went to the outer office and brought back a chair.

"Sit, sit," the judge said. "Now, I can't put the government's fat in the fire unless you are ready to take this thing to trial on Monday. Are you prepared for trial?"

"We're ready," said Watson.

The judge chuckled again.

"I told you about my old hunting buddy out in Wyoming. You probably heard of Mr. Spence? Gerry Spence? He runs a trial lawyers' college out at his ranch in Wyoming for thirty days every year and talks me into going from time to time. He puts me on a stage and has me terrorize two young lawyers while they try to argue a case to a mock jury. I rage at them until they turn white. I degrade and humiliate them by closely questioning them. And afterward we all get drunk. Lots of fun."

Watson smiled and got the wetware willies just thinking about it.

"We have a little skit where we teach the young lawyers the importance of preparation for trial. We fire questions at them until we detect an area of unpreparedness, which as you can guess isn't too tough after you've been at it for forty years the way I have. Anyway, after we find the sore spot, we bring in a couple of hungry Dobermans. One is named Marbury and the other is named Madison. They have these big drop-forged spiked collars on them, and we have some Latin wisdom etched into the iron nameplates. Kind of a long story there, because one year we had a visiting judge who had a prior life as a metalworker, Old Judge Short—dead and gone now . . . funnier than a rubber crutch—anyway he's the one who had the idea."

"Of etching Latin onto the dog collars?" asked Watson with a nervous laugh, dearly wanting to make conversation but unsure about whether the judge was talking about something that had really happened, or something . . . else.

"You bet," chuckled Judge Stang. "Crazy old coot did it with a blowtorch." He laughed. "Whew. We were drunker than fiddlers' bitches that night."

Watson laughed obligingly, as if to say, *Boy, I know that feeling! You have a few beers, and the next thing you know you're pulling out the old blowtorch and looking high and low for some cast-iron dog collars so you can etch some Latin sayings into them.*

"Well?" asked Judge Stang.

"Yes?" asked Watson.

"The Latin. I can tell you, but it's cheating, because—"

Ida appeared and handed the judge a single piece of paper. The judge took it from her and handed it to Watson.

"Anyway, you have to be one promising young defense lawyer to get accepted out at Mr. Spence's college of trial lawyers. But Gerry called me the other day on an evidentiary matter, and we got to talking. I told him about your situation out here and your trip to the Eighth Circuit on this fellow's behalf. Next thing you know, he sent this letter."

Watson took the letter from the judge and read a short letter signed by Gerry Spence, accepting Watson's application to the Trial Lawyer's College for the coming August session. It was signed "Love, Gerry."

"This is real?" asked Watson. "It's not a joke?"

"Jokes are funny," said the judge. "You won't think Marbury and Madison are funny," he added with a conspiratorial chuckle.

"But it says, 'We are pleased to accept your application.' I didn't apply."

"I submitted a verbal application on your behalf," said the judge.

"But—" began Watson, and stopped himself, before he could say, *But I thought you were Ivan the Terrible?*

"This is a dream," said Watson. "Thanks . . ." *Let's see*, he stalled, *I can't really say, "Thanks, man." How about, "Thanks, God!"* "Thank you so much, Your Honor. I've read all of Mr. Spence's books. I'd kill ten prosecutors just to see him argue."

Judge Stang extended his hand. "Congratulations. You're a fine lawyer, which isn't saying much."

Watson felt his hand clasped in the bony grip of Ivan the Incredible.

"Ms. Schweich is a fine lawyer," said Judge Stang. "She does a very good job. But I have higher aspirations for you."

He looked at his ashtray full of scattered cigar butts. "I'll be dead soon," he said. "And I hope to blame it on cigars. But who is going to look after all of these poor, stupid, guilty fuckers the government drags in here every day? Every once in a while, I like to see a good lawyer step up to the plate on their behalf. After I'm gone, when some desperate, guilty incorrigible who's as dumb as a brain-damaged saw mule shows up needing a lawyer, I hope you'll think of me and give him a hand."

"I'll do that, Judge," said Watson. "I promise."

"I know you will," said the judge. "You'll think of me because I'm a desperate incorrigible, too. I'm also meeting with your former boss this afternoon, Mr. Mahoney. He's bringing my chewed sawdust over, and we are going to have a little chat about some irregularities attending your separation from the firm. You stay out of it. We are all discerning professionals," said the Judge. "And Stern, Pale is a fine, old firm—very high caliber. I know they would be constantly vigilant to always and everywhere avoid even the appearance of impropriety in matters of associate compensation, say bonuses, and so on." He paused and winked. "And I know that Mr. Mahoney will be eager to fulfill his duty and rectify any of my concerns about compensation as it relates to the appointment of counsel for indigent defendants. In fact, I know him so well I wouldn't be surprised if along with any bonus money there might not be a little severance pay thrown into the bargain."

Harper appeared in the doorway.

"Come in, Mr. Harper, we're going over our Latin lessons." He crooked a finger and pointed it at Watson. *"Prius vitiis laboravimus, nunc legibus,"* he said. "That's what old Judge Short welded into the dog collars."

" 'First vices we labored with,' " stammered Watson, " 'now legis—' "

"Close," said the judge. " 'We labored first with vices, now with laws.' Mr. Harper, write that down."

Harper's hand went to his shirt pocket for a pen.

"Well, Mr. Harper, you're back, and I trust it took you so long because you've gotten authority to settle every case in the Eastern District of Missouri. While you were gone, I stood Mr. Watson here up in front of an open grave and got his bottom line, and now I am going to do the same for you. Do you have full authority for manslaughter?"

"I do," said Harper, "but only because I assured Mr. Donahue that you would not—"

"Do you have FINAL, FULL, and COMPLETE authority for manslaughter?" yelled the judge.

"I do," said Harper.

"Good," said the judge. "Because Mr. Watson is so young and crazy and inexperienced, he thinks he's got a defendant's verdict here and the beginnings of a glorious career as a criminal defense lawyer."

"With all due respect, Judge," said Harper. "A person was murdered. A disabled person of color."

The judge closed his eyes and touched his silver temples.

"Mr. Harper," said the judge, becalming himself, "your little hate pigeonholes are gone! We don't need to hear about them anymore. If you mention race, disability, or hate again, I will dump this ashtray on the floor, I will pronounce your sins out loud, and I will make you write them in the ashes. Do you understand?"

"Yes, Judge," said Harper, glancing once out the window at the sunlight.

"Now," the judge said, lifting the lid of his humidor, "I know we have a murder victim, that's why this is called a homicide case. But as we go along here, it seems that maybe the government's gone after the wrong perp. What if the wife pulled a nasty on a nasty husband and set his white ass up? You can't turn around and come after her, can you? Because you'll look like legal village idiots and your only witness will become a codefendant. 'Whoops, our mistake. Wasn't a hate crime, it was a marital dispute.' The press would examine your entrails on page one."

"Judge," said Harper, squirming and shifting his weight.

"I'll tell you when I'm ready to hear your arguments. I am having Ida draft up a settlement agreement in this case. The defendant will plead guilty to a single charge of voluntary manslaughter. Mr. Watson has some other incidental language on the medical treatments and the inclusiveness with regard to evidence found at the scene and taken from the defendant's car. I'm sure he has his reasons. It's being typed up now on your letterhead. I foresee that you will be signing it."

"Judge, there is no possible way I can agree to a single charge of manslaughter. Mr. Donahue will—"

"You don't have to sign it," said Judge Stang. "We can do it the old-fashioned way by having a trial on Monday morning with that antic, fun-loving jury who acquitted your drug dealer last week."

"Judge, I—"

"Hold your arguments," said the judge, pausing to light his cigar. "It's a long way from here to Monday morning." He swiveled back around in his recliner and sighed, luxuriously taking in another view of his river. "And we have a beautiful day taking shape out the window. Makes a fella wanna chuck it all and head out to the club for a gin and tonic. Would you care for a chair, Mr. Harper?"

Watson looked at Harper, who suddenly noticed that Watson was sitting in a chair. "Actually, Judge," said Harper, "a chair would be very nice."

"Well, let me know when you're ready to sign the plea-bargain agreements, and I'll have Ida bring them in with a chair."

Harper irritably looked at the top of the judge's bald head. "I apologize, really, I do, Judge, but manslaughter is out of the question in this case," he protested.

"Mr. Harper, I hope you are not in a hurry, because I have a few matters to go over with you and Mr. Watson. And I want to conclude these matters before I entertain your arguments about how you can't offer a plea on a single charge of manslaughter.

"In the car on the way in this morning, I said to Doris . . . Doris, that's my wife, she drives me these days because of my cataracts. Maybe you know her?"

"I confess, Judge, I . . ." said Harper.

"Well then, you've no idea what a keen interest she takes in all the court's business. Why, every evening for going on forty years now, I usually stagger in the door behind her and sit down at the kitchen table, and Doris typically takes one of those big, elegant, long-stemmed white wine glasses with a gold band around the top that we got sixty years ago at our wedding, and she fills it to the brim with Jack Daniel's for me, and then she says, 'Well, Whit, did you receive any amended or supplemental pleadings dealing with joinder or pendent jurisdiction of state claims today?' And I say, 'No, Doris, we don't do a goddamn thing in that courthouse any more, except drugs, guns, and civil rights.' And she'll say, 'Well, Whit, were any of those poor *pro se* prisoners deprived of their constitutional rights today or were any of those jailhouse lawyers filing habeas corpus petitions today, or how about some of that collateral estoppel or res judicata stuff we used to pillow-talk about for half the night?' And I'll say, 'Not anymore, Doris. Time was, if a prisoner didn't get two aspirins on time, we'd have a three-week trial on our hands, but now it's drugs, guns, employment discrimination, and hate crimes.'

" 'Well, then,' she says, 'has the federal government discovered any more substances they don't want people to take for fear it will corrupt their morals and turn them into people of amorality?' She takes a very keen interest in substance abuse," said the judge, nodding vigorously. "Very keen, because she realizes the importance of the government being in control of the chemical makeup of its citizens' bloodstreams."

"Judge," said Harper, despairingly, "we didn't . . . This isn't a drug case. We aren't here to . . ."

"Oh," said Judge Stang, staying him with the flat of his palm, "I know your mission is on an altogether different plane than mere drug abuse. Your mission is to abolish murder and hatred. And you may be just the lawyer I am looking for. You can see that Doris cares very deeply about the administration of justice in these hallowed chambers, so I said to her this morning, 'Doris, I can just feel it in the marrow of these old bones, something different is going to happen today. I'm having a settlement conference this afternoon with two lawyers in that erstwhile hate crime case, which has now become a manslaughter case. And I just know something different is going to happen.' And she said, 'Why, Whit, whatever do you mean? You loathe settlement conferences. You always say it's the same old shit from the same old bulls. What could be different?' "

Harper sighed and lifted his eyes over the judge's head and out toward the window, where white flocs of cumulus clouds were in full sail against a brilliant blue sky.

" 'Doris,' I said," the judge continued, "and tears formed, right here, in the windows of my soul." The lawyers could see his elbows as he apparently pointed at his eyes with his index fingers. "And I said, 'Doris, this afternoon I just know I am going to a hear a brand-new argument from a new breed of lawyer. I am going to hear the most stunning elucidation of fundamental human truths since Aristotle peripatetically paced about the Lyceum and discoursed on metaphysics. This lawyer has impeccable qualifications. He is full to the brim with integrity and oozing ethical punctiliousness from his pores. He is an attorney from the United States Government. His name is Michael Harper, Esquire. He is an Assistant United States Attorney. He is always eager to do the best possible work in my courtroom because he knows if he doesn't I will simply clusterfuck every case he brings before me for the rest of his natural life. Doris,' I said, 'I am going to break my back trying to get the lawyers to agree to manslaughter, but Mr. Harper won't go for it. Instead Mr. Harper will say, 'That is impossible, Judge, and here is why.' "

The judge puffed twice on his cigar.

Harper opened his mouth.

The judge continued talking, " 'And then,' I told Doris, 'Mr. Harper will tell me why. But before he does, my chambers will fall silent. Awe will break out everywhere like the calm before the rash, I mean like the balm before the storm, like the hush that will settle over all Creation before the Second Coming. And Doris said to me, 'Oh, Whit, stop being so dramatic! Get to the point!' And I said, 'No, Doris. You don't understand! Forty years I've waited for the kind of argument Mr. Harper is going to make to me. Forty years I've wandered in barren deserts of legal dust and sand, parched by duplicity and desiccating deception. Forty years I've waited for a messiah! I want to behold the promised land of the new jurisprudence! And Mr. Michael Harper is going to show it to me. He will be my Moses. I am distressed! Only Michael Harper can comfort me. And when death comes for me, Mr. Harper can nod his head wherever he is and say to himself, 'I did right by Judge Stang.' "

Two more puffs on his cigar, and a longer interlude of silence.

Harper again drew a breath to speak.

" 'Then and only then,' I said, 'will Mr. Harper speak. And as he speaks, my heart will beat faster, my eyeballs will fall out of my head, because I will hear an argument from Mr. Michael Harper that will restore my faith in jurisprudence and renew my belief in the fundamental goodwill of mankind. In a single stroke this argument of his will unite social policy with the dignity of the human individual, and it will bring the high concerns of the Constitution together with the lowest municipal ordinance. This argument will be so ingenious, profound, and aglow with particles of sweetness and light streaming forth from the beacon of Reason, that I will stagger out of my recliner and fall to my rickety knees. Sir William Blackstone, Oliver Wendell Holmes, and Learned Hand will walk out of their graves and fall to their knees right next to me! I'll bathe in the light of Mr. Harper's stunning insight and marvel my fool head off that a lawyer and officer of my court is destined to take his place forever as one of history's greatest jurisprudential scholars."

He stopped, placed both of his gnarled hands on the arms of his chair and waited.

"I want to go home and tell Doris I was right. I want to sit down at my dinner table tonight and say, 'It happened! I heard a legal argument that has justified the last forty years of my life.' "

Harper set his briefcase on the floor and put his hands over his ears.

"I'm offering a single count of manslaughter," he said.

CHAPTER 29

When Watson left Judge Stang's chambers, he was no longer a law school graduate with an appointed case. He was a Colossus bestride the Courthouse of the Future. He marched along the corridors of power, down gleaming hallways paneled in limestone and textured marble—a gladiator triumphant in the Coliseum for the New Millennium—the Thomas F. Eagleton United States Federal Courthouse. He didn't see any other prosecutors—they were all probably cowering in little bureaucratic cubbyholes, lest the mighty Watson crush them under his heel. *Maybe I'll give old Gerry a call and let him know how the settlement turned out*, he thought. If Myrna were here, she'd fetch him a wheelbarrow and help him hoist these two big fleshy cannonballs banging around between his legs. Major wood. Instrument of domination.

He entered an elevator and leaned against a cloth panel framed in cherry mullions, sharing his enlarging personal space with other lawyers, courthouse personnel, jurors, and the like—commoners who still had no idea who was standing in their midst. He had to stop himself from clearing his throat and announcing to the group, "Do you realize I just vanquished the government of the United States of America!? Took them to school! Facial humiliation. By myself!" He felt like the young Bill Gates leaving one of those fateful meetings with IBM executive James Cannavino. Big Blue, eviscerated by a twenty-four-year-old college dropout and turbo geek. J. Random Hacker triumphant. *Kicked their ass! With authority. Eat flaming death, Government Warlords! I am CarnageMaster!* Best of all, it was not multimedia with MMX goggles and Active-X plug-ins. It was real. Blood, flesh, bone, and Real Money was looming somewhere on the horizon, he could smell it. His brain was thinking maybe it should insure itself with Lloyds of London.

In the main lobby, he began humming some giddy combination of the Emperor concerto and a tune from his high school days, "Take the Skinheads Bowling," by Camper Van Beethoven. He took a right and headed for the shuttle elevators and the parking garage. He glanced up and saw the snack bar and newsstand concessions where he had paused that fateful day for "refreshments," as Arthur had put it. His former boss now seemed a diminutive, mediocre sort of lawyer, lost in Watson's new long shadow, and it seemed a fitting bookend moment to stop in for another Coke—hoist a beverage in honor of victory and in memory of bondage forsworn.

The same blind cashier was settled on a stool behind the counter, his fingertips skimming another Braille manuscript, his long white cane against the wall.

"Afternoon," said samurai Watson, selecting a twenty-ounce Coke and setting it on the counter. "Coke," he said. "A big one."

Once that bonus comes around, he thought, *I should maybe pick up a hundred shares of Coke.* He could check with R.J. about that, make him proud that his working fool son-in-law was looking to invest some seed money.

The blind man punched buttons on the register keypad.

Watson hoisted his wallet—swollen with twenty-dollar bills from Buck and his lawyer. He pulled out a nice, new starchy one and handed it to the blind cashier, who took it, rubbed it with his fingertips, and paused.

"I'll take some cashews, too," said Watson, snagging a tubular bag near the register and plopping it on the counter.

The blind registrar frowned and rubbed the bill again, while Watson looked over the magazine racks—*Esquire, Glamour, People, George*—all plastered with glossy photos of busty women in slinky dishabille. Babes built for comfort, with billowy bosoms on willowy frames. Elegant enchantresses and spellbinding voluptuaries. Watson heard a beep, but paid no attention because he was soaking up high-tone female flesh by the eyeful.

Ain't it funny how the men's magazines and the women's magazines both *have half-naked babes prominently displayed on the covers?* Call your sociology professor. Probably *means* something. Not that he cared what it meant. He only knew that most of these bedizened silk foxes probably wanted to mate with the kind of guy who got paid hourly wads of cash for stepping on the necks of federal prosecutors. "Alpha! We want you!" they seemed to be saying, displaying cleavages, pursing and pouting their parted red lips, cooching, all but presenting with lordosis. Then the magazine puzzle solved itself in one of those flashes to the new brain that his client was so fond of describing. The men want to *mate* with those alluring babes, and the women want to *be* those alluring babes. Heck of a deal. See Henry Adams, *The Virgin & the Dynamo*. See also Marcel Duchamp, *The Bride Stripped Bare by Her Bachelors, Even*.

"Sir," said the blind man, a troubled look on his face.

"Yeah," said CarnageMaster Watson. *The warrior thirsts! What mundane complications could possibly obstruct the slaking of said thirst?*

"The machine is indicating that your bill is . . . defective," the man said politely. "Do you have another one?"

Watson took the bill back. It wasn't wrinkled, or old, or dirty, or torn, like the bills you can't get change machines to take. It was a perfectly good twenty-dollar bill. Rather than press the issue with a blind guy, he figured it would be easier just to fetch out another, and he did. He had plenty, for once—dozens right there in his billfold, not to mention rip-stop envelopes with plenty more out in the back of the car.

"Here's another one," said Watson, placing the bill in the man's hand. Then his eyes went foraging again among the glossy boobular magazine covers. He didn't even hear the machine beep again, probably because the male visual cortex was orange or hot pink with activity, and auditory was cool blue or purple.

"Sir," said the cashier.

"Yeah," said Watson, tearing his optic nerves from a curvaceous straw-blond vixen on the cover of *Esquire*.

The man was handing back the second bill, as Watson thought, *That fucking machine needs service, man. If it wasn't such a pain in the ass I might buy a few of these magazines.*

"Sir," said the cashier politely, "the machine is signaling that neither of these bills is genuine, and I can tell you that they don't feel genuine either. On the second floor, upstairs here in this building, there are Secret Service currency experts. They are part of the Treasury Department, along with the Bureau of Alcohol, Tobacco, and Firearms. They handle currency matters. If you take these up there . . ."

Watson looked down at the wad of twenties from Buck's lawyer that was fattening his billfold and went into system hang. *THIS PROGRAM HAS PERFORMED AN ILLEGAL ACTION AND WILL BE SHUT DOWN. PLEASE CLOSE THIS SESSION AND REBOOT YOUR MACHINE.*

"It happens from time to time," the man explained in a kind voice. "These counterfeit bills get loose in circulation. The Secret Service will want to know about them. Just go down the hallway there to your right, and back up to the second floor."

Watson's mouth was still open. His fingertips rubbed the bills in his wallet. *PRESS CONTROL-ALT-DELETE TO END THIS TASK AND REBOOT YOUR SYSTEM. YOU WILL LOSE ANY UNSAVED INFORMATION IN ALL ACTIVE PROGRAMS.* He needed a Vulcan Nerve Pinch, a three-fingered keyboard salute and warm boot. *Abort? Retry? Fail?*

"Son of a . . ." he began.

"Don't worry," the man said. "They usually replace them with genuine currency, but first you have to fill out the proper forms, explaining where you got the bad ones, so they can try to trace them and find the counterfeiters. In my opinion, you got counterfeit there, but it's good quality product. Very good paper. It feels very close to genuine texture, just a little too slippery or oily. You could talk me into taking them. Fortunately, the machine never makes a mistake. Not since I've been here. Fifteen? Sixteen years. If Bessie were here, she could tell you."

"Thanks," said Watson. "I'm really sorry about that." He put the Coke back in the cooler and the nuts back in the box. "I'll just head on up and turn these two rascals over to the proper authorities."

"Second floor," said the man. "They're professionals. They'll take care of you."

"Yeah," said Watson. "Thanks again."

Once in the hallway, he glanced over his shoulder with a criminal's furtive terror, wondering if the guy would call the marshals at the security checkpoint just to be sure. *Counterfeit!* He felt his warlord's ballocks shrivel into cowardly cullions. Charges unspooled before his eyes in the bulleted, numbered paragraphs of an indictment with his and Myrna's names captioned at the top: counterfeiting, conspiracy, obstruction of justice, tampering, possession of a controlled substance, and of course, *conspiracy to commit hate crimes,* by participating in the illegal actions of a criminal enterprise. . . . The babes back in the magazine rack were probably thinking, *Gross me out! A criminal!*

He heaved a big sigh when his Honda cleared the tollbooth at the ramp up from the underground parking. Then he pulled over on the side of the street and yanked out the *United States Sentencing Commission Guidelines* and frantically looked up "Offenses Involving Counterfeit Bearer Obligations of the United States Government." Base offense of nine, which meant he could get anywhere from six months to five years. At the next stoplight, he massaged the skin around his skull and tried to knead this crisis gently into his brain.

Memory served up Whitlow's quavering voice from the first interview: *"If I could just get to my car somehow, or if Buck could get to my car. I know I could get some money."*

No shit, Jimmy! Elvin probably brought a load of counterfeit, and Mary had real money to pay for it. The VTD printout of Mary's voice scrolled by on his internal monitor, *"The lessons are too expense if* [expensive?]*,"* and Elvin typing back: *"I DON'T MAKE MORE LESSON BUT THIS LESSON YOU STILL WANT? FOUR FOR ONE? THE SAME AS ALWAYS?"* Four counterfeit twenties for one genuine? Acrobat Printing & Graphics. Elvin Brawley, the "locally prominent artist, an engraver, a craftsman, a black William Blake."

Myrna's voice recollected: *"We still don't know what his priors were, because Dirt's source in the Bureau is on vacation. We should get it well before trial, but in the meantime, we don't know shit about him except he was deaf and into engraving and printing and computer graphics."*

What about Harper? Even Harper had said it, hadn't he? *"You don't want to cut your baby teeth workin' for these jackals. They run guns, fraud schemes, money laundries,* counterfeit *rings. They got silos in southern Missouri full of explosives."* Mary Whitlow's TDD printouts: *"Ready for lesson 12. I have the payment."* Or, *"Elvin, please come for another sign language lesson. I will have the money."* Or how about his esteemed client: *"He weren't no fuckin' sign language instructor, lawyer. I told you that."*

They probably had code words for everything, in case federal agents or the Criminal Investigation Division were listening. Automatic weapons and grenade launchers were probably referred to as parsnips and kumquats, and how about a couple of those heat-seeking, shoulder-launched, surface-to-air summer squash, while we're at it? But nobody wants to get paid in counterfeit, so neither Buck nor Jimmy told their lawyers about that. What was in the briefcases, Buck? Hate literature? I'll bite. Sounds plausible. Mary was just wanting her half of the hate literature back, I get it!

Myrna's voice again emerging from an archived dot-wav audio file: *"According to Buck, this was just a regular drop-off, until Mary Whitlow set Jimmy up for murder."*

Not just murder, either. She gets rid of her asshole husband, Jimmy "VD" Whitlow, and she gets to keep the briefcase full of counterfeit that Elvin had delivered and the briefcase full of real money that she gave in payment for the "lessons." When the Order of the Eagles comes around, she says, "Jimmy hid them somewhere" or "The cops must have took them."

Perfect plan, until Lucy had the car towed, with the briefcases in the trunk. Then Jimmy saw a way to fix her and pay his legal bills and get a nice separate cache of money for him and his bosom buddy, Buck, to strike out on their own.

By the time Watson got to Myrna's place, everything made terrifying sense. He parked the Honda in the back lot, popped the trunk, stuffed all the money into the black leather briefcase, and stormed into her office.

He found her sitting behind her desk, holding her head in her hands—her freckled fingers splayed around flaming hair, grabbing at her skull through the skin, looking as if she were in the throes of the same catalepsy that had afflicted Watson fifteen minutes earlier in his car. She reached into her desk drawer without looking and fetched out her gun. She slid it across the table, covered her face again, and peeked at him through a hole in the mesh of her stubby fingers.

"Shoot me in the head," she commanded. "It's the only way. Do the Kevorkian. Just shoot me."

"You talked to Dirt," said Watson. "And now you know what Elvin's priors were, is that it?"

"Yup," she said, squinting her eyes and bowing her head. "Two aliases with multiple counts under each." She put her head on the desk and covered the back of it with both hands. "Shoot me in the head, first.

Then I'll tell you." She thumped the desk with a fist. "Never mind, I can't tell you. Just shoot me. Hurry! The pain of living is too great."

Watson put the briefcase on her desk, popped the latches, and opened it.

"Remember how Elvin worked at Acrobat Printing and Graphics?" she moaned into her desk. "Some high-end printing joint, computer-generated graphics and reproduction? He's an engraver? He did the printing work for the Eagle Scouts? Guess what his priors were for?"

"I know what his priors were for," said Watson.

She lifted her head and looked at the open satchel. "How do you know? Did Dirt tell you?"

"Nope," said Watson.

"That reptilian client of yours? He told you, didn't he?" She kneaded her temples and sighed. "According to Dirt, old Elvin was the consummate artist. He trained with the best in Singapore. His hundred-dollar bills were so good, Treasury and the Secret Service decided not to bother taking them out of circulation. Elvin made a fortune doing hundreds for the militias under the name of Silas Washington up in Detroit. The Eagles went to him, even though he was black and even though he charged them double." She grinned. "If you want the best, race don't matter, I guess. Silas did five years up in Detroit on reduced charges. When he got out, he moved to St. Louis and became Elvin Brawley. He was long in the tooth, and the government issued the new hundred-dollar bills with the polymer security threads. He retired, but the Eagles found him again and talked him into earning a modest income doing twenties."

"Any word from Buck?" Watson asked.

"Buck does not appear to be getting my messages, so I am going to send a guy over to see Buck and talk to him using an assistive listening device—it's called a nail gun. Cocksucker! I'm gonna—" She put her hands on her chest. "No. I'm not gonna. I'm not gonna tell you anything. You're a decent guy, Joey. I don't want you to know what's going to happen. The only thing you need to know is that every one of those twenties is going to be replaced with real twenties. Swear to God and his big brother. I promise."

The phone rang and she ignored it.

"Try to help a guy in a jam, and you get fucked in both ears for your trouble. Shit!"

"Ms. Schweich," said Tilly over the intercom. "There are two . . . Well, the same two gentlemen who were here last week are back, and they would like to see you. They say it's very important. I told them to call for an appointment. They took the phone from me, asked me for an outline, and called on your line to make an appointment. Just a few seconds ago."

Myrna pushed the mute button. "It's raining barbed wire and butchers' knives around here!" She yanked open her drawer and frantically rifled through cartons of cigarettes and boxes of bullets. "Where's my fucking—? Damn! My holster is at home!" She released the button. "Put 'em on."

"Law offices," she said. She fetched a cigarette and felt for her skull lighter. She fluttered her hand at the briefcase full of bundled money and made big eyes at Joe.

"To whom am I talking to?" she asked. "I mean, with whom am I speaking with? Never mind," she said, "who the fuck are you?"

Watson shut the briefcase and turned around, searching the room for a place to hide it. He went to a likely-looking metal file cabinet and pulled open the lower drawer, where he found a twelve-pack of Heineken and some rolls of fax paper. The briefcase wouldn't fit unless he took out the Heinekens, so he did.

"Look, I told you guys," said Myrna. "Whether you are cops or not, we can't be talking to you about client business. Suppose you were my clients? Would you want me talking to other people about your business? Another thing is my clients make appointments. Does this look like a Legal Aid Society soup kitchen, or what? You want to hire me? I charge by the hour."

She rolled her head around using sarcastic body language in response to whatever she was hearing in the receiver.

"Five minutes. We got trials going on here. Settlement conferences. Come on back, but you get five minutes. Period."

She picked up her gun and looked at it, then looked for a place on her body to put it. "Shit!"

There was a knock on the door.

She set the gun just so inside her drawer, closing it most of the way.

"Enter," she said.

Alpha and Beta, again. Gray flannel and blue serge, respectively. Clean-shaven down to the creases of their dewlaps. White shirts, Egyptian cotton, medium starch. Savory types with tasteful ties. Same busy mirrored shades. Their gait seemed more deliberate this time; they walked in and stood alongside each other, as if they were staking out turf to be occupied until they got what they wanted or their aftershave wore off, whichever came first.

"'Afternoon, ma'am," said Alpha, and with a turned bow of his head, "Mr. Watson."

Beta said nothing—chastened and perhaps disciplined for insubordination and talking out of turn during their last visit. Instead, he made do with a curt nod and contentedly waited for the negotiations to degenerate to his level of expertise: mayhem.

"Some of my clients pay me a healthy retainer for immediate access any time of the day or night," said Myrna. "Everybody else makes an appointment." She puffed her cigarette, then leaned a little toward the drawer and squinted at Alpha through smoke.

"Ma'am, we do not have the delivery. We also do not have a straight story about the delivery. What we do have is a lot of stuff that don't quite add up."

"Whatever the delivery is, I don't know where it is," she said. "And I lost the train of logic somewheres that makes us responsible for supposedly knowing about this shit. Because I represented Buck a few years back? That means I'm supposed to be a lifetime master of Buck trivia? Buck ain't my client. The only client we got is Jimmy Whitlow, and that's because I'm helping this guy," she said with a shrug in Watson's direction.

Joe smiled a tight one in Beta's direction.

"And I see where the paper says that you are something called retained counsel now," said Alpha to Joe. "That sounds like somebody is getting paid lawyer fees by somebody. Is Jimmy paying you?"

"I entered my appearance as retained counsel when I left my job at the big firm," said Watson. "I wanted to work on Jimmy Whitlow's case full-time."

A solid year at Arthur's elbow had taught him the art of stepping right around the standing question and providing an authoritative response that was on topic and beyond reproach, but which also came nowhere near an answer.

"And Jimmy ain't paying you?" asked Alpha.

"If I discuss fees with a third party," said Watson, "I will destroy the attorney-client privilege." As if. His tone was meant to convince them that he would sooner desecrate the temple on Good Friday "Even cops can't break the attorney-client privilege. I'm sorry, but fee matters are privileged information."

"Five minutes is coming up quick," said Myrna.

Beta stirred and flexed under his blue serge. Alpha raised his voice for the first time.

"Ma'am, too many things are not making sense for us. And we ain't leaving until they do." He took one step toward Myrna in a manner calculated to suggest that, if necessary, he would soon be taking more and bigger steps.

"Somebody took the delivery, correct?" he said. "It's got to be Jimmy, Mary Whitlow, Buck, or the cops." He put up a finger for each one and showed them to her. "The only other person who could have taken it is dead. Now, the cops ain't charged Jimmy Whitlow with . . ." Alpha faltered, as if trying to remember his lines, "with nothing else they could have charged him with if they had found the delivery. Mary ain't hiding anywhere. She stayed put. Buck is the one who took off, which makes us figure he is our man. And now Jimmy is getting retained counsel and paying lawyer fees somehow? Mary Whitlow says that Buck and Jimmy must have planned this thing from the beginning. She says they set the . . . person of colored up for a rape. They were probably going to take the money and scoot, but then Jimmy got arrested and the car got towed."

"I'm a lawyer," said Myrna. "Do you know what that means?"

Alpha looked at her and froze up trying to process an unexpected question.

"That means everybody, including you, is a liar," said Myrna. "We don't know if it happened the way you said it happened, or the way Mary said it happened, or the way Buck says it happened. Our job is to get Jimmy Whitlow off of his bullshit hate crime charge. Briefcases were not included in his defense, which means we don't know shit about them, because it ain't our business."

Alpha took another ominous step toward Myrna. "It's your business now," he said. "You just assume it's your business. Because we are making it your business. We are assuming you know where it is and we want it back. Along with any money that either you or him are getting paid by Buck or Jimmy Whitlow."

Myrna exhaled and glanced once at the drawer.

"Boys," she said. "We can't help you find the delivery—"

"Ma'am, you are not listening to me," said Alpha, carefully enunciating his words, struggling to be a professional and explore every possible peaceful solution to his problems before resorting to carnage and human suffering. "I said we will be *assuming* that you know."

"I think I can help," said Watson, when he saw Myrna edging closer to her drawer. He stepped somewhere between Alpha and the front of Myrna's desk. He looked at Myrna. "I need the impound lot inventory sheet," he said to her.

She looked at him. "Uh," she said uncertainly, "I'm not sure we have something going by that name. Would that be something we would even want to have?"

"Give it to him," said Alpha. "What is it?"

Myrna tore herself away from the crack in her drawer and went wading half-heartedly through a raft of manilas on the cart next to her desk, lingering over a red jacket file, wondering what her chances would be of just not being able to find the inventory sheet.

"The keys were in the car when it was towed," said Watson. "No apparent owner because it had no plates and the registration was expired. So at base towing, they inventoried the contents of the vehicle."

Myrna slowly pulled a sheet of paper from the file, then paused and scanned it once more, double-checking for entries that might get her shot in the face.

"Look at the bottom, where it says 'Vehicle trunk,' " said Watson, passing the sheet to Alpha, while Beta leaned over for a peek.

" 'Vehicle trunk,' " said Alpha, reading from the sheet, " 'one car jack, one tire iron, two oil rags, one rubber jug of windshield wiper fluid, one spare tire, a box of tools containing one socket . . . two locked briefcases.' "

"Two," said Watson. "In the trunk of the car while it was locked up in the tow lot," he said.

"OK," said Alpha, in a decidedly unimpressed tone, "that does nothing but tell us that nobody took the delivery or the payment *before* the car got towed," said Alpha. "And we was with Mary when she got the car, opened the trunk, and found *one* empty briefcase with a calculator in it. So all we know now is that somebody got to that car and took both the payment and the delivery" said Alpha. "Which wouldn't be that hard, because it ain't nothing but a fenced-in cornfield. And as we go along, it looks like maybe Buck managed to get to that car. Or maybe *you* or your investigator got to the car, because you got this from somewheres, right?" he said, snapping the sheet of paper. "Which means you had somebody out there looking for the car and the delivery, right?" he said, his tone momentarily acquiring menace as he followed his suspicions to Watson's door.

He heard Myrna take a breath, as her fears about turning over the inventory sheet were confirmed, namely that it might prompt a question like "I thought you didn't know shit about the delivery? Where the fuck did you get this?"

"Early in any lawsuit," said Watson, "the two sides exchange documents. They give each other anything that is evidence or might be evidence. It's called discovery."

Another Arthurian stratagem. Did Watson say that *this particular* document was produced in the course of trial discovery? No way. He'd merely explained the *concept* of discovery at a suggestive and opportune time.

Alpha looked down at the paper suspiciously as if he wanted to take it to a lab and have it analyzed.

"You're right," said Watson. "Any number of people could have gotten to the car in the impound lot. Somebody who worked there, the cops, the FBI, me, you, Buck. I'm sure Mary Whitlow could have managed it if she had to, or she could have gotten somebody to do it for her."

"Sir," said Alpha, using one of the surliest sirs Watson had heard in his short adult life of being so addressed. Alpha's "sir" reminded him of the tone of voice sadistic law school professors had employed in calling him "Counselor" during interrogation sessions governed by the Socratic method, but not by the Geneva Convention. "You talk great, which is what you need to do if you are a lawyer. But so far we still don't know what we come here to find out—where is the delivery?"

"The cops have the delivery," said Watson. "Or so it would seem."

"You said that last time," Alpha jeered. "It was a good idea then, but so far it don't look that way to us. If the cops got it, why ain't Jimmy Whitlow charged with—"

"Counterfeit?" asked Watson.

Both men shifted their weight and tensed at the mention of the word. Myrna muttered something preverbal under her breath.

Watson kept himself from pacing after the fashion of his mentor and instead adopted the voluble earnestness of a pitchman in an infomercial. "The prosecutors were coming after Jimmy Whitlow for first-degree murder with hate-crime penalty enhancers. OK, that puts him at a minimum base offense level of forty-three on the federal sentencing guidelines. Life in prison, gentlemen. Now, why would a prosecutor tack on a measly counterfeit charge on top of that? Counterfeit has a base offense level of nine with sentences as low as six months, especially if they can't prove you made the stuff."

This appeared to give the men some relief.

"But if you can prove they or their organization ordered or controlled the production of the counterfeit currency, the penalties go up fast. But why waste a possession-of-counterfeit charge on one guy they already got on a hate crime murder? For what? If they are patient, the counterfeit might lead to a conspiracy to produce and distribute counterfeit, and the conspiracy might lead to something really big, like a militia. Maybe even a big racist, white supremacist militia, like the Order of the Eagles," said Watson.

Alpha and Beta tensed again and moved closer together. "We are not affiliated with that organization," said Alpha.

"See?" said Myrna to Joe. "And they are telling *us* to cut the shit? I'm supposed to tell them who Buck is, where the delivery is, how much my clients pay me, where I went to grade school, and he can't even admit to being an Eagle."

She seemed to be making her plea to Watson, as if he were the judge of a high school debate.

"We are not affiliated with that organization," Alpha repeated, "but we are familiar with their views." Then he launched into a canned bromide he must have learned at the same charm school where he acquired his careful manners.

"The Order of the Eagles is not a racist organization," he explained. "The Order of the Eagles is not a so-called hate group or a white supremacist organization. Its mission is to restore laws that treat all races equally, and abolish all the new laws that treat some races better than others. The organization believes that the federal government is no longer legitimate, because it has exceeded its powers under the Constitution. Some argue that our current so-called government does not have the authority to tax and spend or to print money, because it has surrendered its authority, debased itself by serving the needs of degenerate special interests."

Was he reading the stuff off of a card? Watson could tell Alpha had a lot more to say on the subject.

"Be a shame if a fine organization like that got hooked up with counterfeit," said Myrna.

"We are not affiliated with that organization. But we are familiar with their views," Alpha stated once more.

"Boy," said Myrna, "counterfeit means the Secret Service comes in. The Treasury Department and those ATF boys just love these militia outfits. We could have Ruby Ridge, Rutger Lupine, and a Waco siege right here in Missouri. I think Joe's right. They're waiting for the mother of all conspiracies."

"In criminal law class," said Watson, "they taught us that conspiracy is called 'the prosecutor's darling,' because as soon as they have evidence of a conspiracy, they're entitled to start hauling people in by the truckload. Conspiracy means you don't have to prove your defendants *actually did* anything, only that they *conspired* to do it. My guess is that's what they are waiting for. A big conspiracy with lots of enhanced counterfeit charges."

"When you say waiting, you mean—?" began Alpha.

"If I had a bunch of counterfeit and wanted to know who it belonged to, I might try not saying anything about it and see if somebody else starts asking about it, or looking for it, or acting like it was theirs, and/or maybe running around town giving people to understand in no uncertain terms that they want it back real bad," said Watson—no special tone to insinuate anything, just plain English.

Beta and Alpha glanced at each other once.

"More talk," said Alpha.

"I can prove that the government has your delivery," said Watson. "If that's what you really want to know." He raised his hand to reach inside the vest pocket of his suit.

Beta and Alpha flinched and unfastened their middle buttons, as if they had to get to the bathroom fast. "Uh," they said. "Maybe just go real slow there, sir," growled Beta, moving his hand inside his coat.

"It's just the settlement agreement," said Watson. He reached slowly inside his coat and withdrew the folded document typed up by Ida, which he and Harper had signed in Judge Stang's chambers.

Alpha drifted away from Beta, so Watson would be at the apex of a triangle, then advanced.

"It's papers, drafted by the government, setting forth the terms of Jimmy Whitlow's plea bargain. Mostly boilerplate legal mumbo jumbo. But take a look at—let's see. There. Paragraph eight."

" 'Scope and inte-gration of the agreement,' " read Alpha, stumbling on *integration*, then forging bravely ahead. " 'This plea agreement disposes of all charges arising out of the incidents set forth in the United States' original Complaint and Affidavit, including charges based upon any and all evidence seized from the premises of the base quarters where the defendant lived with his wife, and any and all evidence seized from the trunk of his vehicle, which was towed the day of the incidents in question."

"Now," said Watson, "look at the top of that document. It says, 'Office of the United States Attorney, Eastern District of Missouri.' I didn't write that," he said. "They did. The prosecutors wrote that. And why do you suppose the prosecutors would be talking about evidence seized from the trunk of Jimmy Whitlow's car?"

Alpha's face blanked and then slowly turned to Beta, who shrugged.

"If I'm the government," said Watson, "I play dumb and see what happens. See if somebody comes looking for it, or goes after people who should have it, namely, Jimmy Whitlow and his wife, Mary, or Buck, or Jimmy Whitlow's lawyer and his redheaded friend. And so far, that's exactly what you guys are doing. Keep it up and maybe the government will bring those charges you're looking for, but this agreement means they will not be brought against Jimmy Whitlow."

Alpha read the paragraph again to make sure he wasn't being hornswoggled.

"If I'm the owner of the counterfeit, I'd be wanting to stay as far away as possible from anybody who had it, or supposedly had it," Watson said. "No phone calls, no retaliation, no pursuit. The last thing I'd do is pester their lawyers," he added with a chuckle.

Alpha and Beta were not amused, but they did seem momentarily convinced.

"If Buck calls you—" began Alpha.

"Ah-ah," said Watson with a cautionary wave. "Who is Buck? Your coconspirator?"

"Never mind," said Alpha. "If we have any more questions, we will come back here."

"If you come back here," said Myrna, "you better bring a retainer, because we are going to charge you double our going rate."

"Yeah," said Beta. *He talked!* "Lady," he said, pointing his finger at her, "you push people."

Right, Beta, Watson was thinking, she pushes people. You mean, like the Empire State Building is tall? *The point is . . . ?*

They closed the door and, swearing audibly back and forth, left through the rear entrance.

She walked immediately to the twelve-pack of Heinekens and tore it open. "Ask me one question," she said.

"What?" asked Watson.

"Ask me, how drunk are we going to get? Just say, 'Hey, Myrna, how drunk are we going to get?' Like that."

"Hey, Myrna, how drunk are we going to get?"

She popped the top off the bottle. "We are going to get knee-walking, snot-slinging, nose-barfing, toilet-hugging drunk." She upended the Heineken and drank half of it with a single inhalation. "In two hours, the only thing you will be worried about is whether the toilet seat is going to come down and smack you on the back of the head."

She handed him a Heineken.

"How drunk?" he asked.

CHAPTER 30

Saturday morning. Face time for Stern, Pale associates. But these days Watson was absent—with pay, as luck would have it. According to voice mail from Ida, he was to get his bonus and six months' severance. Plenty of cash coming in to pay the bills while he was away at Gerry's summer clinic. He and Myrna had listened to the message last night in his office, just after she'd had a conference with W. C. Fields in Watson's well-ventilated bathroom. Myrna may have had a midnight run-in with a toilet seat, but Watson had felt too good to spoil his victory high with drugs and drunkenness. He went home instead, because Sandra was bringing the kids back.

Now it was family face time, and he had his mug buried in a pillow of fragrant tresses in the nape of his wife's neck. She turned half away so they could spoon and curl into each other's curves like two section symbols in the header of a statute. He reached around her and cupped the Forms, one in each mortal paw.

What was the biblical quote? A man shall leave his laptop and his job and shall cling to his wife? And clinging right along with him shall be his kids, it seemed. Benjy had somehow ended up in their queen-size bed after a crying jag during the night. His one-year-old son was trying out his new teeth on Dad's ear, while Sheila wriggled between the adult bodies, working her way up from the bottom of the bed, on a quest for her fair share of attention.

The driveway was being paved in concrete on Monday, and the Memsahib was happy, which meant the family was happy.

"Mommy," Sheila whined, "tell Daddy to move."

Tell Daddy to move? Well, his daughter's priorities were in order. He was dispensable. If Sandra—God forbid!—got cancer and passed away, the family members would each die slow, separate, psychic deaths. Planets without the sun, the center of gravity gone. If *he* died? Well, the next guy might not make as much money. Or with any luck, he might make *more* money.

Watson rolled onto his back and blew a sloppy raspberry into Benjy's tummy. A kid convulsion and rubbery warm limbs grappled Watson's head, smothering him in baby flesh, his face buffeted by the abdominal vibrations of an infant belly laugh.

He heard the laptop's fan whir in the alcove off the bedroom, as it came out of sleep mode and dialed into his service provider to retrieve the morning's E-mail. The laptop—the second penis, the other silicon woman, his little treasure, as in the Bible: "Where your treasure lies, there lies your heart also."

A week or so ago, he was contemplating adultery with a brain scientist, and now his brain was bandying Scripture with itself. See how quickly the world changes?

"Mommy, is Daddy still a lawyer for the criminals?" asked Sheila.

Watson revved up his engine of reason and attempted to formulate a four-year-old rendition of the Sixth Amendment and the right to counsel.

"Daddy feels sorry for criminals, honey," said Sandra. "Nobody wants to help them, so your dad feels sorry for them and tries to help them."

Oh! he thought, *I get it. Now that cash was rolling in from his seamy solo practice, the criminal law business was a badge of good citizenship and human compassion?*

"Oh, I'm glad we're talking about criminals," said Watson, "because that reminds me—don't let the kids answer the phone, I'm expecting a call from Rutger Lupine this morning."

"Stop it," she said.

"No," said Watson. "What I meant to say was I noticed that Sheila was talking to Alexa Finazzo's dad on the phone. He called here looking for Alexa. You know them, right? Her dad is Rudolph Finazzo. He looted a savings and loan and was prosecuted for mail fraud and income tax evasion. I don't think he should be talking to kids on the phone. No, wait! I'm taking the kids and moving out of the house. I can't believe you let them talk to criminals on the phone!"

Watson was pummeled by pillows from all sides. Then he rose to use the bathroom and walked by the alcove on his way to pee. The laptop chimed, indicating the arrival of new E-mail, and his desktop lit up.

The E-mail program was set to auto-open, and the message appeared on the bluish screen just as he emerged from the bathroom: rpalmquist@gage.edu

Dear Joe:

How quickly things change! We could be partners again, if you're interested. Got a call late last night from Montana of all places where a serial killer (of fourteen teenage girls) is due to be executed in two weeks. The neuro wrinkle is a history of head trauma in his youth, but we also need someone to draft up motions and briefs to delay the execution, which—get this—is by *hanging* in Montana.

I'm told the Supreme Court has already ruled that hanging is not cruel and unusual punishment under the Eighth Amendment. Now for the legal wrinkle: The defendant weighs 375 pounds (down from 425), which means hanging would result in decapitation, which *is* cruel and unusual punishment under the Eighth Amendment. Isn't the law marvelous? The warden has the D on a thousand calories a day in an attempt to get him under 350 and back into hanging territory.

Your computer skills would be a big help, too, because we would be zapping drafts of the briefs and memos back and forth from the Legal Aid people in Montana.

Anyway, let me know right away if you're interested.

Affectionately,

RP

It was all he could do to keep from crowing, "Look, honey, a serial killer! I'll bet we could get some bucks on this one!"

Watson reread the E-mail. He was personally opposed to the death penalty and would be proud to be instrumental in helping even one person avoid it. But was he the only techno-legal geek in the country available to make some more paper to file in Montana?

"Affectionately, RP," he read again with a twinge of memory and extinguished desire. If he said yes, he would be back in close proximity to the Brain Venus. He would also spend another week hunched over his laptop, doing research on obese hangings and gruesome decapitations.

"Daddy?" said Sheila.

A murder of crows was making a racket out on his front lawn, which meant one thing—grubs. He peeked through the curtains and saw Oma Hodgkins standing at the property line. She was clutching the morning paper to her chest, staring with terror and loathing as the crows feasted on grubs, ripping up patches of denuded grass from the family Watson's infested front lawn. If he could scan her, the deep, primeval circuits of rage and fear would light up orange and red and white-hot. He would have to go over and have a cup of coffee with her. Console her and apologize for his grubs.

"Daddy?" said Sheila.

He had a lot in common with Oma. She had her lawn and he had his colorful, orderly, software desktop. It would be tough to face her—he would be covered in shame, the evidence of his inferior moral code right there for all to see in his grub-ridden lawn.

He turned back to the laptop, open like a glowing plastic maw in the light of dawn. He clicked REPLY and typed: "Sorry. Can't. Good Luck. JW."

"Daddy? Can I play on the pooter?"

"We're not playing on the computer this weekend," said Watson. "We're going outside to talk with Mrs. Hodgkins. Why don't you get dressed and you can come, too. We can take her a present. Maybe that will help her feel better."

ACKNOWLEDGMENTS

Fred Nietzsche said: "A writer is somebody who possesses not only his own intellect, but also that of his friends." Many friendly, prodigious intellects helped me write *Brain Storm*, especially my editor, Daniel Menaker, and my agent, Gail Hochman.

I am also grateful to Marcus Raichle, M.D.; Helen Mayberg, M.D.; and Rodolfo Llinas, M.D., for introducing me to neuroscience and the various scanning technologies.

Joseph Bataillon, Sheila Hunsicker, Phillip Kavanaugh, Cynthia Short, and David Slavkin were all generous with their legal savvy and their good ideas.

Thanks also to John Albrecht, Mike Becker, Lou Boxer, Liz Karnes, Kate Shaw, and Jeremy Slavkin.

About the Author

RICHARD DOOLING was born in Omaha, Nebraska. He received his B.A. from St. Louis University in 1976 and in 1979 began working as a respiratory therapist in intensive care units. After traveling for over a year in Europe and Africa, he went back to law school at St. Louis University, where he was editor in chief of the *Law Journal*. He practiced law at Bryan Cave in St. Louis for four years.

Dooling's first novel, *Critical Care*, was made into a film directed by Sidney Lumet. His second novel, *White Man's Grave*, was a finalist for the 1994 National Book Award. He is also the author of *Blue Streak: Swearing, Free Speech, and Sexual Harassment*, a collection of essays on the First Amendment and the politics of swearing. His writing has appeared in *The New Yorker, The New York Times, The National Law Journal*, and *Story*. He lives in Omaha with his wife, Kristin, and their four children.

About the Type

The text of this book was set in Palatino, designed by the German typographer Hermann Zapf. It was named after the Renaissance calligrapher Giovanbattista Palatino. Zapf designed it between 1948 and 1952, and it was his first typeface to be introduced in America. It is a face of unusual elegance.